THE LAY OF YOU

a novel by

Corrie MacKay

Content Warning: This novel explores aspects of psychology and mental health and contains occasionally descriptive references to past traumas, including child abuse, physical and mental abuse, cult/religious abuse, sexual abuse, domestic violence, and murder. Please read with care.

Published in the United States of America.
This book contains an excerpt from the forthcoming novel *The Depth of You* by Corrie MacKay. This excerpt has been set for this edition only and may not reflect the final content of the forthcoming edition.
ISBN 979-8-9887445-1-1
Digital ISBN 979-8-9887445-0-4

Cover Design by Katarina @nskvsky
Book Editing and Design by Corrie MacKay

Author Instagram: @writefreemackay
Author Email: writefreemackay@gmail.com

This book is dedicated to every woman who dares to try again. And again. And again. I see you. You are magic. Keep going.

"I think that little by little I'll be able to solve my problems and survive."

- Frida Kahlo -

1

The ambient hum of the road lulled her. Jennifer couldn't remember the last time she'd gotten more than four or five hours of sleep. Her life was an appointment book riddled with tabs and when her head *did* hit her pillow, it was often too full to fall asleep—the next day's tasks, the coming week's concerns, the whims and woes of running a successful company *while* being one of its star attractions. So, Jennifer spent her days exhausted and her nights pretending not to be.

The town car's tinted windows prevented her from seeing out, so the city sped around her in darkness. There was nothing to distract her, nothing but the endless black of the empty leather seat beside her and the glossy dark of the glass partition separating her from her driver and security detail—a charming hammer of a woman named Carolina Roberson.

Jennifer closed her eyes. She was alone, and for the variable length of this car ride, she had no cause to pretend. She would rest.

A familiar chime snapped her awake again. Now, the road was silent. The vibration of movement beneath her feet was gone.

Jennifer shot up and grabbed a compact mirror from the small black clutch at her side, flicked it open and circled her face, checking all her angles. She passed a hand over her hair, the inky black pristine braid that fell to the dip of her back. Her scarlet lips were striking against her fair skin, as was the fresh jasmine bloom pinned to the breast of her slim-fit, raven suit. She caught her own gaze in the mirror, sharp azure under charcoal, and winked at herself—a little ritual she'd long indulged in.

Go get 'em, Gorgeous.

The car door opened as she dropped her mirror back into her clutch, and Carolina stood in the opening, a brick house in a classic-fit, mocha suit. Jennifer took her offered hand and, as she stepped out of the car, her heels crunched and wobbled over dirt and gravel. She steadied her step with Carolina's help and got her first look at their destination.

Port Orford Cedars and Oregon Ash trees speckled the visible land around them, lit by fairy lights strung among the branches. Their towering bodies morphed into shadowy giants as they disappeared into the dark of the acreage beyond. Fresh, wild, and warm summer air, heavy with florals, filled Jennifer's nose as she took in the looming house ahead: an old, triple-story Eastlake Victorian, peeling white with faded purple trim and a wraparound, roofed porch surrounded by bushy lavender. Crickets chirped in a continuous symphony from within the stalks, the sound just as mesmerizing as the hum of the long drive had been, and Jennifer felt a dull ache for home.

How long had it been since she'd last been to Wakefield? San Francisco had proven an entirely different adventure, one she hadn't disliked. In fact, she loved it. She'd found a new home in the city, a new life, a *better* one. But nothing had ever felt like Wakefield. Her first place. Her family place. Fresh air and green trees and every minor blip of seasonal change one could hope to experience—she had Wakefield in her blood. Sometimes, it felt like a sickness.

She smoothed the front of her satin blazer, careful not to crumple her jasmine. "Where are we?"

Carolina cut her a look.

Yes, yes, she knew the rules. *I wrote them after all.* She'd crafted them with care, updating as needed, but some things never changed: no real names, no phones, and no exact locations. It's why the car's windows were blacked out and why the only information she, or any of her employees, ever received about a client came moments before entering their home.

Jennifer could bend the rules if she wished—break them, even. She could know what she wanted to know if ever she cared to know it. It was *her* company, but Jennifer had never considered herself above any other when it came to such things. She did her work as all her employees did and abided her own rules as she expected them to. *Mostly.*

"Right," Jennifer said. "I was just testing you."

Carolina snorted. "If it helps, we're about three hours outside the city."

"Wow." *No wonder I fell asleep.*

"I know. My ass is numb."

Jennifer eyed the house again. She could imagine it might have been something to behold once, but now it sat like someone's forgotten elder, withering away unloved. It certainly didn't scream money. Surprising. Her clients were wealthy people. They couldn't afford her company if they weren't, and this one had to have deep pockets if he was willing to shell out for such a long drive. Her clients paid a mileage fee on any trips over twenty, and three hours outside the city, they were well over the twenty-mile mark. So, why a near-dilapidated house in the middle of nowhere?

"Should I be creeped out?"

"Why? Because it looks like I'm dropping you off at a Victorian murder house miles from civilization where no one will be able to hear you scream?"

"Thanks. You're fired."

"Woman up."

"Double fired."

"Fifty bucks says it's a reno project."

"It better be."

"And a lot nicer inside."

Jennifer grimaced at the tired, sagging face and frame. "I

repeat," she said, lowering her voice as she took Carolina's arm and they made for the old porch, "it better be."

"You've got your panic button if you need it." Of course, she was right. As strange as the situation was, Jennifer didn't feel unsafe, more put-off. The house left much to be desired. She could only hope the man who owned it proved different. Still, the feel of the small remote in her breast pocket comforted her. Carolina was only ever a press away. "You good?"

"I'm good."

"Okay. So, client's name is Fisher."

"A name that actually sounds like a name. Huh."

Carolina glanced at her as they crested the porch, its old body groaning underfoot. "What? You don't miss Mr. Large? Mr. Richard Large?"

Jennifer smiled and shook her head. "How long am I on for?"

"An hour. Private booking with just you and the client, so you'll be staying here."

"Only an hour?" Most of her clients booked a minimum of three and usually more in the vein of five or six, given the particulars she was known for. "After a three-hour drive?"

Carolina shrugged. "I know what I know," she said and rang the doorbell, the chime echoing out from inside. "I'm going to wait in the car, so you can just ping me if you need anything."

"Mhm."

Usually, the door was answered right away, clients eager

to get what they paid for, but not this time. They waited and waited. Nearly five minutes passed in utter, uncomfortable quiet before Carolina cleared her throat. "Maybe he's in the bathroom," she said and rang again.

This time, the telltale tapping of heels followed the chime, and Jennifer's eyebrows ticked up as she and Carolina exchanged a look. A *woman*? Or a man in heels, perhaps. It wouldn't be the first time she'd landed a male client who liked that. Nor would it be the first time a man's wife had discovered the origin of all those massive credit card transactions and intercepted his next visit. It wouldn't even be the first time a man had purchased a session for himself, only to spring his wife on her at the last second in hopes of a threesome. Jennifer was fine with group sex, enjoyed it even. What she wasn't fine with was someone attempting to skimp on the agreed-upon price. Third parties meant double the original payment, and not only that, but all parties directly involved in any booking were required, by contract, to have a complete STI screening on record from no earlier than thirty days prior of their appointment date. No exceptions.

When the door finally opened, Jennifer could only blink and stare. The woman in the frame stood tall like Jennifer but frozen and doe-eyed as a frightened child. Her hair was the color of cinnamon and lightly curled, falling in elegant waves around her cheeks, and she wore a pretty blush to match—whether natural or applied, Jennifer wasn't sure.

Carolina gave a respectful nod. "Mrs. Fisher?"

A string of pearls hung about the woman's slender neck,

complimenting her white cardigan and periwinkle swing skirt, an odd trifecta for her obvious youth but flattering all the same. She wore blush pink heels that matched the gloss reflecting off her lips and the paint coating her nails. To Jennifer, she looked like a dream-girl cutout from a 1950s magazine, a Californian June Cleaver in full, living color. *The kind of housewife one could imagine bending over a counter and—*

"It's Ms., actually. Not Mrs."

Jennifer's gaze dropped to the woman's ring finger to see a slim golden band, no doubt the reason for Carolina's assumption.

"Not anymore."

Perhaps she's recently divorced, Jennifer thought. *Or widowed.* She frowned. How sad that would be, to be widowed so young.

"My apologies, Ms. Fisher," Carolina said. "I have the Director for you."

She stepped to the side, and Jennifer summoned an air of authority. The Director was an imperious woman, arrogant, masterful, and unyielding. It was a persona cultivated over decades, one that lured her clients back time and again, and Jennifer carried it well. But for the first time in ages, she faltered.

The young Ms. Fisher looked terrified, shifting on her heels as her wide, amber eyes kept just shy of making contact with Jennifer's. "Thank you," she said, steadier than expected, "but I don't think I'll be needing her, the, um, *services* any longer."

Jennifer's stomach flipped. *Interesting.* She did love a challenge. "Ms. Fisher, if I may," she said, certain she could calm the woman's nerves if given a chance. She'd had many a bashful client over the years, and even with those who weren't, there was often an awkward adjustment period at the start. "It's natural to feel—"

"Well, thank you again! Sorry! Goodnight!"

Ms. Fisher's sudden outburst barely registered before she disappeared like a ghost into her haunted mansion and slammed its raggedy door in their faces. In her wake, nothing stirred. They stood still as statues but for Jennifer's slow, helpless blinking. *Did that seriously just happen? Am I hallucinating?* Not once in her career had she been turned away by a client, and she'd certainly never had a door slammed in her face by the person who *made the appointment, for fuck's sake!* She had to be hallucinating. But one look Carolina's way told her the truth—it happened—and an odd laugh bubbled up. *Well, shit.* She had never been so utterly bewildered. "I'm actually speechless."

"I just hope she knows she doesn't get a refund for changing her mind."

"Whether she knows or not, she signed a contract."

"Well, I guess it's back home then?" Carolina asked, the two still lingering, awkward and rejected, on the porch. She shrugged. "Long drive. We could get something to eat on the way."

Jennifer frowned at the closed door, something in her unsettled. It was a sick feeling, vaguely familiar, but she couldn't name it. "I guess so," she said and tried to shake it off, but as she followed Carolina down the steps and out toward the car, the feeling got worse. An insistent, nagging sickness that bloomed and spored like a fungus, it started in her gut and spread the span of her in seconds until she felt consumed by it. Then she knew. She was experiencing something she hadn't in years: a heady, bothering mixture of rejection and humiliation.

"What's wrong?"

"Hm?" Jennifer looked over, found Carolina staring at her, forehead wrinkled in concern.

"You stopped," she said. "Is something wrong?"

"No, of course not." As if in protest, the feeling surged, and Jennifer's chest burned. A white-hot flash of anger lit her brain like lightning. "Yes, sorry." She shook her head as she spun back toward the house. *No one gets to make me feel like this.* "No. Excuse me."

"Oh lord."

At the door again, Jennifer jabbed the bell and waited for the clacking of heels again. Her heart thundered in her ears when the sound came, and then she was looking into Ms. Fisher's wide eyes again.

"Step back," Jennifer said before her return could be questioned. She hadn't a clue what she was doing, but she wasn't in the driver's seat anymore. Her ego was.

Ms. Fisher's face reddened as if it were being painted

from within, the color appearing in little splotches along her cheeks and forehead. *Not applied after all.* She squeaked like a captured mouse. "What?"

"I told you to step back, Ms. Fisher." Her voice was crisp and commanding. A fire had crackled to life where the lightning struck. She'd built her pride from the ground up, crafted her confidence with care like a monument to all she'd overcome. She'd be damned before she let some closeted, ill-mannered twenty-something in a poodle skirt make her feel less than. Who did she think she was? It didn't matter. Jennifer was the fucking Director. "Now."

She was almost surprised when the woman did as she was told, taking several steps back into her own empty foyer on the order of a stranger, but Jennifer had seen people do things at her command that would turn some stomachs. It wasn't surprise that she felt, no. It was *thrill*. It was power.

Silence deafened as Jennifer strode through the front door like she owned the place, regal and radiating authority. She closed the door behind her with a nudge of her heel, then took a long moment to smooth and settle her suit. When the tension in the room grew unbearable, she clasped her hands behind her back, locked her eyes on Ms. Fisher's, and advanced. Every step she took, the woman retreated in kind, and Jennifer's thrill heightened.

"Ms. Fisher," she said, voice low and sharp, "I've been doing this a long time, so I've learned how to read people. Their desires. Their bodies. Their pleasures, however particular."

"I...I asked you to leave."

"You didn't, actually." Jennifer took another step. "Would you like to now?" Two more, and she had the woman right where she wanted her, backed into a wedge of a corner where a large, antique armoire met the foyer wall.

"No," came the shaky, whispered reply, and Jennifer was now certain she'd been wanted here all along. Her client hadn't changed her mind. She'd panicked. She'd buckled to a fear Jennifer recognized—the fear of wanting what felt forbidden.

"Well then," she said, inching closer. "Would you like to know what story your body tells?"

Ms. Fisher radiated heat. Her gaze dropped to Jennifer's mouth and lingered, then farther down, scanning the length of her body and back. Her chest heaved, and Jennifer wondered how it would look were the woman bare beneath her—small, pert breasts and supple, creamy skin, freckled perhaps. So very feminine. Jennifer had always been partial to women; unfortunately, their bookings were rare and almost always involved a third-party male partner. Having a woman all to herself for a change would be a dream.

When their eyes met, Ms. Fisher's were dark and wide and struck right at the heart of Jennifer. She looked like a starving stray hovering outside a picnic, wanting and terrified at once, and all Jennifer's ire dissipated. She sighed and closed the distance between them.

"None," she said as she pressed her chest to Ms. Fisher's and was rewarded with a choked moan and a shiver. "There isn't an ounce of pleasure in your poor, neglected body, Ms. Fisher." She freed a hand, let it hover over the curve of a slim waist, the promise of heat. "Only the *want* of it."

The gurgle that rattled and stuck in Ms. Fisher's throat sparked a flare of heat low in Jennifer's stomach. She nudged the tips of their noses together. "Oh, you are my favorite kind of conquest, Ms. Fisher," she said and allowed just a flash of flesh on flesh, lip catching lip. "Unexplored territory."

"I-I'm not...." Ms. Fisher squeaked, and Jennifer tilted a brow.

"Yes?"

"I'm not a virgin," Ms. Fisher said, and Jennifer chuckled low in her throat.

"I never claimed you were." She slowly let her palm connect, curling her long fingers around Ms. Fisher's waist. Sound sang from that slender throat again, a precious whimper, and the low-burning fire inside Jennifer blazed and ran, searing over the curves of her hips and burning at the base of her spine. How long it had been since she'd had one like this? So responsive. So naive. So very eager for what would undoubtedly be her first taste of a woman. "That's the thing about unexplored territory. One can travel it without ever truly learning the land." She clenched her fingers, clumping into the soft material of Ms. Fisher's thin cardigan. "But I am *so* very thorough."

Ms. Fisher whimpered again, but she never reached for Jennifer, never attempted to touch. Her hands remained plastered behind her, braced against the armoire and wall.

"I would have the lay of you, Ms. Fisher," Jennifer whispered and slid her hand around from the woman's waist to the small of her back, walked her fingers up her spine. "Every inch, expertly mapped." Ms. Fisher shuddered against her, the vibration delicious, and Jennifer had to swallow the pleased rumble brewing in her throat. "But...." Without warning, she stepped sharply back and straightened her spine, clasped her hands behind her again. "I never venture where I am not wanted."

Ms. Fisher appeared utterly bereft, mouth opening and closing helplessly as Jennifer gave her a respectful nod then made for the door. *Three. Two.*

"Wait."

Jennifer smirked, devilish and triumphant, but schooled the expression as she turned back. She arched an eyebrow but said nothing.

"What if you *are* wanted?"

This time, Jennifer made no attempt to tame her smile. There was something so innocent and endearing about this young woman, something Jennifer found herself both yearning to nurture and aching to ruin. She sighed again and shook her head. "I require certainty," she said and opened the door to the warm night. "It's a long drive from San Francisco, Ms. Fisher. For the sake of your bank account, and all our time, should you choose to book again, be certain you are ready to surrender. Anything short of that won't do."

With that, she left the woman forlorn and empty of all but her thoughts. And Jennifer knew what those thoughts would be. Filthy. Primitive. She'd had them whispered at her feet like prayer more times than she could count. Oh yes, she would be seeing Ms. Fisher again. It was just a matter of when.

Dosie's knees shook. Her hands, too. She fanned her face, trying to process. Ten minutes had passed since the woman she knew only as "the Director" had stepped into her home as if she owned it, crowded Dosie's body as if she owned that, too, or would like to, and *ruined* her. And with what? Barely-there touches and words. *Words!* A woman had whispered at her, and Dosie felt like she'd run a marathon. Her heart wouldn't calm, still racking wildly about her ribs. Her blood was hot in her veins, itching under her skin, and the material of her dress felt as if it had adhered to her flesh—too tight, too binding.

She curled her fingers around her pearl necklace and brought it to her mouth, a habit she'd developed years earlier. She dragged the pearls back and forth across her lips as she closed her eyes and attempted to calm down. Instead, she ruminated, embarrassed and loathing herself.

Why, *why*, she'd chickened out after everything, every equally unnerving step in the process of booking an escort, was beyond her. She'd been so sure she was ready. All the things she'd thought about every time she was touched by graceless hands or kissed by a messy, scruff-ringed mouth—all those bone-deep yearnings she'd been trapping and taming for years, denying herself—had been right there, ready for her. Finally. And she'd blown it.

Her limited experience left much to be desired, and though she'd kept it a secret for years, she'd never been able to deny to herself that when she'd felt the press of her husband between her legs, she'd wished it was a woman touching her instead. She would imagine a woman's body hovering over her, soft, delicate, and strong. Feminine hands mapping her. Slender fingers probing, stoking her fire. Supple, stained lips tasting her.

Natalie had been the first to suggest an escort. It was late, and they were all tired, their day spent pulling up rank, rotten carpet from an upstairs bedroom and scraping old, lead-laden paint from the walls. So, Dosie had initially dismissed the suggestion as one of those so-called "wild hairs" people got when they were exhausted. But then Kaylia quickly jumped on board, and suddenly, that wild hair was a "legitimately good idea," and her two best friends were nothing if not persistent. It would be *easy*, they'd said. No strings. No judgment. Just sex, learning, experience.

"A way to dip your toe," Natalie told her. "For lack of a better analogy."

Kaylia balked. "Girl, no. I can think of at least three analogies better than that one. Dosie, do not dip your toe into someone. Ever. And please don't let someone dip their toe into you."

"Oh, my God," Dosie had groaned, hiding her reddening face in her hands. "Stop."

"Fingers? Sure," Kaylia carried on. If she wanted to say something, she would say it. "Tongue? Absolutely. Toys? Even better. But girl, please, no toes. I cannot handle you coming back after a night with an escort talking about how hot her *toes* were."

Natalie shoved her. "Stop before you turn her into a tomato." She rounded the large kitchen island where Dosie could still picture her mother, flour-dusted and kneading dough. She slung one arm around Dosie's back. "But for real, there are some great services around, like really high-end ones and discreet, but not like *shady* discreet. Oh, wait, I actually have a number I could give you. I swear it's the best. Like, top-tier service, above and beyond kind of stuff, and they even require STI screenings and everything. So, it's legit, and I mean, maybe it was just my chick, but she also smelled really good. Like, *really* good. And she definitely knew what she was doing."

"You've used them before?" Dosie had asked.

"Yeah, once. It was a gift." She laughed. "Probably the best one I've ever gotten."

Dosie gaped. "Someone *gifted* you sex with an escort?"

"A true friend," Kaylia had said with an approving nod. "It was me. I was the true friend."

Dosie snorted so hard it made her face hurt, and the three of them burst into a loud chorus of laughter. Her sides ached by the time it died down, but she was grateful. It was a perfect ache. She'd never had close friendships outside her family, and she'd only known Natalie for a few years, Kaylia even fewer, but she already felt so connected to them both that she couldn't imagine her life without them.

"What if I don't know what to do though?" Something like this would require Dosie to be brave, *really* brave, but what in her life hadn't? It was her experience, or lack of, that worried her, and on a deeper level: her lifelong companion, trauma. There was no telling what old pains new experiences might bring to the surface, but such things were unavoidable for her. If she could stop herself from looking like a fool, however, that would be great. "What if I'm just a fumbling idiot, and she thinks I'm ridiculous?"

"Who cares?" Kaylia shrugged. "That's the beauty of it. You're paying for a service. Doesn't matter if you know what you're doing or not, only that you have a good time. And trust me, escorts have seen it all. You're not going to be some novel thing for them."

"Okay, but I don't just want to be *serviced*. I mean, I would want her to enjoy it, too. I would want to, you know...*please* her."

"So, tell her that," Natalie said. "Be up front about what you want and what you expect, and then go from there. Just don't overthink it, you know? Don't overcomplicate it, and you'll be fine, and then once you've had the experience, maybe you'll feel a little more comfortable exploring more and figuring out, you know, what all you want and what you might be interested in."

"And if I *can't* please her?"

Kaylia scoffed. "Are you joking? You are the easiest-to-teach person I've ever met. You listen, and you catch on quick, and you don't complain when things are complicated or boring. You seriously underestimate how rare that is."

"And God help you if you aren't the most eager budding queer this side of the Mississippi," Natalie added, poking at Dosie's side. "The day you found out I was gay, I thought you were going to shoot off the floor like a firecracker, you were so excited."

"Well, I never had anyone I could talk to about it before!" Dosie swatted her hand away and laughed. "I mean, other than therapists."

"I know." She grinned. "I'm just saying, you've come a really, *really* long way since the first time we talked about all this stuff, and I know you know that."

Yeah. Dosie nodded. Even a double "really" was an understatement there.

"And I think you're ready. So, you know, if you want to try something like this, or however you want to go about it, we'll support you."

"Hell, we'll encourage you," Kaylia said. "Look at us, we're doing it right now."

Dosie leaned into Natalie's side, craving a physical connection. She'd always been that way, affectionate, handsy. She and her sisters had held hands all the time as girls. It grounded her, grounded all of them, and reminded them they weren't alone. "I love you guys."

"We love you too, girl," Kaylia said. "Just, you know, no toes."

They'd still been laughing when they brought up the website for the service, but later that night, when Dosie's fingers had punched the listed number into her phone, there'd been no sound in her at all. She'd choked on air just trying to get her voice to work and only managed it by forcing herself to focus on the reason she'd called in the first place—that undeniable desire she'd carried in her heart, *and other places*, for years.

Dosie felt that desire crackling through her now as she remained rooted where the Director left her. It popped in her veins like static electricity, warring with embarrassment. Her knees were still shaking. Gods, what had she been thinking? Why had she chosen someone like that? Someone so arrogant, so intense. But then the image from the website came back to her, and heat flashed between her legs. *Oh, right. That.*

The Director was the only name the profile gave. The woman herself stood beside the title, clad in a silky, skin-tight suit as black as her long and wavy hair. Her chest was bare beneath her blazer, the curves of her breasts peeking out and a simple, silver chain dangling between. She wore shiny, black stiletto heels that made her legs go on forever and stared directly into the camera as if she wasn't above jabbing one of them in your eye if she deemed it necessary (or fun). The woman positively radiated power and confidence, and Dosie had wanted her right down to her marrow. No other profile, no other woman, came close to having the same effect. She wanted the Director.

But the moment Dosie had her on her doorstep, heard the chime of the bell signaling her arrival, she'd been inundated with fear and a deep, unsettling shame she hadn't felt in years. It screamed to the surface with dizzying speed, all before anything had even happened, and then she'd felt paralyzed. Everything became stilted and unsure, and she was stuck trying to navigate a body that wouldn't do as it was told while confronting a woman who, also, wouldn't do as *she* was told. And it was confusing. It was *infuriating*.

God, and the money! Not that money was an issue, nor should it ever be again, but to have paid such a price only to turn coward in the end...*ugh*. Dosie wasn't sure she could bring herself to tell her friends.

She sighed and finally pushed herself off the wall, ran one still-shaky hand along the armoire as she passed toward the kitchen. There, she poured herself some water and chugged like it was the last glass of water on earth. It did little to soothe the dryness in her throat, even less for the burn still searing her belly.

Her laptop sat on the countertop, and she flicked it open before she could question herself. It took only a second to pull up the escort site and the profile that had been lingering in her mind for days. Dosie closed her eyes, felt the ghost of warmth against her chest, curling around her waist, puffing against her lips. She brought her fingertips to her mouth and touched, felt it between her thighs as if she'd pressed there instead. She shivered—*Nope*—and slammed her laptop closed. She clearly wasn't ready for this, so she should quit while she was, well, already behind. The Director would just have to be another haunting for her list.

Dosie grabbed her glass and refilled it, carried it with her to the stairs. She carefully slipped off her heels and left them at the base before climbing up. The moment she stepped into her bedroom, she sighed. There were no ghosts in this room; at least, none she couldn't shake. But as she set her drink atop her bedside table and slowly, delicately, began to peel away her dress, she felt it again: desire. It crept through her like warm, trickling water, a slow spread as her palms slipped and scratched down her torso, inch by inch turned bare. She felt the Director's breath on her again, heard the rasp of her voice as if she was right in front of her.

"I would have the lay of you, Ms. Fisher."

Dosie shuddered and pressed harder against her skin, fingers dipping under the sides of her lacy white underwear to drag them down as well.

"Every inch, expertly mapped."

The Director's eyes burned like blue fire in Dosie's mind, so determined, so promising. Dosie hadn't doubted a word the woman said.

"I am so *very thorough."*

She shivered again, trying to imagine what such thoroughness might entail. Timidly, she brought her hands back to her belly, then up to her breasts, cupping their light weight.

She thumbed her nipples experimentally, sucked in a breath as pleasure sparked.

When her phone, long forgotten in the middle of her bed, suddenly sprang to life with a chorus of *quacking*, Dosie screamed like an intruder had just burst into the room and dove for her bed. She flapped around, naked and helpless, for a moment as she tried to cover herself, then stopped cold. Realization.

"Oh my God!" She slammed her face into her mattress and groaned. Her phone. It was her phone, her stupid text alert! She rolled around on her bed until she found the device buried under a pillow and glared at it. Her frustration cooled when she tapped the screen and saw the notification. The group chat.

She scrolled through the extensive back-and-forth that had taken place between Natalie and Kaylia in her absence: an abundance of cheering her on and one-too-many *bow chicka wow wow*'s from Kaylia. Dosie was mortified, not because of their messages—God love them, they were so supportive—but because she didn't know how to tell them she'd screwed everything up. What would they say, what would they *think*, if they knew she'd shelled out thousands of dollars for ten ridiculous minutes of being *breathed on* by a scary hot woman who'd ultimately left her with nothing but a pair of embarrassingly damp panties and even more sexual frustration than she'd had to begin with?

She couldn't. She couldn't do it, couldn't tell them. But

she had to, right? They would know. They always knew when she was lying. *Unless.*

"Unless it's not a lie," Dosie whispered to herself in the quiet room, then she opened her recent contacts.

The drive seemed longer on the way back, the first hour stretching on for what felt like an eternity. Perhaps it was because they'd only just finished the drive *to* Ms. Fisher's home. Or maybe it was due to the surprisingly persistent throb between Jennifer's legs.

She nearly always found a way to garner pleasure from her sessions, even with partners she wasn't attracted to. She was adamant about it, in fact, and encouraged the women working for her to be as well. Sex was their work, sure, but there was no reason they shouldn't enjoy that work. They were in the business of pleasure after all. At the very least, they should know it themselves.

Yes, Jennifer always found a way to enjoy herself, sexually or otherwise, but now she felt riled over utterly *nothing*. Just the scent of a girl, the idea of her. The way she'd trembled at little more than the sound of Jennifer's voice. It was mad and, admittedly, addictive. She had her effects, but it had been some time since she'd seen someone, *felt* someone, react to her the way the young Ms. Fisher had.

She could only hope her instincts were correct. She'd long

since learned not to doubt them, but the longer she marinated, the more she felt an odd prick of trepidation in the back of her mind. What if she'd gotten it wrong? Perhaps Ms. Fisher would not have the fire to call for her again but would shrivel in the heat of Jennifer's wake and recede back into whatever fears had impeded her in the first place. The possibility bothered her.

With a sigh, she cracked open the mini fridge in the back of the town car, her favorite aspect of the vehicle, and removed a chilled tumbler. From a drawer, she collected one of her vintage whiskies, a 25-year-old, single-malt Macallan, and poured two fingers. Her phone chimed from her clutch as she relaxed back into her seat and sipped. A booking. She knew by the sound. Or a cancellation, though those were rare. She didn't usually bother to look. Her assistant, Candace, handled such things, but Jennifer had time to kill and a need to distract herself. It wasn't as if she had any hope of sleep. Her body was too awake now, too sober, and too unsatisfied. So, she took out her phone.

A garbled sound caught in her throat as the booking information loaded on screen, and she saw the name: FISHER. Jennifer spluttered, choking on her scotch as she attempted to swallow before she spewed. She coughed as it went down, then she quickly checked the time, felt her jaw drop.

Jennifer had imagined a few days, at least, would pass before the frightful Ms. Fisher might work up the courage to book again, if she managed to at all. But an hour and a half? Jennifer was shocked. Ms. Fisher had more fire than she thought. Her gaze dropped to the booking date and time, and a white-hot spark ignited low in her gut. *Fuck.*

She jabbed the intercom button above her. "Carolina, where are we?"

"Bay Area side of Sacramento." Her voice crackled through the speaker then smoothed. "Probably about twenty minutes or so outside. Why? Everything good?"

Jennifer grinned. "Everything is excellent, but I'm afraid I'm going to have to ask you to spend the night in a hotel."

A hum whirred to life as the privacy partition descended, and Carolina's coffee-colored eyes found her in the rearview mirror. "What's up?"

"I'm going to have my assistant book us in at the Kimpton in Sacramento."

"Oh?"

"It seems I've outdone myself," Jennifer said, tone bordering on a brag, but she couldn't help it. Her head felt like a balloon, full of the heat wafting up from her—

"No! Fisher?!" Carolina gaped. "Are you fucking serious? It's been an hour!"

Jennifer cackled, feeling witchy. Well, she'd obviously cast some sort of spell. Ms. Fisher could attest to that.

"What did you do, threaten her?"

"Only with a good time." Oh, she was positively vibrating. Sometimes, she *really* loved her job.

"The appointment's not *tonight*, is it? She didn't seriously have us leave just to call us right back, did she?"

"In a way," Jennifer said. "It's tomorrow morning, early."

"A morning appointment?" Carolina was no longer looking at her, focused on the road as she veered into an exit lane to turn them around, but Jennifer could see the astonishment on her face. Her eyebrows had nearly disappeared into her hairline. "That's different."

"Yes, yes, it is."

Carolina chuckled. "Oh no."

"What?"

"You sound excited," she said. "*Too* excited. You're going to ruin that poor girl, aren't you?"

"Only if she asks it of me." Jennifer hid her grin with her whisky as she took a small sip. *And she most certainly will.*

2

Money had always been low on Jennifer's list of desires, but it opened many doors. She enjoyed luxury but didn't need it. In true American fashion, what she desired was convenience. Her days were busy. Her nights? Even busier. She needed what she needed when she needed it, which at times meant she needed it right away, and when one needed something right away, the easiest way to acquire it was with cold, hard cash; or, in her case, the swipe of her platinum card. It's how she managed the knock now echoing through her hotel suite.

She opened the door to Carolina, who appeared pristine despite the early hour and was shadowed by a petite man who did not. He wore oversized glasses, a tired but pleasant enough expression, and a slightly rumpled suit, and his thinning hair stuck out a bit on top. Draped over his right arm, he had a plethora of garment bags and, hanging from his left, an enormous plastic bag packed to the brim with shoe boxes. A smaller, dark green velvet satchel hung from his left elbow—jewelry, Jennifer guessed.

"Good morning," Carolina said. "I have Mr. Clark from Luksus Boutique for you, and yes, I offered to carry something. He refused."

Jennifer chuckled. "Thank you, Carolina." She nodded to the man. "Mr. Clark, thank you for taking such a last-minute request and at this hour, no less. I truly don't make it a habit, but I'm afraid it's a bit of an emergency."

"Ma'am, please," he said with a smile. "We are perfectly happy to attend our private clientele at any hour. We've pulled several pieces for you this morning, and I think you will be pleased with our selection."

"I'm sure." She stepped aside. "Shall we, then?" He hustled past, and Carolina followed.

"Should I call for breakfast?" she asked as she passed, and Jennifer's stomach responded with a loud bellow. "Good answer, because I'm starving."

Jennifer let the door click shut behind her and trailed along. "You know I expect you to have opinions about the outfits, right?"

"Oh, I have opinions," Carolina said, "About everything. Don't you worry, my friend. I'll tell you if it's busted." Jennifer smiled, endeared by Carolina calling her a friend. She'd always struggled with relationships, of any kind, really; rather, she tended toward avoiding them like the plague. But Carolina was hard to shut out, and Jennifer often found she didn't want to. "Not that you *could* look busted, since you've got that whole tall, willowy, regal thing going on."

"You haven't seen me the morning after two too many bourbons."

Carolina chuckled. "Oh?"

"*Oh*," Jennifer said with a pointed look. "From willow tree to gnarly, old oak."

Carolina's laugh bloomed. "Oh no. I'm going to have to see this."

"Perhaps," Jennifer mused as they joined Mr. Clark in the suite's sitting room. "But first, to business."

After nearly fifteen minutes of Dosie's sock-footed pacing from one end of her bedroom to the other, the sound of her shuffling had developed into a kind of ambient music. It was pleasant enough but did little to soothe the rough pulse of anxiety behind her breastbone. Why? *Why* had she thought this was a good idea? She'd booked a freaking escort for lesbian freaking sex at 8:15 in the freaking *morning*. Really? *Really*?

"Really," she groaned and stopped her pacing, smacked her hands over her face and groaned even harder. "Okay." She slapped her cheeks a few times. "Okay." Shook out her arms and hands. "Just stop whining and get dressed already. You'll feel better when you're dressed."

Despite the pile of clothes draped over her mattress, she

was still stark naked but for her socks and had no idea what to wear. She'd been tempted to don her same outfit from the night, or something similar, as was her go-to for stressful situations, but a little voice in the back of her brain whispered she should be more herself this time—more modern, more relaxed. "Relaxed," she huffed at herself. "Yeah, right."

Her mind flashed with an image of the Director's silky raven suit, her bare chest beneath, and shivered. She'd so far been unable to shake the picture for long. She'd hardly even slept. She could only imagine what the Director might greet her in today. And what would Dosie answer with?

She chewed her bottom lip and looked over the items on her bed again. Bounced her knees a bit. She was all nervous energy and heat, one that currently felt more sickly than pleasurable. She rubbed her thighs together and tried not to think about what would be happening in little more than an hour.

Dosie fanned her face and rolled her eyes at herself. "Okay," she said again, exhaling a loud, dramatic breath. "Just *pick* something. It's going to end up on the floor anyway." She fanned her face harder. "Jesus."

Ms. Fisher's quiet, secluded acreage was even more beautiful in morning light, and the sweet smell of lavender in the already warm air heightened Jennifer's excitement. She smiled at the sounds of birds tittering from the trees, a music less vibrant and plentiful in the city. "It's beautiful here."

Carolina nodded beside her as they linked arms and moseyed toward the old porch. "It really is."

Jennifer lowered her voice. "What do you think she does for a living?"

"Clearly something lucrative if she can afford to book you twice in the space of twenty-four hours."

"Trust-fund baby?"

"No way. Trust fund babies live in penthouses. They party on yachts. An old, country Victorian on private land? That's quiet money, earned." She shrugged. "Or, you know, she's the head of an underground criminal organization and just enjoys flipping houses on the side or something."

Jennifer smiled, rolled her eyes. "The house could be inherited. That might explain the state of it." As they stepped onto the porch, she put her curiosity on the back burner and focused. She straightened her posture, pulling her persona to the fore, and turned to Carolina. "Okay. How do I look?"

She always dressed with purpose, usually that of presenting a particular image, but she also dressed to *feel*. Powerful. Dominant. Graceful. Her wardrobe was as much a part of her personality as it was her career, and she took great pride in her selections. Today's selection fit her like a glove, and more importantly, it made her feel like a fucking goddess.

She wore a cotton three-piece suit in midnight blue over a crisp white button-down, with a skinny silk tie and matching pocket square in gold. Dark leather Valentino slingbacks gave her already long legs a few extra inches, and for her hands, nothing but a slim, gold band around her index finger. Her hair hung in loose, shiny waves over one shoulder, the column of her bare neck exposed on the other side, and on her face, only light, neutral makeup but for the shine of gold around her eyelids, which aided her suit in making the blue of her irises pop.

"Hot and terrifying," Carolina said and rang the doorbell.

Jennifer smirked. "Perfect." She had never felt worthier of supplication.

"Let's just hope you're *invited* into the house this time."

"Oh, I'll be invited into more than just her house," she tossed back, and Carolina's firework of a laugh crackled through the surrounding trees.

"Okay confidence. Go ahead then."

"I will."

The door swung open with a groan; only, this time, the woman on the other side appeared entirely different. *Oh.* Jennifer blinked, momentarily dumbstruck and silent. Was this even the same person?

Ms. Fisher wore a white cashmere sweater and skin-tight denim that cut right at the ankle, emphasizing her shiny peach pumps. The night before, her hair had been a cascade of cinnamon curls, but now, it sat in a loose, low bun that left little wisps to wander around her temples and somehow made her appear both older and younger at once. Her fingers ran a nervous back-and-forth over a thin pearl necklace, the only item Jennifer recognized from their first encounter, and her cognac eyes glinted in the morning sun as they landed on Jennifer and stuck there.

"Hi," she said, more under her breath than aloud, and shifted from one foot to the other.

"Ms. Fisher," Carolina greeted. "I have the Director for you."

"Right. Okay." For a moment, Ms. Fisher appeared as terrified as she'd been the night before, but then her gaze tracked its way down Jennifer's body, and Jennifer watched in real time as that terror transformed to want with determination close behind. "I mean, yes, thank you. Thanks." She snickered at herself despite her reddening face, and Jennifer found it terribly charming. "Come on in," she said and moved aside to clear a path into the house.

Carolina excused herself back to the car to wait, and Jennifer stepped inside. She kept close to Ms. Fisher as she entered, her arm just short of grazing the woman's chest, and the air shifted. It tensed. Ms. Fisher took a sharp but quiet breath, and the sound sent a frisson of thrill down Jennifer's spine.

She quickly took in her surroundings, something she hadn't done the night before, and realized Carolina had been right. The home's interior was much nicer than its exterior suggested, though it was clear those nicer aspects were the product of recent renovation. She noted a tool belt hanging over the banister of a narrow staircase and could make out a few paint cans near the edge of the upper landing. The floor and stairs were original hardwood with a dark merlot-colored stain and the shine of a fresh treatment, complimented by the same shade of wainscoting adorning every wall. The ceiling appeared newly treated as well and pitched higher than expected, which Jennifer appreciated. She loathed low ceilings. They'd always made her feel enormous and, on occasion, claustrophobic.

Her eyes found the armoire at the end of the foyer and lingered. She pictured Ms. Fisher pressed into the alcove between wood and wall, her own body crowding and circling; she remembered the tremors, the breath. Jennifer licked her lips, suddenly parched at eight-thirty in the morning.

"Um." Ms. Fisher cleared her throat and smoothed her hands down her sweater. "I guess we can start with good morning."

Jennifer smiled. "Yes, good morning," she said. "I'll admit it's a bit strange for me to say to a client. I rarely have morning appointments."

"Oh." Ms. Fisher worried her bottom lip. "Should I have waited? The time was open on the schedule. I thought—"

"Ms. Fisher, please," Jennifer said, waving away her worries, "I was only saying it was rare, not that it wasn't fine. Would I be here if that was the case?"

A shy smile caused a single, shallow dimple to appear on Ms. Fisher's left cheek. "I guess not."

Darling, Jennifer thought. There was no other word for it, that dimple, or for *her*, Ms. Fisher. Jennifer knew nothing about the woman, truly, and still, it seemed an appropriate descriptor. *Darling*.

Ms. Fisher took the first step, closing the gap between them until scant inches remained, and Jennifer's excitement surged. *Bold,* she thought. *Well, bolder than I anticipated anyway.* She'd half-expected to have to chase the woman around her own house just to get a hand between her legs.

"I wanted to apologize for my behavior last night, um...." Ms. Fisher frowned. "I'm sorry. I don't know what to call you. Do I just call you Director, or do you have a name? That you want me to use, I mean. Obviously, you have a name."

Jennifer chuckled. "Director is fine," she said, "and while I appreciate the apology, I hope that isn't the reason you've invited me here this morning. Because if that is the case, Ms. Fisher, I have to say I'm disappointed."

"Really?" her client asked, a little breathless, and *oh,* Jennifer wanted to play with her like a toy.

She stepped closer, her blazer brushing cashmere, and lowered her voice. "Does that surprise you?"

"Yes."

"And why is that?" Jennifer asked, so close now she could feel the woman's heat, see the quiver that raced across her shoulders. "Do you believe yourself unattractive?"

She swallowed, thick and thunderous in the tense quiet, and something about the wet, heavy sound and the slow bob of her throat made Jennifer's thighs clench. "I guess I just have a hard time imagining that someone like you, a woman like you, might...."

"Want you?" Jennifer asked, and the girl shivered, her body communicating where words failed. It needed, and Jennifer was ready to provide.

"Yes."

"But surely you know how stunning you are." Jennifer touched her—she *had* to—smoothing her fingertips along her client's jaw, the pad of her thumb over the curve of a full bottom lip. "I can't imagine you haven't got a single mirror in this big, old house."

Ms. Fisher's blush returned, deepened. Even splotched with pink, she was lovely. "Thank you."

Jennifer lingered a moment longer then stepped back, delighted when Ms. Fisher's body followed as if chasing her disappearing touch. But she couldn't make it easy. That simply wasn't her way. Her own pleasure demanded desperation—a want so delirious that her clients would beg her to relieve it. Only then did she provide.

"Um, well, can I offer you something to drink?" Ms. Fisher asked, gathering herself. Without waiting for an answer, she spun on her heel and marched toward the end of the foyer as if she'd just remembered that Jennifer was a guest in her home, and she should be playing the dutiful hostess. It both looked and felt conditioned, which Jennifer found curious in someone so young.

"No." Jennifer followed anyway. "Thank you, though."

"I could put the kettle on for coffee. Or tea? I have a few herbal ones and some English Breakfast, I think."

"Thank you," Jennifer said again. "But, really, I'm fine."

"Juice? I have juice," Ms. Fisher said, and Jennifer noted the nervous warble in her voice. She wondered if it was because Ms. Fisher could feel the heat of Jennifer behind her, if the hair at the back of her neck was on end, her heart thumping in her throat with the sensation of being watched, followed. Just on the cusp of capture. Of being ruthlessly devoured. "I could make you a mimosa. I think I have some champagne."

They rounded into a large, open-concept kitchen with a long island in its center. "Do you drink in the mornings?" She made straight for a clear-faced refrigerator stocked to bursting, but Jennifer caught her just as she reached the handles. Her hands curled around the backs of her client's and stilled them.

"Ms. Fisher," she whispered and pressed herself fully against a warm, trembling back. The tip of her nose traced mindless shapes into the back Ms. Fisher's neck as Jennifer breathed her in. Bergamot and hardened honey. She smelled like a lazy day pressed into skin. Intoxicating. Jennifer kept her voice low and silky as her long, slender fingers stroked down the backs her client's hands and under the sleeves of her sweater to rub at her inner wrists, just over the wild jump of her pulse. "Breathe."

"I'm sorry," she said in a whisper, all her body atremble. "I don't know why I'm so nervous."

"This is your first time. It's natural."

A strangled laugh jumped from Ms. Fisher's lips and fogged the glass door of the refrigerator. "It doesn't feel natural," she said, voice pitching into a bodied *whine*, and the sound did wonders for Jennifer's ego—not that it needed stroking. "I feel like I can't control my own body. Like I'm going to jump right out of my skin any second."

"Breathe," Jennifer commanded again and dropped her hands to Ms. Fisher's waist, gripping her. Grounding her. After several deep breaths, the trembling eased, and the woman sagged against her. "Good girl."

"Oh, *God*," Ms. Fisher all but moaned, and the vibrations returned in full force. "Okay, this is happening. It's happening now?"

Jennifer smiled into the woman's hair, thankful to have it hidden as she was certain it would be all teeth. She was far too pleased with the rending of a woman into tremors and ruins. And with what? The sound of her voice. Two sweet little words. She filed away the effect for future use and let her hands slide around to the woman's stomach, splayed her fingers, and yanked her back to hold her close. "We should talk first. Is there somewhere we can sit?" Every inch that *could* touch did. "If not, I'm quite certain my lap will suit you."

Another shiver. Another sound edging on a moan. She nodded and slowly extracted herself from Jennifer's hold. Her legs shook on heels too high for her hazed condition, but she managed to stay on her feet as she led the way to an adjoining dining room and pulled two antique wooden chairs from under a matching table big enough to seat many, *many*, more than one. *Strange.*

"Will this work?" Ms. Fisher asked as she sat and crossed one ankle over the other, hands delicately folded atop her lap.

"Perfectly," Jennifer replied and sat opposite her, enough distance to keep from touching but close enough to not feel oddly spaced. Close enough to keep their heat, the promise of connection. She crossed one leg over the other at the knee, let one Valentino bob as she relaxed back into the chair and watched the bashful young woman across from her.

"Now what?" Her big eyes flitted up to meet Jennifer's, the brown of her irises darkening as her pupils dilated. *My, my,* Jennifer thought. This poor darling was so terribly repressed. And clearly pent up.

"Tell me a secret."

Ms. Fisher's thin, reddish-brown eyebrows furrowed as she shifted in her seat, uncrossing her ankles only to cross them the other way. "Why would I tell you a secret?"

"Trust."

"Trust?"

"You're familiar with the concept, yes?" Jennifer held her laugh when Ms. Fisher rolled her eyes. "Good. So, tell me a secret."

She groaned and covered her face with her hands. "This is not what I expected."

"No?" Jennifer smiled, surprised by how much she was enjoying this. "What did you expect?"

"I don't know. Nothing. Something more...." She dropped her hands and looked at Jennifer as if she might find the answer hidden somewhere in her face, but then she simply sighed and said, "God, you are *so* beautiful."

Warmth spilled through Jennifer's chest. "I'm afraid that is not a secret," she teased. "You haven't stopped ogling me since I arrived."

A choked sound escaped Ms. Fisher's throat. "Oh. *Oh.* I'm so sorry! I'm so sorry, I—"

Jennifer quickly waved away her panic. "No, no, no, stop," she said. "I was teasing you. Besides, this suit was obscenely expensive. I would be offended if it *weren't* properly appreciated."

"Okay." Ms. Fisher laughed, obviously relieved, and as if triggered by Jennifer's words, she let her gaze wander. Jennifer's eyes to her lips. Her neck, the skinny strip of her tie. Then down, down, absorbing every inch. She shifted in her seat again as if alleviating an ache, an ache Jennifer knew well. Arousal. She found it borderline endearing how hard Ms. Fisher was trying (and failing) to keep hers disguised.

"Well, it definitely suits you," she muttered then blushed all the way to her hairline. "I can't believe I just said that."

Jennifer chuckled, a quiet melody that seemed to draw Ms. Fisher toward the edge of her seat. She was hungry for something, anything Jennifer was willing to give her, but clearly terrified of it at the same time. "Tell me a secret, Ms. Fisher."

"What if I don't have a secret to tell?"

"Everyone has secrets." So much tension. It vibrated off the woman in waves, peaking and falling and peaking again. "I think, perhaps, *especially* you."

Ms. Fisher glanced away, stalled. Her manicured fingers, nails painted nude and coated to shimmer, smoothed down the front of her sweater again, a nervous habit if Jennifer had to guess. "I've never..."

"Go on."

Ms. Fisher's eyes were glued to her own hands as if inspecting them for the slightest imperfection, something she could do away with by whatever means necessary. Finally, she slumped and trilled her lips. On an exhale, she admitted, "I've never touched myself."

The confession hung in the air as Jennifer traced over her client's nearly hidden expression. Her downturned lips and wrinkled brow spoke volumes. Confusion. Disappointment. Guilt. Shame. *Need.*

Ms. Fisher was a heady concoction of conflict and desire. Like several of Jennifer's female clients over the years, she'd likely spent her life shrinking her desires and, along with her voice, packing them into a tiny box she could shove to the back of her brain and ignore. She *wanted*, and she felt guilty for wanting. She *needed*, and she loathed herself for needing.

Jennifer rested her chin on her knuckles, elbow propped on the thick wood of the dining table. "Unfortunately, that is the case for many women." When Ms. Fisher looked sharply up at her, Jennifer smiled, slow and knowing. "You can ask."

"Have you?"

"Yes. Often." As if she'd just had the wind knocked from her, Ms. Fisher bowed, shifting forward and back like a thin sheet of metal caught in a storm. Jennifer almost expected to hear a cartoonish, rubbery tone shake from the woman's spine. "And enthusiastically."

"Good lord," Ms. Fisher whispered, and Jennifer had to

choke down a laugh. She had her on the brink of collapse and she'd yet to properly touch.

"But, come now, you can do better," Jennifer said and inched forward until she sat right on the edge of her chair. "A proper secret, please. Something real." She propped her elbows on her knees, folding her hands together under the defined angle of her hard chin, and locked her eyes on her client's. "Something deep."

"I was never able to...." Ms. Fisher hesitated, body taut, then seemed to resign herself to admitting whatever it was. She wouldn't, however, meet Jennifer's eyes. "With my husband, m-my late husband, I was never able to...."

Husband. Ah. That explained the wedding band. Jennifer briefly wondered how she'd lost a spouse so young but decided she neither needed to know nor truly cared. Ms. Fisher was *here* now, and she wasn't in want of a husband. She was in want of a woman. *This* woman. Jennifer, herself.

"Climax?" She received only a short nod from Ms. Fisher's hanging head, and something about it pierced her heart. Instinct took over. She slid from her chair as gracefully as possible and onto her knees. The floor was hard and uncomfortable, and she was certain her suit would wrinkle, but, surprisingly, she found she didn't care.

Ms. Fisher's eyes widened as she looked at Jennifer again. "What are you doing?"

"Deeper," Jennifer told her. "I want you to go deeper."

"H-how deep?"

Reaching forward, Jennifer grabbed the front two legs of

her client's chair and tugged. The chair screeched over hardwood until the peach-colored toes of the woman's pumps bumped against her knees. Jennifer gazed up at her, clocking every minute tick of her lovely, flushed face as it cycled through a breathless string of expressions. "As deep as you can handle."

Ms. Fisher unlocked her ankles and crossed her legs at the knee instead. Her thighs locked together, and Jennifer smiled, a trickle of want tickling at the base of her spine. She moved her hands from the chair legs to Ms. Fisher's denim-clad ankles, then slowly, *slowly*, dragged them up, ringing her calves, smoothing over her knees. She reveled in every tick of movement, every vibration, every quiver her touch evoked like magic.

"I had an affair once."

Hello! That certainly caught her off guard. "Well, well, Ms. Fisher," she said with a rasp of a laugh. Gently, she pried the woman's legs apart, so she could set them back as they were. "You surprise me."

"With a girl. Woman. With a woman."

Jennifer would have laughed, delighted by the revelation, but Ms. Fisher suddenly looked as if she wished she could disappear. She didn't share Jennifer's delight. Instead, she shrank in obvious shame. Jennifer shifted her hands onto the woman's thighs and began a slow, comforting massage.

"I am not judging you," she assured. "I would never."

"It wasn't long after I was married."

"When were you married?"

Ms. Fisher opened her mouth to answer, then closed it again. Her voice dropped to a pained whisper. "Right out of high school."

"Ah." Jennifer nodded. "Young."

"Yeah." She shook her head as if to physically force away a thought, a memory. A frustrated sigh shot from her lips. "Is —is that enough now?" she asked. "Can we move on?"

Jennifer frowned. Something about Ms. Fisher gnawed at her, stirred up sympathies she rarely indulged. Perhaps it was her unwillingness to be forthcoming, especially when Jennifer sensed she was normally an open book. But here, with her, with *this*, she was guarded.

Or maybe it was the way she'd dolled herself up the night before, like TV housewife pulled into a time she had no business being part of. It was the way she looked at Jennifer, was *still* looking at Jennifer, like she could see freedom in her body and craved it, desperately, for herself, but couldn't bring herself to ask for it, let alone have it. It was the way she made Jennifer feel sad and touched at the same time, like a gift from a loved one since passed on. She was an enigma that Jennifer couldn't wrap her head around, and at the same time, she was as easy to read as the words stamped over the entryway to the room they currently occupied: *Home is where you hang your heart.* Jennifer imagined Ms. Fisher had long ago hung her heart out to dry and never once questioned why it shriveled.

Jennifer reached for Ms. Fisher's hands, found her palms clammy, fingers shaking. Jennifer held them tightly. "Did you enjoy it?" she asked as she soothed her thumbs back and forth. "Your affair with this woman, I mean. Did you like how she touched you, where she touched you? I can do—"

"She didn't."

"What do you mean?"

Ms. Fisher squirmed in her seat and blew a heavy breath up over her cheeks. "It wasn't like that. It was more of an emotional affair. I guess."

"So, you never slept with this woman? You never touched or tasted her?"

Ms. Fisher closed her eyes. "No."

"And you never let her taste you?"

Another quiet "No," and Jennifer sighed.

"Director?"

"Yes, Ms. Fisher?"

"I think I'm ready." She opened her eyes again. "You're asking these questions, because you're trying to build trust, so that this can be less awkward. I get that. But I really don't think we need to. I think I'm ready."

Jennifer pursed her lips to prevent a smile. "I see. And what is it you think you're ready for? Be specific."

"For, for you?"

"Is that a question or a statement?"

"I'm ready for you," she said again, and it might have been a declaration were it not for the pronounced crease in her brow.

Jennifer held her gaze and leaned, pushing her breasts against Ms. Fisher's knees. "I disagree."

The crease deepened. Ms. Fisher opened her mouth as if

to protest, but then she snapped it shut again. One corner of her mouth tugged toward a frown.

"You need to go deeper," Jennifer encouraged. "I want a genuine secret. One with consequences."

Ms. Fisher huffed. Her face reddened again as a glossy sheen coated her eyes—for a moment, water, then gasoline. A spark of fury. Her voice pitched upward as she said, "There's nothing. I already told you something I'm ashamed of. What more do you want from me?"

A quiet sound of sorrow, of disappointment, slithered up Jennifer's throat. She swallowed it. "You weren't just ashamed of what you felt for her. You were afraid of it." She eased back, relinquishing her hold on the woman, and stood. Her knees ached from the hard floor, but she showed no sign of it. "Unfortunately, you're still afraid, and fear has no place in pleasure; at least, not where I am concerned." She turned her attention to an ornate clock on the dining room wall. "Our hour is up."

Ms. Fisher jerked as if slapped. "What?"

"I wish you well, Ms. Fisher, truly," Jennifer said and began to retrace her path to the door.

"Wait!" She heard Ms. Fisher's fast, clicking steps behind her. "You didn't give me what I wanted."

"That's just the thing: You don't know what you want." Jennifer walked slowly around the large kitchen island, running her fingers along the edge of the countertop, and allowing Ms. Fisher a beat to catch up.

She arrived flushed and crackling with energy. "Can't you

just tell me what to do?" Her tone took on a surprising edge that Jennifer found both amusing and attractive. "You're the Director, right? So, direct me."

Oh. Jennifer's brow shot up. "Look, while I may not know you, I imagine I'm not misguided in suspecting you've been told what to do and how to feel your entire life. And I think you should determine such things for yourself before bringing in yet another person to do it for you."

Ms. Fisher recoiled like a snake set to strike. "Well, I'm not paying you to think!"

There! Jennifer thought. *There's her fire.* It had needed only kindling and a bit of careful coaxing.

"I'm not paying your ridiculous prices so *you* can decide when I'm ready," Ms. Fisher snapped. "I'm ready when I say I am."

A heatwave rippled out through Jennifer's limbs before rolling back and settling at the base of her spine. She turned sharply on her heel and invaded Ms. Fisher's space. Face to face. Chest to chest. Breath huffing and colliding against breath. "Are you ready now then?" she challenged, and though she was certain of the answer, she hoped she was wrong. Her body was alive.

She advanced as Ms. Fisher stumbled back a step. "Right now?"

Another step back, and Jennifer had her trapped between her arms and the island, boxed in like a captured animal. "Right this very moment?" She curled an unforgiving hand around the back of the woman's neck, dug roughly up into her hair and tugged. The yip it evoked delighted her.

"Because I *will* touch you, Ms. Fisher." She kept her voice low and rich, commanding, so her promise sounded like a threat. Her breath danced over the goose-bumped flesh along Ms. Fisher's jaw as she shifted in until they were melted against one another. She slid the tip of her nose around the curve of Ms. Fisher's ear. "I will touch you relentlessly."

Ms. Fisher vibrated like one of Jennifer's toys, earthquakes wreaking havoc in her bones. Her hands hovered and twitched but didn't touch. So badly this woman wanted her, yet she was afraid to want. She was afraid of her own shadow. She couldn't even touch herself in the privacy of her own home—no witnesses, no expectations, no pressure. It was almost sweet, in a warm, sad sort of way that ached.

"I think you might be right," Ms. Fisher finally, quietly, admitted.

Jennifer lay a light kiss to the hollow of her ear and released her. As she retreated, Ms. Fisher's body bowed like it wanted to reconnect. Her lips parted around depthless breaths, and her eyes began to water.

Fuck. Jennifer's heat cooled in an instant; a wick blown bare. *Please don't cry.*

She did. "I'm sorry."

Jennifer's tolerance for feelings had a low threshold, and the crack in Ms. Fisher's voice struck it like a clapper to a bell. All her alarms started ringing. At the same time, and to her surprise, she wanted to stay. She felt *an urge* to stay.

The mystery of Ms. Fisher taunted her like a present under a Christmas tree, tempting her to unwrap and unravel. What was trapped under all that symmetry and style? What lay hidden at the root of Ms. Fisher's fear and shame, and who was she there, at the core of it?

"Ms. Fisher, I'm going to offer you something very rare."

The woman wiped her tears but said nothing, and Jennifer took the moment to drink her in. Her defeated gaze, and the pulse visibly thumping in the side of her neck. The string of pearls she toggled between her fingertips. The strip of visible flesh at her waistline where her sweater had ridden up.

Jennifer took a breath, her reaction helpless. Whatever it was about Ms. Fisher—her unknown story; the sadness and fear that haloed her like an aura, and the excitement that throbbed underneath; her naiveté; or, that sweet, little dimple —Jennifer was hooked. She *wanted* things, was thinking about things. Couldn't *stop* thinking about things.

"Two options," she amended. "You may choose freely with no argument from me."

Ms. Fisher sniffled. "Okay."

"First, a refund," Jennifer said. "I've made a decision here that I acknowledge you aren't satisfied with. I will not change my mind on this today, but I pride myself on never leaving a client unsatisfied. So, I will offer you your money back, the full amount without conflict."

Ms. Fisher frowned. "The contract said there were no refunds and no exceptions."

"Yes, well...." Jennifer smiled and hoped it offered some comfort. The girl's face still hadn't returned to its natural shade, and as much as she wished to devastate her, she had no desire to do so emotionally. Besides, she'd long ago conquered her own, but she knew what it was to fear desire. This world offered little respite for women and even less for women who craved the touch of other women. She needn't continue the trend. "It's my company. I'll break the rules as I see fit."

A shy laugh. "What's the second option?"

"Touch yourself."

Ms. Fisher blanched. "Now?!" Her voice squeaked. "Here?" She glanced down then up again, then she looked around the room. Whatever she was searching for, she didn't seem to be finding it. "Are you wanting to watch or something?"

"Would you like for me to watch?"

She didn't answer. Instead, she stared at Jennifer as if expecting her to answer for her, predict what she wanted and tell her. Jennifer expected she *did* know what Ms. Fisher wanted, along with a plethora of ways to provide, but she wasn't about to tell her. She *could*, but she wouldn't. Jennifer believed consent should be informed to a reasonable degree and *confident*. She guided clients, ordered them, but she had to have a starting point, and that starting point had to be dictated by the client. Ms. Fisher had no starting point and seemed unwilling to even attempt naming one. How could Jennifer be informed if *she* wasn't?

"Relax," she teased. "I meant this more as an assignment."

"An assignment?"

"Yes. I'm going to leave, and in my absence, now or whenever you choose, I want you to touch yourself. And once you have, once you've *experienced* yourself, then we may try this again with the fee you've paid for today's session held over for the next. If you wish."

Ms. Fisher licked her lips, mouth visibly watering with each breath. She was hungry but didn't know what she was hungry for. She ached but couldn't tell why. She needed but had yet to discover what. She was a mess, a lovely, conflicted mess. "I'm afraid I wouldn't know what to do," she admitted, "or how to start."

"That's something you should explore," Jennifer said. "So, you have your options. Which will it be?"

"Why do you want me to do this?" She sounded so small, so defeated.

Jennifer stepped closer again and brushed her knuckles over the swell of a warm cheek. "Because despite what you might think, I'm not trying to deny you pleasure." She leaned in, lips hovering at the corner of Ms. Fisher's mouth. "I'm trying to help you understand how to have it."

Ms. Fisher shuddered at the delicate kiss Jennifer gave. "Okay," she whispered, and Jennifer retreated to catch her gaze.

"Ms. Fisher?"

"Okay, I'll try."

Jennifer felt a surge of thrill and couldn't help her smile. "Good choice," she murmured then withdrew. She resituated her jacket and smoothed her tie, gave a curt nod. "You know how to reach me."

"Please," Ms. Fisher said, catching her by the arm. "Will you at least tell me how to.... What do I do? Where do I touch?"

"Oh, Ms. Fisher," Jennifer said and took the woman's hand. "Everywhere." She brought it to her lips and kissed each fingertip, thumb to pinky. "Touch everywhere."

With that, she gave one last, promising smile, and left. The heat of the woman at her back dissipated with every forward step, and Jennifer told herself it was only pity, only intrigue, only lust that urged her to go back. She didn't. She wouldn't.

Ms. Fisher would have to come to her.

3

In her Pacific Heights condo, Jennifer lounged on the cushioned seat of a large bay window. The fulgent city lights greeted her in bright pops of colors but cast dimmer and dimmer auras as she followed them out toward the Golden Gate bridge. It was a view that never failed to awe (it had better, given what she paid for it) and one that usually soothed her. She could look out at the lights and the disappearing ocean and remember how expansive the world was, how bright it could be; tonight, however, the serenity of a good view and a tall glass of wine evaded her. There was a heaviness in her chest that she couldn't shake.

It had been more than a week since her last encounter with the diffident Ms. Fisher, but the young woman's face flickered behind her eyes like a spot of light that wouldn't fade. Jennifer could picture her so clearly, it was as if she could reach out and touch her, trace her understated, quivering frown. She could smooth away every fear and follow her fingers with her lips. If only Ms. Fisher would ask it of her. If only she would say the words: *This is what I want. This is what I need. Give me what I need.*

Over the course of her career, Jennifer had learned that, for most people, sex was so much more complicated than they'd ever been taught to expect or handle. A person's entire life and all their experiences—small to large, fleeting to lasting, awful to spectacular—manifested in their sexual lives in a vast and fascinating variety of ways. Sometimes, that made for a wonderful journey of discovery, but the opposite was also possible. Jennifer had seen it firsthand.

It was one of many reasons she was so adamant about clear and enthusiastic consent. Her clients didn't have to know *exactly* what they wanted every step of the way, but they had to know that they wanted to take those steps. It was vital for Jennifer to hear them articulate, to a basic degree, what they were seeking. It wasn't enough to simply be interested or intrigued. They had to communicate in their own words, and they had to be sure.

Ms. Fisher wasn't there yet. Her body communicated, *loudly*, but her effort and ability seemed to stop there. She tiptoed around words like "sex," "masturbation," and "orgasm," like a kid avoiding curses, and wore conflict on her face like a poorly matched concealer. And Jennifer didn't have many rules when it came to sex—she was a strong proponent of never *yuck*-ing another's *yum*—but she was adamant in her belief that consent be conflict-free.

Until Ms. Fisher was ready to shed that conflict or crack it open and face it, until she was able to trust her body and trust her voice and trust Jennifer, they would be stuck in this limbo. Nudging at an old, rusty door reluctant to budge. Jennifer's thoughts looped that door and its story relentlessly, and she realized, with startling clarity, that she *wanted* it open. She wanted to be there when it opened. She wanted inside.

Her friends' laughter both soothed and tortured. It pinged around the cavernous space of Dosie's bedroom as they lay on her bed in their pajamas, clutching their stomachs and slapping at one another as if they'd told the world's most hilarious joke and needed to remind each other, every *three seconds*, how funny it was. And all Dosie could do was sit in a crumpled ball at the head of her bed, red-faced and mortified about what happened but somehow *also laughing*.

She kicked her feet into their sides like an annoyed dog demanding more space. "It's not funny."

"Then why are we laughing?" Natalie pulled her Fleetwood Mac T-shirt up over her face to wipe her own tears away. Her shoulder-length hair, a natural vanilla blonde, was streaked purple and piled atop her head in a loose top knot that jiggled every time she got tickled about something.

"Because you're both assholes."

"You're laughing too!"

"Because I laugh when other people laugh, and I can't help it. You know this!"

"And also, because it was hilarious," Kaylia said and slapped Dosie's foot away. "Masturbation as an assignment. I love it. I can't believe you weren't going to tell us." She crawled up to sit beside her, their backs against the headboard.

Dosie cuddled into her shoulder, under the fall of her longer, shaggy bob—the same espresso-dark as her eyes—and groaned. "I'm hopeless."

"Nah." Natalie stretched along the foot of the bed. "You're just a little repressed."

"Well, 'a little' might be an understatement," Kaylia said. "Let's be real. When you used the hand mirror to look at your vag, you threw it across the room like it was cursed."

"I was just surprised!"

"I know, honey, and that's my point. Nobody's vagina should surprise them that much."

Dosie's blistering whine stirred her friends into another round of laughter. "How am I supposed to have sex with a woman if I can't even...*you know*?"

"You can start with saying the actual words instead of 'you know'," Kaylia said and poked her side. "This isn't elementary school."

"I wouldn't know, because I didn't *go* to elementary school," Dosie grumbled into her shoulder.

"That's what *we're* here for," Natalie said, "to help educate you."

"Right, so repeat after me." Kaylia cleared her throat. "Mas-tur-bate. Va-gi-na. Stay with me here, Dosie. Stay with me. Cli-tor-us."

Dosie snorted. "Ha. Ha. Ha. You're so funny."

"Come here." Kaylia looped an arm around Dosie's back and squeezed her. "I'm just teasing. You've got nothing to be embarrassed about."

"Yeah," Natalie said. "I can't remember how old I was when I found out how close our vaginas are to our buttholes, but I know I had a whole hypochondriac meltdown afterward." She guffawed at herself. "And I *didn't* have a traumatic childhood; well, for the most part. Point being: It's not just you. This stuff's not inherent knowledge. We all have to learn it at some point, and that's not just about our bodies but, like, our boundaries and our rights, too. That we don't *have to* accept anything but what we *actually want*. You know what I mean?"

Dosie nodded. Her eyes burned and watered. "Yeah."

"Ah, Dose, don't cry. You know you've already come so far, right? You know that."

"Anyone who grew up the way you did would be this way," Kaylia said and nudged Dosie to sit up and look at her. "It's only natural that you're a little freaked out by your body sometimes and your sexuality and everything that goes with it."

"Yeah, I know," Dosie said and blew cool air up toward her eyes.

"That's not your life anymore. It hasn't been for a long time, and it won't ever be again. And this place..." She motioned around the bedroom. "...is not *that* place anymore. It's yours now, and nothing ever has to happen here that you don't want to happen."

From the foot of the bed, she couldn't reach much, but Natalie grabbed what she could. She curled her hand around Dosie's ankle and squeezed. "*Ever.*"

The tears fell, creeping down Dosie's cheeks as she finally voiced the fear she'd been ruminating on for years. "What if I'm like this for the rest of my life? What I went through, the things that happened.... You said it yourselves: my childhood wasn't normal, and I'm not normal because of it. And I'm just convinced sometimes I'm going to spend the rest of my life trying to undo the first fifteen years of it, and I..."

A sob barreled up her throat and out, and Natalie quickly crawled up the bed to join them. She and Kaylia, like two human quilts, two precious shields, held her from both directions. Protected her better than anyone prior had ever done or cared to do.

"You are doing everything right," Kaylia reassured. "You go to therapy. You journal. You talk about it when you can. You aren't in denial, and you aren't running from it. You're doing everything you can to heal. It's just a process, and yeah, it takes years. Sometimes, a *lot* of years. But that's okay."

"Everyone has a past, and we can't change that. All we

can do is our best to move forward," Natalie added. "That's what you're doing, and it's what you've been doing for years. I know it's frustrating, but the progress is there, Dose. You know it is."

"I know." Dosie sniffled, frustrated, and wiped at her cheeks. "I'm sorry you guys have to remind me so much."

"Oh, shut up," Kaylia scoffed. "We're family."

Dosie dug a hand into each of their shirts and pulled them as close as possible. "You guys are the best," she mumbled. "You know that?"

"I thought we were assholes."

"Well, yeah, you are, but you're also the best."

"Okay." Kaylia groaned and pushed against Dosie's hold. "That's my sap limit."

Dosie pouted but let her go. "Do you think she thinks I'm crazy now?"

"The escort?" Natalie pulled a face, as if to say '*Seriously?*'. "Um, no. I think she thinks you're hot."

Dosie's eyebrows jumped toward her hairline. Her heart leaped in her chest, and she spluttered—half-laugh, half-gasp. "Okay, now I think *you're* crazy."

"No, I agree with Nat," Kaylia said. "I mean, she offered you a refund, which is basically unheard of in her business, and not only did she offer you a refund, she offered to come back and try again at *no additional cost.*" Kaylia clucked her tongue. "If that doesn't scream, 'I want inside those pretty panties,' to you, then I honestly don't know what would."

Natalie snorted so hard she had to pinch her nose to stop the burn of it.

"And on that note, it's time for wine," Kaylia announced with a grin. "It should be chilled by now."

"I'll help." Natalie popped off the bed to follow. "Dose?"

"You guys go ahead," she said. "I'm just going to wash my face."

Dosie lay back after they left, letting the moment settle before she got herself up and going again. Her eyes still stung, but the chaos in her chest had subsided. Her heart was working its way toward calm, acceptance. With a sigh, Dosie slid to the edge of the bed and sat up.

"Hey, Dosie?" Natalie's face reappeared around the door frame.

"Yeah?"

"You're *so* loved." She smiled easily despite the gravity the words had. "You know that, right?"

New tears welled rapidly as Dosie smiled back. "Yeah, Nat," she said, voice cracking. "I know that now."

Another three nights flew by before Dosie could bring herself to put a hand between her legs without the sole intention of trimming or washing. Pillar candles speckled the furniture, and their small flames cast an enticing glow about her bedroom. It was ridiculous, she knew, but if she was going to do this, she wanted the mood to be right, or as right as it could be when she was utterly alone and entirely clueless.

She lay stiffly under her sheets, naked and unsure of where or how to begin. The longer she procrastinated, the more she thought about what she was doing (or failing to do), and the more she thought about *that*, the more she procrastinated. The vicious cycle had her mind on fire, thoughts exploding like bombs left and right.

Why is this so hard? It's my own freaking body! It shouldn't be this hard. It shouldn't be hard at all. Or awkward. Or shameful. Or anything else. It's just my body. It's just one of its needs. If I can wash it and wipe it and feed it and let someone else inside it, then I should be able to do this.

But then, like a sun streak parting a dark cloud, that voice came back to her. *Her* voice.

Everywhere.

It drifted through her mind like smoke, then down into her body. It settled low in her belly, warm and stirring.

Touch everywhere.

Dosie let free a slow, trembling breath, and brought her fingertips to her mouth. She closed her eyes and traced her lips. Down to her chin. She ran along the edge of her jaw to the space behind her ear, then up into her hair. She scratched over her scalp, back and forth and around, and felt the tension in her body begin to ease.

Her throat bobbed under her fingers as she drew down the slope of her neck. She followed the wing of her collarbone then down again. Her palms began to sweat as she rounded the swell of one breast, then the other. When she circled her nipple with the point of her index finger, a whimper drew up her throat and startled her.

Apprehension seeped in like a breeze, threatening her budding flame, but she did her best to tamp it down. Dispel it. She clenched her eyes and forced another slow, focused breath. As it left her, she rolled one nipple between her finger and thumb. When she pinched down just the slightest bit, she felt a jolt between her legs.

"Oh." It was breathy, barely a sound, until she pinched again. "*Oh.*"

She'd had no idea how sensitive her nipples were, how *pleasurable* it could be to stimulate them. She'd never tried it before, and sex with her husband was always so mechanical. No foreplay. No after-play. No play of any kind, really, and for so terribly long, Dosie believed her role in it to be that of a receptacle and nothing more. Lie down and receive him, allow him *his* pleasure. Her own wasn't necessary; it hadn't even been a thought in her mind, nor ever, obviously, in his. Not that she'd ever blamed him. He'd been conditioned as she had, and neither knew any better.

But Dosie had certainly known worse. So, she never complained. She never even thought to, which meant, at twenty-six years old, she still knew so very little about her body or how to connect with it, and it was only as she experienced her first wisps of pleasure from her own hand that she realized just how sad that was. And how angry she *should've been, should be.*

Dosie brought her hands to her face and pressed at her eyes. "Stop," she said, willing them not to water. "Stop."

With a frustrated cry, she threw off the covers and stood, padded naked to the door and out. She breathed herself steady again as she took the stairs down to the kitchen to grab her laptop. She swiped it off the counter.

"Wine," she told her empty kitchen. "I definitely need wine."

When she returned to her bedroom, laptop tucked under her arm and a brimming Pinot Noir in hand, she felt better. And after a sip (gulp): reinvigorated. She set the glass aside and settled back onto her bed, determined to succeed. God help her, if she had to duct-tape her hand to her vagina to get it done, then she sure as hell would.

Her hands started to sweat again as she opened her laptop and followed the advice that Natalie had given her earlier that day. She used the internet. She opened her search engine and typed the three words in before she could talk herself out of it: *female masturbation videos.*

Her face was lava as the results loaded. "Get it together, Dosie," she said, more command than encouragement. "You're absolutely doing this."

She held her breath and clicked.

When an hour had come and gone and Carolina had yet to pull over, realization settled over Jennifer like a flame. She jabbed the intercom. "Carolina," she said and immediately heard the eagerness in her voice. *What am I? A teenager?*

"Ma'am?"

Jennifer cleared her throat, schooled her voice, and tried again. "Are we headed where I assume we're headed?"

Carolina's knowing chuckle answered. "Excited?"

"I was beginning to think she'd given up on re-booking."

"Is that a yes?"

"I am...cautiously optimistic," Jennifer said, then clicked off the intercom and settled back into her seat. She tried to tame it, but the smile came anyway. She closed her eyes and leaned against the car door, rested her forehead against the window. The strange effect this woman, this terrified, bashful woman, had on her confounded Jennifer. At the same time, she found it equally thrilled and disquieted her.

Two visits with Ms. Fisher and they had yet to even touch beyond brief connections. It was the slowest progression Jennifer had ever experienced with a client; then again, most of her clients were men, and rarely were they shy about sex. She could only recall a few who had been. Even among the much smaller pool of Jennifer's female clients, Ms. Fisher was a unique case. She wasn't the first to need a feeling of trust and safety, nor the first who'd been repressed, or orgasm deprived, but she *was* the first to end an appointment with no sexual contact whatsoever. Not once but *twice*.

Jennifer had had the occasional fleeting crush on a client, when the chemistry was hot, but she knew better than to nurture such feelings, let alone develop relationships with her clients. There were no relationships in her business. There were only transactions. She could care for her clients, but she couldn't indulge that care—not in any way that might be perceived as unprofessional. She couldn't want anything from them beyond a good time, couldn't need anything from them beyond their cash and their consent.

Ms. Fisher had stricken a chord inside her, a rare, fragile note from a rare, fragile instrument. Jennifer wanted to tune and refine her, wanted to play her, wanted to hear all the ways she could sing, and she tried to tell herself it wasn't emotion. It wasn't desire or connection. It was intrigue—the thrill of the chase and the suspense of withholding. The precipice. Dancing along that edge was magic. It was heat. That was what Jennifer was feeling. She told herself as much again and again, because that was all she *could* feel. Ms. Fisher could be played, could be taught to sing, but she couldn't be kept.

There wasn't much Jennifer couldn't afford, but that was certainly one.

The car eventually slowed to a crawl, and Jennifer blinked out of her thoughts. She lowered the partition and looked out the front windshield. The glow of Carolina's phone, mounted on the dash, made it difficult to see much beyond the glass, but Jennifer caught a glimpse of familiar trees. Boughs and branches reached through the dark, stretching over the top of the car as they crept down the lane that led to Ms. Fisher's house.

"You can stay in the car tonight," Jennifer said as Carolina silenced the engine.

"You know I'm not supposed to do that."

"You love reminding me of my own rules."

"Somebody has to."

Jennifer laughed. "You're right, and I appreciate it. But I've been here twice already without a problem. Besides, the woman practically faints every time I look at her, so I doubt she's going to try anything I would need security for."

"You never know." Carolina tutted. "She could be hiding some crazy behind those 1950s dresses and pearls."

"It was one 1950s dress, and I doubt she's hiding anything under it but a perfectly groomed bush, so I think I can manage."

As soon as the words were out of her mouth, she and Carolina looked at one another in the rearview mirror and burst out laughing. "You should crack jokes more often."

Jennifer checked her face in her hand mirror. "I wouldn't want to spoil you." She quirked one brow at her own reflection. *Go get 'em, gorgeous.* "Okay, I will see you in a bit." She stepped out into the warm, breezy night, Carolina's cheeky voice drifting out after.

"Hope you finally get laid!"

The door opened before Jennifer could knock, and there stood Ms. Fisher, primped and pristine. She wore a collared black rockabilly dress that looked like something out of Audrey Hepburn's closet, shiny black pumps, and her signature pearl necklace. *Two 1950s dresses,* Jennifer amended, and felt a smile touch her lips. The girl was gorgeous.

"Hi." Ms. Fisher smoothed a hand over her slick, shiny bun. "Director." Her gaze shot down the length of Jennifer's body, and her posture wobbled. She licked her glossed lips as her eyes drifted back up and locked onto Jennifer's.

Oh. Tingles rippled up Jennifer's spine and spread. *Not so scared after all.*

Ms. Fisher stepped aside, her heels clicking succinctly against the hardwood floor. Her voice dropped a half-octave, and Jennifer's thighs clenched. "Come in, please."

4

The door latching behind Jennifer sounded like thunder, the only noise in a tense silence that rapidly devoured. They stood a few feet apart as little whispers of anticipation tickled the base of Jennifer's spine, but she showed no outward sign of it. Any heightened expression might send the woman across from her running for the hills or tumbling to the floor in a dead faint.

Ms. Fisher gnawed her glossed bottom lip and fingered the small beads of her pearl necklace. "Your, um, driver?" she said, glancing toward the door. "The other woman who's usually with you. She didn't come tonight?"

"She is my driver, yes, but she is also my security detail." Jennifer smiled. "You're not going to cause any trouble, are you?"

Ms. Fisher's laugh wobbled weakly out of her. "No," she said and swallowed thickly, throat bobbing.

"Are you sure?" Jennifer stepped closer, delighted to see the woman's gaze drop in answer.

It dripped like water to Jennifer's chest, from the visible expanse of her skin where her collarbones met to the black onyx stone suspended between her breasts by a y-drop gold chain. Over the curves of her shoulders and down to her hands, short nails crystal clear and shimmering and a petite diamond-and-sapphire gold ring gracing one long middle finger. From Jennifer's gaping navy silk button-down to the jet-black denim painting her long legs and the black leather toes of her Jimmy Choo ankle boots.

Jennifer fought a laugh as she let herself be ogled, Ms. Fisher like a starving Wile E. Coyote hallucinating a freshly roasted Roadrunner. She briefly imagined cartoon vapors steaming off her body and couldn't keep up the fight. Bottled too tightly, the laugh spewed forth, and Ms. Fisher's eyes rocketed back up. They widened with realization, and Jennifer briefly worried she might have ruined the mood before it could even be established. But as her client's cheeks tinted red, Jennifer's amusement was echoed back at her.

Ms. Fisher giggled at herself and pressed a palm to her forehead. Her cheek dimpled with her joy, and Jennifer felt something catch in her chest. She'd thought Ms. Fisher lovely before, but like this, she was radiant.

"I'm sorry." With her free hand, she fanned her face. "You probably feel like a zoo animal."

"On the contrary," Jennifer said as she closed the last of the distance between them and gently pulled Ms. Fisher's hand from her forehead. She stroked her fingers then laced her own through and squeezed. "I feel quite wanted."

Ms. Fisher's breath caught. Her gaze jumped to Jennifer's lips and back as she freed a slow breath and fanned her face harder. "You can't possibly be good for my blood pressure."

"No, probably not," Jennifer said and smiled, hoped it didn't look as shark-like as it felt. "Ms. Fisher..." She leaned in and placed a featherlight kiss on the woman's blush-hot cheek, dropped her voice to a sultry whisper. "...lead me where you want me."

Ms. Fisher turned on her needle-sharp heels, hand tightening around Jennifer's as she led them through the foyer. The destination was a massive sitting room with two tan leather armchairs, a matching sofa, and a dark oak coffee table in-between. Two glasses of wine topped the table, along with a small group of pillar candles that cast an ambient, flickering glow about the room. A fireplace headed the room, its large mantle bare, and a floor-to-ceiling bookshelf that appeared newly built stood nearby. Its shelves were mostly naked with only a few weathered books and a small silver frame, the picture inside obscured by dancing shadows.

The only other decorative piece in the spartan room was a rather large painting that spanned the wall opposite the fireplace. It depicted a nude woman from behind as she sat on a boulder, reaching toward an apple that hung from the bough of a twisted old tree. Jennifer wondered if it was meant to be Eve, yearning for the fruit that would ultimately be her downfall, or if it signified something else, something more, to the curious Ms. Fisher. Any woman, all women, reaching for something they needed or wanted, only to find they couldn't grasp it. Only to have their hands slapped away. Only to be chastised and shamed, blamed for being human and hungry.

"It's bland, I know," Ms. Fisher said, drawing Jennifer from her thoughts. She motioned to the sofa and Jennifer sat, expecting her to join. Instead, Ms. Fisher took one of the armchairs opposite her, easing onto the edge of the seat. "I'm still deciding how I want everything to look, and there's a lot I have to fix, too."

"How long have you lived here?"

Ms. Fisher blew a quick breath up over her cheeks. "That is a loaded question."

Jennifer cocked one slender brow as she took the glass of wine set out for her and settled back into the sofa's soft leather. "Is it?"

"Well, no." She drank her own wine, one large gulp that made her wince. "I guess it's more of a loaded answer."

"I see."

"I'd rather not talk about it though."

"Of course." Jennifer took her in, each visible detail in the candlelight. Ms. Fisher was stiff but not in her typical manner—nervous, yes, but she hadn't shrunk or cowered or avoided. Her hands lay relaxedly in her lap rather than tangled and bloodless, and while her pretty blush remained, it didn't splotch her skin like a rash. She was calmer, more at ease in her body than before, and best of all, she met Jennifer's eyes readily, rather than casting her own to the floor. It was a small progression but a vital one. "Ms. Fisher, I believe you touched yourself."

It wasn't a question. Jennifer was certain.

Ms. Fisher choked on her second gulp of wine and let out a strangled laugh as she returned her glass to the table. She swiped at her chin, catching a bit of dribble with the back of her hand. "You just jump right to the point, don't you?"

"Why dawdle?" Jennifer smiled. "We've only an hour after all."

Ms. Fisher stiffened and frowned. "I thought I booked for three."

"Oh?" Jennifer felt her brows tip toward her hairline. "Did you?"

"Wait. Did you not know?" Her frown deepened. "Maybe I messed something up?"

"It's my mistake," Jennifer said. She hadn't bothered reading the appointment details, and since Carolina didn't accompany her to the door, she hadn't gotten the usual rundown either. "I assumed you'd booked as before."

"Do you need to check anything? I'm certain I paid for the extra two hours," Ms. Fisher said. "But I could ha—"

Sensing a spiral coming on, Jennifer waved her quiet. "No, no, it's my error." She crossed one leg over the other, a sudden heat spilling down her back to spread into her thighs. *Three hours. Promising.* "Dawdle as you like then."

"Okay, good," she said and fingered the material of her skirt, just over her knees. "Um, how's the wine?"

Thick and layered with spice, Jennifer noted. The slightest hint of cherry right at the peak, and as she swallowed, rich plum and a bitter hint of almond. "It's excellent," she said and meant it. "You have fine taste."

"I wish, but no, it's my friend, Kaylia. Her family owns several vineyards around Sonoma and a few in Spain and France, too. She brings some whenever she comes over."

"Ah." Jennifer took a final sip and retired her glass to the table. "Well, Kaylia may be responsible for the wine, but you *do* have taste, Ms. Fisher."

"You think?"

Jennifer settled back into the sofa. "You booked *me*, did you not?"

Ms. Fisher giggled, an honest-to-goodness, ridiculous little giggle punctuated by a snort that made her nose wrinkle, and Jennifer could not fathom why she found it so attractive. "You're a little full of yourself, aren't you?"

"I'm not sure I should dignify that with a response," Jennifer said. "But then, perhaps my response wouldn't be as dignified as you might expect."

Ms. Fisher's smile grew wide and spellbinding. "Try me."

Apprehension sparked in Jennifer's gut. As thrilled as she was with this easy back-and-forth, her client was still fragile, still unpredictable as a minefield. Jennifer was eager to engage, but she recognized the potential for everything going to shit. But no one ever crossed a minefield without taking a risk. "I might have thought to say *you* could be full of me, Ms. Fisher."

The woman's mouth parted in an 'o' of surprise, and Jennifer held her breath. The tension lasted only a moment, though, before Ms. Fisher doubled over and hid her beautiful face in her hands. "I can't believe you just said that," she whined, and Jennifer's breath shook free.

"I thought you liked campy wordplay," she teased. "I seem to recall something about my suit *suiting* me?"

"Don't remind me." Ms. Fisher's voice was airy, her words laugh-split and light.

Jennifer sighed. It was nice, seeing her this way, being with her like this, with such surprising ease. "So, you were telling me of your recent solo activities," she said, drawing Ms. Fisher's face from its hiding place.

Her smile stuttered away, and Jennifer half-expected she would try to change the subject, but she didn't. Her answer was barely audible breath. "Yes."

"And?"

Ms. Fisher drew her bottom lip between her teeth again and nibbled. Her gaze flicked over Jennifer's body again, as if reminding her what she'd miss out on if she chose not to answer. "What do you want to know?"

Jennifer leaned forward, knees nearly touching the edge

of the coffee table. She couldn't deny the thumping in her blood, like a beckoning. "Everything."

"Well, there's not much to tell. I didn't, um, finish."

"That doesn't matter."

Ms. Fisher huffed. "I don't see how that's true."

"What do you mean?"

Her shoulders sagged. "I mean, what's the point if not to reach, you know, a particular end?"

"The point is *pleasure*, Ms. Fisher."

"I told you, I didn't."

"You didn't feel pleasure?" Jennifer softened her voice. She needed to be gentle. Ms. Fisher's exterior was cracked, her seed finally ready to bloom. Jennifer just needed her to open a bit more, needed her to claw her way out of the darkness of the dirt, and burst through the surface. The second she did, Jennifer, like the sun, would sate her. "Not even a bit?"

"Not enough."

Jennifer held her sigh. "Tell me a secret," she said, and Ms. Fisher's eyes rolled so hard, they appeared fully white. It was loud for something wordless, and it absolutely caught Jennifer by surprise. She couldn't help herself and laughed, a bright roar of a sound. As soon as it escaped, she had to resist the urge to clap a hand over her mouth, afraid her reaction would send the woman scurrying back to her burrow, too embarrassed to even poke her head out again.

Instead, Ms. Fisher's lips tugged with a smile. "You

should update your website," she said, her tone one of playful annoyance. "Mandatory confession. I would have shopped elsewhere."

Jennifer laughed again, impressed with Ms. Fisher's newfound fortitude. "Masturbation looks good on you, Ms. Fisher." Her words turned the woman's cheeks red as ripe cherries. "You're beginning to develop a sense of humor."

"I didn't realize this sort of thing was meant to be funny."

"It can be whatever you want it to be."

"What? I haven't gotten a single thing I've wanted from you since the first time you walked through my door."

"How can you expect to get what you want when you won't ask for it?" Jennifer challenged, leveling her with one look. "You won't even say it."

"You said I didn't *know* what I wanted."

"Because you didn't. Do you now?"

Ms. Fisher's gaze, dark in the candlelight, darted back up. It fixed itself hard on Jennifer's chest, the dip between the open buttons at the top of her shirt, then slid up the length of her throat. "Yes," she whispered, and Jennifer felt a jolt between her thighs.

Yes.

She kept quiet, waiting for Ms. Fisher to continue, to speak on her own. But to herself, Jennifer couldn't deny the urge burning in her belly, an eagerness that felt as remarkable as it did natural. Dancing along this edge, waiting to tip, was torture. It was perfection. It was wildly addictive.

"I think I want...." Briefly, she folded in on herself, but sat up straight again and looked Jennifer right in the eye. "I want to kiss you."

It was the boldest she'd ever been, and every brave, simple word of it set Jennifer on fire. Her nerves tingled as if struck by lightning until every inch felt electric. She set her glass down and eased back into the plush leather, keeping her movements and breath slow. Calm. She stretched her arms open in invitation along the back of the sofa. "Well then?"

Nothing. Silence. Every muscle in Jennifer's body tensed despite how relaxed she tried to appear. *Was this it? Was it going to happen? Would Ms. Fisher finally make a move? Any move?*

Ms. Fisher slowly rose to her feet, and Jennifer forgot to breathe. Once standing, she paused, as if decision the move still hung in the air like something she could catch hold of. Something she could ball up and toss and pretend never happened at all. Jennifer could see the debate in her eyes as she lingered in front of her chair, but then slow, determined steps brought her around the coffee table and into the slim space between the table's edge and Jennifer's knees.

They were close now. Jennifer could touch her if she wished, could lean forward and latch on, run her hands right up the length of Ms. Fisher's long, rose-beige legs. Under the flared skirt of her ironed dress. Up. Up. *Up.*

The couch cushion dipped as she sat, positioning herself right on the edge of the seat. Their thighs touched. Then, slowly, *so slowly*, she angled herself toward Jennifer, their knees bumping. A flicker of doubt in her eyes stirred Jennifer into action. If she didn't at least meet Ms. Fisher halfway, the woman was likely to withdraw entirely and *never* try something like this again; as in, as long as she fucking lived.

She sat forward, closer, and Ms. Fisher raised a hand as if to touch her face. Her trembling fingers hovered in the air between them, inching forward then back, forward then back. Her face did the same, eyes hooded and heavy, lips licked over and wet. She *wanted* this. Jennifer wanted it, too, more than she cared to contemplate.

She caught Ms. Fisher's hand and brought it to her face. "Yes," she whispered, answering whatever question it was that caused the woman to hesitate. *Yes, you can touch me. Yes, you can kiss me. Yes.* She molded Ms. Fisher's palm around the sharp angle of her cheek, and the tension broke. It *erupted.* That one touch was like the earthquake triggering the tsunami, an echoing cry provoking an avalanche.

Seismic waves racked her body as she flung herself forward and kissed Jennifer. Right on the mouth. It lasted seconds, *micro*seconds, barely long enough for her to even feel it as Ms. Fisher jerked back like she'd been burned. She didn't stay away long. A moan rocked up her throat and again, she closed the space between them. This time, she cupped Jennifer's face with both hands, one sliding around to the back of Jennifer's neck and pulling. Her chest heaved as she drew Jennifer closer, as close as she could get her, and melted their mouths together.

Jennifer's back tensed and bowed as she experienced Ms. Fisher's kiss for the first time. It was as hot and needy and nervous as she'd imagined it would be, rougher than she'd expected. So intense she could hardly breathe.

She was ruined. Dosie knew it the moment their lips touched. Ruined for anything, any*one* else. These lips were wine and mint, petal-soft and divine. And this kiss? This kiss was a storm. A rupture in her exterior. The devastation of her interior. Her entire life screaming up to a pinnacle it had been clawing toward for ages and roaring like wildfire over the peak, consuming all of her. This, *this*, was what she'd been missing, been seeking, been needing.

A moan left her unbidden, and then everything spiraled. The Director latched onto her, hands smoothing around her waist and digging in, kneading. Then down to her hips. One sharp, insistent tug, and Dosie was in the woman's lap. Dizzied. Hazed. *Is this really happening?*

Every inch of her was wide awake and electric. Her thighs prickled with goosebumps, and chills raced down her back. Her pulse throbbed in her neck and pounded in her ears, beat like a drum between her legs as she straddled the Director.

"*This* is the point, Ms. Fisher," the Director rasped against her lips, then licked along the open seam. "You *knowing* what you want and asking for it. Demanding it."

She nipped at Dosie's bottom lip, then drew back to look

at her. Her eyes were dark ocean magic in the candlelight as she slid her hands farther down. She cupped Dosie's ass through her dress, and smirked.

Oh God. Am I drunk? She had to be drunk. "I...." Breathless. *Hot.* So hot she couldn't think, couldn't process. The Director's hands kneaded and urged her, and her body responded. Every quick tug rocked her against the hard edge of her escort's denim waistband, and the friction set her blood on fire.

And then she felt it: shame. Writhing like a serpent in her gut. Refusing to die.

Dosie whimpered. Her eyes stung, and when next her hips shot forward, the first of her tears fell. Panic hit like a battering ram. She latched onto the Director's shoulders, creasing perfect silk with an iron grip. "I can't," she choked out. Her lungs were moving too fast now, and there were voices in her head. Old voices. Old words. Old terrors.

The Director's touch turned soft as her hands molded around Dosie's cheeks, smearing moisture between her fingers. "Look at me," she said, but Dosie shut her eyes instead.

Fresh, hot tears dropped from her brimming lashes as her hips jerked forward again. Each zap of pleasure made her stomach clench and her skin crawl.

"Ms. Fisher." Sharper. A command. "Look at me."

Dosie opened her eyes and caught her gaze through a wet blur.

"Trust me," she urged, and Dosie's chest threatened to cave in on itself.

She was fully dressed, but she had never felt more exposed. As if all the world, as if *God*, could see her, see what she was doing and *who* she was doing it with. And the heat in her body shifted, no longer pleasure but fire and brimstone—curling around her cells like plague, like damnation.

"I c-can't." The words chattered between her teeth. She stilled her hips but was so tense, she couldn't stop shaking. "I can't."

"You *can*," the Director insisted, and it was so sure, so genuine. "Look at me." She curled one hand around Dosie's hip, kept the other at her cheek, then she nodded, encouraging. "I have you." She kissed the corner of Dosie's mouth, the edge of her jaw. Their eyes met again. "You're safe with me."

Dosie didn't know how a stranger could read her so easily, could know exactly what she needed to hear, what she needed to *feel*, but she didn't care. She was grateful. Collapsing inward, she set her forehead against the Director's and closed her eyes. Grounding herself. "Keep talking," she whispered, and thankfully, her partner needed no further prompting.

The hand at her hip dug in. Long fingers curled into the material of her skirt and began slowly drawing it up like a shade. "Quick and dirty," the Director said, "to ease your nerves."

Dosie second-guessed her own request; the voice puffing against her lips was every bit as destabilizing as it was inspiriting. One hand settled into the dip of her lower back, holding her in place. The other disappeared under the last delicate fold of her skirt, and Dosie held her breath as the Director's palm settled high on her thigh.

"And then, we'll take our time," she promised. "Yes?"

The words warped at the edges as Dosie's head began to spin. She wasn't breathing. The cool tip of the Director's finger was sliding along the edge of her thin, silky panties, teasing the hot flesh where her thigh met her groin, and her brain was glitching. Glitching. Glitching. The finger stopped, and Dosie blinked, rebooting.

Oh. She was supposed to be speaking.

"Quick," she said, nodding as the air wheezed from her. She gasped her next breath like a drowning woman breaking the surface. "Yes."

The Director's mouth was on hers in a snap, giving and demanding in equal measure. Fast, hot kisses peppered the line of Dosie's jaw to her ear as the hand beneath her skirt began to move again, and it wasn't timid. It wasn't slow. The Director shoved her panties to the side and *touched her*.

Dosie cried out at the first brush through her curls. She was wet and swollen like a morning rosebud and sensitive. "Hurry," she panted. Her body bordered on a scream, at once desperate to be touched and not, desperate for it to begin and be over and never stop. For everything, all at once, *now*.

"Shh, Ms. Fisher." The Director licked around the shell of Dosie's ear, nipped at her lobe. "I have what you need."

One fingertip slid down the length of Dosie's slit and back

up. It dipped between her labia and around her throbbing clitoris, and Dosie's eyes rolled back. A low moan built in her throat as the exploration continued, down to her vagina. The Director's finger drew a slow circle around her entrance. Once. Twice.

"So ready for me," the Director husked, and Dosie's hips jerked as if automated. Her clit knocked against the heel of the Director's palm, and fluid gushed from her sex just as she was filled to one knuckle. Only an inch of invasion but good. *So, so good.*

When the finger retreated, Dosie groaned, drawing a laugh from the woman beneath her. "Pretty girl," she murmured, her voice a gritty kind of music that made Dosie's thighs clench. *If sex had a melody....* Then there was a hand on her face, a thumb pressing her chin down so she could be drawn into kiss. Dosie kissed back messily, all teeth and need and then—

"*Unh,*" she moaned as the Director entered her again, a bit deeper this time. Down to another knuckle. She could feel her heartbeat popping against the Director's finger like timed fireworks.

Another brief retreat, and a second finger joined the first. The two tips ringed her with easy pressure then inched inside, just far enough to begin stretching her. The Director's free hand dropped to Dosie's lower back again, arm locking in place around her hip, and began to guide. Forward then back. Forward then back. Every little jerk and glide caused a bit more of the woman's fingers to sink into her.

"Deep breath now."

Dosie obeyed the command without thought or question, and the moment she exhaled, the Director entered her fully. She shouted like a wild thing as the Director's two long middle fingers sheathed themselves inside her with one swift thrust. A second later, they began to move, circling and curling inside as if mapping terrain.

And just like that, Dosie Fisher was being well and truly fucked. Quickly and perfectly debauched in her pretty, girly dress like a common whore until her body took on a mind of its own. She rutted against the Director's waist, sliding up and down the length of her fingers and gripping them, sucking them in further with each downward tilt of her hips. The sound was disgraceful, bawdy. It was fucking *obscene*, the wet squelch and slap of her sex being plundered by two expert fingers and a singular focus unlike any Dosie had ever experienced in any capacity.

Dosie had never heard herself this way, not only the sounds of her desire but her voice. Her words. She was broken moans and staggered pleas. Mewling like something starved, and the woman beneath her was feeding her properly. Feeding and devouring at once, with ease. With clear and maddening expertise.

"I… I'm…" Dosie didn't know what. She didn't know anything. What she was. *Who* she was. What was happening. She felt like she'd lost her mind, even as her body seemed more alive and focused than ever, driven by a tremendous, furious, unrelenting kind of need Dosie had never in her life experienced. It was torture. It was *ecstasy*.

"Oh, I know, Ms. Fisher." The Director touched her like she'd been doing it all her life, panted into Dosie's ear like she hoped to never stop. "Don't hold back," she said and brought her free hand to Dosie's neck. Dug her fingers up into the tight underbelly of her bun and knocked it loose, forced it messy. "I want to hear you."

The fingers inside her suddenly stretched then curled, and Dosie positively *screamed*. Her muscles clamped around the Director's fingers as if trying to lock them in place. Tears burned in her eyes as her breath caught so roughly in her chest that she went lightheaded.

"There it is," the Director moaned and somehow managed to keep moving her fingers, milking every bit of Dosie's pleasure.

Pleasure. Did this even count as pleasure? No, it had to be something else, something more, because Dosie had never, *never* felt anything like this. It invaded. It *consumed*.

Her vision blurred as her pulse pounded in her head, in her throat, in her chest. It bobbed in her belly and hammered between her thighs. It kissed at the Director's fingers like something lovestruck and needy, and for a moment, Dosie feared she might pass out. No oxygen reached her lungs. It refused to go down. It had been choked from her muscles, her blood, her brain, and replaced with nothing but headiness and haze. A strangled whimper shook from her as the last shockwaves rolled through, and then all the world shifted to a manageable rhythm again, slowly thumping back to normal.

Dosie's body dropped, boneless. She spilled like water onto the Director's chest, the spent victim of her perfect torture, and buried her face in the woman's neck. She smelled expensive and feminine but not delicate. Nothing floral or light. The scent was rich and woodsy and mouthwatering, but it was nothing compared to the effect of her pulse—a frantic, excited hop that set Dosie's blood on fire all over again.

"You are stunning, Ms. Fisher," the woman said, voice thick with desire. "Absolutely stunning."

Dosie smiled against her neck, joy and heat reaching all the way down to her toes. "Thank you," she whispered, and she meant it for the compliment, but it was more than that, too. God, it was so much more than that. Dosie felt as if something had finally, *finally*, clicked into place, a feeling she often feared she would never experience outside of fleeting dreams and fantasies she'd been punishing herself over for years. This wasn't just a new experience; it was a revelation.

"Thank you," Dosie said again and kissed the Director's wild pulse. Then again over her jawline. "Thank you." The sharp arch of one cheek. "Thank you." The tears came as she kissed the Director's brow, then the bridge of her nose. Dosie couldn't have stopped them if she tried. Her chest felt like it had a balloon in it. "Thank you." God, she felt dizzy. She felt out of her mind, and if she weren't so drunk on the moment and as loose as the liquid running between her legs, she might've worried the Director thought the same. But she couldn't care, couldn't worry. She could only feel what she felt and press that feeling, with all her heart, into the woman who made her feel it, hoping she understood. *This means something. It means something.* A sob racked up her throat and shook her whole body as she met the Director's mouth with a hard, messy kiss. "Thank you so much."

"Shh." The Director eased her fingers free and pulled Dosie's underwear back into place. She rubbed over the exterior, wiping and massaging for a moment, then down Dosie's thigh, pulling her dress back into place as she went. When she cupped Dosie's cheek with that same hand, swiping her thumb through tears, Dosie could smell herself—a rich, sweet-sour scent that made her mouth water. "It's my pleasure." The Director's other hand rubbed slow, steady circles into her lower back, and Dosie was suddenly overwhelmed with one immense, particular feeling. A feeling she recognized, because she'd been chasing it all her life, only managing to catch it in fleeting moments. Safety. She felt so safe. So incredibly, wonderfully safe.

She whimpered, unable to help it, and to her surprise, the Director responded by pulling Dosie down to her chest, wrapping her in her arms, and holding her. Her nose nudged along Dosie's jaw. A gentle kiss followed. "Slow breaths, Ms. Fisher. With me."

Dosie did her best to match each breath until her body began to relax, heartbeat steadying to mirror the loose, liquid nature of her limbs. Her breath came easier, taming with intent and rhythm, until she felt wholly herself again in this strange, fascinating woman's arms. An almost comical sigh left her as Dosie wriggled her arms down between their bodies and looped them around the Director's back. "That was...." She didn't know, wasn't sure a word even existed that could describe how she felt. Where was a poet when you needed one?

"Agreed."

Dosie laughed and buried her face in the woman's neck again. The balloon in her chest had expanded to fill her entire body. She felt light and airy and, inexplicably, *high*. "I feel like I could float," she mumbled into a clavicle. "Is this what drugs feel like?"

"Yes." The Director laughed and stroked down Dosie's back. "Oxytocin and dopamine, to be exact. The two wonders of the orgasm."

"Orgasm," Dosie mouthed to herself, then she popped up, eyes widening. A smile stretched her lips to the point of aching. She locked hard onto the Director's eyes. "I had an orgasm."

"Yes, Ms. Fisher," the Director said with a smile that appeared downright devilish, and if Dosie didn't know any better, *prideful*. "You most certainly did." Then she locked her arms around Dosie and, with a shocking amount of ease and grace, flipped her over on the sofa.

Dosie sucked in a gasp as her back met the cushion and the Director slid up the length of her, her hips making a home between Dosie's thighs. One hand dug into the cushion to the right of Dosie's head. The other latched onto her chin. The

Director rubbed a rough line over Dosie's bottom lip with her thumb then pressed hard at its center, forcing it down. When Dosie's mouth dropped open, the Director licked inside it, just a flicker of her tongue against Dosie's, a wet pop against the roof of her mouth. She rocked her hips forward, a brief pressure against Dosie's clit, and want rolled through Dosie's body like a hot fog of warning: fire incoming.

"Are you ready for another?"

"Yes."

She would burn.

5

"Do you want to undress?"

"I.... No. Well, I don't know. No, I don't think so. Is that, um, is that okay? If I don't?" Dosie chewed her lip, flexed her fingers around the Director's shoulders. Her pulse still thumped between her legs. "Is that weird? Would that be weird?"

"Uncommon," the Director said, "but not weird."

"Would you be okay with that?"

"Of course." She leaned down and lay a barely-there kiss to Dosie's jaw. "As I've just demonstrated, Ms. Fisher, I don't require nudity to give you pleasure."

Dosie felt a rush of heat in her belly. The ghostly sensation of the way the Director had brought her to completion without ever removing a thing licked at the insides of her thighs. "Right."

The kisses continued, each wetter and hotter than the last. The Director licked her lips then pressed the damp evidence of it just behind Dosie's ear. She opened her mouth just enough to gently suck at the pulse in Dosie's neck, then nipped and soothed and nipped again at the soft skin over her vocal cords, vibrating with the pleasure curling around Dosie's insides like a creeping vine. "Ms. Fisher?"

Dosie jolted, opened her eyes with a flutter. "Huh? What? I'm sorry. Did you say something?"

The Director's laugh was whisper-soft and so intensely arousing that Dosie found herself squirming under the woman's weight. "I asked if you would you like for *me* to undress?"

"Yes." The answer was instant, flying out of her mouth with abandon. "I mean, no. Well, yes, but you know what, no, no, maybe it's better if you don't, because you know it might make me feel like *I* should too just so you're not the only person naked." She laughed at herself. "God, you probably think I'm hiding some huge ugly scar or tattoo under this dress or something, but I'm not. I swear. Or, well, I do have scars, but they're not enormous, and I actually really like my body."

"For good reason, I would imagine," the Director replied as she worked her way up the other side of Dosie's neck. "And I *have* imagined, Ms. Fisher."

"Oh God," Dosie groaned and shuddered. "How do you do that?"

The Director hummed against her throat then licked over the sound. "I have many talents."

"Oh, my *God*." Dosie slapped a hand over her face and bit one of her fingers. "Your voice should be illegal."

The Director chuckled and lifted her head, raised one brow when Dosie peeked at her through her fingers. "Are you sure you wouldn't like me to undress?"

Dosie forced herself to use words instead of worries. "I *want* to see you," she said. "Please don't think I don't." She let her hand shift from the Director's shoulder to the stretch of her neck, warm against her fingertips. "I mean, look at you. Who wouldn't want to see you?" Dosie's entire body grew uncomfortably hot, and she was certain that, from the chest up, she was the color of a sunset, only not as attractive. "I'm sorry. I'm sorry I'm so anxious and awkward." A nervous laugh left her. She hated it—the sound of it, the feel of it in her mouth, the fact that she couldn't hold it in. She hated that it tasted like guilt and fear and failure. "And we thought the orgasm would calm my nerves."

"Ms. Fisher." A gentle, almost sweet sigh sounded above her, and Dosie blinked open her eyes to find the Director smiling down at her. Genuine. *Affectionate*, Dosie briefly thought and felt calmed by it. "Stop apologizing."

"I can't help it."

"I know but try. You have nothing to apologize for."

Dosie's eyes flooded with hot tears, and she blew a cold breath up over them that did little to help. "You must think I'm so childish."

"I don't."

She searched the Director's face for some indication of a lie. "Are you just saying that because I'm paying you?"

"Please, if anything, most people pay me to insult them," the woman said with a teasing grin, and her angled face was so sharp and lovely in the candlelight that Dosie couldn't help feeling a bit breathless at the sight.

"Right." She grew quiet, unsure of what to say next. *Thank you* seemed odd. *Why are you being so nice to me?* Well, that seemed even odder. The Director still herself aloft with one arm, which didn't seem to be tiring in the least, and Dosie, searching for a distraction, ringed one hand around the woman's bicep just to feel it. "Wow. You obviously work out."

The Director stared down at her with a look Dosie couldn't quite decipher. "Ms. Fisher, may I say something personal?"

Shit. "Have I done something wrong?"

"No, no, nothing." She eased back into an upright position again, pulling Dosie with her in the process. They sat knee to knee, one of the Director's hands resting gently on Dosie's thigh, over her dress, and the other reaching for her glass of wine. Instead of taking a drink, she handed the wine to Dosie. "Have a drink."

Dosie took the wine and drank.

"I have no intention of insulting you," the Director said. "It's just an observation, but one could argue it's an observation I have no business making, let alone saying."

"Oh. Well, okay. That's okay. Go ahead."

"Good, because I want to make it clear to you that I don't think you're childish. I never have. But I *do* think you're repressed. And perhaps, even, a bit traumatized."

Dosie's throat thickened and ached around a growing lump. She set the wine glass back on the table, too afraid to spill it with her shaking hands, and curled her knuckles into the sofa cushion instead. "Oh."

"I've seen it in many women," the Director said and abandoned Dosie's thigh to comb her hair back from her face. "Closeted queer women who struggled with their identities. Battered women who wanted comfort but couldn't handle the touch of another man. Women repressed by conditioning and shame and abuse. I've seen it all, really." She sighed and took Dosie's face between her hands, looked her right in the eyes. "I don't know what your history is, Ms. Fisher, and I don't need to. But please hear me when I tell you that you *never* need to apologize for how, when, or with whom you heal the hurts that others have caused you. Never."

Dosie's heart was a hammer in her chest, pounding so roughly that it hurt, and it made her want to be reckless, foolish, fun; something other than what she'd always been, *who* she'd always been. It felt like fear and courage pressed into one, scary and inviting at the same time. "Dosie," she whispered, the hammer's pace increasing.

The Director's brows knitted together at the soft reply. "Dosie?"

With that feeling coursing her veins, Dosie buried her

hand in the Director's silky blouse and pulled her closer until they were only a breath or two apart. "My name," she said and bumped their noses together. She laughed at herself, quiet and proud. "Well, Theodosia, actually. But everyone calls me Dosie."

The director's back bowed, and her eyes closed. Her hands slid from Dosie's cheeks to the back of her neck, fingers funneling up into the tight ball of her bun. She yanked without warning, pulling Dosie's hair with one sharp flick of her wrist. A bobby pin fell to the sofa cushion; another caught and dangled in Dosie's freed, messy hair.

"Dosie," she whispered, and opened her eyes again. They were ocean blue and starving, and that was all it took.

Dosie dove at her, kissed her as if it could set her free, and it certainly felt like it could. Everything felt hot and hazy and *possible* against this woman's lips. Dosie wanted to live inside her kiss until it burned all her fear away. Until it made her new and bold and *ready*.

God, she was suddenly *so* ready.

"Please," she panted into the Director's mouth. "Please touch me."

The groan the words pulled from the Director's throat only drove Dosie higher, ran her hotter, *fucked her up*. She couldn't think, couldn't breathe. The Director's kisses were fierce and determined. She crowded Dosie again, easing over her to press her back into the cushion.

"Where?" she prompted. "Where do you want me to touch you, Dosie?"

Dosie was shaking. Every time the Director said her name, she heard it with her whole body. "Touch me where you want to touch me," she managed to say through trembling lips, between molten kisses and sharp, nipping pulls at her bottom lip. "That's what I want."

One hand fisted in Dosie's hair while the other raked down her side toward the bottom of her dress. "I want inside you, as deep as you'll let me go," she said, and a garbled sound choked in Dosie's throat.

It wasn't just her hands that were shaking anymore. Her thighs twitched, the muscles in her legs jumping at every brush of contact, every promise of more. The Director's voice was like blood in her veins, rich and driving.

The woman's fingers latched onto the skirt of Dosie's dress and hiked it like before. As her hand slid under, she hovered her mouth over Dosie's, flicked her tongue across Dosie's top lip. "I want my tongue on you."

A painful tremor screamed its way up Dosie's spine and back down, pooling at the base like acid, hot and achy and *eating her alive*. She had never wanted this way. She had never even known it was possible to want someone, something, *anything* this way. "Oh God, I feel like I'm losing my mind," she said, half-moan, half-laugh, and the Director responded by gripping her panties and giving them a tug.

"Let me take these off," she said, and Dosie couldn't tell if it was a command or a plea. Some odd part of her wanted it, strangely, to be both. "Let me have you in my mouth."

Dosie could do nothing but pant and nod.

"Say it."

"I.... Yes, t-take them off."

The stuttered words were like a trigger. Jennifer felt explosive with the girl's name ringing in her head. In her business, her life of aliases and secrets, such a thing was a gift. It was precious. It was trust. She quickly shimmied Dosie's panties down her long legs and over her heels. Her mouth was already watering. She tossed the garment to the side then reached for her own shirt.

"What are you doing?"

"Relax," Jennifer said, setting one hand atop Dosie's thigh to reassure her. With the other, she expertly undid several buttons of her shirt. "I just need to get something."

Dosie frowned. "From inside your shirt?"

Jennifer chuckled and opened one silky side to reveal a lace-cupped breast, which Dosie promptly ogled like a hormonal teenager, and a small leather pouch she wore strapped over one shoulder and resting against her ribs.

"You have a tiny purse in your shirt." Dosie said with a gleeful squeal. "What for?"

"Protection," Jennifer said as she took a red, paper-thin packet from the pouch and held it up. "Do you know what a dental dam is?"

"Like what they use when you get a root canal? The little sheet thing?"

"Exactly. It will prevent any crossover of fluid, but it's thin enough that you'll still have plenty of sensation." She opened the packet, eyes darting between Dosie's cycling expressions and her own work, conscious of both. "Are you okay?"

Dosie assured her with a nod. "Just a little nervous. Excited though. I've never done this before. I mean, no one's ever...you know."

"Performed oral on you?"

"Yeah. That."

Jennifer knew nothing about her client's prior experience, only that she'd been married and no longer was. She knew nothing about the man to whom that marriage had taken place, only that she wanted to throttle him for never bothering to make Dosie sing with pleasure, every rhythm and tune hidden inside her body and waiting to be coaxed free. Only that she damned anyone who ever could have refused this woman the euphoria she deserved.

"Would it help ease your nerves to know I've been wanting to do this since I first laid eyes on you?"

Dosie's lips parted around a silent gasp. "Really?"

"Oh yes."

"Honestly, I don't know if that helps or makes it worse." Dosie laughed, her head dipping back to expose her neck, and Jennifer found her so incredibly attractive that she nearly dropped the packet. She focused and freed the dam, then eased off the couch and onto her knees. There was just enough space for her to kneel between the coffee table and sofa. "May I?"

Dosie trembled like a slow-growing earthquake but gave her consent without hesitation, much to Jennifer's delight. She moved easily at Jennifer's urging until she was in a partial sitting position with her head and shoulders against the sofa's back and her ass shimmied down to the cushion's edge, knees encasing Jennifer's shoulders. She looked messy in her prim, pristine dress with her half-collapsed hair and wide eyes. Like a debauched housewife in need of a smoke. *Fuck*, Jennifer thought as her mouth started to salivate.

"Close your eyes." There was no need to heighten the girl's anxiety by having her watch the somewhat awkward process of application. Jennifer had no desire to send her spiraling back into a panic, so she made quick work of it. She flipped up Dosie's dress just enough to see her, and what a sight she was. Just as she'd expected, Ms. Dosie Fisher had a neatly trimmed bush the color of roasted cinnamon, dewy and glistening in the candlelight. Jennifer could have stayed right there, staring, indulging, but she didn't linger, didn't allow time for Dosie's nerves to fester. She smoothed the dam over her weeping sex, making sure to cover every part of her, then flicked her dress back down and squeezed her thigh. "Good girl."

Dosie opened her eyes, looked as if she'd been placed under a spell. Her pupils dilated as she stared at Jennifer. "Why is it so hot when you say that?"

"Because you want to please me, so it makes you wet to know you have."

Another choked sound of pleasure cracked in Dosie's throat and whimpered its way free. She threw an arm over her eyes and said, "God, just do it already before you kill me with your voice alone."

On her knees, Jennifer dipped her head under Dosie's dress and breathed her in fully for the first time. *Fuck.* Her pussy was like a swollen fruit, ripe for plucking. Devouring. She smelled tangy and natural with just a hint of soap and salt from sweat, and Jennifer found the scent intoxicating. She settled her mouth over her and stroked up the length of the dental dam, pushing the material into Dosie's slicked hole. Her eyes rolled back as she licked her way up and ringed Dosie's clitoris.

It pulsed against her tongue as if Dosie's heart was right there at Jennifer's mercy. She cried out when Jennifer sucked her clit into her mouth, and her hips bucked so hard that Jennifer had to lock one arm over her waist to hold her down. She flicked her tongue in fast succession, pressed the flat of it as harshly as she could and dragged it roughly up and down, ran circles around Dosie's entrance and pushed inside her. She devoured her until the girl was all but fucking her face, one hand ground down into the sofa and the other latched onto the back of Jennifer's head like she might go flying off into outer space if she lost her grip for even a moment.

"Please," Dosie panted above her. "Please." She whined, frustrated and hot. "I want more."

Jennifer moaned. Hearing a woman say what she wanted had always been sexy; hearing *this* woman do so was like a firecracker going off in Jennifer's brain. Then another between her legs. She sucked Dosie's clit roughly into her mouth and earned herself a delicious shout. God, she wanted to touch herself, but she wasn't sure how far she could push before she pushed too far and turned Dosie's pleasure back into panic. *Baby steps*, she reminded herself and clenched her thighs together.

Dosie's breath pitched up into a desperate, almost feral whine as Jennifer dropped back down to run the edge of her opening. "Oh, God," she groaned. "Oh, my *God*."

Jennifer chuckled, open-mouthed, as she flattened her tongue and dragged it back up the girl's slit. Amazing, how often people called out for God when they were with her. She tugged Dosie's clit between her lips again, flicked mercilessly with her tongue until a cry cracked the air like lightning, and the hand in her hair fisted. Dosie's thighs clamped around her head, squeezing her jaw like a vise, and trapping her ears. The world muted as the girl came so hard that it gushed against the dental dam and leaked down, slicking her ass and the cushion beneath. Jennifer felt it seep a spot into the neck of her blouse, and she'd be damned if she didn't admit, at least to herself, how incredibly aroused that made her.

The tension released a moment later, and the world spilled back into Jennifer's ears in a haze of whimpers and ragged breaths. It was the most intense orgasm Jennifer had witnessed, let alone caused, in some time, and it was the epitome of divine. Jennifer wanted to see it again, as many times and in as many ways as she could. She lay delicate kisses over sensitive flesh, delighting in each responding twitch, then drew that straining little bud between her lips again. The slightest bit of suction, and another, smaller orgasm—quick like the strike of a match and just as hot—pulled a furious, *desperate*, whine from her client.

Dosie's body shook as coming down from her orgasm had caused the temperature to plummet. "Oh wow," she huffed. "Wow. Wow." She lifted her head up and looked down at Jennifer as she slipped back out from under Dosie's dress. "*Wow*."

Jennifer smiled, and it must have appeared as mischievous as it felt, because Dosie's sweaty brow crinkled.

"What?" She panted. "Why do you look like that?"

"Like what?"

"Like you have nefarious plans."

"Oh, I do, Ms. Fisher," Jennifer said, and in a flash, was on her feet again, shifting Dosie onto her back. Smooth and silent, graceful as a panther, slid atop her. She took Dosie's mouth in a fierce kiss as she reached under her dress, quickly peeled the dental dam from her sticky cunt, and tossed it aside. A breath later, Jennifer was inside her.

"Fuck!" Dosie shouted and nearly wriggled herself out of Jennifer's reach, but Jennifer held on and thrust into her even deeper.

"Such a dirty mouth. What else can you scream for me,

hm?" She added another finger, slipping her long middle digit in to fill Dosie up, two wide and as deep as she could get them. "How does that feel? Do you like that?"

"*Mm.*"

"Words."

"Y-yes."

"I knew you would," Jennifer said and withdrew to her fingertips before slowly pushing in again.

"*Yes,*" Dosie gasped, her mouth dropping open. Her brow furrowed. Formless sound burbled in her throat. And then she did something that stunned Jennifer. She tossed her legs in the air, wrapped them around Jennifer's back, and locked them in place, feet crossed at the ankles so one pretty heel dug into the top of Jennifer's jeans. She grabbed every part of Jennifer she could find and held on as she tilted her hips to meet each thrust. "Yes. Oh God, *yes.*"

Jennifer hadn't felt such delicious tension in her spine in ages. Her skin was electric, her mind nothing but fog and desire. Dosie kissed her greedily, *hungrily.* Dosie kissed her like it was her first kiss and her last kiss at once, something she wanted to remember, something she wanted to keep. She kissed Jennifer like she wanted to leave some part of herself behind, an impression, an imprint. The thought that she might, that she *could,* terrified her.

When Dosie climaxed again, Jennifer nearly followed on the high of it alone. Her nerves were on fire. Her muscles trembled. There was a steady pulse between her legs. Dosie's hands dug into her skin through her shirt, and her heel had slipped under the band of Jennifer's jeans to scratch the top of her ass. Jennifer's fingers ached where they were still buried, squeezed bloodless by Dosie's satisfaction. Every zap of pain enhanced her pleasure.

The tension broke with a final whimper, and Dosie melted into the cushions. Jennifer barely managed to hold herself up long enough to free her fingers, then she collapsed onto the sofa as well, half on top of her client, and half beside her. Dosie's body still shook; in fact, it began to shake harder, so hard the girl's teeth chattered.

Jennifer attempted to move, only to be yanked into a tight hug. "Okay," she whispered. "Okay. You're okay." She wriggled her arms under Dosie's back and eased their bodies over so that they lay side-to-side. "That's better. Okay. Just breathe now."

"I can't s-stop shaking."

"It's only adrenaline." Jennifer the cupped the back of her head, lay her cheek on top of Dosie's. "It will pass. I promise."

"I'm sorry."

"What did I say about apologizing?"

"Sorry."

Jennifer sighed. "Why are you sorry?"

"Cuddling your clients to calm them down probably isn't in your job description," she said through staggered breaths. Her voice broke. "I'm sorry if you feel obligated to do that for me. I hope you don't. But even if that's the case, I'm really grateful. This.... Well, this hasn't been easy for me."

Jennifer wasn't sure what to say, so she said nothing. She hurt, and this pain didn't heighten her pleasure. Her chest felt porous and weak, as if it could crumble to ash if she was squeezed any harder. The woman in her arms was so wide open, even curled in a ball as she was. Her sincerity, her terror, her want—Dosie Fisher decorated every part of herself with how she felt, not just how she felt on the surface but how she felt at her core. It was in her voice, in her eyes, in her touch, and it affected Jennifer in ways she wasn't sure she wanted to scrutinize. But it had been a long time since anyone had managed to make her feel so touched, especially someone who hadn't actually *touched* her, and Jennifer felt the value of her work keenly in that embrace.

A few breaths more, and Dosie's body lay tame again but for the errant muscle spasm. She eased her grip and rolled onto her back, wiped the sweat from her forehead. "Do you?" she asked after a moment, staring up at the ceiling. "Feel obligated?"

"No." It was out of Jennifer's mouth before she'd even bothered to put thought to the question. But there it was—the truth. She felt no obligation to this woman, only desire and a strange, nagging sort of affection she found both disconcerting and addictive. "I feel honored." That, too, was the truth, and she didn't regret saying it, even if it did feel a bit like crossing a line. "To be trusted with not only your pleasure but your care as well is something that moves me deeply. I don't take such things lightly."

Dosie's eyes watered. "That's really nice." She shook her head at herself as she sighed and wiped her tears as soon as they fell. "Thank you for being so nice to me."

Jesus. What was she supposed to say to that? Jennifer couldn't think to respond. What kind of life had this girl lived that she could be so surprised by basic decency? *That she's thanking me just for being nice to her?*

A lump formed in Jennifer's throat, a telltale sign of crying that she responded to by clearing her throat and promptly changing the subject. She brushed a few errant hairs from Dosie's cheek, then traced over her chin to trail down her neck. The pearls strung over Dosie's collarbones were warm between her fingers. "You know, few women wear genuine pearls anymore. Considerably fewer of your generation."

"I know." Dosie took Jennifer's hand from her necklace and kissed her fingertips, one after the other, and Jennifer wondered if she could smell herself there. She wondered if Dosie liked it, wondered what she would taste like with nothing between them. Just wet flesh on flesh. Jennifer scolded herself for thinking about it. She was already going to be a throbbing, uncomfortable mess for hours, until she could return home to tend to herself. Her mind needed to stop making it worse. Jennifer refused to masturbate in the car with Carolina on the other side of the glass. "I lied to you."

Jennifer blinked, pulled back to the moment. She

propped herself on her elbow and studied Dosie's face. "Is that so?"

"When I told you there was nothing else." She chewed her bottom lip, looked away again. "That I had no more secrets."

"Oh." *Obviously.* "I know."

Dosie's head jerked to the side. "You do?"

"We all have secrets," Jennifer said and shrugged her free shoulder. At the ripple of movement, Dosie's dark eyes dropped to Jennifer's chest and lingered.

"I'm glad you left your shirt open," she said as if suddenly entranced, and Jennifer couldn't help laughing.

"Well, I am in the business of pleasing," she said and reveled in Dosie's answering grin. In the deep dip of her one dimple. "And, just so we're clear, you are never under any obligation to share your secrets with me. Even if I ask."

"Ask?" Her delicate fingers wrapped around Jennifer's hand and held it. "I think 'demand' might be more accurate."

"Yes, well, most who book with me *like* being told what to do, or did 'The Director' not give that away?"

"No, it definitely did," Dosie said as she massaged the back of Jennifer's hand. "I guess I just thought those demands would be more along the lines of, like, 'spread your legs', or something sexier. Not 'tell me all your secrets'."

"First of all, I did not ask for *all* of your secrets." She ensconced herself in Dosie's tangled, half-free hair just to breathe her in. It had been a while since her last time with a female client. She'd nearly forgotten how good and natural a woman could smell, especially a woman in the aftermath of sex. "And second, those two demands are not mutually exclusive. I will happily tell you to spread your legs any time you like, Dosie, including *whilst* you tell me your secrets."

The woman in her arms giggled, snorted, then giggled even harder. Jennifer resisted its infectiousness, but found her lips spreading, throat bubbling with sound. In seconds, she was laughing right alongside the girl. *Damn.*

"I want to tease you for saying 'whilst'."

"You could," Jennifer said. "Or, you could tell me this secret you clearly have on your mind to share."

"I could," Dosie agreed. "I definitely could, but I'm not sure I want to, yet."

"Is it that you have a 1950s housewife fetish?" Jennifer asked, playfully jabbing her clothed breast. "Because, I have to tell you, it isn't subtle."

Dosie pushed herself into a sitting position, and when Jennifer attempted the same, shoved her back down and cackled. It was familiar, that shove—friendly, comfortable, like Jennifer was someone she truly did trust—and something about the casual intimacy of it, the way Dosie's hand lingered before slipping away, made Jennifer's breath catch. It made her head swim. *Strange.*

Meticulously, *pointedly*, Dosie prettied her dress, trying and failing to smooth out her wrinkled skirt. "*That* is another story entirely," she said and took a huge drink of Jennifer's wine, large enough to choke her. She spluttered but managed to swallow. "I should probably try to quench my thirst with water, not wine."

Jennifer recognized the choking, the words, the whole scene for what it was: a deviation, a distraction. She wasn't going to be privy to whatever secret Dosie was keeping; at least, not yet. There were limits, and Dosie, an exquisite creature only just realizing she *had* a shell, let alone coming out of it, had pushed her own quite far enough for one night.

"I'll get a glass," she said and stood. She stopped just long enough to scoop the discarded dental dam and package from the floor, then disappeared through the nearest doorway. Her voice floated back like a trail of smoke. "Do you want one?"

"Yes, please." Jennifer sat up and ran a hand through her hair, fanned her chest with her open shirt. As she stood, she became acutely aware of the sticky situation in her pants. "Jesus," she muttered and adjusted her underwear. In one smooth gulp, she downed the rest of the wine, then she buttoned her shirt and followed the one responsible for the mess.

In the kitchen, Dosie looked up from the sink where she was filling a second glass with water. "My legs feel like Jell-O," she said. "I almost fell over."

Jennifer tried not to feel smug. No, she didn't. She loved feeling smug. "Yes, that happens," she said with a smirk, "especially after four orgasms." Four orgasms, and barely a scrap of clothing removed. Jennifer hadn't even taken her boots off. Shameless pride burned in her chest. It itched in her fingers. Pulsed between her thighs.

"I didn't know I could do that. I mean, have that many orgasms in a row." Her neck and cheeks pinked in patches as she said the words, and she looked like she wished she could explode into a million pieces, but Jennifer was proud that she'd said it.

"Oh, you can." She eased around her to wash her hands, dried them on a towel hanging over the sink. "And many more," she said, laughing when Dosie choked on her water. She drank some of her own and checked her watch. Five minutes over Dosie's allotted session. *Damn.* She was shocked Carolina hadn't shown up at the door, knocking. Jennifer was nothing if not prompt, and Carolina was nothing if not cautious.

Then again, Jennifer knew Carolina was aware of her little...*preoccupation* with Ms. Fisher. Dosie. *Dosie.* Jennifer said the name over and over in her mind. It was an odd name, cute. Jennifer wasn't entirely sure she believed it was real, but she hoped it was. She liked the way it sounded, the way it felt on her tongue.

"I am afraid it's time for me to leave," she said and hoped she didn't sound as disappointed as she felt.

Dosie didn't seem to mind showing her own disappointment, all but crumpling right there at the kitchen counter. "Oh," she said with a pitiful frown. "Yeah. Of course."

Jennifer caught her gaze. Dosie's eyes were big and dark as molasses with her pupils still dilated. She was beautiful, messy and flushed and just a little bit awkward, and Jennifer wanted her.

"I guess I'll walk you to the door then."

"Thank you."

Neither moved for a moment, caught in the spell of their staring and the drive to drag things on just a touch longer. But then Dosie turned and led her on, and they made the short walk in silence, shoulder to shoulder along the length of the foyer, the backs of their hands brushing, knuckles knocking together. They were nearly to the door when she stopped and took Jennifer's arm. "Wait." She frowned as if questioning herself and wrapped her fingers around her pearl necklace. "Did you like it?" When she met Jennifer's eyes again, she looked sick with nerves, but her head was up. Her back was tall. "Being with me, I mean. I wanted to.... I wanted you to enjoy it, too."

Jennifer's head spun. Her body flooded with heat. She wanted this woman more than she had even properly begun to process, and here she was, trembling in front of her, asking if she'd enjoyed being with her. Touching her. Being inside her. Giving her the first orgasm of her life. And the second. The third. The fourth. Had Jennifer *enjoyed* it? She'd fucking *reveled* in it.

With a single step, Jennifer had her wrapped in her arms, a hand in her hair. Dosie's back thumped against the foyer wall as Jennifer crowded and kissed her breathless. "Yes." She slipped her thigh between Dosie's legs, under her pretty dress and right up against her sex. When her denim soaked through, Jennifer remembered the girl's underwear was still in the other room. *Fuck.* She kissed her greedily, sucked

Dosie's tongue into her mouth and imagined it was her cunt again.

Dosie moaned, rutting down against her thigh, and Jennifer knew she had to stop. They were out of time. They were *over* time. She sighed and eased her leg back down, kissed Dosie's cheek, over her eye, the little space between her eyebrows. Foreheads resting together, Jennifer closed her eyes and cupped Dosie's cheeks. "Yes," she promised a final time. "When you're ready, I will show you just how much."

She didn't let herself linger. "Goodnight, Ms. Fisher." One last kiss, a flash of lip on lip. "*Dosie*." And then she left.

Carolina was halfway up the porch steps when Jennifer emerged from the house. "Oh, I was just coming to check on you."

"Thank you," Jennifer said and knew she sounded out of breath.

"Are you alright?"

"Fine." *On fire. Confused. There's a drum in my vagina, and that woman, that sweet, ridiculous, gorgeous woman is responsible.* She swept past Carolina and down the steps, toward the waiting car. "Let's get going."

Carolina blessedly asked no questions and said nothing when Jennifer beat her to the car, wrenched open her own door, and all but threw herself inside. She couldn't talk about it, likely wouldn't even if she could. Jennifer wasn't sure where to begin processing how much she'd felt, how surprised she'd been to feel it. She pressed the button to raise the partition and settled back into her seat, blew a harsh, cold breath up over her face.

Part of her ached to shove a hand down her pants and relieve herself. Another part, strangely, felt like crying. Jennifer distracted herself with her phone instead, bringing up her search engine and quickly tapping in a name. DOSIE FIS—she deleted and started again—THEODOSIA FISHER. She was sure it would prove fruitless besides a social media account, if that, but she was curious.

When she clicked to search, it took barely a second for the internet to take that curiosity and detonate it like a bomb.

There she was: her client. Younger by a decade or so, maybe more, but it was her. She had the same cinnamon-colored hair, the same roasted-honey eyes, but here, she sagged as if trying to hide herself from the world. Her full cheeks looked like they'd been vacuumed hollow from the inside and were streaked with tears as she was led in her thin, patched clothes to a waiting police car, and suddenly, Jennifer was terrified. She was also painfully invested.

Dosie on the steps of a courthouse, microphones shoved in her face, eyes wide like a cat's in the night and skittish. Dosie shielded from a crowd of paparazzi while leaving a hospital. Dosie in a hospital bed, her gaunt cheeks and dark circles making her eyes appear cartoonishly large and sad. Dosie in the back of an ambulance, spattered in what could only be blood. Jennifer cycled through picture after picture, unable to look away. But it was the headlines that struck her the hardest, the context to every picture rapidly taking shape in her mind. Bolded lines and links, one after another, screamed out at her, words popping like blown fuses in front of her eyes, setting her brain aflame.

Feds Raid NorCal Commune after Escaped Child Makes Claims of Widespread Abuse

Nine Arrests Made in NorCal Cult Case; CDSS Stays Silent

Medical Examination of Hand-of-God Children Suggests Years of Sexual Abuse, Experts Say

California Department of Social Services Subject to Massive Investigation in Cult Case

Teenage Daughter's Testimony Seals the So-Called Prophet's Fate

Hand of God Children v. State of California Reaches Shocking Conclusion – Largest Settlement in State History

Theodosia Fisher, Daughter of Fallen Hand-of-God Prophet, Pens Painful Memoir

Jennifer dropped her phone into her lap and sank back into her seat. She'd known, *guessed*, that Dosie had suffered somehow, but she'd never imagined anything like this. That sweet, terrified face filled her mind as she pressed shaky fingers over her eyes and felt tears coming. Dosie's voice played on loop in her ears. Her gentle courage. Her trembling need. '*Thank you*,' she'd whispered over and over, words Jennifer had felt in every part of her body, gratitude and desire that had flattered and shaken her and made her want to do and be and *give* more. But now....

The lump in her throat was jagged, clawing and jabbing with every swallow. Her stomach roared its protest to every word she'd read, every haunting picture that now sat in her vision as if painted there. The first of her tears fell. Jennifer thought of Dosie's warm body against hers, delicate and needy, nuzzling into her like an animal seeking shelter, affection, care, and her stomach plummeted with realization. The lump in her throat went down like a shard of glass.

What she'd given Dosie, what she'd shared with her, had been so, *so* much more than pleasure.

6

The knock she'd been waiting for was loud and frantic, as expected, and Dosie nearly killed herself racing down the stairs. She dove for the door the second her feet hit the landing, and when she yanked it open, a bottle of champagne was thrust into Dosie's face with its shiny foil topper glinting under the foyer lights. A second bottle appeared beside it, and then Natalie stuck her grinning face right between.

"We're about to pop some corks like that escort popped your gay cherry!"

Dosie's nose wrinkled despite her laugh. "Ew."

"For the record, I told her not to say that," Kaylia said as she shoved past them both with an oversized, and undoubtedly overpriced, Italian leather bag slung over her shoulder. "Where's the corkscrew?"

"Why do you need a corkscrew?" Dosie waved Natalie in, so she could close the door. "It's champagne."

"For the two bottles of wine I have in my bag, girl," Kaylia said and led the way to the kitchen. "Honestly, it's like you don't even know me."

"She wants the corkscrew on the counter in plain view, so we don't lose it like last time."

Dosie suddenly felt as effervescent as the bubbly they were about to consume. "Oh God," she giggled. "How drunk are we getting?"

"Whatever amount of drunk gets you to spill the deets," Natalie said as the group entered the kitchen. She grabbed three large wine glasses hanging from the underside of the upper cabinets, while Dosie dug the corkscrew from a drawer and tossed it on the countertop.

"That part," Kaylia agreed as she pulled two large bottles of red from her bag.

"Did you pack any clothes in there?" Dosie asked. "Or just the wine?"

"Are you kidding?" Natalie took the bottles, placed them one by one in Dosie's cooler. "She's got like a week's worth of outfits in there. She does the Marie Kondo, rolly-polly thingy."

"It works," Kaylia said with a shrug, then she turned her gaze on Dosie. Scrutinizing. "So, I have to say, we've been here five minutes, and honestly, Dosie, I expected more."

"What? What do you mean?"

"You're acting like a revelation hasn't occurred," she said. "A sex revelation."

"A sexelation," Natalie provided.

"Exactly. You're way too calm."

"Eh," Natalie said and grinned. "Maybe she's just that freshly-fucked kind of calm."

"It's been three days, you guys."

Kaylia scoffed. "So? If the sex was top tier, then three days is like three seconds. I've had top-tier sex glow that lasted three *weeks* before. It was that good. Like, people *said* I was glowing." She pointed to Natalie. "She said it."

"Maybe I'm just keeping my glow on the inside. An inside glow." Dosie buried her face in her hands, groaned and laughed at herself. "How am I supposed to act? It was sex. There was sex."

Natalie tutted as she worked on the foil top of one champagne bottle. "You and I and Kaylia and whatever surfaces in this house you got down and dirty on all know it wasn't just sex. Stop trying to downplay it. You were excited. I mean, scared shitless, yeah, but excited. We want to be excited with you." She froze. "Wait. You didn't do it on this countertop, did you?"

Kaylia laughed out loud as Dosie groaned harder into her hands.

"The island is way too high for that," she said, and Kaylia barreled over again.

"Well, you *said* she was tall," Natalie said, finally

managing to clear the foil from the bottle's neck. "And *you're* tall, so...."

"All surfaces are suitable for sex if you believe in yourself," Kaylia said, and Natalie stuck her tongue out as she strained across the island to high-five her. "Side note: Dosie, what are you wearing?"

Dosie looked down at herself. "What's wrong with jeans and a T-shirt?"

"Um, everything is wrong with jeans and a T-shirt when we specifically told you this was a pajamas-only affair."

"Kaylia, you're wearing Gucci," Natalie said, grunting as she tried for a third time to pry the champagne cork free.

"Yes." Kaylia rolled her eyes. "Gucci *pajamas*. Look at this silk."

"And a full face of makeup."

"So, now it's a crime to want to look cute? I brought my bonnet. I'm serious about the sleepover. Chill."

Natalie laughed. "Oh shit! Look out!"

Kaylia ducked just in time to avoid getting dinged as the cork shot free of the bottle and flew by her head. Champagne foamed over the lip of the bottle and spilled down the side, and Natalie quickly positioned it over the waiting glasses. As she poured one after another, Kaylia turned her attention back to Dosie.

"So, now that the bubbly's pouring, tell us: how *was* baby's first orgasm? We've been dying to know."

"Dying," Natalie agreed. "It was basically all we talked about on the drive over."

"And it was a *long* drive."

Dosie shook her head at them. "And neither of you found that weird?"

"Of course, it's fucking weird," Kaylia laughed. "I wasn't even this excited about making my first million."

"Those silver-spoon baby problems," Natalie interjected, making Dosie smile.

"But *as I said before...*" Kaylia rolled right through the teasing. "...a revelation has occurred, and since we know you won't be properly thrilled for yourself, it's our job to be thrilled *for* you."

"Also, it's been a little minute since I got laid," Natalie said, "so part of it is just me shamelessly living through you."

"If I talk about it, my face is going to melt off."

"You would be cute faceless. It's fine," Kaylia said. "Now, suck down some of this ridiculously expensive champagne, and tell us all about your first life-changing orgasm, and *we* will respond with all the fanfare you and *it* deserve."

Dosie puddled on the countertop and hid her face in her arms. She was tempted not to say a word, but her friends had driven all the way out to be with her, to celebrate this milestone in her life that, for some, might not mean much, but for Dosie.... What she'd shared with the Director had not only been an awakening into the world of pleasurable sex, but a thorough conquering of so many fears. A shifting in her body, in her *being*, when she'd so long felt the structure of her upbringing like restriction in her spine, paralysis of her muscles and of her dreams.

"Four," she murmured as she heard the scrape of a champagne glass being slid across the island.

Natalie chuckled. "Um, what was that? You're going to have to talk to us, Dose, not your arms. We don't care if you look like a lobster."

When Dosie dragged herself out of her hiding place, Natalie and Kaylia both were mid-sip of their champagne. "I said 'four'," she told them, reaching for her own glass. "It was *four* first life-changing orgasms."

All at once, Dosie's kitchen *erupted*. Kaylia snorted champagne up her nose then burst into a fit of coughing, while Natalie spewed her drink across the island like a broken sprinkler giving one last spurt before its untimely demise. And all the while, Dosie watched, red as a beet and fanning her face, gulping down champagne to try to douse the fire inside. It didn't work. She was hot and embarrassed and delighted, and something ballooned in her chest that felt a little like pride.

"*Four*?!" Kaylia shouted the moment she was able. "On your first fucking time? Okay, I'm sorry. Wait. She got you off four goddamn times? As in one, two, three, four?"

"Well, it wasn't like it was *her* first time," Dosie said, and Natalie raised her glass.

"Cheers to her. That's putting in the work right there."

"Honestly, it was so fast, I'm not even sure it qualifies as work," Dosie said and managed to turn even redder. "And that was with, like, two miniature panic attacks mid-process, which she was actually really nice about."

"She better have been."

"Damn right."

Affection trickled through Dosie like cool water. Her shoulders caved as tension and heat seeped from her muscles and skin, and she sighed. "I really love you guys." They had never made her feel like a freak, not even when she most felt like one herself. "You know that?"

"Uh oh," Natalie teased. "I feel a group hug coming on."

Kaylia made a show of scrunching her nose. "Feel something else," she said, and the air crackled with laughter again.

The world fizzled down to the clinking of glasses and the music of friendship, and for a perfect moment, the life Dosie had lived before, didn't matter. It didn't even exist.

In the week since her last encounter with Dosie Fisher, Jennifer had canceled two bookings, something she rarely did. She could count the number of cancellations she'd ordered over the last two decades on one hand. But she was distracted and uninterested, and while she'd always prided herself on working through *whatever*, something in her now refused. There was a wall that wouldn't buckle, a door that wouldn't budge, sealed inside its frame. She just wasn't in the mood for company, not of any kind.

She'd hardly left her condo, stalking the large space like a wild animal that had trapped itself by accident. She had too much energy but no motivation to properly expend it. And that book. Always in sight, sitting in her peripheral or in the back of her mind, and while Jennifer hadn't touched the thing since bringing it home from the bookstore, it might as well have been glued to her body. Like a cursed object, it bespelled her, and she both longed and loathed to explore it: Theodosia Fisher's memoir.

Something about Jennifer reading it felt like a violation of her client's privacy. Dosie had shared her story with the world, but with Jennifer, she'd been hesitant to share much of anything. Beyond the vulnerability exposed during sex, Dosie had given Jennifer little information about herself, and even that vulnerability hadn't necessarily been voluntary but rather a natural result of what was happening. A cracking in Dosie's exterior. An opening of a chapter she'd never dared to write or even fully imagine. But when the option to share was given to her—*tell me a secret*—she'd evaded it, giving only minor things, barren hints of something greater. Maybe Dosie didn't care if the world knew her secrets; maybe it was Jennifer, specifically, whom she didn't want to know.

Jennifer tried to tell herself she was being paranoid, overthinking it, but every time she thought about opening the book, Dosie's face would flash through her mind. Her vulnerable, tear-filled eyes. Her jittery plea for Jennifer to hurry, to help her get through something that was difficult for her but that she so desperately wanted.

"I can't stop shaking."

She could still feel the ghost of Dosie's warmth against her chest, the echoes of her grip on Jennifer's arms, clinging to her for support, for safety. For an understanding that Jennifer could only properly give with her body. Words weren't enough.

Jennifer face-planted into her couch. She was coming apart at the seams and had no idea why. Why did Dosie Fisher haunt her so? She'd had clients with trauma before, their bodies and breath riddled with it, their needs defined by or despite it, and she was always affected. But she'd never been shaken. Not like this.

A loud chime jolted Jennifer from her torment, and she peeled herself off the couch to buzz Carolina into the building. Jennifer wasn't one to confide in others. She didn't get close with anyone, not since her sister, but Carolina had come to feel like something in the vein of a friend, and Jennifer was afraid she'd lose her mind if she didn't talk to someone. Maybe a friend was exactly what she needed. After a week of canceling work to stay home and torture herself, the problem persisted, so someone needed to fix it. Fix *her*. Friends did that, right?

"Hey, I brought food," Carolina said when she arrived at the door. The scent wafting off the bag she carried made Jennifer's stomach growl, and she realized she'd gone the whole day without eating. With a sniff, she went from oblivious to starving, and briefly considered vacating her comfort zone to hug Carolina. She didn't, wouldn't. She hugged her clients on occasion, when asked to or during aftercare, but that was work. Personally, Jennifer thought of hugs much like she thought of flies. Did they serve a purpose in life? Yes, so she didn't begrudge them their existence. But did she want them anywhere near her? *No, thank you.* Unfortunately, a hug-swatter had yet to be invented.

"Never would've guessed you owned sweatpants," Carolina said as she toed off her sneakers. "I mean, they probably cost more than my car, but still: sweatpants."

"They're from Target, actually."

"Sure."

Jennifer shoved her toward the kitchen and diverted to the table to grab Dosie's book. She glared at it a moment, then picked it up, surprised it didn't hiss or explode or burn her fingers on impact. *Dear God.* She rolled her eyes at herself. *I'm having a fucking breakdown over a book.*

"Did you know about this?" she asked when she entered the kitchen.

"Know about what?" Carolina looked up from the foiled food she was unpacking to the book Jennifer all but shoved in her face. "What is that?"

"So, you didn't know then?"

Jennifer watched as Carolina's eyes scanned the cover, watched her eyes widen and her brows inch up her forehead.

"Fisher, as in your client? Ms. Fisher? Fifties-dress-wearing, scared-of-her-own-shadow, lives-in-the-middle-of-nowhere Ms. Fisher?"

"Mhm."

"No shit!" She snatched the book from Jennifer's hand

and read the title. "*The Prophet's Daughter*. What does that mean?"

Jennifer flopped onto one of the barstools surrounding her kitchen island. "You've always lived here, right? In California?"

"Los Angeles, mostly, yeah. Modesto, 'cause I lost my whole-ass mind for a minute. Don't ask. Then here. Why?"

"You'll probably remember this then," Jennifer said. "I started to remember it myself after I did a few Google searches. I mean, I remembered it being on the news, but it was before I moved the company here." She waved a hand. "Anyway—the Hand of God. Do you remember that?"

Carolina had just turned the book over to read the back cover when her head shot up, mouth gaping. "Are you serious? No!"

"No, you don't remember it?"

"Of course, I remember it," Carolina said. "It was *insane*."

Jennifer's stomach knotted. "Yeah."

"And not even just because of the cult stuff," Carolina said. "There was a whole mess with, like, Social Services involved and stuff. The state ended up paying a *huge* settlement to the surviving kids. Negligence or something, I think. I don't know, but I'm pretty sure it was the biggest payout in California history. My mom was obsessed with this story when it was on the news. She probably has this book." She stopped and frowned, put the book down as if it had suddenly doubled in weight. "Fuck." Her hand rose to her mouth as her eyes grew larger. "Oh *fuck*. So, she was...." The hand dropped to her chest where she rubbed over her heart like she was soothing an ache. "She was one of the kids? She was one of *his* kids?"

Jennifer tried to respond, but a boulder had lodged itself in her throat and refused to go down. The thought of the funny, dimpled, tender woman she'd held in her arms being mixed up in something like that tortured her to silence. She nodded.

Carolina stared and stared. Dumbfounded. "Have you read it?"

"No."

"Are you going to?"

"I don't know. I'm conflicted."

"Yeah, no shit." She rounded the island to sit beside Jennifer, their food forgotten. "I would be, too." They sat in silence a moment. "Jen?"

"Hm?"

"Her house," Carolina said, brow dipping again. "All that land. Do you think...?"

Jennifer sighed, felt a prickle in her eyes and blinked it away. "That's the conclusion I came to as well."

They stared at one another, wordless horror passing between, until Carolina's face shifted. A surprised dawning. "You care about her."

Jennifer wanted to deny it, but when she opened her mouth, no words came. No sound emerged. She closed it again, which was confession enough.

"I mean, I knew you were invested, more than usual," Carolina said. "But you feel something for her, don't you? Something real. That's why you've been canceling bookings."

"It was only two."

"That's two more than you've ever canceled in all the time I've worked for you."

Jennifer shook her head. "It doesn't matter what I feel, how I feel, *if* I feel anything. I would never act on it. That's crossing a line."

"Uh huh," Carolina said, giving her a pointed stare. "And if she books you again?"

"What? I'll do my job."

"Oh, you must not have gone to church growing up like I did."

"Meaning?"

"Meaning, 'The spirit is willing, but the flesh is weak,'" she said and leaned over the counter to grab the food, threw a napkin at Jennifer's face. "Or in non-spiritual terms: Don't go to the grocery store when you're hungry. You will do the thing you swear you won't do. Every time."

Jennifer crumpled. "Buy the ice cream?"

"And the doughnuts, too."

The cavernous dressing room filled with the sound of steps.

"Let's pull another of these, then something with a wider leg as well, I think."

Dosie froze inside her large, curtained stall, one leg in the high-waisted butterscotch palazzos Kaylia had insisted she try and the other still naked, dangling.

"And if you could bring in a few blouses as well, that would be great, Poppy. Thank you."

Dosie's jaw dropped. Heat slithered through her belly like a snake. *The Director.*

"Of course. I'll be right back with those."

Poppy click-clacked away with purpose.

"Dose?"

Panic rushed through Dosie's system like a bucket of cold water dumped over her head. She had to slap a hand over her mouth to stop herself from squawking like a chicken.

"She had them pull, like, ten more things, so—you're in this one, right?"

A gap appeared in the tall curtain hiding Dosie from view, and despite knowing it was Natalie, she still jumped like she'd been shocked and tripped over the palazzos. She caught herself before she could fall as Natalie stepped in with a bundle of clothes and said, "Oh good. I'm not walking in on a naked stranger."

Dosie launched herself at Natalie and capped a hand over her mouth. The bundle of clothes tumbled to their feet as Natalie's hands shot up to Dosie's elbows, and her eyes bulged. "Don't say my name," Dosie whispered. "Okay?"

Natalie nodded, and Dosie let her free. "Are you having a breakdown right now?"

Dosie couldn't blame her for asking. She was acting

deranged, and she knew it. But the woman she'd literally *paid to give her orgasms* was right next door. The woman who'd held and soothed and *changed* her as if it was the easiest thing in the world. How was she supposed to act? How was she supposed to *feel*? Out of her mind seemed appropriate.

"Seriously, though. Hey. You're worrying me." Natalie took Dosie's hands, squeezed. "Are you having one of your flashbacks or something?"

"No, sorry," Dosie said, shifting on her feet in her white cotton bra and panties. "I'm sorry. It's...." She pointed toward the wall, the adjacent dressing room.

Natalie's face scrunched, upper lip curling in bewilderment. "Huh?" Then her mouth opened into an 'o'. "Oh, shit! Is there someone famous in there?" Dosie wanted to melt into the floor. Natalie's version of whispering was her regular volume in a raspy hat. "Who is it? I love seeing celebrities in the wild."

A nervous giggle shook from Dosie's throat. This was hopeless.

"Dude, I read that Julia Roberts got a place in Presidio Heights, and that is my wife. I will die."

"Here we are." They froze as Poppy's voice sounded from next door. "A wider leg in your preferred navy, and I went ahead and pulled a pair in our darker sage as well."

"Oh, thank you."

"And the blouses. Darker tones to your preference, and I took down one of our softer silks in peach as well, in case you're feeling adventurous."

"Poppy, I say this with respect: If peach is your idea of an adventure, you need to get out more."

Natalie looked at Dosie blankly, mouthed, *"Who is it?"*

Poppy laughed, good-natured. "I should've known. Sorry, Ms. Dupont. I'll take it back."

Fireworks burst in Dosie's brain as Poppy left again. *Dupont.* Oh, this felt like dangerous information, classified information for which Dosie did not have clearance. There was a reason the escort service used titles instead of names. She was never meant to know The Director's identity, not any part of it, and now she did. It both excited and terrified her. *Dupont. Dupont. Director Dupont.* A shiver ran through her. *Why is that even hotter?*

"It's her," Dosie whispered and pointed again.

"I don't know what that means."

"Nat," Dosie groaned as quietly as she could.

"I'm sorry. I need more words."

"Her as in...." She bugged her eyes out. "*Her.*"

"Oh, okay, right, right," Natalie said, though Dosie could tell by her voice and the complete lack of change in her face that she still had no clue. "Oh, wait. *Oh!*"

"Finally! I thought I was going to have to spell it out for you."

"Sorry." Natalie snickered. "It's been years since I've had to be fluent in Gay Panic."

Dosie scoffed and shoved her. "It's not gay panic. It's...."

Natalie raised her eyebrows. "It's...?"

"I don't know. It's just panic. Regular panic."

"Regular, *gay* panic." Natalie waggled her eyebrows. "Do you think if I hover long enough, I could get a peek of her? I mean, not naked or anything. I'm not a creeper. But I honestly can't remember what she looks like. We looked at way too many pictures that night."

"Will you focus? I am freaking out!"

"Okay, sorry, but what's the problem? Why are we panicking?"

"Because it's *her*," Dosie hissed again. "We've had *sex*. A lot of it. Okay, well, not a lot but more than once, and for me, that is a lot of sex. Especially when only one of us knows the other's name!"

"Okay, but—Wait, what do you mean? Did you tell her your name?"

"Yes," Dosie said and felt her body temperature spike to unhealthy levels. "I mean, I booked with just my last name, but it was weird being called Ms. Fisher by..." Dosie refused to look in the mirror, knowing she'd look like a crab, as she lowered her voice so much Natalie had to lean in to hear. "... the person who was *inside me*."

Natalie pinched her lips together in an obvious attempt not to laugh. "Well, yeah, but people usually give fake names for that kind of thing. I mean, unless they're booking for actual escort services, like to an event or something. Or if they're famous, so there's really no point."

"Well, I didn't think of that," Dosie said and shoved her. "Thank you for reminding me how naïve I am."

"Come on." Natalie chuckled. "You've been in the news.

Your book was a bestseller. I mean, you're not Julia Roberts, Dose, but a lot of people still know you."

The words hit Dosie like a punch to the gut. "Do you think *she* knows?" Her mouth went dry. "Do you think she—"

"Googled you? I mean, she probably assumed the name you gave her was fake, so I doubt it. Even if she knew it was your real name, I don't know why she would look you up. Unless she was just curious, I guess." She sighed. "But obviously, yeah, it's possible."

"Oh God." Dosie buried her face in Natalie's chest, pulled the edges of her blazer around her head until she was hidden inside. "Why did I do that?" Her pulse was unsteady, like it couldn't decide if it wanted to race or retire. *She knows. She knows. She knows. She knows.*

"Hey." Natalie nudged her up again, laughed at her mussed hair. "You're not ashamed of your past," she said as she smoothed the wild strands. "So, why would it matter if she knew?"

"Because." Dosie's voice cracked pitifully. "I don't want the way she looks at me to change."

Natalie's expression crumpled. "Oh."

"I'm not stupid." Her voice sounded small to her ears, every part of her shrinking under the dark cloud expanding overhead. "I know I'm paying her, and she gives me what I pay for, but when she looks at me, it feels *so* good. Like, somehow, *I'm* desirable to her. But if she knows..." She sagged, ached. Her shoulders felt like they'd been tied to her feet. "... she'll just look at me the way everyone else who knows does.

Like I'm someone who needs to be protected. Like I'm fragile. Like I'm broken. And I know I'm not. I know I'm...but everyone else...." She huffed. "No one *wants* broken things, Nat. No one looks at broken things the way she looks at me."

Natalie briefly turned her face away, cleared her throat. "Put your clothes back on. Let's get out of here."

"But Kaylia—"

"Will understand," Natalie said. "I promise." She discreetly wiped her face and cleared her throat again. "Just meet us outside when you're ready." Then she squeezed Dosie's hand and left.

Dosie breathed, relieved. Maybe they could find a café nearby, sit and have tea. A moment to think would be good, a place to talk. She blinked up at the ceiling to force away tears. *Okay. You're okay. All you need to do is get dressed and go.* She grabbed her original outfit and started pulling pieces on. *And get out of here without bumping into the Director.*

She blinked, stricken. She still had to get out of the dressing room unseen. What if the Director was still next door? What if they left their stalls at the same time and bumped right into each other like something out of a movie? It could happen.

A tickle in her belly told her, on some level, she *hoped* that was exactly what would happen. She wanted to see the Director, just a peek of her. Part of her wanted more than that —to touch her, talk to her. As terrifying as that was with paranoia now rooting around her brain, Dosie couldn't deny she wanted it.

"When you're ready, I will show you just how much."

Dosie shivered. Energy pulsed between her legs. *Maybe she doesn't know. Maybe she'll look at you the same way she always does. Maybe—*

"Stop," she snapped at herself and shut her mouth. The Director was not her girlfriend. She was an escort. *You can't feel things for her. Stop.*

Jennifer's chest was rubble. Dosie Fisher's voice was a dirge in her soul, heavy, mournful words that hadn't been meant for Jennifer's ears but that she'd heard all the same through thin walls and flimsy curtains. At first, she'd thought nothing of the hushed voices. Recognition came slowly, then all at once, and Jennifer had been dizzied ever since.

She didn't know what to do. Part of her was sure she should stay where she was, stay hidden until Dosie left. Another part felt an immense urge to *put herself* in Dosie's way. What she'd overheard broke her heart, and the wound was still throbbing.

"No one wants broken things."

Fuck. How could she leave those words unchallenged?

The neighboring curtain squeaked with movement again, and Jennifer's body decided for her. As quick, timid steps skirted past, she jolted to her feet and out of her stall. Dosie was already almost out of sight, scampering like a cat avoiding a dog. And since Jennifer was the dog, she chased.

"Dosie," she croaked and watched the girl stumble over her own feet.

"Um, hi," Dosie said as she spun around. Her eyes were golden brown as they dropped to Jennifer's tits and stuck there.

Oops. Jennifer had been sitting thunderstruck in her dressing room for ages. She'd forgotten she was only half-dressed. *At least I have a bra on today.*

Dosie licked her lips, then returned to Jennifer's eyes. "Hi."

"Hi," Jennifer said back, unable to think of a single other word in her entire extensive vocabulary. Her mind was a speeding bullet, too fast for clear thought. So, she was left with emotion—unbridled emotion—the likes of which Jennifer hadn't grappled with in ages.

Unlike her, Dosie was fully dressed, but Jennifer found she still needed to take in every inch of her—from her wide-leg jeans to her black-and-green flannel, oversized and knotted at the waist. Jennifer swallowed and dragged her gaze up again, said nothing. Why was this so difficult? Finding words to make conversation—she'd done it countless times in her life. But her tongue was paralyzed. Her stomach was in her knees.

Dosie's gaze pinballed around the room as she laughed, breathy and forced. "So, um, is it weird seeing a client outside of a session?"

Say something. Say something. "It happens." *Smooth.*

Dosie nodded. "Oh okay." She rocked on her feet,

frowned. "Then why do you look like that?

"Like what?"

"Like you've seen a ghost."

"I...." Jennifer swallowed again. Her throat felt like it had been put through a shredder.

Dosie's shoulders fell. Her beautiful face crumpled. "You looked me up, didn't you?"

Don't look at her like she's broken. Don't look at her like she's broken. "Yes."

For a moment, time slowed. It stalled. Their eyes locked, and they were caught there, suspended in a connection Jennifer felt down to her cells.

"Okay," Dosie said, and her voice cracked. Reality jerked into motion again. Time barreled forward. "Okay." She sounded like defeat personified. "Well." She shrugged, and Jennifer's nerves jumped as if triggered.

"Dosie."

"Please don't," Dosie said, eyes slamming shut. "Please don't say you're sorry or that you can't imagine what it must have been like or any of the things everyone always says. I just, I didn't ever want to hear those words from you. I didn't want you to pity me. I just wanted you to...." She pressed two fingers to the bridge of her nose and forced a breath. Every word vibrated. "I wanted you to want me."

Jennifer's skin could have sparked. She felt electric. In two long strides, she had Dosie by the back of the neck, reeling her in, enveloping her like fire—snuffing out the oxygen they needed with a furious kiss. Her mind swam with emotions too garbled to decipher, but her body was a swarm of adrenaline and need, and *that*, she understood.

Every step was instinct as she shuffled backward into her dressing room, pulling Dosie along with her. She yanked the curtain closed, rings screeching along the rod, then pressed Dosie roughly against a mirror. There was moisture on her lips, her cheeks, the tip of her nose. Tears. Hers or Dosie's, Jennifer wasn't sure, which terrified her. She hadn't felt so off-kilter, so exposed, in years.

"I want you," she panted into Dosie's frantic kisses. She siphoned a moan from the girl's throat as she tugged open her jeans. "I want you."

"Oh, *God*."

The zipper cried. Jennifer felt delirious. "Yes?"

"*Yes*," Dosie wept, and a second later, Jennifer's fingers were in her curls, spreading her dewy lips.

"I want you," she said again, voice edging on a whine she couldn't contain, and pressed Dosie's clit like a button. She promised it over and over as she ringed Dosie's sex then speared her. One finger. Two. Dosie shouted and moaned, and Jennifer clamped a hand over her mouth to quiet her. "I want you," she panted against her neck as she plundered the girl, using her knee to increase the pressure. "I want you so badly, I can't think." She sucked her neck, her jaw, her top lip, and shook all the way down to her marrow. "Dosie, I can't *breathe* for wanting you."

And that was all it took. Dosie came around Jennifer's fingers with a vicious clamping of her muscles and a muffled cry against Jennifer's palm. She gripped Jennifer's shoulders, fingernails digging into exposed skin, but Jennifer didn't care.

"I want you," Jennifer promised as the climax waned, and Dosie shuddered in her arms. She pulled her fingers free and wrapped her arms around her, drew her close. "I want you."

A quiet sob melted into the skin of Jennifer's neck as Dosie concealed her face there. "I'm not a victim anymore," she whispered, quiet but firm, and Jennifer tightened her grip. "I'm a survivor."

"I know," Jennifer said and buried her nose in Dosie's hair. Her scent was like a hot bath, working away tension. "I'm s—"

The sharp clearing of a throat was so jarring that Dosie gasped. The two shot apart, eyes snapping to the curtain.

"Is everything alright?" Poppy asked from the other side, and Dosie blushed so hard, she turned purple.

"I have to go," she said and quickly fastened her jeans. "I'm sorry. My friends are waiting."

"It's okay," Jennifer told her, too rattled to say anything else as reality decked her in the face like an angry ex. She'd just finger-fucked a client in a boutique dressing room, and she *hadn't* been paid for it. She'd simply done it because she wanted to. *Needed* to. *Oh God.* "Go."

Her nerves sparked like frayed wires. *What did I just do? What did I just do?*

Dosie darted through the curtain, revealing Poppy on the other side, arms stacked with new options for Jennifer. She said nothing as she flitted past and disappeared, leaving only awkward silence and a racing heart behind. Poppy's disapproving eyes met Jennifer's. One of her perfectly tweezed eyebrows shot high, and while it wasn't in Jennifer's nature to feel embarrassed, she couldn't deny the heat in her chest and cheeks. Still, she summoned what little pride she had left and said, "Some privacy?"

7

Dosie woke to the sun on her face. The hammock hugged her sides as she stretched and twisted and breathed the morning air. She'd not slept outside in ages, but she'd been floating on the high of being wanted for days and felt like treating herself to a night of wine and stargazing. Her glass had been abandoned somewhere on the ground after her yawns grew more frequent than her sips, and she'd snuggled under her old quilt and let the breeze and the crickets sing her to sleep.

A slow smile spread Dosie's lips. Today was the day; or rather, *later that night* would be the night. The night she would see the Director again.

Only three days had passed since their surprise encounter in San Francisco (and the scandalized expressions on her best friends' faces when she walked out of the boutique with kiss-swollen lips and an unfortunate wedgie), but Dosie hadn't been able to make herself wait any longer. In fact, she'd waited only *two* days before she found herself on the escort service's website again, clicking to book. She hoped that wouldn't make her seem desperate for the Director's company. She *was*, but she didn't want to *seem that way*.

Dosie pulled her quilt over her head and squealed, kicked her legs like an excited child. She rolled herself out of the hammock, picked up her discarded wine glass and the slippers she'd worn the night before, and headed toward the house. She had hours before her appointment with the Director, but her mind was already buzzing. *What should I wear? What should I say?* Should she mention what happened in San Francisco? It had been, well, far from professional, to say the least, but the Director hadn't looked or sounded like she regretted it. Then again, she'd been focused—very focused—and regret didn't typically set in until after.

Dosie's heart accelerated, as she considered, for the first time, if the Director might regret what happened between them at the boutique. It took seconds for her to spiral, even less for the nausea to follow. *She regrets it. She regrets it. She regrets it. She regrets it.*

"No," she told herself as she latched onto the door jamb of the now-open back door and steadied herself. "Stop." She closed her eyes and slowed her breathing, gave herself one long, deep inhale, freed it with a loud *whoosh*. Recited one of her therapy mantras. "You know these are only thoughts, and thoughts are not facts. This is just your brain processing anxiety. It will pass. These are only thoughts, and thoughts are not facts. This is just your brain processing anxiety. It will pass."

A few more repetitions, and her heart began to settle into its natural, painless rhythm again. She was able to swat away her doubts like flies buzzing at her ears. She'd seen the Director's face after all, had the woman's own words still thumping at the back of her head like background music.

"I want you."

"I want you."

"I want you."

Those weren't thoughts. Those were facts.

Dosie smiled to herself again as she made her way through her house to the stairs. She had a few things she wanted to get done before her date—*appointment*. There were boxes in the living room that still needed unpacking, a load or two of laundry in her hamper, and she'd wanted to get a yoga session in, too. Her back had been hurting from all the renovations. *But!* First things first, she intended to try on every article of clothing in her closet until she found the exact right amount of seduction. What the exact right amount *was*, she hadn't a sliver of a clue, but she damn-well was going to give it her best.

Perhaps something that screamed *we've done it before, but I can't get enough of you and I'm pretty sure you also feel the same way?*

Or *I'm finally ready to see your boobs and maybe also touch them.*

I don't even know your first name, but I think this might be what love feels like. Hm? What? I didn't say anything. Who?

Dosie blew cold air over her cheeks, burning like coals. She chuckled nervously at herself as she trekked up the stairs to her room. Thirteen hours and counting. Plenty of time to get her shit together. Right?

Ass in the air, Dosie was two deep, meditative breaths into her *ardha sirsasana* when the doorbell rang. She tapped her phone with her toe to see the time. Was she expecting a delivery? Had she ordered something and forgotten? *Knowing me, yes. That's exactly what I did.*

Dosie snorted and walked her hands back to a forward fold, slowly unrolled herself to standing. Her heart rate was up from the last twenty minutes of yoga, a bit of sweat soaking into the thick band of her sports bra, but she felt good. She ran a hand over her messy ponytail and used her tank top to wipe her forehead as she made for the door.

The bell chimed again as she entered her foyer, and Dosie frowned. *Somebody* was impatient. "Coming," she called, a little winded. When she opened the front door, she lost her breath entirely.

Standing in her open doorway, the Director was framed

by blue sky, tinged fuchsia from the first streaks of sunset. She wore a skin-tight sleeveless charcoal shirt that left her toned arms on generous display, paired with soft-linen, wide-leg dress pants in a deep navy. The pants sat high on her waist and made her already long legs seem even longer, and on her feet, she wore a pair of charcoal slingbacks with a sharp, pointed toe in brilliant white. Her hair was slicked back and shiny, spilling down her spine like dark water and leaving all her angles beautifully exposed. She stood with her arms loose, hands tucked in her pockets with the gray-faced, teak-wood watch adorning her wrist just peeking out from behind the fabric. She was lithe as a draping willow and just as natural —exquisite.

And I'm a mess! Her hair was *blah.* Her face was *bleck.* Her boobs were sweating. Her vagina was also sweating. She hadn't shaved her legs yet! She was supposed to have more time. Two whole hours! *Help! Someone. Anyone.* If she could just get a half-hour, an hour tops.

"Ms. Fisher?"

Dosie blinked and shook her head, realizing she'd been standing opposite the woman for a solid minute, just gaping at her. "Sorry." Her voice squeaked. She cleared her throat and forced an awkward laugh. "I wasn't expecting you. I mean, *yet.* I wasn't expecting you yet. Are you...."

Her mind raced with *whys.* Was it possible the Director had come early because she was excited? *God, no. Don't be ridiculous, Dosie.* Maybe she'd come by to cancel? Something could have come up. *Wouldn't she just have called?* What if—

Dosie blanked as she became acutely aware of what was happening across from her.

The Director's gaze had dropped like an elevator, passing over every level of Dosie's body from her sweaty neck to her naked toes and back. Her lips parted as she assessed, tongue darting out to moisten, and suddenly, Dosie wasn't so keen to fix anything. She was sweaty and messy and wearing nothing impressive, and apparently, that was *just fine*.

"Yes, I realize I'm quite early," she said, her voice just a touch strained as she finally met Dosie's eyes again. "I apologize."

"Um, no problem." Dosie fought the urge to clench her thighs together. "Is everything okay?"

The Director hesitated like she wasn't sure she wanted to say whatever she was about to say. Eyes conflicted. Lips thinned. And Dosie's stomach dropped. The flush of desire chilled to ice. *No.*

"Ms. Fisher," she finally said, and Dosie flinched. *Why is she avoiding my name?* "Perhaps we should talk inside?"

Dread pooled in Dosie's gut, but she did her best to keep calm. She stepped back, opening the door a bit wider, and gestured the Director inside. What else could she do?

"I don't understand."

The downward arc of Dosie's lips felt like sandpaper on Jennifer's skin, and the urge to soothe it, soothe both, hit like a hammer. She resisted. Little space existed between them as it was, standing only a foot or two apart in the daylit foyer, and she'd caved to her impulses enough already. *It's what got us in this mess.*

"You came all the way out here to tell me you won't take my appointments anymore?"

Jennifer cleared her throat, her insides dry. "Ms. Fisher," she said and steeled herself, "I crossed a line with you, a line I've crossed only once before in my career and after which I vowed never to cross again. Yet I have, and I—"

"You regret it?"

Jennifer's chest heaved as she tried to force in a breath too light to sink. Her head felt hollow and hot. "I shouldn't have done it." It was all she could think to say, because when she'd tried to form the word *yes*, she found herself unable. It would have been a lie, a cruel one. She *had* crossed a line, but she couldn't regret it. Touching Dosie Fisher was like fantasy bleeding off a page and into three dimensions—Jennifer felt magic in every stretch and shiver of her. She also felt like she'd been thrust into a world she wasn't built for. "For what it's worth, I'm sorry."

Dosie stood stricken, staring like half of her expected Jennifer to crack a smile, tell her she was teasing. When she didn't, Dosie expelled a loud, strangled breath and said, "What are you sorry for? Fucking me in a dressing room without getting my credit card information first?"

Jennifer winced but regained herself. "Ms. Fisher, I—"

"*Stop it.*" It was forceful, blunt, and it caught Jennifer off guard. "Stop." Weak. Broken. Jennifer's heart went into freefall. Discomfort itched in her spine, crawled over her skin like a rash, sickly hot and ugly.

"Stop what?"

Dosie's face, her neck, the visible parts of her chest—every inch of flesh Jennifer could see was splotched in red. The brown of her eyes was glossed and dark, her eyelids pink-rimmed and glistening. "Calling me Ms. Fisher won't change what happened. If you crossed a line, then you crossed a line. Reverting to formalities won't pull you back to the other side of it."

Jennifer felt cracked down the middle, a gap spreading to expose her. "You're right," she said. "Dosie."

Dosie closed her eyes at the sound of her name, and tears dropped at the pressure, skated down her cheeks. "Thank you."

The urge to touch her, to close the distance and capture her, *comfort* her, had never been stronger. Jennifer *ached* with it. There were many things she could say, could do, but nothing seemed apt. Nothing felt appropriate or honest or right or *real*. The world seemed tilted more harshly on its axis than ever before, and all Jennifer truly wanted to do, if she couldn't take back her words, if she couldn't change her mind, was *run*.

"I need you to tell me something." Dosie's quiet voice rocked the silence. Her eyes opened again, and she settled one hand over her stomach as if trying to soothe it while the other went to her neck. To the space where her pearls typically lay. Only, they weren't there, and Jennifer realized this was the first time she'd seen Dosie without them. "I need to know if you meant it, what you said."

"What I said?"

"That day, in the dressing room. Did you mean it?"

Don't ask me that, Jennifer pleaded inside her mind. Her own words were suddenly like thunder in her head. *"I want you so badly I can't think."*

This wasn't a road they should go down, not when she was trying to make a clean cut—reverse, go back to before. It wasn't a road they should go down, but Jennifer had been the one to point out the shortcut in the first place. *"Dosie, I can't breathe for wanting you."* She sighed, heavy and raw, and nodded. The simplest, swiftest motion, yet it somehow shifted the air.

Dosie's gasp was silent, just a motion of her lips and a widening of her eyes that caught Jennifer like a hook in her chest, a tug at the heart of her. A sudden gripping pressure between her legs. It wasn't shock or surprise. It was something deeper, more familiar to Jennifer. Dosie's silent gasp was pure, full-bodied *pleasure.*

For a moment, Dosie stared at her like a glitched video. Her throat dipped with a thick swallow, and her eyes flitted madly about the room. They returned to Jennifer as Dosie pressed a hand to her forehead and propped another on her hip. She looked, briefly, like a woman who'd rushed to the store only to forget what she'd come for. "Well...." Dosie said and sniffled. The hand cupping her forehead slid back, smoothing over her ponytail. "I guess you'd better come upstairs then."

Jennifer blinked. *Wait. What?* Surely, she'd misheard. "Upstairs?"

"Yes, it's where I keep my bed," Dosie said, and despite how nervous she appeared, she sounded resolved. She moved around Jennifer to the old staircase. The creak of pressure on the first step made Jennifer weak. "I already paid. If this is the last time I'll see you, I want to at least get my money's worth."

Her body bowed, the tension in her spine like a taut wire stretched to capacity. She was certain, even as she followed, that a single step more into Dosie's orbit—into her bed, her body, her *life*—would break her. She took that step anyway.

They made the climb in silence, the only sound that of the staircase's complaints. Jennifer couldn't recall a time she'd felt this way following a client to their bed. Every nerve was singing and alive, searing hot under her skin, twitching beneath and around her muscles. Her breath was hot in her chest like mid-summer air that refused to soothe. She clutched the banister as if it was the only thing anchoring her feet to the ground, her body to this space, and all the while, Dosie said nothing, and never once did she look back.

Their silence continued down the skinny corridor at the top of the stairs, the wood still creaking and thumping under their feet. They passed three closed doors before they reached the last one on the right. The door was ajar, and Jennifer could make out the edge of a dresser through the slit. She stopped as Dosie did, hovering just outside.

She chewed her bottom lip, hesitating, then pushed the door open to reveal a rather large space, large enough that Jennifer would wager it as the home's master bedroom. She was certain once she made note of the sizeable, connected bathroom with a peekaboo view of a clawfoot tub. The bed in the room's center was larger than necessary for a single woman, but Jennifer couldn't find fault with it. Her own bed was obscenely oversized given she'd not shared it with anyone in, well, *ever*. The air was pure Dosie Fisher, that lazy-day smell that made her bones feel liquid and warm. Jennifer had only just begun to revel in it when something struck her.

This house. The land. Maybe even this room.

Her heart spasmed, a jolt of pain beneath her ribs, but she did her best not to show it. If Dosie could be here, live here, fuck here, love here, then certainly, so could Jennifer. This wasn't her home. It wasn't her past. It wasn't her pain or her trauma or her burden. This, simply, was Jennifer's job, and she would fight through every nerve in her body, every aching bit of empathy pressing her from the inside, to remember that, so that she could do her job well. If she was going to walk away from Dosie Fisher for good, the first person she'd felt a genuine connection to since she was a literal teenager, she didn't want the girl's memory of her to be of her back as she left or of her nerves rattling the walls like an earthquake. She wanted the tremble only in Dosie's thighs, wanted the devastation dialed to the precise sear of Jennifer's mouth on Dosie's sex. Jennifer cleared her throat and met Dosie's gaze. She wanted Dosie to remember only pleasure, and for herself, only Dosie's joy in receiving it.

"Are you okay?"

Well, shit. Clearly, she'd not masked her emotions well enough. Or... Was it possible Dosie could read her that well? Past Jennifer's carefully constructed composure to what lay beneath?

Oh, she shouldn't have followed. How was she going to cut herself away now? How was she going to banish the ghost of Dosie's eager, nervous body from her fingertips when she couldn't stop reaching for it? When it wouldn't stop reaching back? How was she going to do this with as minimal damage as possible? Not only to Dosie but to herself. She was screwed. They both were.

Jennifer turned toward Dosie at the foot of her bed and held out her hand. "Come here."

She didn't hesitate, taking Jennifer's hand to be drawn closer. Her breath trembled when Jennifer leaned in. It shook over Jennifer's lips and bolstered her, *encouraged* her. Dosie's nerves, always so sensitive, and Dosie's nerve, always surprising, pressed *that* feeling into Jennifer's chest—the feeling she'd come to associate, in such a short time, with only this woman. A breathless kind of need. The need to protect her, to care for her, to respect her. To *give* to her anything, everything she'd been denied. Anything, everything she'd missed out on. Anything, everything she'd wanted or could ever want. Jennifer felt the impulse strongly. It was singular, exceptional, and she'd been ruled by it since Dosie's first act of caving, torn between fascination and fear.

Screwed, indeed.

When the tips of their noses bumped together, the tiniest sound rattled from Dosie's throat, and Jennifer closed her eyes, let the brief music of it wash through her. Dosie began a slow exploration of her fingers, whether deliberately or not, Jennifer wasn't sure. One by one, she stroked them, base to tip in silence. "I was thinking," she whispered, and tingles shot down Jennifer's spine, "earlier today...."

She drifted back into silence, so Jennifer opened her eyes. A flurry of relief cooled her nerves. Dosie was exactly as Jennifer had only just been. Her eyes were closed, lips parted. Her body stood frozen but for the hand she worked over Jennifer's, digit by digit by digit and back.

Jennifer could take her in properly now, unafraid of the things she felt stirring inside painting her face like tattoos. She could look, *revel*, unabashed and unburdened by whatever Dosie might've found in her gaze. She dipped in to kiss her, just the barest press of flesh, and the quiet gasp it elicited went straight to her sex.

"What were you thinking?" Jennifer asked, low and breathy.

Dosie kept her eyes closed, fingers stroking, nose rubbing. "I was thinking," she began again, and her bottom lip shook and shook, "that I haven't touched you enough."

The words scorched down Jennifer's spine, bubbled in

her belly. She moaned, and Dosie's eyes snapped open. Her hands stilled, fingers gripping tightly instead.

"Is that something you would like? Me touching you?"

Jennifer tried to keep her voice from trembling and failed. "I think you know it is," she said as she brought her free hand to Dosie's face, stroked her thumb along the swell of her soft cheek. "But is that something you would like?"

"Yes." The answer was so quick, a puff against her lips, that Jennifer nearly missed it. Dosie's eyes widened as if she'd surprised herself, then she laughed. The sound floated over Jennifer's ears like a caress, inspiring her own smile. She would never understand how with little more than an embarrassed giggle, Dosie Fisher could make her feel so mad with affection.

"I hope I'm not the only one of your clients who embarrasses themselves this often."

Jennifer's smile grew until she felt it wrinkling her nose, crinkling around her eyes. "No, you would be in good company, I'm afraid."

One of Dosie's hands jumped to mirror Jennifer's, cupping Jennifer's cheek as if to insulate her joy—keep it, protect it, savor it. "Oh," she whispered, and her cheek dimpled. Her eyes caught the last glints of sunlight as it disappeared beneath the window. "You are *so*...."

"So?"

Dosie's forehead crinkled. "I don't know," she said and leaned closer. "I really don't know." Their noses nudged again with a barely-there zap of static. "I just know I want it." Her eyes pinged back and forth, gaze searching Jennifer's, seeking something Jennifer hoped she both would and wouldn't find. "I want you." She freed Jennifer's hand to frame the other side of her face, fingertips curling around the back of Jennifer's jaw. "*You*. Not an escort, not the...the sex. It's you. I want *you*."

Oh, this was bad. *Bad, bad, bad.*

"Is that okay to say?" Dosie whispered, and Jennifer was sure she would never breathe again.

She did. One swift, caving exhale that sounded perilously like, "Yes."

Jennifer had no time to question it, not a chance or dream of backpedaling, because Dosie was touching her now, on her own and as she pleased. It was the boldest she'd ever been, and Jennifer could do nothing but stand still. Stand still and be touched by this woman. Stand still and feel her body vibrate with desire. With sorrow. With pride.

Dosie's hands sloped down Jennifer's neck and over her shoulders, fingers bunching gently in the soft fabric of her shirt. "Can I take this off?"

"Yes," came her reply once more, little more than air. She was in the current now, pulled in by the tide. She would stay with this to its conclusion, and hopefully, when she emerged on shore, she'd still be breathing. "Dosie."

Dosie's eyes found hers. "Are you okay?" she asked, fingers stilling over Jennifer's stomach. "Do you want me to slow down?"

Just like that, the ache Jennifer felt, the anguish, had a

name: *Care.* Unlike all who had come before, Dosie cared about Jennifer. Openly. Constantly. As timid as she was, as terrified as she could be, she never failed to ask Jennifer for consent, to ask Jennifer if she wanted, if she needed, if she could, if she *would.*

"I'm okay," Jennifer said and hated the way her voice squeaked. She danced her hand up Dosie's bare forearm to her elbow, her shoulder to her neck. "Are you? Because I want you to be sure, Dosie. You weren't ready for either of us to undress before, and I want you to know that it's fine if you aren't. I don't want you to feel rushed or pressured to take a step you aren't ready for just because you won't be booking with me again. You should feel ready, regardless of who you choose to take those steps with."

Dosie softened. She lay her hand over Jennifer's heart. "Do you talk this way with all your clients?"

"No," Jennifer admitted. "Just you."

"Not even the one before?"

"One before?"

"You said you'd only ever crossed the line with one other client," Dosie explained. "Was it like this with them, too?"

"No." Jennifer brought Dosie's hand up to kiss her palm then the inside of her wrist. "The way I crossed the line with her was not how I've done with you, Dosie. In fact, I wish I'd been gentler with her. It might have made for a better outcome."

"So, why are you like this with me? Because you think I'm fragile?"

"You *are* fragile," Jennifer said, and before Dosie could protest, pressed a finger over her lips. "That doesn't mean you aren't also strong. You are. But intimacy, including the physical kind, is a tender thing, and not everyone has the capacity to be as nonchalant about it as others, especially when other factors are at play."

"Factors like growing up in a cult?"

Jennifer had to catch her breath at the question. Hearing Dosie say the words out loud was like being slapped in the face with a truth Jennifer had been choking on for days. A history she'd yet to reconcile with what she'd shared thus far with this damaged, perfect person.

"Dosie."

"I'm ready," Dosie said, and it was clear. Fearless. Adamant. "Please believe me. I want this. And I want it with you."

Jennifer searched her eyes for any hint of doubt but found none, so she toed off her heels to stand at nearly even height with her young lover. "Okay," she said and brought Dosie's hands back to her belly, to the top of her pants. "Take it off then."

Dosie tugged Jennifer's top from her pants, eyes fixed on every inch of flesh she exposed as she pulled the material up and up until Jennifer was lifting her arms for it be pulled over her head and discarded. Her hands returned to hover over Jennifer's bared abdomen, not quite touching as she shook with nerves. When they connected, Jennifer's nerves jumped.

"You're so warm."

"No, your hands are just freezing."

"Oh." Dosie grimaced. "Sorry. They're pretty much always like that. At least it's not my feet though. I don't think they've been warm a day in my life, even with socks on. Even with *shoes* on."

"Yes, I'm glad you're not caressing my stomach with your feet." She laughed at Dosie's horrified look, her teasing pinch over Jennifer's hipbone. "Though, if you want to know, you wouldn't be the first to try it."

"Oh *no*," Dosie said with a gasp that turned into a giggle. "Really? Another client?"

Jennifer nodded. "One thing you learn quickly in my job: People are strange, especially where sexual stimuli are concerned. We just are."

"I got turned on by a peach one time," Dosie admitted with a blush that turned her borderline blueberry, and Jennifer's lips began to pull and pull. "Literally, all I was doing was eating a peach. It was so weird." She groaned. "I can't believe I just told you that."

"Dosie."

"I *know*."

"No, that's actually much more common than you think."

Dosie's jaw dropped, then a sly smile touched her lips. "You're messing with me. Peaches?! People are turned on by peaches?"

"Well, a variety of fruits, but yes," Jennifer said. "It makes sense if you think about it. Some fruits are visually comparable to sex organs. Some are *texturally* comparable to sex organs. The sounds we make when we eat them."

"Right." Dosie nodded, gaze drifting then snapping back. "So, peaches...."

Jennifer raised a brow, lowered her voice to a teasing rasp. "Are pretty," she said and kissed the corner of Dosie's mouth. "And pink." Another kiss to her cheekbone. "And soft." A slow trail of kisses to her ear. "And *wet*."

Dosie shuddered. "Okay. I see your point." She shook her head at herself and pinched Jennifer again. "You like to rile me up."

"I do."

"And all this time, I thought the peach turned me on because I hadn't eaten in three days." She laughed at herself. "Not because I was gay."

Jennifer's mind imploded, thoughts spiraling toward Dosie's childhood, the thing she'd been trying and failing to put out of her head for days. Anyone else, and her first guess as to why they'd gone three days without food would've been that they'd been as stupid as any other young adult and spent those three days gorging on alcohol and drugs and *sex* and simply forgetting to eat altogether. But with Dosie, all she could think was *abuse*. Not the kind inflicted on the self *by* the self, for fun or whatever motivation, but the kind that stemmed from neglect, from punishment. From another person's hands; in this case, those of Dosie's own parents.

"Wow." Dosie's voice pitched up, breathy and surprised. "I don't think I've said that out loud before."

Jennifer ignored the sick feeling in her gut and put her focus back to the moment. "Said what before?" Her fingers itched to touch, so she did, sliding over Dosie's tank top, down her sides. "That you're gay?"

"Yes," she whispered, and her eyes watered. Her one dimple appeared, deepening as she smiled.

"Come here," Jennifer said, and Dosie walked into her arms. She tugged Dosie's ponytail free, buried her face in the falling waves as they embraced.

"I hope I don't smell bad," Dosie said with a chuckle that vibrated against Jennifer's shoulder. "I was doing yoga when you got here. I'm sweaty."

Jennifer carded her fingers through Dosie's hair, then made a point of sniffing her, one long, slow inhale up the length of her neck and into her hair again. "Mm." She squinted her eyes as if considering. "Mhm."

"Well?"

"Amazing."

"Oh, really?"

"Yes," Jennifer said. "Very gay."

Dosie's explosive laugh made her feel like she was ten feet tall. With a soft sigh, she said, "Thank you," and melted against Jennifer's chest. Her hands mapped Jennifer's back as they fell into silence again, swaying to nothing.

It was a kind of intimacy that had never come naturally to Jennifer, one she'd avoided most of her life. But with Dosie, it was different. *She* was different. Intimacy, in any form, was more with Dosie Fisher than it had ever been with anyone else. Most days, it scared Jennifer. But now, in what she knew would be their last appointment, she felt an urge to embrace it. This was how she would say goodbye.

"Tell me a secret, Director Dupont."

Jennifer pulled back. "What?"

"I heard it at the boutique."

Right. The boutique. Jennifer's stomach flipped. The dressing room flashed through her mind. A spark popped between her legs. Guilt burned in her chest. "Ah."

"I'm sorry," Dosie said. "At least it's only your last name. You can still be all mysterious."

Jennifer pursed her lips, amused. "I bought your memoir," she confessed. "Does that qualify as a secret?"

Dosie's lip curled. "Buh. I was afraid of that."

"I haven't read it." Jennifer ran her finger along the girl's cheek. "It felt too intimate, like something I should only do with your consent."

A touch of a smile graced Dosie's lips as Jennifer traced over them as well. "I'm pretty sure signing the publishing contract was me giving consent for people to read my story."

"Your *direct* consent," Jennifer said. "Specifically, for me."

Dosie's breath left her in a soft, audible rush. Her hands gripped Jennifer's sides. Her voice trembled. "You're kind of amazing. You know that?"

Jennifer closed her eyes, relishing Dosie's touch and tone, her proximity. She found herself yearning for it to continue, for it to last. For it to progress. God, she wanted. She *needed.* "Dosie."

"Yeah?"

Jennifer twisted one arm behind her back to pop open her bra, pulled a strap down.

"Oh," Dosie croaked, and when the thin lace dropped to their feet, her gaze went with it. Her lips parted, tongue moistening. "Oh."

"Touch me," Jennifer whispered and guided Dosie's hands to her newly exposed flesh, curled her fingers around her breasts. And when Dosie's wide-eyed gaze finally drifted back up, Jennifer had to kiss her.

It was compulsion, she'd swear it, like a hook in her gut, tugging and reeling her in. She had to be closer. Had to touch her. Taste her.

When their lips met, Jennifer moaned and pressed in hard, licking into Dosie's mouth like she was trying to map her flavor. She cupped her hands around Dosie's and held them harder against herself, encouraged her to knead and massage, taunt her stiffening nipples. She wanted to touch and be touched in a way that left nothing to the imagination. A touch that could communicate exactly where they were headed.

Dosie whimpered as if overwhelmed, not that Jennifer could blame her. She knew she was everywhere. Her tongue in Dosie's mouth. Her breasts in Dosie's hands. Her nipples rubbing, straining against Dosie's fingers. Her scent and bareness and desire—Jennifer was surprised Dosie was still on her feet.

"Are you alright?" She slowed to gentle, closemouthed kisses here and there. "Is this too much?"

Dosie's reply barely shook the air. "Yes."

Jennifer stilled. "Yes, you're alright, or yes, it's too much?"

"Both." Her eyes met Jennifer's, pupils dilating with her arousal. "Would it make sense if I said it's too much and not enough at the same time?"

"Yes. Do you want to stop?"

Dosie flexed her fingers around Jennifer's breasts then slid down to her stomach, to the top of her pants. "Literally never," she whispered and dipped under the waistband.

"You're feeling bold today," Jennifer said with a slow smile.

"I'm freaking out on the inside."

"Don't freak out," Jennifer said and brought her hands back to Dosie's, helped her unclasp her pants. She watched as Dosie's eyes dropped to see them drag the zipper down together. Jennifer's navy lace underwear peeked, and Dosie took a quiet, sharp breath. Jennifer rubbed and massaged her wrists. "Just breathe and listen to your body." She slid Dosie's hands to her hips and guided them down, pushing her pants to the floor.

Dosie took a deep breath as Jennifer's hands found the hem of her tank top. She lifted her arms as Jennifer shimmied it over her head and cast it to the floor as well. "I have scars," she blurted, and Jennifer stilled. "On my back. I just wanted you to know."

"Okay," Jennifer said simply. Bodies were always marked —scars, freckles, tattoos, birthmarks. Everyone had stories in their skin. She grasped the damp bottom of Dosie's sports bra. "May I?"

Dosie choked on her reply. "Yes."

It was work, removing the tight material, but when Jennifer finally managed it, she was rewarded with the glorious sight of Dosie's small, perfect breasts and her pert, pink nipples, pebbling in the cool air. Her slim belly disappeared into the thick band of her yoga pants and quivered with every breath she took. Jennifer splayed her fingers over the vibrations, and Dosie keened toward her, eyes wide, mouth open. So desperate to touch and be touched that the slow pace she required to keep her nerves in check was clearly bordering on torture.

"You're beautiful."

Jennifer couldn't deny she liked it—a maddeningly slow pace for a maddeningly addictive woman. And the slower they went, the longer she could hold onto this, this strange connection they had and the way it floated through Jennifer's body like a warm breeze. When it wasn't striking between her legs like lightning.

"I'm going to touch you here now," she said, inching toward the bottom swells of Dosie's breasts. "Is that okay?"

Dosie whimpered. "Please." When Jennifer cupped her breasts, her back bowed. She was velvety smooth to the touch.

Perfect. Her mouth shot open as Jennifer pinched one nipple between her fingers, and whatever stillness they'd known shattered like glass.

Dosie's hand shot forward and hooked the back of Jennifer's neck. With a low whine, she rocked herself forward and swallowed Jennifer up in a dizzying kiss that nearly knocked them off their feet. They stumbled their way to steadiness again, and all the world thinned to this one moment. This one kiss. This one desire-drunk woman. Little mewling vibrations sang into Jennifer's mouth, and all her thoughts chiseled to a single, haunting command.

More.

8

Heat.

A match lit under her skin.

A single flame held captive on fingertips dragged the expanse of her, catching on nothing, on *everything*—a flash-quick burn devouring her like easy kindling then settling in to smolder. She was embers and birch now, blazing steadily under the Director's touch, stoked by the press of her, the breath of her, this slow, torturous ruin painted over with pleasure. This heat, Dosie was certain, would leave nothing in its wake.

They stood partially undressed at the foot of Dosie's bed, quiet but for their uneven breaths and the swipe of skin on skin. The Director's chest molded against Dosie's back as she encased her from behind. One strong arm looped her, hand greedily cupping her breast, while the other explored, palm dancing down one side and up the other. The Director dipped and rolled over the bumps of Dosie's ribcage, then smoothly snaked down the center of her, the pad of one finger stroking from chest to navel.

"So soft," she whispered into the fine hairs at the back of Dosie's neck. She kissed her there, openmouthed, and Dosie moaned.

"Don't stop."

A low chuckle rasped from the Director's lips. "Oh, darling," she said, and the affectionate term threatened to buckle Dosie's knees. "I've yet to even begin."

Dosie keened. "I feel like I'm on fire."

"Good," the Director said as her fingers skated under the band of Dosie's yoga pants. "Because I refuse to suffer this alone." She kept going, her seeking touch gliding under the thin material of Dosie's panties and into the coarse thick of her, and the room seemed to shake along with Dosie's bones. As if the Director's words manifested themselves in the air, the floorboards, the walls, in Dosie's own racing blood. "The way I want you. It's torture." She mouthed Dosie's pulse like a half-starved creature coming to feast, sucking bruises into tender flesh as her middle finger teased Dosie's slit, then descended. She moaned, her contained stature losing its measure as she ringed Dosie's slick entrance. "It is fucking *exquisite*."

The shudder that rippled through Dosie's body rolled

from the base of her skull to the tingling arches of her feet. She had never known want like this, had never even known such an experience was possible. How pleasure could be so dialed in, so precise as to be painful—the pleasure not only of being touched this way but of the truth she could hear in the Director's voice. Knowing *she* was the one who had undone her. With nothing but her body, her natural self. *God,* it was invigorating.

Despite the weakness in her legs, the trembling that wouldn't stop, Dosie turned in the Director's arms, and pushed their chests together. Kissed her roughly. Held her close and tight, fingers digging in wherever she touched, making prints. Marks to endure.

Dosie had said so many goodbyes in her life, more than anyone should ever have to, but this one... This goodbye, she knew, would linger. It would last. It would ruin her.

"Do you want me inside you?"

The words siphoned the breath from Dosie's lungs with startling ease. Yes, *yes*, she *did* want that. God, she wanted it more than words or shivers or the gentle, unconscious bucking of her hips could possibly express, but there was something Dosie wanted even more. Something she'd been working up the courage to ask for, to have. Something, at this point, she felt she might wither without, especially now that she knew this would be their last time together. Her last time with this woman, who she hardly knew yet craved like a drug, like the wonder of freedom after years of captivity.

"No," she whispered, and the Director stilled. Her dark brows furrowed in the waning light of Dosie's bedroom, a question pulling her lips apart, but Dosie gave her no time to speak it. No time to worry or fear or wonder. She shifted her hand to the thin band of the Director's lacy underwear and curled one finger under. "I want to be inside *you*."

A strangled sound emanated from the woman's throat, and her sharp blue eyes widened. Her bottom lip dropped, breath huffing free. Dosie captured every minute change, every tick of surprise, and reveled in the ability to inspire it all with only a few desire-drunk words whispered with intent.

"Please let me," she said, and when the Director answered with an honest-to-God whimper that nearly sent her to the floor, Dosie knew she had her answer. Still, she wanted, *needed*, to hear her say it. "Do you want me to?"

"Yes. God, Dosie, *yes*." The Director's slick, sticky fingers curled around and gave the gentlest tug to Dosie's wrist, encouraging her to move. "Please."

Dosie's mouth went dry. Her throat strained around a lump. Her stomach leapt and fluttered and leapt again. God, she wanted this. She'd craved it for *years*, and now? Now she was but a mere few inches from having it. She was dizzy with the development, every cell vibrating, every thought heady. How much she yearned to feel the warmth of this woman, the wetness she could only hope to find waiting between her thighs.

"Let's do this properly then," Dosie said, emboldened.

She backed up until her legs hit the foot of her bed, then sat. Slowly, she crawled herself backward, and the Director followed without beckoning, slinking up the bedspread like a panther on the prowl. Dosie would bet all her fortune that that image alone had sent some former clients to their early graves. The bliss and terror of being wanted and hunted—no one person should have such power, such allure, and yet.

The Director rolled onto her back, pulling Dosie atop her as she did, and suddenly, Dosie was staring down at a goddess. Her desert-dry mouth watered again as she took in the long dark hair pooled over her pillow, every sharp, feminine jut and angle catching evening shadows—desire-heavy blues gazing up at her with such affection. The steady thump between Dosie's legs quickened as she absorbed every detail. How... How would she ever be able to have another after this? How would she ever desire anyone more than she did this woman?

"Can I?" Dosie whispered, fingers toying again with the Director's last scrap of clothing.

The Director huffed a laugh. "If you don't, I might implode."

Dosie dragged the lace down and was greeted with a sheen of moisture in the dying light, the glistening evidence of the Director's desire for her. And despite hoping for it, despite some part of her expecting it, *knowing* this was what she would find, Dosie was still startled. Still thrown. "Oh," she said, unthinking. The lump in her throat was back.

"Oh?"

Dosie's gaze flicked up to the Director's, then down again. "You're...."

One of the Director's perfectly manicured brows ticked up. "Wet?"

Dosie nodded. "Very."

"That's a good thing, darling."

"No, I know that." Dosie jabbed her thigh for teasing. Her heart pounded at the use of 'darling' again, but she told herself not to read into it. "I *know*. I just...."

The Director sat up and took Dosie's face. "You are gorgeous, and yes, I want you. I told you that myself, and now you can see it. You can *feel* it. So, touch me."

"I might be bad at it," Dosie whispered, so soft it barely had sound.

"I'll help you, but as long as it's you who's touching me, it could never be bad."

A wave of affection crashed through Dosie's chest, pushing and pressing and *jarring* her heart. *Oh no.* There was no *way* she was coming out of this unscathed. When the Director left, she would be taking a piece of her with her. A piece of Dosie, sliced right from her soul without even a wound. Dosie resigned herself to the pain of it because she wanted this, wanted *her*. Perhaps some part of her always would.

"Touch me, Dosie," the Director implored again. She kissed the corner of Dosie's mouth, sucked her jaw. "Touch me the way I know you want to."

As she eased onto her back again, Dosie stretched alongside her, hoisted on an elbow, and steeled her nerves. She set her hand on the Director's warm thigh and began. Up, up, up. Over a sharp hipbone and back down. She raked her fingertips through trimmed, soft curls, then ventured in.

Her breath stuttered over her lips at the first touch of wet flesh, at the jump of the Director's clit under her fingers. A whine worked from her throat when she slid a bit lower and found what could pass as a hot spring. Her head dropped to the Director's chest as all the air shot from her lungs and refused to return.

"Oh wow," she croaked and rimmed the woman on instinct, fingertips circling the well, wetting themselves.

"Do you like that?" the Director whispered, her own fingers digging into Dosie's hair. "Feeling what you do to me?"

"Yes." Her voice strained. "*Yes.*"

Dosie's body was a livewire as she pressed one tip in and immediately felt the Director's inner walls latch on and pull. She crackled with energy, felt drunk with power. The Director's hips rocked up, seeking more, and Dosie knew she was absolutely, irrevocably *hooked.* Nothing could ever compare with this. This surge and surrender, merged into one. It was an absolute, whole-body experience—from the wet tip of her finger to the hammer in her chest.

She teased a second finger, then pushed, inching in, knuckle by knuckle, until she was buried. "Oh *God,*" Dosie moaned as strong muscles flexed around her fingers. "I'm inside you."

"Yes, you very much are," the Director said and tugged Dosie's hair. Then again, harder, yanking Dosie's head back, so their gazes met. "Kiss me." She reeled Dosie in by her hair, caught her in a searing kiss, and while her tongue probed, her hand caught Dosie's between her legs and told it to move.

No apt description existed in Dosie's mind for what the inside of a woman felt like, to be gripped by her strength and desire, pulled in and hungered for, giving and aiding in what would surely find its way to unmitigated, unparalleled, *unrelenting* bliss. It was destabilizing, intoxicating. She never wanted it to stop.

"I *love* this," she moaned as she explored, curling her fingers, experimenting with pace, and the smile it earned her was downright wicked. One particularly pointed thrust, and that smile shattered around a sound so guttural that it curled Dosie's toes.

"*Fuck.*"

"Good?"

"So good." The words shot through Dosie's body like an electric current. She curled her fingers again, then replicated the thrust. "*Yes.*"

"What else?" Dosie whispered and sucked the woman's collarbones, the swells of her breasts, operating on instinct. Madness. Affection. Her eyes rolled back when she drew a nipple between her lips and felt the Director's pussy clench in response.

"I need to feel you." She urged Dosie's legs apart to slot one of her own between and wriggled a hand down her pants again. "Oh, you're soaked." Dosie whimpered and bucked her hips erratically. Her breath shot from her body as two fingers entered her in one swift, easy stroke, and then they were moving. "Stay focused. Match me."

It was all Dosie could do to keep from collapsing as she tuned herself to the Director's rhythm. Her fingers ached. Her wrist was screaming. Twitches plagued her muscles as her pulse turned war drum, beating against the fingers sheathed inside her, and a fog had infiltrated her brain.

They panted in time, mouths hovering just outside of a kiss, lips wet and trembling beneath the static rub of nose to cheek. Flesh on flesh on flesh. Everything was heightened. Everything was wired. Dosie could feel rapture vibrating in her bones.

"Come for me," the Director ordered, leveraging her hips for more pressure. "I'm close. Come with me."

She arched off the mattress, lips parted in a silent cry, and that was all it took. Dosie gasped into her own climax, choked on nothing. They peaked together in quiet tension, and it was the most transcendent experience of Dosie's life—baptized anew in the Director's pleasure. It rolled through the woman's body like a too-hot summer breeze, and when they shivered back to calm, she was dappled with sweat and shadow, and Dosie could not look away from her. She'd done this, given a woman pleasure, genuine pleasure, and she needed to capture every second of it, cement each image in her mind for keeping. When she played back her memories at the end of her life, she wanted them to be good ones. Riveting ones. The moments that took her breath away. *This* moment. This *woman*. Dosie never wanted to forget.

"Mm," the Director hummed, content. "Thank you."

Dosie sniffled and laughed. Her eyes burned. She dropped her chin to the Director's chest and rested there, just between her breasts. "Thank *you*."

"How do you feel?"

She didn't know. So many things. Too many things. She felt unbridled and dangerous and alive and—an unbidden giggle jumped from Dosie's lips. *Oh no*. She felt it rising in her throat like foam, a spiritual release to match the physical. Up and up. Dosie snorted, then dissolved into another laugh. It grew and grew, vibrating against the Director's chest until it finally seeped in to infect her too. They bubbled like idiots, still buried inside each other. High on the dopamine flooding their brains.

"I haven't come that fast in a long time," the Director said when the fit ended, and Dosie didn't miss the surprise in her voice.

She grinned wide enough that her cheeks began to ache. "When you say things like that, it makes it very hard to stay humble," she teased. "And that was my first time, so you know, I'm worried about developing a complex."

"Wow. One orgasm, and you're full of yourself, hm?" The Director poked her sides until Dosie squirmed and caught her hands. Their fingers locked, then softened. "You should be naked," she said as she stroked down Dosie's palms to her wrists, touches too gentle to be anything other than care.

"I'm *half*-naked."

The Director scoffed and flipped their positions. "Do you know the definition of 'half'?" She quirked a brow as she hovered over Dosie, hair slung messily to one side, and grabbed her waistband. "Not enough. May I?"

"Did you find that in a dictionary?" Dosie teased as she lifted her hips to be stripped of her last bits of coverage. She'd expected to feel anxious about it. It was the first time she'd been properly naked in front of another person in years, since before her husband died. Instead, she felt brave and feminine and sexy. *Safe*. She felt free.

"You are stunning."

Dosie shivered at the gravel in the Director's voice. Their breasts rubbed together, sparking new sensation between her thighs. "You would know all about stunning," she said and pushed the Director's hair back so she could see her better. "No one should be this gorgeous. It's dangerous."

"Is it?"

"I bet people have offered to sell you their souls just for a kiss, haven't they?"

The Director's smile was bright white in the dark, so sexy it was nearly painful to endure. Her grainy laugh sang through Dosie's body like a symphony. "And you? You don't think you're dangerous?"

"I haven't been dangerous a day in my life."

"Oh, you have," the Director told her. "You *are*."

Her hands skirted up Dosie's sides, featherlight caresses that both tickled and aroused. She drew circles around the small hills of Dosie's breasts and nipples, then skated up to her throat. She descended then, took Dosie's bottom lip between her teeth, sucked then bit then kissed as if trying to soothe away a wound. "You terrify me, Dosie."

Dosie's chest tightened. Her stomach bottomed until it felt like it was melting into the base of her spine. "Oh."

Kisses peppered the line of her jaw. The Director's voice became a hot, wet whisper in the shell of her ear. "I want you."

White-hot lightning straight to Dosie's core. "You just had me."

"Again," the Director moaned. "Let me have you again." She retreated, sitting back on her knees, and urged Dosie to roll over so that she was on her stomach instead, arms curled under her head like a pillow. "Perfect."

Confident fingers pressed to the plane between her shoulder blades, then dragged down her bumpy spine to the top of her ass. A second later, they were replaced with the Director's mouth. A whisper of a kiss in the peach-fuzzed dip of her back caused every nerve in Dosie's body to flare. She jerked. A moan tore from her throat. Another kiss, another jolt. Even a breath there made her feel as flimsy as a toothpick and ready to snap.

"So responsive," the Director murmured over her hip bone. "You have no idea what that does to me."

Dosie ground her forehead down into her arms and fought the sudden urge she had to jut her ass back. "You have *every* idea of what you're doing to me."

The Director's chuckle breezed over her ribcage and back down to the dip. "I have many ideas of what I'd *like* to do to you." The words were barely a lilt in the air before the Director's teeth were sinking into Dosie's ass cheek with sharp delight.

Sound poured from Dosie's throat, and she thrust back, unable to fight it. She *needed*, and the needing made her brave. "Then put them to action before I pass out. Please."

She expected the Director to laugh or tease her, torture her more with alternating featherlight kisses and stinging nips. Instead, the woman pushed her thighs apart stroked Dosie's needy cunt from behind. No pressure. No invasion. Just a slow, torturous gathering of sticky heat.

"Do you trust me, Dosie?"

It was said aloud, not a whisper in the dark but something bold and hopeful and, yes, *dangerous*. Dosie should've been surprised by her easy answer, but she wasn't. She believed, without doubt, that the Director would take care of her. "Yes."

As soon as the word left her lips, the Director's coated fingers shifted from her throbbing sex to the slit of her ass. Dosie stiffened as one wet tip found her hole and teased it. She couldn't help the sound she made—a garbled mess half-buried in her arm.

"Relax," the Director instructed.

Dosie closed her eyes, implored her body not to resist. There was so much she didn't know about sex, so many things she'd never tried and had, for many years, imagined she never would. There were so many things she'd been taught to fear or reject that she now knew she'd never had reason to demonize. She'd been free of that life for over a decade, and still, every day was a process of un-learning and learning anew. It had taken her nearly six years to even be able to say the words "Oh my God" without flinching, without guilt for taking the Lord's name in vain. And now, it was a minor addiction. The little burst of freedom, of rebellion, she felt every time the words slipped her lips excited her, and she wanted more. More freedom. More rebellion. More sex. There was so much she wanted to explore, and if ever there was a time, if ever there was a partner, it was now, and it was *her*.

So, Dosie swallowed her doubt and relaxed. As the rigidity in her body eased, another gentle probing began. One wet fingertip pushed without entering then retreated again.

"No one's ever had you here." It wasn't a question. "Would you like to try?"

Dosie flushed with white-hot embarrassment and desire, a strange, heady combination that made her head spin. "Will it hurt?"

"No. Not with me."

"Are you sure?"

"I am. There will be pressure, but you shouldn't feel any pain. If you do, we'll stop. We will stop any time you want to, whether you need to or not. Okay?"

"Okay." Dosie breathed into the crook of her elbow, tried to slow her heart. "Okay, we can try."

"Will you look at me, please?"

Dosie heard the waver in her voice for what it was: *worry*. She tilted her hips so she could look over her shoulder. The Director was a tall shadow poised behind her, eyes like black water as they caught hints of moonlight. Her breasts sat high on her chest, nipples attentive, and the dark thatch on her pelvis disappeared behind the curve of Dosie's own ass. It was an image torn from a fantasy, and it sapped the humiliation from Dosie's body in an instant, leaving her with only desire.

"You're shaking, and I can't tell if it's because you're excited or scared," the Director said, slowly massaging Dosie's thigh. Her other lay statically on the curve of her ass. "Are you sure you want to try this? I will be happy either way, Dosie, so don't say yes if you mean maybe."

It was an odd position to swoon in, ass in the air with a woman's thumb in her crack, but Dosie couldn't help it. She knew it was fucked up, the way it affected her to have a sexual partner caring enough to make sure that she was present and willing and *eager*. It should be a given for any person, an *expectation* for all people. But it wasn't. Dosie had known that all her life. So, with affection and gratitude soaking her system like a warm summer rain, she sat up on her knees and molded her back to the Director's chest. She turned her face to nuzzle the woman's cheek, buried a hand in her dark hair, and pulled her in for a slow, soft kiss. "Yes, I want to try it," she said and kissed her again. "With you."

With one last kiss, she dropped onto fours and clenched her fingers around the bunched-up folds of her mussed fitted sheet. She'd barely managed to find her balance when she felt the Director's teeth latch onto one of her ass cheeks, and Dosie jerked so hard that she nearly collapsed into the mattress. She moaned and lowered her forehead to the bed, bowing her back into a sharp bend that pushed her ass higher.

"What a view," she heard the Director murmur and couldn't help grinning into the sheet. "I'm going to go inside now." Her voice was pure sex. The simplest words, something clinical even, sounded like pornography when wrapped in her dulcet tones. "Don't hold your breath."

Dosie hadn't realized she *was* holding her breath and laughed. It huffed out of her as the Director's fingertip returned to her perineum to catch the dewy remnants of Dosie's earlier orgasm. She dragged a wet trail back to her ass to ring and coat her tight hole. Once. Twice. Then she was inside.

Another, harsher, breath fired from Dosie's lips as the Director slowly penetrated her ass to the first knuckle then stopped. It eased back out, then in again. Out, then in again. There was so much pressure. Dosie felt invaded and full and nervous, but just as she'd been promised, there was no pain.

"Are you ready for more?"

"Mhm."

"Yes?"

"More, yes."

The Director's finger sank deeper, up to the second knuckle, and Dosie whimpered at an unexpected spark of pleasure. *Oh, I could like this.* When her entire finger was inside Dosie, her other hand settled over one of her cheeks and squeezed, gripping Dosie's ass like she owned it. "I want you to rock your hips forward, Dosie, just a bit, and then ease back for me."

Dosie traded biting her lip for her bedsheet as she leaned away from the Director and felt the woman's finger slide out of her until only the tip remained. She couldn't hold her moan when she shifted back again and took it all in one slow stroke. She *definitely* liked this.

"Beautiful," the Director whispered. "Again."

A delirious sort of thrill buzzed in Dosie's brain. This woman was having her fuck herself in the ass on her finger. And Dosie was doing it, *eagerly*. She couldn't *not*. Everything from the waist down now housed her pulse. She throbbed in places she didn't know she could throb.

"Now, touch yourself."

Dosie was not prepared for the explosive effect the words had on her. She jerked, hard, and slammed her hips back, spearing herself on the woman's finger. A feral whine left her, the sound of a starving animal, as she smashed her face harder into the mattress and raced a hand down her stomach. When she found her straining nub, her hips jumped again, and there was no helping it. She rubbed with abandon, sloppily working her clitoris like she was trying to churn butter until the Director's breathy command stopped her.

"Easy now," she said. "Find your control. When you control your body, you control your pleasure."

Dosie forced herself to slow and focus, letting herself be guided so that each stroke felt deliberate, hitting right where she needed it. But just when she found her stride, the hot grip of the Director's free hand on her ass disappeared. A second later, those missing fingers were poised at her vagina. *Oh, God.*

"I'm going to take you here as well," she said and slipped two tips in. "Do you want that, Dosie?"

"Yes."

"Yes? You want to come with me filling you in both places?"

"Yes. *Yes.*" Dosie felt like she was losing her mind. She panted, felt tears burning in her eyes and had no idea why. "Just do it already!"

The Director drove into her like a hammer to a nail—hard, fast, *precise*—and Dosie shouted. The angle made it deeper than she was expecting and took the breath right out of her. She barely got it back before she was given another rough stroke, then another. The pace escalated, the Director pummeling her vagina while the finger she'd buried in Dosie's ass turned slow, deliberate circles. The combination was potent, too potent—euphoric to the point of hysteria—and Dosie quickly became lost to it. Flotsam caught in an immense tide.

Her voice sat like a rock in her throat, right on top of her pulse, as she mindlessly thrust her hips back. Everything bubbled, boiled. She was so full, so *full*, she couldn't think.

"Control," she heard the Director say again, but that wasn't a possibility anymore. Not for Dosie.

"I can't," she sobbed. "I can't. Please."

Nothing existed anymore, least of all control. Her body was not her own. It was driving itself, writhing on the woman's fingers and hurtling toward an end she feared might actually *end* her. Her stomach coiled like a snake prepared to strike. "I'm going to—"

Shock white.

Brightness burst behind her eyelids as pleasure exploded through her body. The cry that left her was little more than a mangled thump to her own ears as the room, the woman behind her, the entire world dwindled to the drumbeat between her legs. Her lungs seized at the height of it, muscles so tense she was sure she'd pass out, but then the tension drained like someone had yanked a plug, and she collapsed, limp but conscious.

"Breathe, Dosie," the Director said as she eased her fingers out, dragging another whimper from Dosie's throat, then lay a kiss between her shoulder blades. "Just breathe, love. I'll be right back."

Dosie said nothing. She was a frayed wire, twitching and sparking, just synapses and nerves randomly firing as she lay in a heap. Oxygen slowly staggered its way back into her lungs, painful at first, then soothing, and new tears welled in her eyes. The world spilled back in in thumps and twitches, and Dosie heard the water running in her bathroom. A second later, the faucet switched off, and then her steps were padding back across the room.

The bed dipped. A hand settled into the low of her back. "Talk to me. Are you okay?"

A tide of emotion swept through Dosie, dragged her down and under. She wasn't sad, wasn't scared, wasn't anything but spent, and yet, she was a breath away from sobbing into her mattress. She couldn't move, her body a puddle in her bed, muscles dead. She could only lie there and *feel* and cry her fucking heart out. "I'm sorry," she choked out. "I don't know why this is happening."

"Shh. No," the Director murmured as she stretched alongside her. "Don't apologize." Her hand, cool to the touch and now scented like Dosie's cherry-almond soap, brushed Dosie's hair back from her face and lay against her cheek. "It's normal. Your body is just overwhelmed, and your adrenaline is crashing. A lot of people cry when they experience this. Okay? It's nothing to be ashamed of."

Shame. The moment she heard it, thought it, Dosie felt it. She'd just experienced the height of pleasure doing things she'd been taught were dirty and sinful, and she'd done those things with another woman. Her stomach dropped. *No. Stop. What was and what is are not the same. Stay here. Be here. Be here with her.*

"Let me get you some water. I can go down to the kitchen."

"No," Dosie said before she could stop herself. Truly, water sounded divine. Her throat was a desert. But she couldn't bear the thought of being alone, not even for a moment. "Stay, please." She couldn't see the Director's face, her own eyes still tightly closed, but she heard the woman's sigh and felt her weight settle beside her again. "I need...."

"What do you need?"

"Hold me?"

The Director said nothing, only wriggled her arms around and let Dosie snuggle into her chest. Dosie's tear-stained cheek smeared over her breast, but she didn't seem to care. Her fingers funneled in Dosie's hair, scratched at her scalp in long, soothing strokes until Dosie's body began to lull.

"We didn't do anything wrong," she whispered, and while she hadn't meant to say the words out loud, she was glad she did. She needed to hear them.

"No, Dosie," the Director said and held her tighter. "We didn't do anything wrong."

A soft kiss landed on her forehead, and Dosie felt all her anxiety, all her worry, all her spiraling, damaging, painful thoughts seep out and away until she was utterly empty.

And emptiness had never felt so *good*.

The steady chirping of crickets was a lullaby Jennifer felt down to her bones. *Home.* She'd not been back in years. But on occasion, when she lay in her bed at night, the itch of nostalgia would creep into her brain, and she'd find herself slipping away into used-to-be's and never-again's. Walking the gravel driveway to the old manor, surrounded by trees. Sitting on the porch in her favorite swing, listening to the groan of aged wood in the wind and the crickets calling from the shrubbery, toads croaking somewhere nearby. She would think of her parents, harder now to remember than ever before, but mostly, she would think of Lauren.

The thought wasn't always a welcome one. Jennifer's memories of her came in little flashes—fleeting smiles and too-loud laughter, late-night Scrabble and clever advice, the unbearable weight of absence. She'd welcome them only to reject them again, bury her face in her pillow and try to forget. Drown herself in booze or books or masturbation, anything to distract her, get her out of her head.

But in this moment, she had only the quiet and the crickets, a placidity that both soothed and unsettled her. Even here, even now—or perhaps, especially here, especially now—as she lay in a bed that wasn't her own with a woman who wasn't hers either, she couldn't shake her memories. Her racing thoughts. Her fears, so adeptly buried, managed to break through again like seedlings seeking sunlight. Her chest grew tight, breath thinning, and Jennifer knew she needed to leave. She couldn't feel like this, not here. Not with anyone. She needed to be alone. Soon. *Now.*

Dosie's weight on her chest was warm and heavy after an hour of stillness, and despite how urgently Jennifer needed to leave, she was loath to move. She stroked Dosie's hair back from her face one last time. Her features were lax with sleep, serene, and Jennifer wished she had her phone. She wanted to remember this, this moment, this face, this girl. A mental image would have to do. It would have to last.

She shimmied out from under Dosie, careful not to jar her too much. She hadn't wanted to do it like this, sneaking off without a word, but maybe it was for the best. No awkward, painful goodbyes. Just a quiet shadow slinking away, leaving Dosie to the echoes of her pleasure, memories and experience she could take with her as she moved on with her life and continued growing, continued learning. Found someone to love and to love her in return. Properly. Deeply.

A hand shot from the dark, latched around her wrist. "Please don't do this," came the raspy whisper in the dark.

Jennifer startled, then froze. "I thought you were asleep."

The grip around her wrist tightened, thumb pressing into Jennifer's pulse. "Please."

With a heavy sigh, Jennifer eased back onto the bed, not as before but still close. She turned her wrist, slid her hand up to lace their fingers. "It's time for me to go, Dosie."

"Don't take this from me." It was so quiet, so earnest, a plea to crack Jennifer's resolve. "Not yet. I want more. I need more of this. More of *you*. Please."

Fuck. Jennifer's heartrate spiked. Her stomach felt like it was somehow both in her knees and in her throat. *I need to leave.* "It's not a good idea."

"I know," Dosie whispered. "I know it's not."

Jennifer groaned. "Then why are you torturing us both by dragging this out?"

"I'm sorry."

"Don't be sorry." She released Dosie's hand to cup her cheek instead. "Just accept that this is how it has to be. Okay?" She swiped her thumb over Dosie's bottom lip and thought about kissing it. She didn't. "You've come a long way in our time together. You should be proud of that. You've done so well. But I've given you what I can, and now, it's time to move on."

"But—"

"Dosie, this isn't a relationship," Jennifer blurted and sat up. It was a simple fact, yet she hated herself for saying it. "This is my *work*, and I've been happy to work with you, truly, but now that work is finished."

"What if I paid you?" Dosie asked as she sat up beside her, a hand on Jennifer's arm. "For what happened in the dressing room?

"What do you mean?"

"That's what's bothering you, right? That we were together when you were, um, off the clock? Not in a professional way, is what I'm trying to say."

"Yes, I follow, and yes, that's part of it." Jennifer frowned, confused. She'd expected backlash, upset. Tears, even. Not a proposition. "But—"

"So, if I paid you for it, then it's like it was a session, right? Like this one or any other. Would that fix it?"

"Dosie."

"Come on. You can't tell me you don't have repeat clients you've seen for months. I can't be the only one."

Jennifer stuttered over her own breath. This was not how this was supposed to go. Dosie wasn't supposed to push back, not like this. Knocking at Jennifer's walls with perfect sense. "No, you're not. I have clients I've seen for years."

"Then what? Is it me?" She took a breath as if bracing

herself. "Is it because of my past? It, it freaks you out? It makes me less attractive to you?"

"*No,*" Jennifer all but snapped at her. "Dosie, God. Did it *feel* like you were, in any way, unattractive to me when you were inside me earlier?"

"Well, no," Dosie squeaked, and Jennifer didn't need light to know the girl's face was bright red. "But maybe you're just really good at your job!"

Jennifer huffed. "I certainly thought so, but if I *was*, then I wouldn't still be here."

"Why are you?"

The sigh that left her bordered on a growl as Jennifer determined to simply tell the truth. She may as well, since it was clear Dosie intended to drag it out of her, one way or another. "The problem isn't your past. It isn't attraction. You *know* I'm attracted to you. The problem is that you're annoyingly easy to become fond of."

"It's a problem to be fond of me?"

"Yes."

"Geez."

"Stop." She knocked Dosie's shoulder. "You know what I mean." She looked away, somewhere neutral that would allow her to get the words out. "It's not a problem to care about you. You deserve to have people care about you. But it *is* a conflict for my work. I don't do attachment, ever. It's a hard boundary for me, and normally, it isn't difficult to abide."

"But it is when you're with me?"

Jennifer could feel Dosie's gaze boring into the side of her face, but she kept her eyes averted. "I know why you chose me, what drew you to my profile, and your instincts weren't wrong. You *are* attracted to authority. You respond to it eagerly, and down the line, you'd likely be an excellent professional match for me. But you're just not there yet. Right now, you still require a lot of affectionate intimacy to feel safe, and that isn't a bad thing, but it isn't what I do. It isn't for me. Do you understand?"

"So, stop." Dosie's hand found hers. Their fingers slid together with an ease that made Jennifer's skin itch. Sometimes, when Dosie touched her, it felt almost domestic, like they'd done it a thousand times before and would a thousand more. Like they'd known each other for years instead of months. "Treat me like any other client." The words hit Jennifer's gut like an angry fist. "Be the Director if that's who you need to be. I will respect it. I promise."

Jennifer shook her head. "You can't promise that."

"Yes, I can, because I *do* feel safe with you now. I *do*. God, *look* at me." She grabbed Jennifer by the chin, forced her to meet her eyes in the dark. "Listen to what I'm saying: I trust you. I don't even know your name, but I trust you. Completely." Her grip softened then fell away, dropped back into Jennifer's lap to find her hand again. "I trust you with my body. I trust you not to abuse it, because I *know* you won't. I know that with everything I have in me. Do you understand the magnitude of that? I'm not...." She exhaled slowly, steadied her voice. "I don't want to pressure you. I hope it doesn't feel like that's what I'm trying to do. I just need you to understand what this means to me."

Jennifer's chest felt weak, like her ribcage might crack or cave in at the slightest jump of her heart. She resigned herself to the devastation. "I do understand," she admitted, "but say it anyway."

"Will it change your mind?"

"I don't know," Jennifer said and squeezed Dosie's fingers. "But it might."

Dosie's eyes widened in the dark. "Is that what you want? For me to change your mind?"

Jennifer shivered, said nothing, which Dosie clearly interpreted as confirmation.

"My first sexual experience was a violation. I was eight years old." Jennifer inhaled sharply and closed her eyes, fought the instinct to say she was sorry, because she knew Dosie wouldn't like it. The grip on her hand turned painful. "Nearly every sexual experience I've had in my life has been that way. Even when I was married, sex wasn't my choice. I did what I thought I was supposed to do. You are the first person I feel like I've *chosen* to have sex with, and it's been one of the most liberating experiences of my life. Even when I'm scared, even when my thoughts go dark and my anxiety takes over, I still feel free, because I *know* I'm safe with you. I will do whatever you ask me to do when it comes to your boundaries. I will respect them, I promise. I'm just very much not ready to give this up. Please."

The sting of tears was back, burning in Jennifer's eyes

with a vengeance. She blinked them away again, shook her head. "Why must you be so competent with communicating your feelings?" She let herself collapse against Dosie, foreheads together. "Why can't you go the typical route and just kick me out of your house? It would make all this much easier, you know."

Dosie chuckled. "Years of therapy." She brushed a bit of hair from Jennifer's face, let her fingers skate down her shoulder and back up, gently stroking. "You should try it. Everyone should."

"My therapy is mostly expensive whisky and whipping men on their behinds until they cry."

Dosie's laugh was like sunshine spilling into the room. "What is that saying? To each their own?"

"No, really. It's an excellent stress reliever," Jennifer said, latching onto the light, desperate for it. "You get to smack people, and they thank you for it."

"You're trying to change the subject."

"Yes, I am."

"Okay, can I just say one more thing?"

"For fuck's sake," Jennifer whispered, and Dosie snorted, cupped a hand over her mouth to trap a laugh. Jennifer kind of hated her for how cute she found it.

"I'm sorry."

"Fine."

"I just want you to tell me you'll think about it," she said. "Really. That you'll think about everything I said before you decide, for sure, that you don't want to book with me anymore." Her hand found Jennifer's again. "I really want to have a healthy sex life, and you can help me learn how. You steady me. You make me feel grounded and brave, and I'll try things with you. I'll try things I know I'd never try with anyone else. I want that."

Jennifer's heart slithered up her throat and onto her tongue, stuck there. "How can you feel grounded..." She drew Dosie closer, breathed her in. She smelled like sweat and sex, and it made Jennifer dizzy. "...when I feel so completely untethered?"

Dosie's quiet gasp gave way to a rush of breath she pressed into Jennifer's lips. She kissed like a sinner coming to confession, so giving and honest that it felt like something sacred. Jennifer let herself sink into it, told herself it would be the last. It would be the last, and so, it was okay to prolong it a little. She should enjoy it, so that when the memory surfaced from time to time, she wouldn't feel the urge to push it away. She would smile, maybe even indulge.

When it was over, a calm settled over them. It was thick, like a scent in the air, but not unpleasant. Dosie followed Jennifer's lead, the two redressing in silence, Jennifer in the clothes she'd come in, and Dosie in a clean, baggy T-shirt and a pair of sweats, sans underwear. She looked comfortable, relaxed, *so* goddamn beautiful. Jennifer couldn't let herself linger. She might not leave at all if she did.

Dosie walked Jennifer down the hall, down the stairs, and into the foyer where she opened the door. The warm night air floated in, smelling of trees and dewy grass, and the cricket sounds came rushing back, a louder symphony than before. The silence broke with their song, and Dosie sighed beside her. "Thank you," she said, "for tonight."

"Of course."

It wasn't late, Jennifer knew. By the time Dosie had fallen, sated, against her mattress, the actual appointment time they'd originally set had only just begun. But it felt like the middle of the night. It felt like a new night altogether, like days had passed since she'd followed Dosie up those creaking, old stairs; quiet confessions having frozen them in time.

"I trust you."

She stepped out into the night as Dosie leaned against the door, watching her go. She didn't know what to say. *Goodbye* felt wrong. *Goodnight* did too.

"Ms. Fisher," she said and tilted her head reverently. "It's been a pleasure."

Dosie's smile was easy but toothless, joyless. "Goodnight, Director."

And Jennifer couldn't explain it, but as she walked away, down the steps of the porch to the sound of Dosie's door closing behind her, something inside her shifted. Something cracked. Something *broke*.

"Goodnight, Director."

The words rang in her ears, discordant.

"I don't even know your name, but I trust you. Completely."

She was nearly to the car when her feet turned back, unbidden, and her heart ratcheted up to an unhealthy speed, a painful one. Her tongue felt swollen in her mouth as she retraced her steps to the porch, to the door, and when her fist knocked against wood, her stomach roared in protest. In terror. In *need.*

What am I doing? What the fuck am I doing?

Her thoughts spiraled, brain on fire, as the door pulled open again, and there stood Dosie, brow wrinkled in confusion.

"I trust you. Completely."

"Did you forget something?" she asked, and just like she'd done the night they met, Jennifer let herself into Dosie's home without invitation. She stepped right over the threshold, right into Dosie's space, driven only by the awful, maddening *care* coursing her veins. Her hands found Dosie's waist and pressed her back, back against the door as it swung wide and thudded into the wall.

"Oh," Dosie gasped, the sound like a pinball pinging about Jennifer's body with unrelenting speed. Striking everything. Her hands shot up, one latching onto Jennifer's shoulder, the other sliding under the messy fall of Jennifer's hair to her neck. "You're trembling."

Jennifer lay her forehead against Dosie's and breathed roughly against her lips—ragged breaths that offered no relief. Her palms were sweating. "Dosie."

It was little more than breath, than hope, than a plea for this to stop. For it to continue.

"You're safe with me, too," Dosie said and nuzzled her cheek. "Whatever it is, you're safe with me."

"My name," she croaked and tightened her grip, gave herself over, "is Jennifer."

Dosie shuddered against her. "Oh," she said again, breathless. "Jennifer." Her nails dug in as she anchored Jennifer to her, kissed her with wide, smiling lips. Perfect, *awful* joy in the dark.

9

"Did God ever speak to us? Yes, He did. He spoke to Adam, the first man. He spoke to Noah, who built the Ark. He spoke to Moses, who parted the sea. So, why, why, *does God not speak to us now? Why does God stay silent now when His children have become so lost?*

The Good Book tells us that God sent his only Son to become His presence here on earth, to become and embody his Word. Jesus was the Word, and when Jesus died on the cross, the Lord made plain that from that point on, He would only communicate by a pouring of Spirit and only with those of His choosing. Congregation, I'm here today to tell you, I am Chosen. I am awash in Spirit, my friends, and I tell you, it's unlike anything you could ever imagine.

God has chosen me to bring in his flock, to guide them from the wickedness of this dying world and onto the only path to salvation. Brothers and sisters, if you will follow me, if you will hear God through *me, then I promise you this: I will enrich your lives with His holy light, and there will be no more pain. There will be no more suffering. There will be no more loss or ugliness or greed. Through me, God will provide—for you, your children—and your joys will be multiplied. Your sorrows washed away. I will be God's Word here on earth, and I will be God's Hand. And my friends, my flock, as the Hand of God, I say to you now, I will make for you a home, a true home, and so long as you reside within that home, you shall never be alone again."*

This was the start of it, of everything. I listen to that voice as it plays on my mother's old recorder, and it sounds so different—younger, kinder. But I hear the man I knew as well. I hear him in rich persuasive notes and promises too utopian to be real, and now, thanks to the beautiful, *terrible*, gift of hindsight, I can hear the threat there, too.

I can hear the start of something sinister.

Samuel Alan Fisher recorded this sermon in the summer of 1985. It is the first known record in which he designates himself as a prophet of God. Ten years later, nearly to the day, the so-called Prophet would pull me from my mother's laboring body in a horse trough on a half-dead ranch outside of Sacramento, California. And for the next fifteen years of my life, his voice would become the melody I am most familiar with. And the man himself? He would become the nightmare I never dreamed I could escape.

My name is Theodosia Fisher, and I am the third

daughter of the man in the recording, the man known as the Prophet. I am a child of the Hand of God Disciples, and I am a survivor of nearly two decades of physical, emotional, psychological, and sexual abuse at the hands of both.

My father was not a prophet. My cult was not a community. We were not the chosen ones.

We were the awful secret that shocked the world.

Jennifer snapped Dosie's memoir shut and tossed it to the side. It hit the couch cushion with a thump only a moment before Jennifer's face did. She'd only read the preface, yet anxiety already prickled at the back of her neck. It slithered in her gut like something alive. And, of course, she knew why. The content would disturb her, break her heart even, but Jennifer had read horrors before. She'd *lived* horrors, seen them with her own eyes. It was the person telling the story.

Dosie Fisher was the why of her disquiet. What Jennifer *didn't* know was the why of the why. *Why* did Dosie affect her so much? Why was it so easy for her to get under Jennifer's skin?

Just as she'd told Dosie, she did not do attachment. She didn't make connections, not of that nature and certainly not with a client. In truth, Jennifer shied from most types of connection. She'd not bothered with personal relationships in some time, nothing beyond the occasional catch-up, the little windows into her mind that she sometimes gave Carolina. But now, her body and mind screamed at her to not only connect with Dosie but to latch onto that connection like a lifeline.

She growled into her couch cushion. What a fucking mess she'd gotten herself into, and all because of her ridiculous pride. Because she'd had her chance, hadn't she? That first night, that first encounter—Dosie had panicked, tried to cancel. It was Jennifer who'd insisted; Jennifer, whose ego had been wounded by rejection, whose body had been insistent, whose words had dared; Jennifer, who'd pushed her way through Dosie's door and ignited something that now refused to be snuffed. It was Jennifer who'd seen Dosie as a challenge, her shy, eager body as a map toward still-buried treasure. She'd wanted to crack that girl's exterior and her entire world, unearth every desire, and leave her with ruins. Devastation she would spend the rest of her life trying and failing to replicate.

Yet, somehow, it was Jennifer who found herself dangerously close to disrepair. She'd cracked *herself* in her eager endeavor, it seemed, and pieces had been quietly crumbling ever since. It scared Jennifer. It infuriated her. And the only way she knew how to respond was to withdraw. Clean. Swift. It was already done.

But *fuck*, Dosie's face. Her earnest voice begging Jennifer not to abandon her yet. Promising Jennifer whatever she needed in exchange for only more of her. Taking Jennifer's face in her hands in the dark quiet of her foyer and kissing her, not as an escort, not as the Director, but as only herself—the person she was when the labels fell away.

Jennifer felt sick to her stomach. Was she punishing Dosie for something that was her own fault? She'd asked for only one thing—Jennifer's expertise. She craved it. She needed it. She deserved it. Jennifer believed that.

Dosie deserved every pleasure, every chance to find herself properly, and she deserved to do that with someone she trusted and desired. Jennifer was that person. There were things she could teach Dosie that could change her relationship with her body and with pleasure, things that could literally change her life for the better. Jennifer had seen it before. She'd *lived it* before. Was she really going to let one odd little crush get in the way of that?

For all she knew, especially given her history, her affection for Dosie was fleeting. Like any other wisp of emotion Jennifer felt, any little passion that became temporary obsession, it would pass. She would help Dosie and, in the process, have her fill of her, and then the itch would dissipate. The need would wane. The affection would fizzle, and everything would go back to how it was, how it was supposed to be.

Everything would be all right.

Wouldn't it?

Jennifer rolled onto her back and sighed, grabbed Dosie's book again and flipped past the preface to the first chapter. *Maybe I shouldn't.* What if reading it made things worse? Made her care about Dosie even more? Or maybe it would make her trauma clearer, allowing Jennifer to focus because the importance of the work would be foremost in her mind.

It was the same loop she'd been circling for days—read it or don't—toiling then reconciling then toiling again. Jennifer ran her palm down the smooth, cool page, heard her own voice waffling in her mind. *Read it or don't. Read or don't.*

Finally, she made a choice.

"It's one in the afternoon," Dosie said as she slumped against her kitchen island. "I should not be this drunk."

Kaylia scoffed. "Please. You spoke before the entire California State Legislature this morning. You deserve to be this drunk."

"I agree," Natalie said as she picked at the remains of a massive charcuterie platter. She popped a grape in her mouth, then a hunk of gouda, spoke with her mouth full despite Kaylia's twitching eye. "You hate public speaking, but you do this stuff anyway, because you don't want kids in fucked-up situations like yours to fall through the cracks again. Like, who deserves to be drunk at one in the afternoon if not you?"

"I appreciate your support," Dosie said, the slightest slur in her voice. "Both of you. Really, I do. And all the nice things you're saying. So nice. But I feel like a floaty ball of static." Natalie opened her mouth to say something, but Dosie quickly waved her quiet. "No, it *isn't* a fun feeling, even if it sounds like it might be." She whined at Kaylia. "Why do you always make the mimosas so strong?"

"Because I love myself."

Natalie pointed at Kaylia's abdomen. "Not your liver, though."

"She's okay," Kaylia said and shrugged. "I'll chug some water later."

"Your liver is a girl?"

"All my parts are female."

"This is a weird conversation," Dosie said and wriggled where she sat, uncomfortable. She was still clad in her pistachio swing dress and pearls. She'd long-since pulled the pins from her hair and abandoned her too-high heels, but she'd do just about anything for some sweatpants and a T-shirt the size of a tent, some fuzzy socks for her freezing feet. Anything *except* walk up the stairs. "But since we're talking about it, I think my ears are boys, because they really like girl voices."

Natalie snorted. "No, your ears are just gay, Dosie. Like the rest of you."

Dosie smiled drunkenly. "Yeah."

The muffled ring of her phone had her smacking her chest and waist. Her dress had no pockets, but her inebriated brain did not care. She huffed. "Where is it?" *Oh, wait!* She yanked it out from under her thigh and blinked at the screen. Her stomach sank. "Unknown number."

"Maybe it's a political call," Natalie tried. "Or, like, your usual run-of-the-mill scam dial. Don't think the worst."

"I've had this number for a year now. I really thought they'd given up."

As the phone began its fourth ring, Kaylia snatched it from Dosie's hand. "Let's just have a chat, shall we?" She smoothed her silk button-down for no reason and cleared her throat. In the two seconds it took for her to accept the call, her expression transformed from her toothy, too-many-mimosas-at-brunch smile to her there's-a-reason-I-get-paid-the-big-bucks one. "Dosie Fisher's phone. Kaylia Davis, attorney at law, speaking."

Across the table, Natalie snickered. She grabbed another grape and chucked it at Kaylia's head. It smacked her shoulder and bounced away, but the girl didn't flinch. She raised her left hand to flip Natalie off, then carried on speaking. Her diction was crisp, her tone sharp. The switch had been flipped, and she was *on*.

"Yes, I would be happy to pass the phone to Ms. Fisher once I know who I'm speaking with and what your intended business with my client entails. And before you answer, know that my client does not engage with press, on or off the record, without prior vetting, and no, there are no exceptions. She won't be answering any questions concerning her past or any ongoing legal matters in relation to said past. Is that clear?"

Dosie laid her cheek on the countertop. The surface was cold and soothing. "I hope I don't have to change my number again."

"Nah, you won't," Natalie said. "Kaylia will scare them off."

"Until they Google her name and see she's just my IP attorney."

"What private business are you referring to?" Kaylia's brow wrinkled. A half-second later, it shot up. "You can't say?

Wow. How original of you. Well, if that's the case, I'm afraid I can't put you through to Ms. Fisher."

Natalie prodded Dosie's shoulder. "Who do you think it is? Ridiculous answers only."

Dosie willed the room to stop spinning, but it refused. So, she closed her eyes instead. "Um, the lottery people? Telling me I've won a billion dollars?"

"Nah. You've got enough money. If anyone needs to win the lottery, it's me."

"Well, how do you know I wouldn't just give you all the money if I won?"

"That does sound like the kind of annoyingly charitable thing you would do."

"You're welcome."

"Do you actually play the lottery?"

"No," Dosie laughed. "But you said ridiculous answers only. It would be ridiculous to win the lottery when you don't even play it."

"I'm thinking Vogue."

"Vogue?"

"I don't care if you're calling on behalf of someone else," Kaylia said. "I still require a name and a purpose. Cough it up or give it up. I haven't got all day."

"Yeah," Natalie said. "They're doing a spread on cult couture, and they want you as the centerpiece."

Dosie giggled. "Cult couture."

"Someone put some lace on a baptismal robe, and now it's fashion."

The giggle bloomed into a full-blown belly laugh, until Dosie could do nothing but wheeze and clutch the countertop, which her friend seemed to interpret as encouragement.

"I don't know why you're laughing," she said. "It's serious, Dosie. Is fashion not important to you?"

Kaylia smacked her hand over the microphone end of Dosie's cell phone. "Will you two shut up already? You're killing my vibe." When they ducked liked properly shamed children, she went back to the call. "Mhm. Okay. Can you repeat the name, please? Just so I'm clear on it. Thank you." She capped the mic again, looked at Dosie. "Dupont? Do you know that name?"

Dosie shot off the countertop so fast, she nearly toppled over. "Give it here!"

Bewildered, Kaylia handed the phone over, and Dosie fumbled it like a ball she couldn't get a grip on before managing to land it at her ear. "Yes? Hi? Hello? This is Dosie Fisher?"

Natalie chuckled. "Is she asking them or telling them?"

"Who is this Dupont person?" Kaylia picked up a baby carrot and crunched it. "Do you know?"

"Sounds kind of familiar," Natalie said and crunched a carrot of her own. Obnoxiously. "But not really ringing any bells."

Dosie couldn't drown them out, so she raced from the kitchen into the foyer. Her body was on fire, but she no longer felt drunk. Only hopeful. So, *so* hopeful. "Hello?"

"Oh! Hello!" a woman's voice replied, and Dosie's shoulders caved. It wasn't the Director. *Jennifer*. "My apologies. I was briefly distracted. Is this Ms. Fisher?"

"Yes, and you're not Jennifer Dupont." She shivered as she said the name, a jolt of thrill working through her as she remembered those three quiet syllables, murmured in the dark. "Who are you?"

"Right, no, I'm not Ms. Dupont," the woman said with a kind laugh. "I'm her personal assistant."

"Oh." Dosie's shriveling hope bloomed again. "Oh! I'm so sorry. What's your name?"

"Not a problem. My name is Candace. It's a pleasure to meet you over the phone, Ms. Fisher. My apologies for any issues with your attorney before, but we pride ourselves on discretion here at Allure, and I didn't want to reveal anything you may have wished to keep private."

"Right. No. Thank you. I appreciate that. What, um, what can I do for you?"

A thought popped into Dosie's mind, and her hope seized. Dread crept in like vines and bound it. *What if this isn't a good call?* What if Jennifer had asked her assistant to call Dosie to let her know her account had been canceled? She'd known it was a possibility, that Jennifer wouldn't come back. That she might never see her again, never touch or kiss her or *be* with her again. But she hadn't let herself believe it, not really. She'd held onto the idea that the Director would reconsider, that she would—

"Ms. Dupont has requested that I contact you directly to

ask if you would like to book an appointment for the coming week."

Dosie blinked. *Wait, what?*

"Ms. Fisher?"

"Oh, yes!" Dosie blurted. "Yes, of course." Did she sound too eager? "I mean, um, that would be great, yes. Thank you."

Candace chuckled. "Wonderful. Let's get that scheduled then. Would Wednesday evening work for you? Or Ms. Dupont can do Friday if that works better?"

Dosie, thankfully, managed not to squeal. Barely. The Director was coming back. They didn't have to stop, and Dosie could continue to learn. She could continue to *feel* and explore, and the Director would help her. *Jennifer.* Jennifer, who she trusted despite knowing so little about. Jennifer, who made her feel things she'd never even known were possible.

Jennifer was coming back.

When Dosie finished the call, she bounced like a ball into the kitchen only to find it empty. But the back door was open, so she followed it through to the backyard, where Kaylia and Natalie lay in the hammock, staring up at the treetops and the cerulean sky.

"Any room for me?"

When they were all squished into the hammock, Natalie's arm around Dosie's shoulder and Dosie's leg looped over Kaylia's, Natalie said, "So, care to tell us who this Dupont person is? Or should we keep guessing? Because Kaylia thinks it's some kind of media thing—"

"Or medical," Kaylia said. "Who else plays the 'can't disclose private information' card that hard?"

"Um, lawyers," Natalie said, and Kaylia guffawed.

"Point."

"It's her," Dosie told them. "The Director."

"*Oh*, see I knew that name sounded familiar. We heard it in the dressing room, didn't we?"

"Who cares?" Kaylia said. "Why was someone calling you on behalf of your escort?"

Dosie sighed, blissful and drunk, and Natalie balked.

"Dude, have you been holding out on us?" she asked, jabbing Dosie's side.

"Maybe a little," Dosie confessed. "Or a lot." She covered her face to hide her idiot grin, and that was all it took. Two jabs this time, one from each side.

"Spill!"

It was a bad choice.

Jennifer had known it the moment she started reading, but then she'd read six chapters in as many days and couldn't convince herself not to carry on to the seventh. Even the early chapters haunted her, mild as she knew they'd be once she got through the rest. Dosie's highly sensitive nature made her recollections rich with sensory detail. Her descriptions, despite never rising to a level Jennifer would deem graphic, created sharp, layered imagery that still managed to wound and invade and linger.

The book followed her into her appointments, caging her mind like a prisoner so that Jennifer could hardly focus, barely enjoyed herself. Even beating the unholy hell out of Mr. Maddox with her favorite braided flogger had done little to break her brooding. She could only hope her performance hadn't suffered. She was sure it hadn't, but the thought that her clients might have been able to tell, in some small way, that she'd been "off" during session nagged her. It needled. Jennifer Dupont had only ever been one thing in session: exceptional. Anything less was unacceptable.

"You're thinking so hard, I'm surprised I can't hear your thoughts." Carolina's teasing voice over the intercom startled her. The partition lowered, and the setting sun spilled through the car's windshield. Carolina's shaded eyes turned toward the rearview. "You want to talk about it?"

Jennifer dropped her head back against the seat and grumbled.

"Is that a no?"

"No," Jennifer said. "It's an 'I don't know what the hell I'm doing anymore, so what is there to talk about?'"

"You having second thoughts about keeping Fisher as a client? Because we're nearly there, but if you want me to turn around, I can."

"No, though I feel like I *should* want to turn around."

She didn't, wouldn't. Jennifer had known by the time she reached Dosie's third chapter that she'd be booking with her again. But truthfully, the book had merely tipped her over an edge she'd already been skirting. It was Dosie's quiet, determined pleas, the ones she'd made to Jennifer during their last time together that had made the decision. They'd looped Jennifer's mind like a broken record since the moment they were spoken, and all she'd been able to think since was that Dosie Fisher was owed pleasure. Life owed her pleasure—immense and exceptional pleasure—but Dosie would only take that pleasure from someone she trusted.

Jennifer was that someone.

All Dosie needed was a little more time with her. She'd asked for nothing beyond what Jennifer was willing to give, and she'd paid every penny ever billed. There was no reason to deny her, except that Jennifer didn't *want* to deny her. Anything. Ever.

That was the reason.

"Jennifer?"

"Hm?" Jennifer looked up. *Too late. Decision made. You're doing this.* "Sorry?"

"I said, 'Are you still reading her book?'"

"Oh. Yes."

"How is it?"

"Taxing. I've been spacing it out." She ignored the impulse to dig out her mirror and check her face. She was a confident woman who loved herself, but sometimes, when she looked at her reflection, all she saw was too-sharp angles and a wide jaw, tired eyes, and little, creeping age lines. Long, lanky limbs and bushy hair that refused to be tamed.

No, she wasn't about to give herself anything else to obsess over and pick at. She had enough flitting about her mind already. "Did you know her father had twenty-one children?"

"Jesus."

"With five different women."

"And only one with a memoir?"

Jennifer's stomach bottomed as a passage she'd read came back to her. *"The morning the compound was raided, I woke with seven brothers and thirteen sisters, most of whom I'd helped raise. By the end of the day, only nine of us were still breathing. Today, as I sit here writing this, only four of us remain."*

She closed her eyes, thought of Dosie. Her wide, bubbly smile and the dimple it formed in her one cheek. Her eyes that changed colors in the light, a spectrum of honey and molasses. Her embarrassed giggle. Her excited one. Similar but not the same. Her kindness. Her courage. How was it that someone so gentle and funny and *good* had come from such horror?

"Carolina," Jennifer said with a heavy breath, "am I being foolish?"

Normally, she wouldn't ask such things. She liked to keep her emotional cards, her desires, her doubts, close to her chest. But now, in the quiet of the car with only the hum of the road and Carolina's calming presence, she felt compelled to show her hand.

"For continuing with Fisher?" She took a deep breath as if

considering, let it out with a shrug. "I think you're doing what you think is best for her, which—"

"Is, in and of itself, odd," Jennifer finished for her. "I know."

"I wouldn't say odd. Just different. You're always attentive to your clients' needs, but with Fisher, you seem to want to privilege her needs over your own comfort. It's—"

"Foolish."

Carolina chuckled. "You suck at guessing what I'm going to say."

"I thought I was doing pretty well."

"Different doesn't have to be bad. Or foolish. Sometimes, different is just different."

Jennifer processed the words as she watched the sun disappear below the horizon. "I feel responsible for her," she said after a moment.

"You want to help her."

"Help her," Jennifer agreed, nodding. "Guide her. Protect her while she explores the things that she's been afraid to all her life."

"And you *like* her," Carolina said simply, and Jennifer felt as if she'd taken a knee to the gut. Her diaphragm seized, and her throat turned brittle. Her mouth went chalky, and she couldn't say a word as Carolina lowered her sunglasses just enough to catch her eyes in the rearview. "You know that's okay, right?"

It absolutely was not.

"It's okay to care about someone," Carolina said again,

plainly. "And I don't mean in the way you always care about your clients. I mean, in a *real* way. It's okay."

Was it?

No. It wasn't okay. It wasn't *safe.*

"Jennifer?"

Her heart shriveled, its beat an unsteady flutter. She didn't want to talk about this anymore. She didn't want to *think* about it anymore.

"You can walk me to the door tonight," she said instead of all the things, any of the things, kind things, grateful things, that she could have said. And with the press of a button, she closed the partition and found herself alone again.

10

Right away, Dosie could tell things were different.

Jennifer Dupont, dark hair disappearing in a slick braid down her back, was as pristine as ever in the open doorway. She wore navy linen pants and a flowy, white silk button-down complemented by white leather loafers with a gold buckle over the top. Her blouse lay unbuttoned at the top, and a single pearl at the end of a golden Y-chain hung in the gap. Dosie admonished her mind sharply when it dared to imagine that that pearl was for her.

It's not. Things are different.

Different, because yes, Jennifer was as gorgeous as ever, but her posture was stiff and her face expressionless. The energy coming off her was odd, withdrawn—far removed from the primal sort of chaos and control she'd somehow always managed to wield at once, the spirit Dosie found so addicting. It's absence set her nerves alight.

You wanted this, she admonished herself. *You were the one who said she should treat you like any other client. So, she told you her name. So what? It doesn't change anything. You're still just a client, and she's giving you what you agreed to. So, suck it up and go along.*

"Ms. Fisher," said the woman on Jennifer's arm, but Dosie was distracted by the large black duffle bag slung over her shoulder. "I have the Director for you."

"Yes, hi." Dosie tripped over her own tongue and willed herself not to turn scarlet because of it. "Um, thank you. Come on in." She watched as the mysterious black bag was passed to Jennifer, and Jennifer stepped over the threshold. The other woman waited until she was inside, then turned to leave. On instinct, Dosie called out to her. "I can get you something to drink! If you want? Or a snack?" She shifted awkwardly as both Jennifer and the other woman looked at her like she'd grown a second head. "Um, is that okay to offer? I feel bad that you have to sit in the car for hours doing nothing while we...." She choked back whatever it was she might have said, and there was no amount of control that could stop the blush from devouring her cheeks. "Anyway, um, I can bring something out for you, if you want."

The woman gave a surprised chuckle. "I appreciate that, Ms. Fisher, but I'm fine. Thank you."

"Oh, okay, sure. Are you sure?"

"She's sure," Jennifer said and closed the door. "Now, where to?"

They settled in the living room, because Dosie didn't think she could have Jennifer in her bed again, not if things were going to be like this. Different. Less intimate. Her bed felt too personal, and part of Dosie wanted to keep her memory of them together in it pristine and singular. If she couldn't have her like *that* again, she would have her elsewhere. Somewhere neutral.

"You look amazing."

"Thank you," Jennifer said as she dropped the black bag on the floor beside the sofa and sat. "You do, too."

Dosie wasn't sure she believed her. She'd wanted Jennifer to know she was comfortable with her, that she'd meant it when she said she trusted her, so she'd gone with simple jeans and a loose black T-shirt, hoping to appear more relaxed. She'd even forgone her pearl necklace, her anchor, which now felt like a stupid decision. Her fingers itched to latch onto it. She felt exposed. Still, she wasn't about to argue with a compliment.

"Thank you."

Silence enveloped them, somehow still loud. *Now what? How is this supposed to go? How am I supposed to act?* She tamped her nerves, hunted for something to focus on. Found it. "You have a bag this time."

Jennifer offered her first smile of the night, and while Dosie knew it was only courtesy, it instantly soothed. "Yes."

"Do you want to tell me what's in it?"

"Props," she said, and the smile shifted to her typical smirk, which comforted Dosie even more. *See, we can do this. It doesn't have to be* too *different.* "In case you want to try something new."

Curiosity struck, drawing Dosie to the bag like a magnet. "Can I?" she asked as she dropped to the floor beside it. When Jennifer nodded, she pulled the zipper and peeked inside. *Don't bug your eyes out*, she told herself as the first thing they landed on was a large, curved dildo, already harnessed. *Don't bug your eyes out.* More dildos of varying sizes and shapes. A variety of small vibrators. Some weird metal clamps that made Dosie's body hurt just looking at them. *Don't bug your eyes out!* A wooden paddle with holes drilled through it. A ball of twine. Some silk and satin ties. Several things she couldn't identify at all. Then a long and skinny black stick that she recognized immediately.

"This is a riding crop." She pulled it from the bag and twirled it between her fingers. They'd had a few horses on the compound when she was growing up, but her father never let the girls ride them. So, they'd watched from the fence as he taught them to obey just as he'd taught her—with sharp smacks and sharper words. "Like for horses. Right?"

"It's a riding crop, yes, but not for horses."

"You hit people with this?"

"Only when asked to."

Dosie fiddled with the flat end, smoothed over the soft leather. "Does it hurt?"

"That would depend on your tolerance," Jennifer said, "and your preference. It doesn't have to hurt, but it can."

"Why do people want you to hurt them?"

Jennifer shrugged, and Dosie nearly rolled her eyes. How did she make a shrug—*a shrug!*—look sexy? "People are strange," she said, as if it summed up the entirety of everything. Perhaps it did. "Some get their pleasure from pain. Some from inflicting it."

"Do you?" Dosie asked, not entirely sure she wanted to know the answer. "Do you get pleasure from hurting people?"

Jennifer held Dosie's gaze for one long, silent moment, and Dosie got the impression that she was searching for something in her eyes. What that was, she didn't know. "Sometimes."

A tickle of pleasure fluttered in Dosie's gut, surprising her. The idea of pain didn't seem attractive to her, but the idea of Jennifer Dupont experiencing any kind of pleasure, whether it be from pain or otherwise, very much *did.* "Why?"

"It isn't so much about the actual pain as it is about the control of it," Jennifer explained like a professor launching a lecture she'd given countless times before. "Controlling when and how you experience pain and to what to degree. Controlling who gives you pain. Controlling how you deal *with* and deal *out* pain." Her voice briefly softened. "As you know, some people have spent a great deal of their lives in pain with no control over or say in it. Taking control over it can be empowering. Ultimately, it's about that power. The power of agency even while in, or perhaps especially while in, pain. Does that make sense?"

Dosie didn't answer, couldn't. She dropped her gaze to the floor as a familiar feeling invaded. *Shame.* It spilled through her blood like a virus until every inch was infected. She knew pain, intimately, and she'd never had control over it, but imagining *wanting* that pain made her feel dirty.

"Dosie." Jennifer tugged the crop from her hands and set it aside. She placed her fingers under Dosie's chin and nudged her face up again. When their eyes met, Dosie had to tell herself not to lean in. Not to feel things she shouldn't. "If you want me to, and only if you want me to, I will inflict pain," Jennifer said. "But I will *never* harm you. Do you understand?"

"Yes." Dosie grabbed Jennifer's hand before it could slink away. "Thank you for taking the time to talk things through with me. I'm sure it's annoying, having to explain everything, and me being so—"

"Stop, Dosie." Jennifer eased her hand away. "It's my job," she said, and cleared her throat—the sound of a crack forming in Dosie's soul. She took up the riding crop again. "Now, would you like to try this or not?"

Don't dwell, Dosie told herself and blinked away the sting in her eyes. *Focus.* She looked at the crop, considered. While she could admit she was curious, a more insistent part of her mind throbbed red with warning. Outlines of memories she wished she could forget began to take shape. She shook her head, hoping to dispel them before they filled in.

"No, please," she croaked and hated how weak she sounded.

"Okay," Jennifer said simply and returned it to the bag. When she turned back to Dosie, she smiled easily, seemed open and pliant as ever, but Dosie could feel that she was guarded. There was a palpable barrier between them now, a thin layer of distance carefully applied like paper over a wall. Whatever had been brewing between them, and Dosie still wasn't sure what that was, now felt tamed and muffled, and while Dosie ached to uncover it, hear it loud and feel it fully, she knew that wouldn't happen. Not this time. Never again. Not with this woman.

This was business. This was work. This was pleasure *paid* for, a contract between two parties. It wasn't and wouldn't be anything more.

"And just so we're clear," Jennifer said, shaking Dosie from her pained thoughts, "you can always change your mind. About anything." She lay her hand on the bag. "Now, is there anything in here that you do want to try or that you want to ask about?"

For days, Dosie had thought of nothing else. What she wanted to try. What she could do and have done. What she could ask for and *how* she might ask for it. She'd cycled through images in her mind—Jennifer, the last time they'd been together, when she'd broken Dosie's world open with stiff nipples and wet heat. Dosie had remembered and ached and *imagined*, and she'd also, possibly, spent a bit too much time on the internet. Sex was so much more expansive than she'd ever realized, and now she had too many ideas and not enough nerve.

"Ask for anything," Jennifer said, as if sensing the chaos in her brain. "There's no need to be ashamed or scared or even timid. Okay? There's no judgment here. Whatever it is, if it's within my power and comfort to give, then you will have it."

Dosie licked her lips. *Just pick something. Do something. Say something.* "Sit back." One of Jennifer's dark, angled eyebrows ticked up, and the sight made Dosie's spine jerk. "I want...." *Pick something. Pick something.* Jennifer eased back into the soft leather, and an idea sparked, just not in Dosie's mind. Her cunt throbbed. "I want you to teach me how to touch myself."

The words hung in the air like scent, an overwhelming aroma that dizzied Jennifer, and before she could reorient herself, Dosie's T-shirt was on the floor. She was gloriously bare underneath, and her pretty, peach nipples perked as if eager to be seen. So, Jennifer looked.

Scarlet splotched Dosie's chest and splattered up her throat, and Jennifer half-expected her to chicken out. Pride ignited in her belly when Dosie simply fanned her face, took a breath, and popped open the button on her jeans. Her eyes were warm carob as they locked on Jennifer, and then visibly sweaty hands shimmied the denim down her long, pale legs. When she was down to only her underwear—a scrap of carmine cotton that sharpened the red in her skin—she hesitated.

Jennifer held her breath, scared she might shatter their spell with the slightest movement. In the full brightness of her living room, Dosie Fisher was being braver than she'd ever been, and Jennifer wasn't about to give her any reason to doubt herself. In fact, she was desperate for it to continue.

She chewed the inside of her cheek to stop herself gasping when Dosie stepped into her space, their knees bumping, then turned around. A series of thin, white lines marred the space between her shoulder blades, the scars she'd mentioned but that the dark of her room had made difficult to see. Jennifer didn't get much of a look this time, either, as Dosie's ass sank into her lap, and then they were molded together—Dosie's back to her chest, thighs on top of thighs.

"Show me," Dosie whispered, chest heaving as she pulled Jennifer's hands to her belly. The heat in her skin made Jennifer feel drunk, and she wondered, not for the first time, if Dosie had any idea how powerful she was. "Show me how to pleasure myself."

This is fine. I'm fine. Her clitoris felt like a pin cushion, her heart, too, but she was fine. *I'm working. This is work. Focus, and do your work.*

It was a struggle to keep distance like this, but Jennifer would be damned if she didn't try. She kept her body static, torso frozen, as she folded her hands over Dosie's clammy, trembling fingers, and began to guide. One hand she left where it was. The other, she slinked up to Dosie's chest, then higher, up the slide of her neck, over her soft jaw. She pressed Dosie's fingers to her own mouth, dragged them over her lips.

Dosie licked her own fingertips, catching Jennifer's in the process. When she deliberately sucked both inside, Jennifer's eyes fluttered. Neither she nor Dosie spoke a word as she guided Dosie's fingertips back down to her chest to ring and knead her breast. Jennifer closed her eyes and encouraged Dosie to circle her own nipple, prod it, rub it. Pinch it between her fingertips. Dosie gasped with the pressure, so Jennifer urged her to do it again. She dragged Dosie's hand to the other breast to serve it the same attention. The same punishment.

As Dosie teased herself under Jennifer's hand, the quiet of the room seemed to expand. It magnified. The walls tightened. The room shrank. The air thinned. Until there was nothing but them and what they were doing. This slow, exploratory touch. Dosie's heartbeat thumping in her back so that Jennifer could feel it in her own chest. Dosie's hands moving beautifully under hers, doing as they were bid without even a word of command. It was perhaps, Jennifer realized with breathless shock, one of the most erotic moments of her life.

"Talk to me," Dosie whispered, her head falling back onto Jennifer's shoulder. "It's too quiet."

Her scent infiltrated, clean and mild like she'd recently showered, and Jennifer couldn't help herself. She nuzzled into her, breathed her deeper. "Pleasure is a full-body experience," she said, voice low and throaty. "You can manifest it anywhere." She led Dosie's hand to her lips again. "Here." Then around to graze over her ear, down to the baby-soft hairs on the nape of her neck. "Here." Over the sharp wing of her collarbone and down to the flat plane between her breasts. "Here."

A weak whimper sounded next to her ear, and Jennifer felt it like touch, like a whisper of a fingertip testing the waters between her legs. She fought not to clench, not to think of her own needs. This wasn't about her. It was about Dosie. Dosie's pleasure. Dosie's needs. Not Jennifer's. Not *theirs*. There was no them.

With her other hand, she guided Dosie's fingers from her stomach down. "Here," she said as she skirted over cotton and the crease between Dosie's thighs. "Certainly here." Dosie kneaded and gripped herself under Jennifer's hand and swallowed so thickly that Jennifer heard every inch of the journey down.

When she urged Dosie to cup herself over her panties, Dosie's quiet whimper became a moan, a sound so rich it made Jennifer's teeth ache. Oh, she wanted. She *craved*. She soothed her own ache with a slow, measured breath and pressed Dosie's fingers down, encouraging pressure. "But orgasms," she said, "the *best* orgasms, begin and end with the brain."

She drew Dosie's fingers to her waistband, but Dosie, herself, shoved them under. Jennifer stilled her hand. "Stop. Excitement is good but control it. Don't let it rush you." Dosie took a breath, and Jennifer relaxed her grip. She slid their fingers through Dosie's coarse hair. "Now, you can touch as much as you like, however you like," she said, "but what matters most is where your mind is."

Slowly, she parted Dosie's first two fingers and positioned them over her labia, could almost feel the soft, swollen skin through her. She imagined it was her own hand touching, rather than guiding. "Think about what you want," she instructed. "*How* you want. How you *need*." Over and over, she guided Dosie's fingers to stroke but never pushed, never applied any pressure to where she was certain Dosie needed it most. This was about exploration. "Picture in your mind what excites you. The sounds you like. The scents. The drag of skin on skin. The feeling of wetness at your fingertips. The thump of your heartbeat in your ears. The taste of another's tongue in your mouth."

Dosie's hips twitched. Her breath shallowed. She pressed her fingers harder against herself and whined like she was being denied something she deserved.

"Can you see it?" Jennifer asked and gave Dosie's fingers the slightest push. "Do you have your picture?"

"Yes." Her thighs clamped around their hands. "Tell me what to do."

"You know what to do," Jennifer said and pushed the heel of Dosie's hand down into her clit, causing her to cry out. "Listen to your body. Give it what it's asking for."

Jennifer smiled as Dosie's hand immediately took over. Her own went soft, now a static blanket over unguided actions as Dosie dipped her fingers into her vulva and spread herself open. Kneaded her clit like a woman possessed. She skated down to circle her slick entrance, and when she briefly penetrated herself, Jennifer imagined the digit sinking into *her* instead. Her hips jerked in response, and Dosie jumped to her feet. Jennifer was about to apologize, but then the girl was in her lap again.

She straddled Jennifer's thighs, facing her, and dug her hands into Jennifer's shirt. "Let me take this off," she said then did so. Her sticky fingers latched onto the top of Jennifer's pants and tugged, just enough to take Jennifer's hand and shove it under. "Touch yourself."

Fuck. Since when did Jennifer like being told what to do? *Who cares? Touch yourself.*

Dosie didn't hold Jennifer's gaze as she went back to messily rubbing her own clit. She focused, instead, on the bulge between Jennifer's legs, Jennifer's hand moving inside her pants, stroking herself. Dosie absorbed the sight like she was witnessing a miracle, eyes wide and crimson in her cheeks. The tip of her tongue darting out to wet her parted lips. Her breath dying prematurely as it burst in and out of her. She was a vision.

"Go inside," she said, and Jennifer felt herself flood. Pleasure made Dosie bold, and boldness had never been more beautiful. It had never been more *arousing*.

Jennifer's pants were tight around her wrist, but she made it work, pressing a finger inside herself, up to the first knuckle. No resistance. She was soaked. She added another, penetrating herself as deeply as she could manage.

"Are you inside?" Dosie panted.

"Yes." She crooked her fingers to hit the ribbed flesh of her g-spot and gasped.

"*Fuck*," Dosie cursed, and Jennifer nearly came on the spot. "Me too."

Jennifer knew. She *heard* it, the wet, sucking sounds of Dosie impaling herself. And the harder she fucked herself, the more her scent permeated the air. Jennifer breathed it in, and her mouth watered. "Dosie," she said without thinking, her body expelling the name like a last-ditch prayer.

Dosie's forehead dropped against hers, slick with sweat. "I want you to come," she panted, voice pitching at the end so that it peaked into a whine. "I want you to say my name when you do."

Dear *God*, what was happening? Dosie was coming alive, coming into herself in the most vibrant, dizzying way, and Jennifer was absolutely floored by it. Entranced by it. She was a breath away from coming so hard, she feared she mi—

"Fuck, *Dosie*," she choked out as her orgasm hit like a blow to the gut. The wind expelled harshly from her body, and every muscle turned to stone, every nerve to fire. The room spun. Lights burst and died and flickered back to life again as she gushed around her fingers. Her heartbeat thundered in her ears as Dosie cried and tensed above her, and all the world halted.

It lasted seconds. Seconds that felt like minutes. Minutes that dragged into hours. Hours that spawned years that became their whole lives. It was everything, and it wasn't enough.

They crumpled into the couch, Dosie a heap on Jennifer's heaving chest, both their hands still buried in their underwear. "That was my picture," Dosie panted and kissed Jennifer's shoulder. "You, like this." Another kiss under her ear. "You're so beautiful when you orgasm."

Jennifer closed her eyes and tried not to let the words infiltrate, float around inside her like possibilities and promises she wasn't willing to indulge. She lifted her free hand to Dosie's cheek and rubbed her thumb along its slope, hoping it would communicate all the things she couldn't put into words. Things she wasn't sure she could even define.

And then Dosie began to giggle. It was the most jarring, precious sound, and Jennifer almost hated her for it. For the affection that flooded her chest. For the urge that rose to hold her and kiss her. For the desire to do something utterly childish, like tickle her just to make the sound last longer.

With an exaggerated sigh, Dosie pulled her hand from her panties and slid off Jennifer's lap to her side. Jennifer freed her own hand and wiped it on her bare stomach. And then they sat. Silently. Thigh to thigh. Shoulder to shoulder. Just breathing together. Just *being* together.

Jennifer watched Dosie's pinky finger twitch her way, acutely aware of how close their hands were, resting atop their thighs. She expected Dosie to close the gap, take her hand and hold it. But then the pinky retracted, and Dosie set her hands over her own belly as if to help them avoid temptation. She was holding Jennifer's boundaries, those spoken and sensed, refusing to ask for intimacy she didn't truly need.

Of course, Jennifer felt grateful, but on top of her gratitude sat guilt. Like oil spilled over water. *No. You have nothing to feel guilty for. Boundaries exist for a reason.*

This was work. This was business. They could both abide that. They *were* abiding it.

"Do you want something to drink?" Dosie asked. "Water?"

"Yes," Jennifer said, grateful for the distraction from the discord in her mind. "Please."

When Dosie stood on shaky legs, she reached out just long enough to squeeze Jennifer's shoulder instead of her hand. "Thank you," she said, "for doing that with me." Then flitted away before Jennifer could utter a word.

Silence fell over the room again, thick and unyielding. Jennifer cupped her hands around her knees and leaned forward. She breathed slow, deep breaths until she felt like herself again.

In the kitchen, Dosie washed up and pulled two glasses from a cabinet. She nearly dropped them both when her hands began to shake. Glasses safely set aside, she folded her fingers together at her chest and squeezed. Her body hummed with nervous energy, and her face was too hot. Her heart was beating too fast.

She wrapped herself in a tight embrace and closed her eyes, holding herself because she couldn't ask Jennifer to. She couldn't ask for anything more than what she'd already been given, and *God*, she'd been given everything. Jennifer's orgasm, coated in Dosie's name, detonating her own, both so intense they'd been helpless to do much else than tremble. Clutch each other as pleasure spilled over the threshold in warm, gushing waves that drowned out the world.

But the adrenaline was waning now, and Dosie could feel her doubts and insecurities creeping in again. All her worries and shames and fears. All her guilt.

"Stop thinking," she whispered to herself. "Stay present."

The glass pitcher in the fridge was full to the brim and cold. It offered some relief as Dosie stuck her cheek to it and breathed. Her jelly legs wobbled underneath her as she carried it to the glasses and filled them, and when she returned it, her reflection caught her eye. She stopped and stared at herself. A wonky beige blur in stainless steel. Dosie found it oddly pretty and wondered if that was how the Director saw her—a pretty, curious thing. A limited-edition novelty to be fleetingly adored.

"I want you so badly, I can't think."

Jennifer's voice, needy and loud in the silence of that dressing room, floated through her mind as if to defend the woman's honor. Dosie smiled, shivered. Their time together would be temporary, but the want was real. It would last.

When she was ready, she picked up the full glasses and headed back, trying all the way to keep the thrill she'd just felt in her mind and not focus on her doubts and anxieties, on the fact that her boobs were out. She was about to walk topless into the living room with a serving of drinks like a waitress at a strip club. *Wait. Strip club. Stripper.* Her instinct had been to banish the thought, embarrassed by it, but strippers were sexy. Right? Strippers were confident and bold.

Strippers made sure you remembered them.

She kept that in mind as she sauntered (or what she imagined a saunter would look like) back to the Director. *Confident. Bold.* Maybe she would have another peek in that bag. Maybe they would try something new. Maybe, the next time they came together, Dosie would say the Director's name.

Maybe *Jennifer* would let her.

In the few seconds it took to get to the living room, her confidence waned. Some days, it required constant stroking, lest it fizzle like a spent match. Thankfully, seeing Jennifer's gaze drop, however briefly, to her chest quickly replenished her flame. Dosie smiled and handed her one of the waters.

"Thank you." Jennifer drank greedily.

"Can I look in your bag again?"

The glass stalled at Jennifer's lips. "Of course," she said as she set the glass aside. "Is there anything in particular you're curious about?"

"There are a lot of things I'm curious about."

With a velvety laugh, Jennifer leaned back into the couch and stretched one arm along its back. She crossed her legs at the knee and smiled, and Dosie was not prepared for her body's reaction. The embers of her earlier pleasure burst into bright fire, such instant heat that she felt it in her chest and her neck, her cheeks and the backs of her ears, the top of her head. It was in her blood, and in her *thoughts*. Her brain flooded with it, forged images with it, sounds, sensation—little sparks of memories. *Jennifer on her back beneath her. Jennifer's face between her legs. Jennifer fucking her against a mirror.*

Dosie shook her head as if it might force a breeze through her ears to cool down her brain. But she made the mistake of looking at Jennifer—the actual Jennifer, sitting right in front of her—and she may as well have doused herself in gasoline. Jennifer's eyes, normally such a soft, sky blue, were cornflower and slate, the colors deepened and hazed and thinned to skinny rings around broadened black. The high arches of her cheeks wore a faint blush, and there was a knowing little smirk on her mouth as if she knew what Dosie was thinking, as if she could *see* every wicked little picture playing out on her forehead like a silent movie. It made Dosie feel *dirty*, and to her surprise, dirty felt good.

"May I make a suggestion?"

"You can do anything you want," Dosie blurted, and Jennifer's eyebrow ticked. *Jesus*. No one had the right to look that elegant and intimidating at once, especially not when they were wearing nothing but suit pants, a bra, and a braid. How was that fair?

"In that case," Jennifer said, "how would you feel about a strap-on?"

Dosie's mouth went dry. The downy hairs at the back of

her neck and in the dip of her lower back prickled. *Good lord.* "Are..." She cleared her throat. "...you going to wear it?"

Both Jennifer's eyebrows tilted. Her lips parted then closed then parted again. "Would you like to wear it yourself?"

Dosie nearly swallowed her tongue. Despite her question, she hadn't considered that option. But *oh,* she was considering it now. Her eyes shut as her mind was yanked into the image like a too-close star sucked into a vacuum: her hips strapped, just as she'd seen on the internet, something considerable between her legs. Canting into Jennifer, disappearing inside her glistening sex, deeper than she could ever reach on her own.

"Okay, breathe," Jennifer said, and Dosie opened her eyes again. "A topic we can revisit another time?" She chuckled and bent to grab her duffle bag, lifted it onto the couch. "Considering you just glitched at the first mention."

Dosie laughed at herself. "Yeah." As sexy as the thought was, she had no experience with strap-on dildos. She had no experience with dildos at all, or any other sex toy. She'd never even seen a vibrator in person until the first time she'd visited Kaylia's house. The girl had an entire collection of them displayed on a shelf in her bedroom. Dosie didn't want her first experience to be her *failing* to make Jennifer come because she didn't have a clue how to go about it. "But you can wear it."

"Wonderful." Jennifer lifted her bag onto the couch and began to pull a variety of dildos from inside, each sealed inside its own clear container but for one that was already secured to a harness. "Do you have any triggers related to this style of sex?"

Affection sprouted like a seed in Dosie's chest, but she suffocated it. *She's doing her job. Asking is part of her job. It's not personal.* "Um, well, none that I know of," she said as Jennifer laid the dildos out on the coffee table. "I mean, I've never experienced one, but then, you know my sexual experience is limited."

Most of the triggers she'd established in therapy were rooted in words and ideas, sensory experiences like sounds and smells, and sometimes, rarely, locations. Her sex-relaxed triggers had always been rooted in thoughts, never the actual *act.* Ineffective and mechanical as the sex with her husband may have been, it had happened without issue.

"Is that okay?" Dosie asked. "That I don't know? I mean, should we not do it just in case?"

"Of course not," Jennifer said, soft and encouraging. "We can do whatever you like. It's just best to be prepared when we can be. But I do want you to tell me if there's a particular response you prefer in that type of situation. I know it can vary, but is there anything specific that you want me to do or say? Anything you've found that consistently helps soothe you when you're experiencing anxiety?"

"Guided breathing works if it's mild. Or compression, like a good, tight hug. Outside of that, I have mantras I use, but they don't always work if the anxiety is really bad. Sometimes, I stick my face in the freezer. A blast of cold to kind of knock me out of my head. You know?"

"I may have to try that sometime," Jennifer said, then she tapped the edge of the table. "Okay, so how about this? I'm going to slip into the kitchen to wash my hands, and while I'm gone, you can choose the size and shape you think you'd be most comfortable with. How does that sound?"

"Okay," Dosie said, hoping she sounded less nervous than she was. It wasn't like it would be her first time having penetrative sex with something larger than a finger or two, but it had been a while since the last time. "Sure."

Jennifer stood and lay a hand on Dosie's bare shoulder, squeezed. "Try not to overthink it."

"And give up the one skill I've mastered in life?"

Jennifer chuckled and, to Dosie's surprise, bent to kiss the side of her neck. "Just try," she whispered, then she headed for the kitchen.

"Director?"

"Hm?"

"Any advice on how to choose?"

"Feel," Jennifer said, stopping to look back. "Sight can be deceiving, so test the weight and girth with your hand." She grinned, so much more relaxed than before. It comforted Dosie. "Trust your instincts, not your libido."

And then she was gone, and Dosie was left staring at seven different dildos the way she stared at all the different cupcakes in the bakery when she was on her period. How was she supposed to choose? There were different colors and shapes, sizes, and materials. One of them even looked like it was made of glass, which was a bit unnerving, but at least it looked doable. The last one Jennifer had taken from the bag had been a hard *no* the second Dosie saw it. At *least* ten inches long and as big around as a fist—if Dosie was honest, it kind of scared her.

A much smaller one, iridescent with a slight curve, kept drawing her eye. It didn't look to be any more than five, maybe six, inches long, an inch around. It seemed like a good place to start, so she unpacked it and took it in her hand. Immediately, she understood why Jennifer had told her to do this. It didn't feel at all how she imagined it would. It was soft, almost squishy, more akin to a partial erection than a full one. She returned it to its container and selected another, this one similar in size and curved as well, but with a bigger tip and much more firmness. Not too firm. It had some give but only enough to make it pliable. It felt good in her hand.

"Excellent choice."

Dosie fumbled the toy but caught it. "Really?"

"Of course," Jennifer said as she rounded the sofa. "I wouldn't own it if it wasn't."

"You're so cocky."

"Says the girl holding the cock."

Dosie snorted hard enough for it to hurt. "Ow." She pinched the bridge of her nose as she laughed. "Don't do that me."

"I'd apologize, but I'd be lying. Now, is that your choice?" She pointed to the dildo, and Dosie nodded. "Okay, then..."

She dug what looked to be a complicated tangle of brown leather straps and gold metal from her bag. "...I will put this on." She set it out on the table, and it took a more recognizable shape. The harness. *Oh, right. Obviously.* "And while I do that, you can decide where you want to do this. Oh, and grab a condom and some lubricant. They're in the front pocket."

Dosie frowned. "A condom? For a dildo?"

"It's just a precaution," Jennifer said as she toed off her shoes, then unbuttoned her pants to drag them down her long legs. "Vaginas have a delicate pH balance. It's hard to know what will upset it. I stick with water-based, all-natural lubes, but the toys themselves can cause irritation. Not always, but it happens. So, a bit of protection doesn't hurt. Do you know if you have an allergy to latex? I have other types of condoms if you do."

"No, no allergies," Dosie said with an easy shake of her head, lips stretching with a smile.

"What?"

"What?"

"What are you grinning about?"

Dosie shrugged. "It's just nice to be able to ask questions and get answers without having to feel awkward and embarrassed about it. When I started all this, I was afraid I would feel like I was constantly annoying you, because there are so many things I don't know, but you don't make me feel like that at all. You're so patient and prepared and knowledgeable, and it just makes it all, sex, *everything*, so much less.... Terrifying doesn't seem like the right word, but it's the first that comes to mind. Does that make sense?"

"It does." Jennifer hooked her thumbs in the waistband of her silky charcoal panties, and Dosie had to avert her attention to the bag.

Seeing Jennifer fully nude in a well-lit room might be a bit like staring straight into the sun—beautiful but unsafe. What if she fried her brain? What if the image spotted her pupils like one of those little neon specks that sometimes floated through her vision, and then for the rest of her life, her naked escort would be transposed over everything she looked at, like a sticker on a window?

"Women are taught not to explore this part of ourselves, and even when we do, we have no education to guide us," Jennifer said as Dosie pulled a selection of condoms and lubricants from the bag and looked them over. *Ooh! Banana flavor! Wait. It's not going in my mouth.* "What they gave us when I was in school was a joke. Fear tactics and judgment. Still mostly the case, unfortunately. And forget about anything queer. It's like we didn't even exist."

Dosie looked up at the first jangle of the harness. She couldn't help herself. It was instinct. *Dear Father in Heaven, have mercy on your sinful child, for I am weak and—Stop!* She'd worked for years to break the habit of praying when overwhelmed, and it happened less each year, but some routines were so deeply embedded that they'd become as natural as getting a drink when she was thirsty. *I'm definitely thirsty.*

Jennifer stood stark naked on the other side of the table, unabashed as she buckled a leather strap. Oblivious to the fact that someone was dying of dehydration right in front of her. "It's an annoyingly long process with a genuine leather harness already," she said, then glanced up, a smirk on her lips, "but I can drag it out if you're enjoying the show."

Oh no. There was the affection again, blooming in her belly like a flower. Several flowers. An entire field of color. *Damn it. Damn it.* Somehow, inexplicably and without anyone's consent (certainly without Jennifer's), Dosie's heart had become involved. She cared about this woman. She really, *really* cared about her.

"Nope," she squeaked, face burning, as she looked away. She could do this. She could tamp it down, control it, prevent it from growing. She had willpower. She just had to use it. "Thanks though." *Or... a distraction. I need a distraction.*

So, she rifled through the bag again, came up with a small, turquoise-colored object that she couldn't identify. "What's this thing?"

Jennifer glanced over. "Vibrator," she said then went back to adjusting the straps around her thighs. *Don't stare. Don't stare. Don't stare.* But it was hard not to. Seeing how free Jennifer was in her own skin, how confident and relaxed she was in her natural body—it was magic. Even with all her therapy, Dosie doubted she'd ever find her way to such a place. There was too much history in her skin, too much trauma in all the places that she now struggled, and sometimes succeeded, to love.

"A vibrator?" She fiddled with the skinny curved legs protruding off the toy's thick oval center. "It looks like a June bug." She wasn't prepared for Jennifer's loud bark of a laugh, nor for the pleasure it sent spiraling through her system. She looked up, face flushed with the satisfaction. "What? It does! It has little legs."

Jennifer finished securing the harness, and it fit her as if she'd had it custom-made for her hips and thighs. "Wow." Maybe she *had*. This was her job after all. Dosie had heard of writers who'd had custom chairs made since they sat so much. Why not a dildo harness? "That looks really good on you." Her gaze fixated on the thick metal ring clasped at the apex of Jennifer's thighs, waiting to be filled. "Like, *really* good."

A seductive smile painted Jennifer's mouth like art. "It will look better once it's properly equipped," she said, *promised*, and crossed toward her.

Dosie's nipples perked, stiffening to the point of pain, and she remembered she was completely topless. She watched Jennifer's eyes drop, watched her smile expand until she was shark-like, then the vibrator was being snatched from her hand and suddenly Jennifer was right beside her. Dosie tried desperately not to think about the fact that the woman's bare ass was on her couch. She tried not to judge herself for finding it arousing. Then again, she was rapidly growing accustomed to the fact that she clearly found everything about Jennifer Dupont arousing. Everything. Things she'd never even thought could *be* arousing—like ribcages and kneecaps, collarbones and forearm veins and freaking *earlobes*, for God's sake.

"The 'little legs'," Jennifer said, amusement clear in her voice, "or some people call them wings, serve a purpose." She stretched the limbs open a bit wider and turned the object over in her hands. "The whole device is meant to be hands-free, so the center portion is set over the clitoris, while the wings are secured just inside the labia to hold it in place. This way, the clitoris can still be stimulated while the wearer and their partner engage in other activities."

"Like what?"

"Like exactly what we're about to engage in."

"Oh." Dosie licked her lips. "So, you could put this on me while you...." Her gaze dropped to the harness.

"Indeed, I could," Jennifer said as she wrapped her strong, slender fingers around Dosie's chin, drew her gaze back up. "Would you like that..." Her voice dropped, tone deepening to a buttery-rich melody that made Dosie's spine tingle. "...Ms. Fisher?"

Dear Father in Heaven, have mercy on your sinful child, for I am weak and—Goddamn it!

"Yes."

The fireplace sat empty and cold, and they'd yet to even begin, but the air already boiled. Sweat slithered down Jennifer's spine as she hovered over Dosie, a hand braced on each side of her head. The floor was hard beneath them, the single, thick blanket Dosie had tossed down not quite enough to cushion their bony parts. But Jennifer didn't mind. There was a certain allure to the dichotomy between soft flesh and an unforgiving surface.

She looked down at the weight between her legs, the fullness of her measure spread over Dosie's mound and already slick. She followed it, base to tip, then beyond, absorbing the sight of the girl lain out beneath her, hair pooling over blanket and hardwood. The overhead lights reflected in her swollen pupils as she gripped Jennifer's shoulders and bent her knees around her thighs. *Beautiful.* Jennifer absorbed every detail in perfect stillness, as if she was afraid it might disappear with the slightest motion, the smallest, quietest huff of air. In her held breath, she was heat and desire and the kind of thrilling, nauseating terror that came from needing something she couldn't name. Wanting something she was certain she shouldn't want.

"I didn't think you would come back." Dosie's voice was whisper-soft, an easy breeze against Jennifer's chin. Her grip loosened as she slid a hand from Jennifer's shoulder to her jaw, her cheek.

Jennifer swallowed the words that barreled up her throat. *Neither did I.*

"I'm glad you did."

So am I.

How could I not be?

I like doing this. I like being here.

With you.

She said none of it.

"Director?"

Something pulled in Jennifer's chest at the sound of the title, the way it sat in Dosie's mouth like sand that needed sifting. The treasure was beneath it. Her name, the one she'd given Dosie in a whisper that she could still sometimes taste when she thought about it. But they were as they needed to be, and Jennifer accepted it.

She slid a hand between their bodies to grasp her temporary cock and slowly raked the tip through Dosie's slit and down, down to the inviting heat of her. "Yes?"

Dosie's breath stuttered over her lips. She followed it with her tongue as Jennifer pressed the large tip inside just enough for it to burn. "You *will* come back again," she said, eyes locking on Jennifer's, searching, *hoping*. "Won't you?"

"Focus, Dosie," Jennifer said and lay a feathery kiss under her eye, then another at the corner. Another in her hair. "Be here now." She didn't want to talk about such things, wouldn't. She couldn't detach herself enough from Dosie to treat her like any other client as requested, but she could maintain some distances. Some barriers. If they wanted this to continue, she had to. "Be here with me." She nosed along Dosie's cheek as she pulled her hips back enough for her cock to fall free then pushed it in again.

Dosie gasped with the brief invasion. Her grip tightened.

"Are you ready?" Jennifer sucked Dosie's neck, scraped her teeth over her pulse. She retreated again, let her tip draw delicate little circles in wet flesh. "Tell me you're ready."

"I'm ready." Dosie shuddered beneath her, and Jennifer lifted her head so she could see her properly.

This time, as she pushed inside, she sank deeper, a good two inches of her shaft devoured. Dosie's animalistic grunt made her clit jump behind the harness. She watched Dosie's face as she slid in a little deeper, reading her expression like a how-to guide. When her forehead scrunched and her breath stuttered, Jennifer held still, gave her a moment. "Okay?"

"I'm okay."

"Sure?"

"Yes."

Another inch, and Dosie's lips pulled with a sharper grimace. Jennifer stopped again. "Don't hold your breath," Jennifer said. "You're too tense. When there's oxygen in your muscles, they relax."

Dosie's breath burst out of her like air from a popped balloon. A deep, loud inhale followed then, slowly and with control, she let it go, and her muscles loosened a bit around the toy but not much. She tossed an arm over her eyes and huffed. "I'm sorry."

"Don't be. Just tell me what you need."

Dosie swallowed loud enough for Jennifer to hear, then slid her arm from her face to look at her. "Before you, I hadn't been with anyone since my husband. And you've only used your fingers until now. I think I'm just a little overwhelmed by the size."

Jennifer nodded. "That's okay. Is it too much to the point that you want to stop? Or do you want to give it a moment and see if you can adjust? We can try a different size or position, too. More lube?"

"I think I can adjust." Dosie's fingertips were sweaty when she lay them against Jennifer's cheek. "Let's just take it slow, okay?"

Jennifer let a smile slide over her lips. "Okay." She knew just what to do, just how to help Dosie relax into the pleasure of having Jennifer's cock inside her. She dipped her voice into a rasp. "You should know..." She sucked the corner of her mouth. "...that you feel *so very good* around me."

A sudden, soft gasp sounded from Dosie's lips, and Jennifer's smile grew. She hid in the fall of Dosie's hair as she sucked and nibbled her way down her neck and back up. "The way you're gripping and pulling me," she said and slowly rocked back her hips until just the tip was inside, then forward again, just a bit. A little back. A little forward. "Like you're desperate to have me inside you." Back. Forward. Millimeter by millimeter, Jennifer slowly gave everything and nothing at once. "God, you want every inch of me inside you, don't you, Dosie? You want me so deep. You want me to come so hard."

Dosie's next gasp shattered around a positively *filthy* moan. Her thighs clenched around Jennifer's waist as her perfect cunt flooded and stretched. "Okay, okay, I think I want—I'm ready for more," she panted, and Jennifer bit hard into Dosie's shoulder as she gave her the final length in one swift thrust.

"Oh!" Half-sob. Half-moan. Dosie ringed her legs around Jennifer's hips, locked her ankles over the top of her ass, and Jennifer used the shift to angle herself deeper. Her leather-strapped mound collided with Dosie's clit as they slotted like puzzle pieces, and Dosie's second cry may as well have been Jennifer's. She felt it in her cunt.

"How's that feel?" She pumped her hips shallowly, building friction. "Does that feel good?"

"It's starting to." Dosie jutted up to meet her, and Jennifer grabbed her hips to hold her in place. Pressed right up against her, she made a tight circle with her hips, grinding Dosie's clit while she was buried inside her. "Oh *God*, it's *really* starting to. Do that again."

Jennifer's eyes rolled back at the words, at the sudden surety in Dosie's voice. "Do what again?" She kneaded Dosie's thigh, sucked the corner of her mouth. "This?" Another grinding circle with her hips, and she was rewarded with a pleasured groan and kiss so deep it made her feel faint.

Dosie's arms looped her neck and yanked her closer. Her fingers clawed into Jennifer's hair, messing her braid, but she didn't care. All she cared about was the hot, wet panting in her ear, the insistent heel digging into the top of her ass as she began a slow, steady rhythm with her hips. Every thrust teased her with near-perfect pressure, the base of the dildo thumping against her clit, and every sound she made in response seemed to drive Dosie higher in her pleasure. A perfect chain reaction—Jennifer was drunk on it.

"You have no idea how good you feel," she said as she landed a particularly harsh thrust, and Dosie all but screamed, muffling the sound on Jennifer's shoulder as she bit down, hard. The zap of pain nearly brought Jennifer to orgasm. She buried her face in Dosie's neck again, breathing her in—sweaty and salty and familiar and *perfect*. "Or how many times I've fantasized about doing this."

Fuck. She hadn't meant to say that, to confess it. But God, she'd wanted to. She suddenly wanted so much, she felt sick with the wanting. She felt unnerved by it. And wild.

"Director," Dosie moaned, and pleasure detonated through Jennifer's body like a bomb. She cried out and felt Dosie's fingernails dig into her skin. "*Yes*." Dosie rutted against her hard, breath ragged, and then— "Oh, God. Oh, G—There!"

Jennifer nearly came again, just hearing those words. "That's it." She stilled, waiting for the tension in Dosie's body to pass, then slowly pumped her hips to ease her down from her high. Her own pleasure was still zinging around her body, and Jennifer was ready for more. She was desperate for it.

She grabbed the hands-free vibrator Dosie had discovered and set it over Dosie's sensitive clit before it could stop twitching. She secured the wings at the labia as Dosie lifted her head and looked between their bodies with hazy eyes.

"What?" She laughed. The melody was breathless and tired, *beautiful*, and it only stoked Jennifer's fire. "More?"

"Always," Jennifer said with a grin.

"You're crazy."

"I want you coming again before you've recovered from this one."

Dosie's entire face was the color of a beet. She covered it with her hands and groaned. "If I don't *die* first," she said, and Jennifer melted. *Why does she have to be so cute?*

She pulled Dosie's hands from her face. "Trust me," she said. "When you see stars, it will be because you're flying, not because you've died." She sealed the vow with a slow kiss as she reached between them again and turned the vibrator to its first, gentlest setting. Clearly, it wasn't gentle enough, because Dosie's entire body jerked, and a moan that hinged on a shout rocketed from her throat.

"There's no way," she said, voice shredded and near hysterical already, even as she attempted to impale herself further on Jennifer's motionless cock, still buried inside her.

"Yes, there is," Jennifer said as she turned the vibrator up another notch and began to fuck her properly again. Dosie was so wet that every thrust sounded obscene. "Stay with me."

"Oh my—I can't." Her body said otherwise, gripping and tugging at Jennifer as if she was eager to have her inside her. "I can't."

"You *can*," Jennifer promised and pumped her hips harder. "I can feel how close you are already. So am I."

"*Fuck*," Dosie cried, actual tears streaming down her

cheeks as she latched onto Jennifer's hips to tug her cock more forcefully inside herself. "Please. Please."

Jennifer shifted just enough to angle the tip and drag it along the vagina's sensitive anterior wall and watched Dosie's gorgeous, dark eyes flutter, watched her wet lips tremble. "How badly do you want me to come, Dosie?"

"Please, I want it so—*Ah!*" Dosie jolted as if struck by lightning the moment Jennifer flicked the vibrator to its final, highest level. Its hum turned to a violent buzz, adding chaos to the already raucous sounds of harsh breaths and slapping, sucking flesh. "I feel like I'm going to explode."

"It's going to be so good when you do."

Dosie whined. "It's so much."

"Too much?"

"No. But, God, *yes*. I can't. I *can't*."

"You *can*," Jennifer insisted. "Concentrate. You're *so* close, Dosie. We're so close. You can take it."

Dosie froze.

As if someone had dumped a bucket of ice water over her, her breath caught roughly in her throat and every part of her tensed. Her nails dug into Jennifer's skin until the flesh split, drawing a hiss from Jennifer's throat, and then Dosie was simply gone. Still and silent and *gone*.

Jennifer stopped immediately, chills racing down her spine. "Dosie?" She switched off the vibrator. "Dosie?" Her hammering heart shot into her throat as she cupped Dosie's cheek but heard and felt no response. "Come on, love. I need you to answer."

Dosie's chest still heaved. Her body shook around every rigid muscle. But her mouth only lightly gaped, wordless, and her eyes wouldn't focus. They stared up, unseeing and lightless. No recognition. It was the eeriest thing Jennifer had ever seen, and it sent her stomach barreling toward her knees so fast that she almost gagged.

Traumatic responses weren't foreign to her. She'd had triggered clients before, but it had never been like this. Dosie was like a corpse beneath her now, and Jennifer was still inside her. Everything about it made her skin crawl. Worse, she didn't have a clue what the trigger was, so she didn't know what to do other than hold still for fear of jostling her lower half and making the situation worse.

"Dosie," she tried again, thumb soothing along her cheekbone. "Can you hear me?"

Nothing.

Damnit. Damnit! Jennifer did her best to keep her panic internal, but she could *feel* her heart beating, *hard*, and there were pinpricks in her eyes. *What do I do?* Dosie was near catatonic, so guided breathing was out. That left two options, both of which would require Jennifer to move, and that scared the hell out of her.

Still, she had to do something, didn't she? What if Dosie needed medical attention? What if she wasn't triggered at all but having a stroke or a fucking aneurysm? What if—*Stop. Keep your fucking head on. Focus.*

"I have to move." She kept her voice soft and measured even though she was shaking—partly because she was worried and partly because her body was still wired by their activities. The disparity dizzied her, a sick heat invading until nausea screamed in her gut. "Dosie? I need to move so I can help you. Okay? I'm going to pull out, and you're going to feel it but only for a second. Then it'll be over."

No answer.

Fuck. "Okay, here we go," Jennifer said and eased her hips back until the toy slipped free. "There. It's out. You're okay. Just hold on a little longer for me." She quickly removed the vibrator, too, and rolled it off onto the floor. She had little room to move as Dosie's grip on her hadn't relaxed in the slightest. It hurt, but the hurt didn't matter. Jennifer cared only about getting to the next part, the part where Dosie came back to her. She didn't care how much pain she had to endure to get there. "Just a little longer."

She knew she wouldn't be able to get the harness off, so she wrestled open the metal snaps at the front and pulled off the cock ring instead, the cock along with it. It too, she rolled aside. "Okay," she said as she settled herself back in place, pressed against Dosie everywhere she could be. "Okay. Come here. Come here." She wrestled her arms under Dosie's back and let her full weight drop onto her chest. "I've got you. You're safe with me, remember?" Dosie needed compression, so she squeezed her until her arms strained and she could feel the girl's heartbeat like a fist against her breast. "You're safe."

She wasn't sure speaking helped. Dosie hadn't yet responded to anything she'd said, so Jennifer stopped talking and simply held her. She held her for several long, intensely quiet moments, held and held her until it felt as if hours had gone by. And then finally, with a whimper, Dosie returned.

"Dosie?" Jennifer eased her grip. Her arms trembled with exhaustion as she lifted herself up. "Can you hear me?"

Dazed, coffee eyes blinked themselves clear then slowly darted until they connected with Jennifer's and focused. "Jennifer."

Jennifer's heart both shrank and grew in the span of that one word. Her name, broken, on Dosie's lips. "Yes, I'm here."

"What happened?"

"I don't know. I think I triggered you," Jennifer admitted, guilt flooding her gut even though it had been a genuine accident. "I'm so sorry, Dosie."

"No, it's...." Dosie shook her head, furrowed her brow. "I.... Will you let me up?"

"Of course." Jennifer rolled off her, and Dosie sat up. "Do you want to talk about it?"

"Huh?" Dosie looked back at her, expression dazing again. "What?"

"Your episode? Or...? I don't know what you prefer to call it. Do you want to talk about it, about what triggered you?"

"No, I—no."

Jennifer wanted to touch her but didn't, too afraid it might trigger Dosie again. She could soothe herself later. "What can I do? How can I help?"

Dosie visibly trembled as she raised her hands to her cheeks and wiped her tears dry. "I think I just need to go splash some water on my face." She stood, pausing once she was on her feet, and looked back. She kept her gaze from Jennifer's, focusing on the floor instead as, in a voice as sweet as it was strained, she said, "Can you be gone when I come back? Please?"

A painful shock hit Jennifer square in the chest, sending electric tremors out through her limbs, but she fought not to let it show. If that was what Dosie needed, not to be comforted by Jennifer but to be rid of her, then she would have that. "Yes," Jennifer said, voice cracking as she formed the word.

Dosie's only reply was a curt nod before she walked out of the room, leaving Jennifer naked and alone. Reeling from how quickly the night had shifted. How quickly their satisfaction had soured, their pleasure turned to plight.

Jennifer refused to cry, the stinging in her eyes yielding nothing but irritation. She refused to *feel*, as she got to her feet, shucked off her harness, and gathered her things. She dressed faster than she had in ages and was in the foyer before Dosie had even been gone five minutes.

Guilt and worry burned in her lungs like toxic smoke as she stood just inside the door, forehead digging into the wood. She didn't feel right about leaving, not when she'd seen the state Dosie was in, but she didn't feel right about staying either. Dosie had explicitly asked her to leave. Her knuckles whitened around the doorknob. She had to, didn't she? Dosie told her to go, so she needed to go. She had to go. *Go.*

Jennifer forced herself to turn the knob and stepped out into the night.

The moment she heard the door close, every ounce of tension in her body turned liquid. Dosie melted down the wall at the top of the stairs, naked and hurting in places she shouldn't. Hurting in ways she couldn't yet name or understand. *What just happened? What just happened? What just happened?*

"*Dosie-girl.*"

She spasmed and sat up, eyes wet and wide, searching for the root of the voice. That voice. It was in the walls and the ceiling, in the creak of wood beneath her. All around, she heard it, even as it echoed from within.

"*Quiet now. Quiet.*"

Dosie sobbed, batted at her ears. Her heart thundered in half-beats, and her breath burst in and out, refusing to stick or expand or soothe. A prickling erupted, screaming up the lengths of her arms until she flapped her hands furiously, desperate to rid herself of the sensation. It wouldn't go. It wouldn't stop. It wouldn't *stop*.

"*You can take it.*"

A phantom pain lanced between her legs, and she flopped onto her side. "Stop it," she howled as she pulled her knees to her chest, held them so tightly that her joints ached. "Stop," she cried into the floor, over and over until her voice fractured and fell apart.

How sleep found her like that, she'd never know.

11

The night shuddered. A nauseating glaze permeated Jennifer's surroundings as the air wobbled unnaturally around her. Every step she took felt foreign, as if her feet had gone numb. As if the ground was floating away from her, and she was helpless to keep up with its flight. Her heartbeat was a dream, a nightmare, throbbing in her fingertips and thundering in her ears.

How she managed to find her way to the car and then inside it with even a modicum of composure, she hadn't a clue. She wasn't in her body; rather, she wasn't *fitting* in her body. She wasn't comfortable in it. Everything felt too tight and too loose at once. Her senses, somehow both wired *and* dimmed, wreaked havoc on her sanity.

When the privacy screen lowered and Carolina's greeting came through, it was like an odd series of thumps against the sides of Jennifer's head, the words disappearing in notes too warped to ring clear. Not that Jennifer could have otherwise responded. Her tongue was swollen and useless. Her throat choked around nothing.

Except she *was* responding. Jennifer could feel her mouth moving, her vocal cords vibrating. Her head was nodding, crisp despite how sickly drunk she felt. It was as if she'd somehow split herself in two, half of her devoured by the wild of what she was feeling and the other half dutifully piloting her from one moment to the next.

The small part of her brain still rooted in awareness knew what was happening. This was anxiety. It was only anxiety. She wasn't ill. She wasn't dying. She was still in control. She just needed to slow her breathing. She needed to calm her heart, get a handle on her thoughts. De-stress her system.

But Dosie's dazed face was stuck in her mind like a poster plastered over a wall. Her empty eyes. Her terrifying absence. The cold shiver of her voice as she'd asked her to leave now sat in Jennifer's spine like a lightning rod—trembling and hot, stricken.

And then the flashes began.

Jennifer jabbed the button to close the privacy partition. It had barely cleared before she pitched herself forward to put her head between her knees. Her stomach rolled like a river. Her skin itched.

The hand on her back, gently pushing her toward a door the color of a robin's egg.

"No." Jennifer cringed. "No." She sucked in breath after breath, trying and failing to steady herself.

"Jennifer, I'm fine."

The voice in her head was distorted. Time had curled around it like ivy until its colors were only blips and splashes between long stretches of blankness. Nothingness. Vacancy. Still, it struck her. It rang in her like an alarm bell. It took her right back to that day.

"Come here. Give me a squish." Her sweater was scratchy against Jennifer's cheek, the bulk of it unnatural for the season. Her hand drew circles between Jennifer's shoulder blades, warm through the thin material of her old running shirt. "You know how he gets. But it's Glass. He always comes around."

The rumble of the road as the car drove along only made Jennifer's nausea worse. Her unease grew. Her eyes burned with tears she couldn't blink or will away. Her esophagus felt like it was coated in acid.

"Go on now. Get out of here." Lauren's laugh sang stiffly, as if it couldn't find the right key. "Give us some time to fuss at each other, and then we'll be good as new."

Hot and cold warred along the surface of her skin as her gut balled itself up like a fist. Sweat dappled her forehead. She gagged and jabbed the intercom. "Pull over!"

As the car lurched to the curb, Jennifer threw open her door and heaved. Spilled herself onto the asphalt shoulder. She couldn't hear herself gagging or the cars zipping by or the splatter of her vomit against the ground. She couldn't hear the words on Carolina's moving lips or feel the fingers she could see curling around her arm. The only noise in Jennifer's ears, in her mind—the only sound in the world—was a phone ringing. Ringing and ringing and ringing. No static. No greeting. Just an endless ringing that had haunted her for years.

"Jennifer."

Fingers snapped harshly in her face. She winced, cried before she could stop herself. It was devastated, deep, ejecting from her body the same way the splatter on the ground had done, and then all the world rushed back in again. Rapid bursts of color, sound, sensation.

Carolina was squatted on the side of the road in the open door of the town car, Jennifer's vomit pooled between her polished shoes. She had one hand braced on her knee and the other cuffing Jennifer's arm. "Hey, you good? You get carsick or something?" Another sob lurched up and out, and Carolina's eyes stretched wide as Jennifer capped a palm over her bitter breath. "What the hell, Jen? What is wrong? Tell me right now. Are you sick? Are you in pain?" She grabbed Jennifer's other hand and squeezed, *hard*, right over her pressure point. Instantly, Jennifer's heart began to calm. "Get your shit together and talk to me right now or I'm taking you to the hospital."

Jennifer let her hand fall from her mouth. "There was an incident."

"An incident? You mean with Fisher?" Carolina's voice took on an edge. "Is that why you came flying out the way you did? What did she do? Are you hurt? Did she hurt you?"

"No."

"Did she try something without your consent?"

"No, no, nothing like that," Jennifer said and turned her hand in Carolina's so she could send a reassuring squeeze back. "You know I'd have called you if I felt unsafe."

"Do you want to tell me what happened then?"

"I…." Jennifer's mind filled with that image again—Dosie beneath her, alive, *ecstatic* with pleasure, then still, so very *still.* Saliva flooded her mouth as a fresh wave of nausea stirred. Every cell in her body screamed for her to go back, to check on Dosie, to make sure she was safe. Fix whatever she'd done to cause that awful stillness. Those empty eyes. That quiet plea for her to leave.

Go back. Go back. Go back.

Instead, Jennifer forced a slow, long breath then eased back into her seat. "No, it's nothing," she said. "I'm good. I'm okay." Another breath. She pretended not to hear Carolina's frustrated sigh. "We should be getting home." She pretended not to hear the door slam. "Thank you for checking on me," she muttered into its echo. She pretended she wasn't exposed and raw and scared out of her fucking mind.

She could still hear the phone ringing.

Maybe it had never stopped.

Crimson and purple crescent moons dappled her hips, perfect impressions of Dosie Fisher's fingernails. Jennifer dabbed at them as she stood naked in front of her mirror, the bright lights of her bathroom shining down. The cotton ball she'd soaked in peroxide was cool to the touch. It soothed and stung at the same time.

Her reflection stared back at her with tormented eyes, and Jennifer hated it so much she couldn't stand to look. The cotton ball fell from her hand as she gripped the edge of the sink. Panic brewed quickly in her chest, a simmer to a boil in no time at all. "Oh fuck." She hadn't experienced this much anxiety in years. Her chest felt like it was going to explode. "Fuck. *Fuck.*" The room spun. "What did you do?" The air swooped. "What did you fucking *do*?"

She gritted her teeth and bowed her head, forced her breath to slow until the spinning dwindled to a gentle sway. Jennifer told herself everything was okay. She was okay. Nothing terrible had happened. Nothing terrible *would* happen. Dosie was fine. Jennifer was fine. They were both fine. Everything was fine.

She told herself again as she left the bathroom and turned off all the lights. She told herself again as she slid into bed. She told herself again and again as she lay awake in the dark, knowing she wouldn't sleep.

Four days.

Dosie stared at the shadows on the wall as the light waned, watched them grow long and odd until they devoured the last of her bedroom's afternoon glow, and she was left in the dark again. Four days had passed since her episode with Jennifer, and Dosie hadn't been able to drag herself out of bed for any purpose other than relieving herself and forcing a bit of food down her throat. She had just enough presence of mind to know to maintain the most basic functions of survival. Beyond that, she was a ghost. Not the haunted, roaming, unsettled kind, but the trapped kind, incapable of shifting from the shock of whatever trauma had led to their passing.

It wasn't the first time something like this had happened. Discovering new triggers was always hard, especially when they brought buried memories to the surface. Dosie had many carved into her like trenches, filled over the years with loose dirt and rain until they'd been mostly hidden, innocuous—her mind's attempt at obscuring what it could not process or purge. Her early years of therapy, right after she'd left the compound, had been like navigating a minefield. No keen noses sniffing out dangers. No detection. No aid.

Every blast stunned, tore that obscurity away like skin stripped from bone. Awareness. The awareness of what had been done to her. The awareness of things that she had experienced and seen and learned. That awareness was mad-hot and violent and sometimes, in some ways, worse than the enduring had been. Clarity gave her horror where she'd once had normalcy, and Dosie had been certain, at times, that she would not survive the shift in perspective.

Nearly three years had passed since the last time Dosie stumbled onto a new trigger, since the last time a memory as cutting and raw as *that one* had jumped through her bones like fire and crept like ice into her veins. The warring sensations bewildered her body, overwhelmed it, and she ended up trapped in a state of inaction. She couldn't move, couldn't think. Could *only* think. Could only panic. Could only struggle to breathe or wait to die, or both.

She knew it would pass. Her own history was proof. She could survive this, this feeling, this echo that wouldn't stop cycling about her brain. She just had to get herself to snap out of it. Out of the memory. Out of the past. Out of the pain.

"*Dosie-girl.*"

A shudder scored Dosie's spine. Her eyes snapped shut as she forced a breath. "It's not real," she murmured to herself, nose not even wrinkling at the foul scent of her breath wafting up. She was accustomed by now. For four days, she hadn't showered or brushed her teeth or picked the crust from her eyes. She'd done nothing but lay in her bed and stay alive, listen to herself cry. "It's not real."

She was desperate for sleep. She was also terrified of it.

"*You can take it.*"

And so, the cycle continued, and Dosie burned and froze and stank and *sank*. And stayed right where she was.

The sky was cloudless and painted with sunset. Weeds crept up her calves and over her knees, ticked under the hems of her terry-cloth shorts. Dosie had finally dragged herself out of bed but not out of the past; in fact, she now stood waist-deep in it. No one had been to this part of the property in years. Dosie hadn't either, not since *that* day. The last day. The worst and best day of her life—the day she'd lost everything and gained an entire world.

Even when Dosie had bought the property, committed herself to replacing old horrors with new happiness, she'd not been able to go certain places. Never past the old stump. Down the dirt path, now grassed and bushy. Out to the place where she'd been born and where, fifteen years later, she'd died as well; at least, part of her had. Why she'd felt compelled to go there on *this* day, after however many hours, weeks, *months* she'd spent in bed, she didn't know. Except that the past seemed to have taken the place of her pulse, and she felt owned by the rhythm of it.

The field was wide open and severely overgrown, nothing like how it used to be, but the air still vibrated with energy. It crept into Dosie's lungs as she stared out at weeds and sky and saw the past transposed over emptiness, so vivid she felt as if she could reach out and feel wood. Brass. As if she could turn a knob and open a door, smell the hot, woodsy scent of burning white sage and frankincense and myrrh.

A warmth bloomed in her chest, every delicate edge of it tainted with dread.

Screaming.

Her mother was screaming.

Dosie heard it like a distant storm, something just at the

edge of her consciousness, of her senses. It pulled at her back, tugged at her gut.

Her father's voice. "Do not run!" The shine of metal around his waist. "Do NOT run!"

Dosie winced as a dull popping crackled in her ears like static.

Screaming.

"Quiet now, Dosie-girl. So, so quiet. It'll all be finished soon."

The lump in her throat suffocated her. Dosie gagged as her legs gave out, as thick grass and bramble poked and prodded and swallowed her, hid her from the world she was desperate to crawl her way back to. Her thoughts scattered, memories bleeding into other memories faster than she could sort them, and she could do nothing to stop it. She could only hold on for dear life as her world spun, shifted yet again on its axis, and flung her about the dark vastness of space.

"Dosie?"

Dosie blinked and found herself in the overgrown field again, nothing but swaying weeds and Natalie's face right in front of her. "Natalie? Are you really here?"

"Yeah, I'm here, Dose." Natalie's hands were clammy around Dosie's cheeks. "Feel me? Can you stand up?"

"No." The ground was firm. It was the only thing keeping her from spinning off into nothing, into *everything*. "No."

"Okay." Natalie swatted away weeds and a few thorny bits and sat. "You need a mower, dude. If you hadn't trampled all this down coming out here, I probably wouldn't have even found you. Your yard is freaking massive."

"Yeah." Dosie still felt dazed, *gripped.* Her limbs were numb but tight. Every nerve, tweaked and relaxed at the same time.

"Are you okay?" Natalie's hand found Dosie's knee. "What are you doing out here?"

Dosie shook her head. "I don't know. I can't remember."

"Okay. Is there something out here that you were maybe looking for? Can I help?"

Dosie frowned. "What are you doing here?"

"I came to check on you."

"Check on me? Why?"

"Your therapist called me. I'm your emergency contact, remember? She said you missed two appointments."

"Oh."

"And that you weren't taking her calls. When you didn't answer mine either, I just decided to come out. I'm glad I did. Dose? Can you look at me?"

The haze fractured at the crack in Natalie's voice, and Dosie felt herself slide fully into her body again like liquid filling a container—a jarring rush. Tears dropped from her lashes as she blinked herself more aware, and when she focused on the face in front of her, she found it.

"Hey." Natalie's broken voice shook itself into a relieved laugh that Dosie felt in her bones. "Hey, there you are. Oh, fuck man, that scared the fuck out of me."

Dosie latched onto Natalie's hands. A second later, she

was in her arms, in her lap, clinging like a koala. As if a dam had buckled, everything raging inside her spilled out with a fury. She cried so hard her body shook, so hard her breath broke every sound into something desperate and dying.

"It's okay," Natalie promised, holding her tight. "Everything's going to be okay. You know you're safe, right? Can you say that?"

"I'm safe."

"Do you believe that? Say it 'til you believe it, Dose. I'm not going anywhere."

Dosie said it until her tongue felt numb. *I'm safe. I'm safe. I'm safe.* She said it until her breath found its rhythm again, until her heart slowed. She said it until she believed it, and all the while, Natalie sat with her, holding her and letting herself be held in return, promising security and connection and care.

Dosie sniffled as she found her way back to herself, wiped her eyes and leaned her forehead against Natalie's. "Thank you, best friend."

"Always, best pal." Natalie patted her back. "Now, are you ready for help?"

With a heavy sigh of relief, Dosie nodded. "Please."

"Okay." She crawled to her feet and pulled Dosie up with her. "Let's go call your therapist, dude." She laced their fingers together and headed in the direction of the house. "Should we order some food?" she asked, grinning. "Being the hero of someone else's emotional crisis always makes me hungry."

A laugh burst from Dosie's lips, and a tremulous thread of joy knotted itself around her heart.

Jennifer made her way through the lobby of the Hyatt Regency with ease. Several of her clients, past and present, worked in the financial district, so she was familiar with the area's hotels and bars. The Hyatt was a popular choice, and Jennifer made an impressive number of men weep into their crisp, white sheets.

Carolina walked sedately beside her as they made for the elevator. Neither said a word. It had been that way for days, at least ten since Jennifer got her shit together enough to get back to work. The woman was reliably professional, but her blunted, clipped greetings and detached client rundowns raked at Jennifer in all the places she was already raw. The little distance they'd devoured over their time working together crept back between them as if it had never gone, and Jennifer hated it.

She knew why it was happening. She'd had the opportunity to *share* (as friends supposedly did with each other), to ask Carolina for help and accept it, and instead she'd shut her out. She wanted to apologize; at least, part of her did. Part of her wanted to explain herself, confess what happened that night, and why it had bothered her so much. Part of her wanted to say so much, *ask* so much, find her way to those benefits of friendship she was always hearing about. But the other side of her, the parts that were colder, sharper, more logical, more *cynical*, recoiled from even the idea.

Jennifer was starting to wonder if her insides would ever harmonize again. The constant discord disrupted everything so that nothing felt satisfying. Nothing felt good. Nothing felt right or safe or stable. She needed it to let up.

In the elevator, Carolina broke the silence. "Client's name is Carson." She cleared her throat. "*Mrs.* Carson. You good with that?"

The urge to *talk* hit Jennifer like a brick. Instead, she licked her teeth and nodded. "Why wouldn't I be?"

"You haven't had a female client since—You know what, nope. Not my business." Carolina huffed, and Jennifer's chest felt like a house of cards caught in the breeze. "It's a two-hour appointment, as I'm sure you saw on the agenda. I'll drop you at the door then wait at the bar in the lounge. You need anything, you know what to do. You've got your Panic, right?"

The small light overhead flicked, seventeen to eighteen. "Carolina...."

"What? You forgot it?"

"No. I have it."

The elevator dinged with their arrival to the nineteenth floor. "This is us."

Jennifer swallowed whatever it was she wanted to say, still unsure, and stepped through the opening doors. She firmed her spine and set her jaw. Summoning the Director and finding comfort in her fortitude. "On your lead then."

As she followed Carolina down the hall, she cycled

through memories of prior sessions. Times when she'd felt powerful, when she'd been flying high on a job exceedingly well done, when clients had thanked her for helping them as if she'd descended from the heavens. Times when she felt like her job had genuine purpose, the ability to help people, to ease an anxiety or mend a marriage or even save a life—maybe not in ways that made her a hero in most people's eyes but that mattered, nonetheless. Times when she hadn't fucked up but had shined.

By the time they reached their destination, she was better. She strutted the last few steps, feeling not quite ten feet tall, but maybe six and a half, six and three-quarters. She felt sexy, at least, though she often felt that. Still, her gunmetal gray leather pants and steel blue bowtie neck blouse were working for her, and the Ferragamo pumps gave her another few inches to add to her confidence. But then Carolina knocked, and the door swung open as if triggered, and every bit of Jennifer's swagger stuttered, suffocated, and died.

Dosie Fisher stood in the open doorway like a perfect cardboard cutout of a 1950s trophy wife. Twisted back in a smooth, braided knot, her hair sat centered at the back of her head and gleamed in the hall's fluorescent lighting. Her apricot swing dress had a white cape collar and matching cuffs to end its three-quarter-length sleeves, and there wasn't a wink of a wrinkle to be found in the fabric. In fact, it appeared to have been starched to the point of inflexibility. Her long legs were bare but shiny, as if freshly moisturized, and on her feet, she wore apricot pumps, just as lustrous. Little makeup adorned her face, just enough to soften her features, and around her neck sat, unsurprisingly, her pearl necklace.

She looked like a doll, stood just as stiffly, and as gorgeous as she was, the sight of her done up this way caused a pang in Jennifer's chest that vibrated out through her body like an electromagnetic pulse. She felt fried and stupid and numb and *broken*, and she barely registered a thing that followed. Not Carolina's greeting or the words exchanged. Not steps or sounds or scents, just one minute, she was floating, drifting, dazed, and the next, she was closed inside a hotel room with a beautiful, trembling girl who both looked like herself and didn't.

"Hi."

Jennifer took a breath, tried to steady herself on the exhale. "Hi," she said. "You're here."

"I was advised to get out of my house for a few days," Dosie said, and she sounded just the way she had the night Jennifer met her. Small. Bottled. Trapped somewhere inside herself with only her voice echoing up from the deep. "By my therapist."

"Oh." Jennifer's stomach lurched. The hairs on the back of her neck stood. "Because of what happened?"

"Yeah."

"Oh."

"Yeah."

Jennifer swallowed her questions and moved, closing the

gap between them. She didn't touch, didn't know if she should or could. She just needed to be closer, close enough to feel Dosie's warmth. See her every little tick of movement.

It was Dosie who broke the last barrier, her hand finding a home on Jennifer's bicep. Then higher. She cupped Jennifer's cheek, said, "You look beautiful," and it felt like a door opening.

"I was worried about you," Jennifer whispered. "I'm still worried about you."

Dosie answered with a sad, breathy laugh—sweet but too empty, too lifeless to be hers. Her body still stood too stiffly, as if she couldn't bring herself to relax, as if she was afraid to, and her tame smile never reached her eyes. God, she looked tired.

"I know," she said. "Your assistant called me three times to see if I wanted to make an appointment. I have the voicemails to prove it."

"Oh." Heat flooded Jennifer's chest. "Right. That."

"How do you think I found out you never check your appointment details? I think Candace likes me."

Understanding dawned. "Mrs. Carson. Right." Then she frowned. "But why a fake name? Why wouldn't you want me to know it was you? It's not like I wouldn't have taken the appointment." She grimaced. *Three fucking calls from my assistant. God damn it.* "Obviously."

"It's not a fake name," Dosie said. "Carson was my married name. Zeb. Zebadiah Carson. That was my husband's name."

"Oh." Jennifer didn't know how to feel about that; her stomach sank regardless.

"And the reason is complicated. I'm not sure I understand it myself yet. I didn't want you to come here knowing it was me, because I—I don't know—I didn't want you to come with expectations."

"Expectations?"

"For how things would be between us, I guess. For us to be, well, *us*. I'm sorry. That sounds like an *us*-us, and I know we're not. But—"

"Yeah," Jennifer said, thumbing Dosie's mouth to prevent a spiral. "I get it."

"I can't be me right now," Dosie whispered, "and I can't be us, because I can't talk about what happened yet, and I know we need to. I know you'll say we need to before we do anything, but..."

Yes, as loath as Jennifer was to have any manner of emotional conversation, some things required discussion. If nothing else, she needed to know what she'd done, the trigger she'd tripped that had ruptured their delicate *whatever* and left them with only debris. How could she possibly have sex with Dosie without knowing the trigger? What if it happened again? She'd gone over it a thousand times in her head and still didn't know, but then, she wasn't sure she even remembered everything she'd said or done in the heat of the moment.

"...I just can't yet. I hope that's okay. If not, I'll understand."

Jennifer's worries locked in her throat, held in place by Dosie's pleading eyes and the tension in her frame. She forced them down—all her reservations, concerns, *guilt*—and nodded, and when Dosie's shoulders sagged with relief, she knew she'd made the right choice.

She took Dosie's hand, braided their fingers together. "Tell me what you need."

Dosie was certain that *this* was not what her therapist meant when she'd told her to get away for a few days. Out of her house? Yes. To a different city? Sure. To a hotel? Fine. To a hotel where she would pay for sex with the woman who'd, unfortunately, helped her discover the latest trigger to disrupt her life? Eh, it likely wouldn't have made the list of advisable behaviors if presented as an option in session.

What, exactly, she was searching for or why she thought she would find it in sex with Jennifer Dupont, she didn't know. So far, all she had was a half-assed, half-written plan and a huge risk of triggering herself again while already in a vulnerable state, but.... *I don't care.* She was doing the work, would always do the work, to tend to and mend her wounds, but sometimes, she just needed to feel what she felt in whatever reckless, ugly, or messy way she felt it.

Hand in hand, she led Jennifer through the large hotel room, switching off lights as they passed so that only the city's glow through the window remained. At the foot of her large, temporary bed, she turned and put her back to Jennifer. If she was going to get through this, she couldn't see Jennifer's face. She felt too many things looking into Jennifer's eyes. Good things, *wonderful* things. Maybe that was what she needed, but it wasn't what she wanted—not when she felt this way—broken, tainted, desperate, *hopeful*.

"I don't want you to try to take my clothes off," she whispered and felt Jennifer sidle up behind her, her chest to Dosie's back. Her hands settled on Dosie's hips. "Don't kiss me on the mouth."

Jennifer's thick swallow was audible. "Okay."

"Just stay like this, okay?"

"Okay." Jennifer didn't move but for a slight tremble working the length of her. Dosie could feel it at every place their bodies connected. "What else?"

"I want you to put your fingers inside me." She closed her eyes, relieved the words came out unhindered. She'd practiced this part, at least. It was hard for her to say things that felt—as her father used to say—like "wicked words." Vulgar words. Sinful ones. She said them anyway and felt proud of herself.

"I want you to make it hurt," she said and felt Jennifer stiffen. Heard her breath catch. But no protest was made. No argument. "I want you to make me feel so much that I forget who I am."

"May I say something before we begin?" The hands at her hips slid up to her waist. One palm flattened over Dosie's stomach and tugged, fitting her ass into the bend of Jennifer's body. When Dosie nodded, Jennifer kissed the back of her ear and said, "You are still safe with me. No matter what happens, you are always safe with me."

The words struck a chord deep in Dosie's chest and, for a moment, she felt the resonance of it vibrate her shadows into softer, kinder shapes. She sank fully against Jennifer's chest, the only answer she could give. She knew it would be enough.

Per Dosie's instructions, Jennifer didn't attempt to undress her. Silent as the grave, she hiked Dosie's dress to the juncture of her thigh, shoved her panties to the side, and roughly pressed her dry clit. It twinged, an uncomfortable pleasure that shot her breath from her lungs. Jennifer scratched through Dosie's pubic hair then slid between her labia and spread them open like a book she wanted to read.

"Do you want a safe word?"

Dosie bit her lip. Her stomach twisted itself into a knot. "Dosie-girl."

For a moment, Jennifer froze. But then she mouthed Dosie's neck, sucking and tasting her, and carried on with her work—fingers mapping Dosie's vulva as if memorizing it. And Dosie felt dirty. She felt awful and gross and excited and safe, and she wanted, she *needed*, more. A shout tore from her lips when Jennifer suddenly pinched her clit, a zap of pain pinging around her pelvis. The shout leveled into a thick, throaty moan, and Dosie flushed with humiliation. She'd never imagined she might want something like this—she'd had enough torment to last a lifetime—but *God*, she did. She was desperate to replace the pains she'd never wanted with ones she'd asked for, ones she could receive and bear on her own terms. At any moment, if she wanted this to stop, it *would*. She could whisper, and it would be done. That one little name that had haunted her all her life could be her saving grace rather than her nightmare.

She stumbled forward as Jennifer rubbed over the swell of her ass then hiked her dress again from the back. Dosie's hands found the windowpane and braced as her panties were tugged open from another angle, and two of Jennifer's long fingers probed her from behind. Then they were inside. Her vagina stretched around the sudden invasion with a searing jolt of pain, and Dosie let out a vicious cry. A breath later, pleasure followed. It was odd pleasure, pleasure hollowed out and filled with agony, and it felt incredible.

"More," she demanded, and Jennifer withdrew to the tips to thrust in again. Her other hand began a brutal rhythm over Dosie's clit, fast, tight circles that threatened to tear the thing off. And make Dosie see stars. She was dripping in no time and delirious with need. "*More.*"

The fingers abusing her clit dropped to her cunt where Jennifer's other hand pumped with abandon, and Dosie's lungs faltered. Her heart stalled. *Is she going to—*

Dosie collapsed into the window with a strangled gasp as Jennifer wriggled two more fingers inside her vagina. Two from the front. Two from the back. She was open wide and feverish hot. The cool glass mashed against her cheek did little to soothe. And all the while, the woman stoking her heat said nothing, only panted against her neck. Every breath was like a static shock, heightening Dosie's pleasure.

That pleasure transcended to overwhelm when Jennifer's thumb roughly probed her asshole. Dosie howled as the thumb pushed inside and immediately picked up the rhythm of Jennifer's other fingers. She whined and rutted against Jennifer's wrist, slotted between the window and her own swollen vulva. It provided an incredible amount of pressure against her clit, and with the simultaneous invasion of her cunt and ass, Dosie found herself speeding toward some awesome, terrible inevitability. She had no idea what it was, because it had to be too massive, too much, to be orgasm. She wasn't sure she *could* come at this point. She was so wet, so full, so overstimulated, that there could be no focus or rhythm or thought. Everything hurt and everything felt amazing, and she didn't care if she came or not. She didn't care if she never caught her breath again if it meant this would continue. Her muscles cinched around every digit, locking them in place, milking them for more—more pain, more pleasure, more *everything* until it obliterated her. She wanted to be drunk on it. Wasted. *Gone.*

She came.

It didn't hit like a wave but a rupture, right at the core of her, pressure building and releasing at the same time until the rupture gave way. She lost all ability to function as her vision went white and she spasmed. Her vagina clamped viciously around Jennifer's trapped fingers until she heard the woman groan behind her, then at the slightest expansion, they were gone. In one swift move, Jennifer pulled out of her, all five fingers that had been buried inside, and Dosie shouted so hard and so loud that she was certain someone would call the front desk to report a possible violent crime. A warm jet of liquid spurted out of her, chasing Jennifer's fingers, and soaked through her panties and down one thigh. She heard Jennifer's gasp followed by a low, pleased moan at her ear, and then, with a whimper, Dosie collapsed.

Jennifer felt it the moment Dosie's legs gave out and quickly scooped her up, both arms looped around her middle. "I have you," she said and pressed her fully to the window, molded against her back. She lay her forehead against the glass beside Dosie, their breaths fogging in circles close enough to merge, and resisted the impulse to nuzzle her.

Little pops of sound punctuated Dosie's breaths, whines and whimpers and grunts as she trembled down from her peak. "I feel like there's a hammer between my legs."

"I'm not surprised. That was an impressive climax."

Everything had been impressive. From the moment Dosie had opened her mouth and demanded her pleasure, told Jennifer exactly what she'd needed and how she needed it, Jennifer had been stricken and off-center and *proud* and hot, and now she was also sopping wet and *aching*.

"Normally, I would be embarrassed to ask you this," Dosie panted, and Jennifer tensed, "but I'm not sure I'm even alive anymore, so I'm just going to ask. Did I pee on you? Because it didn't *exactly* feel like I was peeing, but it also kind of felt like I was peeing."

"Oh." Jennifer snorted. The sound bloomed into a laugh. "I'm sorry. I was just bracing myself for something bad. No, love, you didn't pee on me. You ejaculated."

Dosie made a choked sound at the back of her throat. "Excuse you," she said, and Jennifer laughed even harder. "Has that happened to you before?"

"To me personally, or to one of my clients?"

"Either? Both."

"Yes, and yes."

"Oh. Is it that common?"

"I wouldn't say common, but I wouldn't say *uncommon* either. Perfectly natural either way. How did it feel?"

"Intense." Neither turned toward the other, both with their foreheads to the window, eyes on the city outside, but their cheeks brushed. Dosie's hair tickled at her ear. "A little scary. I think I stopped breathing." She squeezed Jennifer's forearms. "I'm glad I didn't pee on you."

"Me too."

"It was amazing." Her cheek pressed a bit harder, and Jennifer closed her eyes. Enjoyed it. "Thank you."

"Was it what you needed?"

"Yes."

Jennifer's body buzzed. Her brain prickled, still hormone-flooded and hyper aware of every connecting point of their bodies. She could feel the comfort Dosie found in her arms, even if she wasn't voicing it, even if neither would ever acknowledge it, and the words spilled onto her tongue before she could stop them. "I didn't want to go. That night."

"I know."

"I felt sick for days after I left," Jennifer admitted in a whisper. "I couldn't stop thinking I should have stayed. I should have...." She calmed when she felt Dosie's nose bump against her cheek, her breath puff across Jennifer's face instead of the glass.

"I'm okay," Dosie promised and kissed Jennifer's jaw.

"Are you?" Jennifer held her tighter. "Really?"

"No." Dosie's lips rubbed over her jaw again, not quite a kiss but something. A touch. Reassurance. "But I will be. It just takes time. And therapy." She sighed. "Lots of extra therapy lately."

"Will you tell me what the trigger was?"

"No," she said with such ease that Jennifer couldn't help but be proud despite the way her stomach lurched at the answer. She was being shut out. Jennifer knew the importance of respecting boundaries. It was the foundation of her career after all. But there was that little voice in the back of her head, the one that sounded so much like her sister.

"Jennifer, I'm fine."

There was the ringing that wouldn't stop, spilling into her head at random times of the day and night. It pushed at her own boundaries and begged her to override them all. Everyone else's, too, if it would assuage this constant pressure in her chest. She didn't. *Wouldn't.* She'd never violated another person's autonomy, and she had no intention to start. The ringing could fuck off and take her whole past with it.

"I'm still processing it is all."

Oh. See? Stop fucking jumping to conclusions. Jennifer forced a breath. "Right. Okay."

"It's late," Dosie whispered, and Jennifer's minor relief plummeted to its death. She knew a dismissal when she heard one. "I should try to get some sleep."

Jennifer eased off her, glanced at her watch. Only an hour had gone by, the second hanging in front of them like ripe fruit they wouldn't pluck. She gave a hum of acceptance and slipped away to the bathroom to wash her hands; thankfully, it was her only task since she hadn't undressed. The last time they'd been together, the awkwardness of being dismissed while naked and harnessed had left a sour taste in Jennifer's mouth, and she wasn't keen to have such an experience again. Even the thought made her ill.

When she returned, Dosie was neat again, if slightly wrinkled. She fiddled with her fingers at her waist for a moment then hid them behind her back. It was too dark to see her blush, but Jennifer could picture it perfectly in her mind. "I wanted to tell you that it isn't your fault," she said. "What happened at my house and what's happening now, none of it is about you, okay?"

Jennifer's throat tightened. "Okay."

"People forget sometimes that seeing someone else's

trauma can be a kind of trauma itself. Especially when you, um, when you care about the person."

A shiver ran Jennifer's spine. She did care about Dosie. How could she not? Here the girl was, actively traumatized and still making sure that *Jennifer* was okay. God, yes, *yes*, of course Jennifer fucking cared about her. As if that word, that idea, could even begin to approach what she felt for Dosie Fisher. *Fuck. Fuuuck.*

"And when you're, you know, involved, the way you were when it happened," Dosie continued then huffed at herself. "I'm sorry. I really don't want to talk about this, but I need to make sure you know that it wasn't your fault, and you didn't do anything wrong."

Jennifer's eyes burned and watered. She knew if she tried to speak, her voice would crack, so she nodded instead and watched relief nearly drop Dosie to the floor. She walked on wobbly legs at Jennifer's side all the way to the door, and neither said a word. They didn't even touch. Somehow, Jennifer still found it comforting.

"I'll see you tomorrow then," Dosie said as she opened the door, and Jennifer felt a jolt in her chest. *Another booking?* She knew she had a booking the next night but hadn't checked the name. *Carson*, she now expected she'd find. Jennifer masked her surprised and nodded, left Dosie's hotel room with her body still humming and a strange sense of dread swirling in her gut.

When she entered the hotel lounge, she spotted Carolina immediately. Rather than wave her over to leave, Jennifer crossed to the bar and sat beside her. "Your best single malt," she said as the bartender arrived. "Neat. Thank you." She glanced to Carolina. "Do you want something?"

Carolina held up her soda. "I'm good."

"Do you want something alcoholic?"

"I don't drink on nights I drive."

The bartender placed Jennifer's drink in front of her, and right away, Jennifer was tempted to down it, the quickest way to get it into her system and start the process of numbing her senses. But the thought of wasting quality whisky by treating it like a cheap shot made her cringe, so *no*. She would savor it and calm herself down naturally. Maybe she could also find a way to blunt the edge she'd whittled between herself and Carolina.

The whisky was smooth and oaky and went down like warm butter, and Jennifer closed her eyes in relief. The comfort of something familiar. "I'm not good at this," she admitted as she set the glass back on the bar, rotated it between her fingers. "Having friends. Being a friend. I don't do friendships. I don't do relationships of any kind, really." Saying the words made her itch. She hated feeling exposed in this way. "If I'm honest, I find the idea of being voluntarily vulnerable with others borderline excruciating. In a non-sexual way, at least."

"I'm not going to have sex with you, Jennifer," Carolina

said and sipped her soda. "No matter how much you beg, so you might as well let go of that dream now."

Dear fucking God. Jennifer snorted through a laugh and dropped her head into her hands. She was going to need another drink; several, in fact. However many drinks might allow her to, as Dosie had sought to do, forget who she was—that was how many drinks Jennifer needed. If for only an hour or two, she could forget her life, forget her fears, forget every ridiculous feeling wriggling about her insides like a tangled, teeming blob of parasitic worms, then maybe she would.... *I have no fucking clue, but it has to be better than this. I can't keep feeling like this. I can't. I can't.*

"You okay?"

"No," Jennifer admitted and took another drink. "I'm trying to say I'm sorry for shutting you out. I don't know how to be a friend."

"Yeah." Carolina's gaze remained with the lounge's small crowd, shifting from one occupied chair to the next. Jennifer knew little about the woman outside of work, but she did know that before Carolina went into private security, she'd been military. It showed, not only in the way she held herself, but in her alertness. "I figured that out about you a long time ago."

Jennifer laid a hand on her arm. "Will you let me try anyway?"

The waiting, a bubble of silence growing around them in the middle of a murmuring room, was torture. But then Carolina turned in her seat, knees bumping against Jennifer's, and rested her elbow on the bar. Found Jennifer's eyes. "So, *Mrs. Carson*, huh?" Her mouth tugged up at one corner. "What's that all about?"

A rich laugh bubbled up Jennifer's throat, and all the tension she'd been holding onto released. "It was her husband's name, apparently."

"Uh huh, and what's *that* all about?"

"He died."

"Oh. Well, damn. How?"

Jennifer frowned. "I don't know, actually."

"It wasn't in her book?"

"I still haven't read it all. The worse things get, the more breaks I have to take."

"Is it graphic?"

"Not really." Jennifer downed the rest of her drink. "She doesn't go into much detail about the abuses. She doesn't have to. It's easy to imagine. Terrible but easy. I think it's more because it's her. It's horrifying, all of it, but I picture *her*, specifically, enduring it, and I...." God, she hated this. She felt like she'd been skinned alive, and all her nerves were exposed, but she ignored the instinct to fight it. To cover herself up again. "I can't breathe when I think about her life there," she confessed. "I get lightheaded and dizzy and sick to my fucking stomach, and I have to stop."

Carolina didn't say anything for a moment, just offering a smile that Jennifer couldn't quite read—something tossed between amusement and pity. Or maybe it was something else entirely. Maybe Jennifer was projecting. Then: "I see."

"You see? See what?"

"Now, what would be the fun in telling you that?"

Jennifer gaped. "Really?" She raised her hand to call the bartender again. "This is friendship? You *not* helping?"

"Who says I'm not helping?"

"Oh, shut up." As she watched the bartender refill her whisky and listened to Carolina's teasing laugh, she remembered something. She looked at the woman beside her. "You said I was going to ruin her."

Carolina's laugh fizzled as she frowned. "That was forever ago," she said. "And you know I didn't mean it like that."

"No, I know. It's fine. I just...." Jennifer's eyes watered as she palmed her refilled whisky tight enough to test the glass. "It's *me* who's been ruined, Carolina." A wet, hollow laugh jumped free as she choked back tears. "She's ruined me."

12

Dosie stood in front of the large mirror mounted on her hotel room's wall. The red-and-white plaid halter swing dress she wore—or as Natalie had once dubbed it, her "sexy tablecloth dress"—was one of her favorites. It fit snugly around her waist and breasts and had a flattering flare at the hips, and though it had taken her years to build up the courage to wear it, she'd always felt pretty in it; more than that, she'd felt *hot*. But as she waited for the Director's knock, she instead felt faint. The dress's tight embrace choked her, and she watched in horror as her exposed arms and shoulders bloated into odd, oblong shapes in the mirror. The scars on her upper back writhed as if they'd come alive, and she was certain that if she could see them, they'd be doused in neon and set alight like fireflies.

She knew what was happening. Her therapy session that day had been particularly brutal. Fifty minutes of uprooting herself, digging through her past for all the shrapnel left behind and overlooked. Some pieces took longer to become symptomatic, and they were harder to pin down. Harder to clarify. Often, they were harder to face as well.

Every time she discovered a new trigger, she had to adjust her schedule. Her therapy sessions increased in frequency and left her dehydrated and tired and irritable. Sated, though, which made all the difference. It still surprised her, years into it, the relief each session provided even when it was frustrating or hard. Or painful. That bit of purging never failed to make it easier to breathe, easier to stand up straight. The sick feeling waned. The shadows crackled around light.

When the knock finally came, Dosie shot for the door in her bare feet. "You're fine," she muttered to herself, clutching her pearl necklace harder with every step. "No. You're better than fine. You're great. You're *excited.* This dress looks freaking amazing on you. Hi!"

As always, Jennifer Dupont was a breathtaking sight. She stood arm in arm with her security detail and looked effortless in her shredded black skinny jeans and crisp white tee. Her jacket was military-style, the same black as her denim and her studded-leather ankle boots. Her dark hair was secured in a shiny, slicked French braid, and though she wore a bit of makeup, Dosie could see faint shadows under her eyes. Had she not slept? Was that because of *her*?

Dosie felt a pulling in her chest. She wanted to ask, wanted to know. She wanted to say she was sorry, even if she had nothing to apologize for. *Do I? Have I done something wrong?*

Once everyone was greeted, Jennifer stepped inside, and Dosie closed and chained the door behind her. The moment the chain stopped rattling, the room plunged into a silence so consuming and awkward that it made Dosie's skin prickle. It made her spine cringe. Oh, she didn't like this. No. Their rhythm was off. It felt wrong, like they were trying to connect from opposite sides of a concrete wall. It had been the same the night before, but then, Dosie had needed it. Now, she wanted it the way it used to be, the way *they* used to be. But she couldn't ask for that, *shouldn't*.

Don't.

She didn't. She walked Jennifer through to the bed as she'd done the night before, nixing any source of light along the way. At the foot of her bed, in only the glow of the city, she forced her nerve and grabbed Jennifer by the open edges of her jacket and drew her close. *Don't*, she warned herself again, but she was already trapped in the lure of Jennifer's eyes, the hint of peppermint on her breath.

"We didn't kiss last night," she whispered. "I miss it."

Jennifer closed the gap, nudged the tip of Dosie's nose with hers and seemed as comforted by the touch as Dosie was. *Stop. Don't.* "We hardly spoke or saw each other at all."

"I know." Dosie framed her cheek. "I'm sorr—"

"No, don't. Please. Don't apologize."

"But things feel weird between us."

"Shh." She looped Dosie's waist to melt their bodies together, rubbed the tip of her nose again. "Just kiss me."

"Jennifer."

A shudder moved through Jennifer's body and into Dosie's. "Kiss me and tell me what you need."

Dosie muffled her moan with Jennifer's mouth, kissing her hard enough to feel her own teeth digging into her lip. But Jennifer was there, taking her measure and adjusting it, commanding it to control itself. She slowed their kiss to a smooth glide of wet flesh, the occasional flick and taste. It was deep and intoxicating but easy too. Just slow enough to be natural and somehow both satisfying and frustrating. A gorgeous push-pull that took Dosie right out of her head and into space. She could've cried.

"I think…." *Don't.* "I think it's actually just the kissing that I need." *Too late.* "Is that okay?" She hadn't expected to want something soft after the way she'd needed it the night before, but it had been a long day, and she'd worked through a lot. She was rubbed raw, and she was tired. And Jennifer was so warm and so gentle and so very beautiful despite looking like a deer caught in headlights every time Dosie said something even fractionally tender. "Can we lay down with our clothes on and just…." She stopped at the barely contained panic seeping into Jennifer's expression.

It was clear Jennifer was trying desperately to appear neutral, but Dosie saw so much in her face. Apprehension, in the pulling line of her lips. Fear, in the wrinkle and dip of her brow. Longing, in the wet fullness of her eyes. *Longing.* It was *that* that pushed her to keep going. She knew there were professional boundaries, and she didn't want to cross them, but she *did* want to lean really close to them and give a nudge or two. And maybe that was awful of her, but she felt awful, so why should she be anything else? Maybe, for once, she could throw caution to the wind, and maybe Jennifer could too. Maybe they could *both* be a little reckless with their boundaries.

Dosie ran her thumb along the shallow curve of Jennifer's bottom lip. "Just kiss me and hold me for a while? Please?"

Blue eyes slipped shut as Jennifer dropped her head forward again, bumping against Dosie's and resting. "Dosie." Her breath stuttered, voice so low that it hardly made a sound. "Why do you do this to me?"

Dosie shivered. "Why do you let me?" With the slightest tilt of her chin, their lips touched. Just a flash of flesh on flesh but still enough to make her ache. "*Jennifer.*"

A wet moan hit the air a second before Jennifer moved. Her hands dropped to Dosie's hips then down to dip beneath her dress. She found purchase at the backs of Dosie's thighs, just under her ass, and all but tossed her up into her arms. Dosie grunted as she ringed her legs around Jennifer's waist and felt her clit collide with the thick metal button of her jeans. She rutted once against it before she could stop herself and heard Jennifer practically purr in response. It very nearly made her do it again. Instead, she settled her weight on the arm under her ass and let the hand curling up into her hair pull her into another kiss.

Slowly, Jennifer turned toward the bed and inched forward until her knees touched the comforter. She propped one up on the mattress and began to crawl up the bed, Dosie still curled around her. At the top of the bed, she lowered Dosie into soft white and let her own weight curtain over her. It was the most sensual moment of Dosie's life. The softness of it, the control, the timid connection they'd always seemed to have now correcting itself, finding its rhythm again, rocking around them like music slowly boosted through an amp. Everything felt attuned to their frequency, all the world shifting to the right wave and riding it.

Jennifer Dupont kissed her as if she was born to, and for just this one night, maybe nothing else needed to matter.

Little involuntary twitches in Dosie's hands made Jennifer chuckle. One was buried under Jennifer's shirt, rucked up out of her pants. The other lay open in the scant space between their chests, Dosie's pinky finger curled around hers. Jennifer raised her hand to run her finger down the bridge of Dosie's nose. "Are you falling asleep?"

Dosie opened her bleary eyes. "How'd you know?"

"You're twitching."

"Oh." She curled her hand around Jennifer's waist. "Maybe." Her lips stretched with a smile, and Jennifer felt the pull of it in her chest. "Would that be terrible of me?"

"No." Long, lazy kisses and gently roaming hands had

ticked an hour of their time away. They had an hour left, but again, Jennifer sensed it would reach its end prematurely. The sheer ache she experienced at the thought of having to leave was enough to make her feel sick. "Roll over."

Dosie blinked at her, sleepy and confused. "What?"

"Roll over," Jennifer said again, voice cracking a little. She couldn't stand to look into Dosie's eyes, because she already felt like she was falling. Dosie's soft face, the clear affection she wore in her expression as if she'd never been taught its power, could far too easily deceive Jennifer if she let it. Deceive her into thinking that a crash wasn't inevitable, that she could just fall and fall, and Dosie would fall right along with her. Endlessly. Breathlessly. No, there was always an end point. There was always a crash, and Jennifer needed to brace herself for it. She needed to accept it. "I'll hold you until you fall asleep, and then I'll go."

Go home and pretend she wasn't hopelessly without purchase. Maybe, if she could just allow herself this, this one last night with Dosie falling asleep in her arms, then tomorrow, in the harsh light of day, she could finally do what needed to be done. She could choose not to return. She could choose to set them both free. And then maybe the crash wouldn't be so bad.

Maybe they could both just walk it off, not much worse for wear.

"Okay," Dosie whispered, then she turned over and wriggled herself back against Jennifer's chest. She fit as if she'd been clicked into place, a preset part of Jennifer's structure, a perfect match. Jennifer had long since discarded her boots and jacket and now tangled her legs and feet with Dosie's. She could feel how cold Dosie's bare feet were through both their socks.

"Do you even have circulation in your feet?"

Dosie laughed. "Stop! I told you they were like that. Warm them up."

"Fine." She topped Dosie's feet with hers. "Better?"

"Mhm."

The quiet settled over them again, a little less easy than before. There was a bit of tension now, slowly growing. The tension of Jennifer's impending exit. The tension of the truth sinking in—the truth that they'd spent an entire session kissing with their clothes on, and now Jennifer was wrapped around the girl like a security blanket, entangled with her, sharing her warmth, her solace. Even if neither of them acknowledged what it looked like, what it *felt* like, they both knew what it was.

Intimacy. An intimacy that, despite what they told themselves, had tipped over its physical bounds and become something it was never supposed to become: *more*. This was more. *They* were more. More than anything Jennifer had ever had or known before. More than anything she'd ever even imagined possible for herself.

"Are you sure this is okay?" Dosie asked as if she could read Jennifer's mind. *Or my heartbeat. Is it racing*? "Jennifer?"

"No," she admitted, and Dosie's body went rigid under her arm.

"Oh." Her voice tightened. "Do you want to stop?"

Jennifer stared at the back of her, taking in the shine of her hair in the city glow, the freckles speckling her shoulder. The style of her dress left her upper back bare, putting her skin on beautiful, moon-washed display, and Jennifer's eyes caught on the marks there. She'd glimpsed them before but now saw them clearly—a mural of long, pale scars painting the space between Dosie's shoulder blades like stars streaking a night sky. Most were razor-thin and straight as arrows, but a few were wider and more uneven, as if the wounds that had formed them had struggled to heal.

"No," she whispered again as she let herself touch, trailing her fingers over one of the wider scars. She didn't expect the shiver that traveled Dosie's spine and sent it bowing. She stilled her touch. "Sensitive?"

Dosie's hair swished over the pillow as she nodded. "Always." The sudden drop in her pitch made Jennifer's stomach flip.

"Pain?"

"No, not bad sensitive, just sensitive."

"But does it bother you?" Jennifer leaned in to replace her fingertips with the tip of her nose, traced it over another scar. "To have them touched?"

"No."

"Kissed?" She followed with her mouth, and goosebumps pebbled Dosie's skin. Another shudder coursed her body, and

Jennifer felt every ripple of it as if they were riding the same electrical current. The high it gave her, turning this woman on—not as if flipping a breaker but as if slowly cranking a flashlight until it glowed—was consummate. Incomparable. She couldn't help craving it. She couldn't help chasing it.

Dosie's spine arched, ass jutting back into the pocket of Jennifer's hips. *Fuck.* Her body was so responsive, one of the most responsive Jennifer had ever worked with. Every little touch made her twitch. Tremors ran her body like a fault line at the mere sound of Jennifer's voice. There wasn't a doubt in Jennifer's mind that if she wriggled a thigh between Dosie's legs, she'd soon have her denim dampened. *High indeed.*

"I wasn't comfortable showing them for a long time," Dosie said, and Jennifer kissed her again, just the slightest brush over one wider, gnarled scar. "I'm still not sometimes. I like my body. I mean, I don't think it's ugly or anything. But I don't like to be stared at. Does that make sense?"

Jennifer hummed a confirmation and curled an arm around her, kissed her way up the back of her neck. "I quite like to be stared at, myself."

Dosie's stomach quivered under Jennifer's hand as she laughed. "I know."

A natural quiet settled in as they lay still in a perfect envelope, or so Jennifer thought until she realized the woman in her arms was a bit *too* still. Her back wasn't moving. Her stomach wasn't either. She was holding her breath.

"What's wrong?" Jennifer whispered, and the breath gusted free.

"Aren't you going to ask how I got them?"

Oh. "No."

"Because you don't want to know?" she asked, and Jennifer noted the sudden strain in her voice. *Shit. Was that the wrong answer?* "Or because you already assumed my father gave them to me?"

She had to stop herself from gasping. Dosie's voice wasn't angry, only agitated, *nervous*, but they'd never spoken of her past before, nothing beyond the barest thread of a detail. Jennifer momentarily found it hard to breathe. "I wasn't assuming anything."

"Then why haven't you asked?"

"Because it isn't my business." She tightened her hold, flexing her arm to pin Dosie to her chest, and hoped the extra pressure would quell the girl's anxiety before it grew. "If you want to tell me, that's your choice, and I'll gladly listen, but it's not my place to ask you those questions, Dosic. And even if it was, even if we were...." She choked on whatever she might have said and corrected course. "I would never ask you about something potentially traumatic, not if I didn't need to know the answer."

Dosie remained quiet a moment, then the tension leaked from her body, and she sighed. "You're afraid to trigger me again."

It wasn't a question, but Jennifer answered anyway. "Yes."

"That's why you were so quiet last night."

"Yes."

"When we...."

"Yes."

"I thought things were just awkward because of what happened, but you were deliberately being quiet, weren't you? So you wouldn't trigger me."

"Yes."

"Stop saying yes!"

Jennifer winced. "I'm sorry."

"No, *I'm* sorry," Dosie groaned and grabbed her arm. "I'm sorry. I didn't mean to snap. I shouldn't have snapped." Her thumb drew circles on the back of Jennifer's wrist. "It's just that, if the hell I've been through didn't break me, you won't either."

Jennifer turned her hand at Dosie's urging, let her knot their fingers together over her chest. "I don't have to break you to hurt you, you know."

"I'm not that fragile."

Jennifer's throat constricted. The words rushed up anyway. "I am."

Instinct sparked hard. *Run.* She'd had it for years, that burning prickle at the back of her neck any time she felt the slightest bit of attachment to someone. It happened rarely, but when it did, she'd always yanked it like an obstructive root and cast it aside, refusing to nurture something she knew would have only fleeting life before a cruel, inevitable death. She'd never had reason to doubt that instinct. It kept her safe. But with Dosie, she found she couldn't follow it either. She was rooted to the spot, stuck in a tug-o-war between her inclination and her affection. Both relentless. Both screaming at her—*run, stay, help, touch, forget.*

"Oh, Jennifer," Dosie whispered, and all that chaos turned static. "What are you so afraid of?" She brought their joined hands to her lips, kissed Jennifer's knuckles, and the static turned to silence. "Tell me your secrets."

"I had a sister." As the words eased out of her, she was certain they took little pieces of her soul with them. "Lauren. She died when I was seventeen." A furious stinging erupted in her eyes and throat. "She was my favorite person."

Dosie's soft kisses returned, one knuckle after another and back. "What was she like?"

"My opposite." Jennifer took a breath, steadied herself. "You wouldn't believe me if I told you how I used to be."

"Try me."

"Shy," Jennifer admitted, a sad laugh bubbling up as she remembered the way she used to carry herself. "Horribly so."

"Really?"

"Yes, to the point that it sometimes severely interfered with my life. I ended up in the hospital once for a UTI because I didn't want to tell anyone I was in pain. I was septic by the time I was treated."

"Jennifer!"

"I know. It was bad."

"I can't even imagine you as shy. It doesn't seem possible."

"I told you."

"But your sister wasn't?"

"No, she was loud and full of herself. And bossy."

"So, exactly the way you are now?"

Jennifer laughed, the sound cracking down the middle as the first of her tears fell. "Yes, but she was also funny and artistic and generous, and after our parents died, she was my entire world."

"Oh, God." Dosie's grip on her tightened. "You lost your parents, too?"

"In a car accident."

"How old were you?"

"Fourteen."

"I'm so sorry, Jennifer," Dosie said, and for the first time in Jennifer's life, the words didn't feel like a cheese grater being dragged over her skin. She heard in them something she'd never heard before. Understanding. Weighted and real, the kind of understanding gained only through experience. "Did you go into the system like I did?"

"No, we moved in with my aunt, my dad's sister, which wasn't bad. She was kind and made sure we had everything we needed, but she'd never wanted kids, and it showed. So, we kept to ourselves, mostly."

"You took care of each other."

"Mm." She nodded, felt an odd comfort in the bumpy back and forth of her forehead against Dosie's spine. "But my aunt lived in a different town."

God, what am I doing? Why was she still talking? Why was she telling her all this? Why couldn't she stop digging her own grave, burying herself alive? She was going to tunnel herself so deep, she'd lose sight of the surface, and then how would she ever get free again?

"It was close to the one we grew up in, but we still had to change schools. That's how we met Glass."

"Glass?"

"His last name."

"Oh."

"His first name is Orwell."

"*Oh.*"

"Yeah." She sniffled, squeezed Dosie tighter. Immediately, she felt the pressure returned, as if Dosie was telling her to keep going, that she was listening, that she *had her*. "He was in Lauren's class, and he was full of himself, so naturally, she had to date him. But he seemed nice enough, and he was always making Lauren laugh. He made us *all* laugh and at a time when we were really struggling just to get through the day."

"What happened?"

Jennifer could have laughed at the development. It just seemed so wild. Only moments ago, Dosie had been drifting to sleep, and now she was wide awake, asking Jennifer about her most wretched wounds. And what was Jennifer doing? Bracing herself to yank her whole ugly history from its cobwebbed box and give it to her. How, *how*, had it come to this? How had it gotten this far?

And that's when Jennifer realized something: She didn't care. She didn't care that she was spilling her guts. She didn't care that they were on a time limit. She didn't care about anything but the thumping of Dosie's heart beneath her palm, and the way she took Jennifer's pains and held them, and so, for once in so terribly long, she wasn't shouldering them alone.

If she truly was burying herself alive, why did it have to feel so fucking good?

"She dropped out of school to marry him," she said. "My aunt had been renting out our old place since my parents died, and they moved in there. Lauren wanted me to live with them, but Glass said he wanted some time for them as newly-weds, so I didn't."

Every word felt like something violent and alive being purged from her body. Some kind of foreign body or parasite. A lifetime of sickness.

"She came over every Thursday for pizza night, and we talked on the phone almost every day. But then she started skipping visits and calls, and when I tried to go to her, it was never a good time. She had plans, or she had to work. She was always busy, and even when I got her on the phone, he was always in the background, talking at her. Telling her to hurry up or hang up, to stop talking so loudly, to stop talking about *him* even though she hardly ever said a word about him. I...."

Nausea sparked like a struck match as the memories rushed back. *The hand on her back. The robin-egg blue door.* The more she spoke, the more vivid they became.

"The Lauren I knew would've told anyone who tried to tell her what to do to fuck off, husband or otherwise." Jennifer's heart began to pound again. "But she didn't."

"Come on. Give me a squish."

A cry choked in Jennifer's throat. "I still don't know why she didn't."

Dosie tried to roll over, but Jennifer locked her in place. "Don't, please," she said and pressed her forehead harder into Dosie's back. "I haven't talked about this in years. I don't think I'll be able to get it out if you're looking at me."

"Okay. That's okay." She put their hands to her chest. "Keep going."

Jennifer closed her eyes, focused on the thump of Dosie's heart under her hand. "The last time I saw her, it was the middle of August, but she had on a big, bright blue sweater." *Thump-thump. Thump-thump. Thump-thump.* "I didn't tell her I was coming. I knew she wouldn't let me if I asked, so I just showed up. The house was wrecked and smelled like smoke. There was a lamp on the floor, and the TV was cracked, and the remote was stuck in the wall where he'd thrown it. And I... I will never forget the feeling I got. This sick, *sick* feeling. Heavy and thick and sinking, like I was slowly drowning from the inside." Her mouth watered despite how dry her throat felt. Every breath she took seemed to evade her lungs. "But I didn't say anything."

The hand on her back.

"Glass wasn't there. She said they'd had a fight, and that things had gotten out of hand. That it was her fault, and it wasn't a big deal. He'd drive around for a while, blow off some steam, and when he came back, things would be better. He'd be calmer. He'd be sorry. And I knew that was a lie, but I still didn't say anything. I was so fucking incapable of speaking up, I just...." Jennifer shook her head. "I just helped her clean up his fucking mess, and then I let her push me out the door."

The robin-egg blue door.

"I can still hear her sometimes," Jennifer whispered. "Telling me not to worry. Telling me she was fine. Telling me to go home."

"Give us some time to fuss at each other, and then we'll be good as new."

"And I did. I went home." Her eyes seared, fresh tears flooding. Shame lanced through her chest like a hot blade. "I tried to call her that night, but no one picked up." Her mad, aching heart crawled up her throat onto her tongue. "The phone just rang and rang." She blew a cool breath up over her burning cheeks, but it offered no relief. "And I just sat there with that fucking feeling, and I didn't say anything. I didn't *do* anything. I didn't call the police. I didn't tell anyone. I wanted to, but every time I tried, I would get so anxious. I was, I don't know, terrified that I was overreacting or that I might somehow make everything worse."

"Oh, Jennifer." Dosie's voice was so soft. Her thumb ran Jennifer's wrist like a windshield wiper, steady, hypnotizing. Jennifer focused on the rhythm, like a distant light in a dark tunnel, guiding her toward relief. She just had to say it, just had to get the words out, and then it would be done. It would be over.

Except it would never be over.

She couldn't change anything.

She couldn't get her sister back.

"The next morning, there were cops at my aunt's door."

"Jennifer, I'm fine."

"He'd apparently bought a hunting knife while he was out blowing off steam."

"He always comes around."

Bile bubbled at the top of her gut, but she held it down. "He stabbed my sister twenty-two times, barely an hour after I left her." Dosie flinched so hard that it jostled them both, and they tightened their grips on each other. "That guy who always made her laugh, made us all laugh. He.... And I...."

The mattress dipped as Dosie rolled in her arms. Jennifer blinked her teary eyes open to see a face just as streaked as her own, and an odd, unexpected sense of calm settled over and into her. Dosie said nothing as she wiped through her own tears then Jennifer's. No '*I'm sorry.*' No '*It wasn't your fault.*' She just pulled Jennifer closer and kissed her cheek, her wet, sticky jaw, the corner of her mouth, and somehow, that was so much better. A heavy breath that felt like it started in her toes eased up and out of her as she rolled onto her back, and Dosie rolled right along with her.

Her clammy fingers trembled as they slid under Jennifer's top and over her abdomen, trailing her stomach back and forth. She kissed down Jennifer's neck and slid a knee between her legs, found the button of her jeans and worked it open. "Let me make you feel good," Dosie whispered against her chest. "Let me try, Jen. Please."

"Fuck." Jennifer sobbed as a strange sensation began to

burn in her chest. Something achy and awful and hopeful. "Yes," she whispered, and Dosie kissed her as if it was the first time. Or the last time.

When she slid her fingers inside Jennifer, neither woman made a sound. The room, the world, was so quiet, as if it was holding its breath. Dosie lay her cheek right against Jennifer's, her forehead pressed to the pillow. They were nothing but slowly shallowing breaths and gentle motion as Dosie explored Jennifer's sex with her fingers and thumb, knee knocking against the back of her hand to apply more pressure. It was a slow, silent journey to the softest orgasm Jennifer had ever had, and when it was over, she felt cracked in half.

Dosie turned her face to kiss Jennifer's cheek, fingers still sheathed inside her. "I did it to myself," she quietly confessed. "The scars on my back."

Jennifer flinched, caught off guard. Clearly, Dosie felt she needed to break herself open as well. She wrapped a hand around the back of her head, pulled her closer. "Why?"

She didn't ask out of judgment but confusion, concern. She'd never even considered that Dosie might have been responsible for the scars. Fear struck like lightning. *If she's done this before, would she do it again?* Jennifer couldn't bear the thought of Dosie harming herself. She couldn't bear the thought of Dosie being harmed at all.

"Penance."

Fuck. Jennifer's chest felt like it might cave in. What was she supposed to say to that? How was she supposed to react?

A loud knock startled them, and Jennifer jerked up to

check the clock on the bedside table. "It's Carolina," she said with a sigh. "We're twenty minutes over time."

"Oh." Her face crumpled. "That means I have to take my hand out of your pants."

"Unfortunately, yes."

With a dramatic groan, Dosie pulled her hand free and flexed her fingers, wiped them on the bedsheet. "I'm sorry for keeping you over time," she said as Jennifer sat up. "Do I need to, um, pay you extra or something?"

To Jennifer's surprise, the question speared her. Her back bowed as she caught her breath. A sick feeling trickled through her. "No, that won't be necessary," she said, sharper than intended, and slid from the bed. Awkwardness rushed in as if a dam had broken, and Jennifer all but ran for the bathroom. "Could you tell Carolina I'll be right out?"

She slammed the door shut behind her before she could hear Dosie's reply.

It took her nearly ten minutes to clean and compose herself, but she finally felt neat enough. The bedroom was empty when she emerged, but Dosie had lain her jacket out on the bed for her with her boots on the floor just below. Affection warmed her heart. *I shouldn't have snapped at her.*

Ready to go, Jennifer found Dosie waiting for her beside the door. It was closed, the little entryway dark, and when Jennifer stepped into her bubble, Dosie grabbed the open edges of her jacket and pulled her close. "Do you have everything?"

"Yes."

"Okay." She shifted her weight like she was too nervous to hold still. "Okay." She didn't let go. "Are you okay?"

All the hurts coursing through Jennifer numbed at the sound of that one earnest question. She set her finger under Dosie's chin, tipped her head up to catch her eyes. "Are you?"

"I think I hurt your feelings before, when I asked about paying extra."

"Dosie, stop. You didn't do anything wrong. I was—"

"No, listen." She pulled Jennifer closer until their chests were separated only by Dosie's hands in her jacket. "I think I hurt your feelings, and I think I know why. Or at least, I know why it hurt *me* to ask you. I don't think we can do this anymore. I don't think we should."

Whatever numbness Jennifer had felt split around new pain like stone about a chisel. "What?"

"I was wrong about this. Us."

"What do you mean?"

"I thought I could respect your wishes and be professional," Dosie said, "that what I was getting from my sessions with you was enough, and that *enough* was worth smothering the way I feel every time I see you." She slid her hands up to Jennifer's jacket collar then onto her neck, fingers spanning. "Every time I touch you."

"Fuck," Jennifer breathed and let her own hands fall to Dosie's waist.

"God, when *you* touch *me*." Little quakes in Dosie's fingertips vibrated into Jennifer's skin, sank right into her soul. "You were right, that first night. You said you would have the lay of me, and you do. You make my body feel so good, Jennifer. I can't even tell you. I don't have the words. But it's not just my body. It's everything. When I *think* about you, I—"

A heavy knock thudded the door beside them, and Dosie jumped. She laughed at herself, broken, helpless, and gripped the back of Jennifer's neck. "You have to go."

Jennifer couldn't speak. She wasn't sure she was even breathing anymore, so she did the only thing she could think to do. She kissed the girl.

They fell against the wall, clutching one another like they'd been tossed into freefall, seeking purchase, and Dosie sighed into her mouth. She set her forehead to Jennifer's and said, "I'm pretty sure I'm falling in love with you."

Fuck. Fuck!

Jennifer's heart raged. It thrashed. It floated. It did and *was* everything at once. She felt frozen at a thousand miles an hour. Her breath was tight in her lungs, and her stomach was in her feet.

Another knock came, and Dosie turned her face away, wiped her eyes. "Go," she said and nudged Jennifer toward the door. "She's waiting." When she looked at Jennifer again, she smiled, beautiful even if it was forced. "You have to go."

"Dosie," she managed to croak but could think of nothing to say. And *too many* things to say. Her head was a mess, half-cracked with shock and lit up with wonder like a Christmas tree. Her body buzzed with energy and terror and thrill.

"I'm okay," Dosie said as if she knew Jennifer needed to hear it and took her hand. Kissed it one last time. "Go."

Jennifer wanted to tell her that they could talk soon, that they *would* talk soon. Instead, she choked on nothing and turned to the door. She didn't let herself hesitate when she tugged it open and stepped out, leaving Dosie alone with the echoes of her confession.

She was halfway to the elevator, her pace furious, when Carolina caught up to her. "I'm sorry," she said, "if you're mad about the knocking. You're forty minutes over. I was starting to get worried."

"It's fine," Jennifer said, and it was.

Except, *no.* Nothing was fucking *fine.* Nothing in her entire world was fine.

Everything had just been ruptured beyond repair, and there was no going back. They couldn't ignore or pretend or fuck away a love confession. They couldn't erase the night they'd had. They were in each other, under the surface, and there was nothing professional about it, nor could there ever be again.

When the elevator doors closed them inside, a heavy, familiar foreboding snaked its way through Jennifer's body and settled there.

13

The saturated washcloth plunked into the bathwater with a mild splash. Dosie scowled as she scooped it up again and wrung it out, slapped it over her face to inhale its steamy heat. "I'm pretty sure I'm falling in love with you," she said to the empty bathroom and cringed. Water heaved around her as she kicked her legs like a mid-tantrum toddler. She yanked the cloth from her face again, let it disappear into the water like jetsam on a turbulent wave, and growled at herself. "I'm pretty sure I'm in love with you. *Why*? *Why* did I say it like that?"

She briefly wondered how long it would take the hotel cleaning staff to find her body if she died of mortification in this tub.

"You couldn't have just said you have feelings for her and left it at that? You had to say you were in love with her? No.

No! You didn't even say that! You said you were pretty sure you were falling in love with her. *Pretty sure.*"

She whined and sloshed and sank. Heat engulfed her. Water rushed by her ears. Then she burst free again, shouting, "I mean, what *is* that?! The worst way *ever* to express your feelings?" She pushed her sopping hair off her face and rolled on her side, head just above water. Bunched her knees to her chest. "Why did I say it like that?"

Why had she said any of it at all? Done any of it at all? Why had she let herself carry on with things? Booking appointments when she knew she was too attached, when she knew she was triggered, when she knew she wasn't in complete control of her emotions. God, she knew better. She knew better. She *knew* better. And now she'd said things she couldn't take back, pushed them over lines that couldn't be uncrossed. And for what?

What if nothing came of it? What if she'd read everything wrong? What if Jennifer didn't feel the same way or *any way* about her, and all she'd done was make a complete fool of herself?

No. Stop. Stop it. She wasn't going to let herself spiral anymore. Even if nothing came of it, Dosie had every reason to believe Jennifer felt something for her. Something real.

Hadn't it been Jennifer who'd started things in the dressing room? Jennifer who pulled them over that line? Hadn't she said they couldn't continue after, that it was a bad, bad idea, then continued anyway? Hadn't she followed Dosie to her bedroom when she could've walked away? Hadn't she held Dosie and kissed her and whispered to her in the dark, such precious, private things?

"How can you feel grounded when I feel so completely untethered?"

"My name is Jennifer."

"I was worried about you."

"I had a sister."

When Jennifer spoke to her like that, when she gave herself over in little moments and timid words, Dosie could swear there'd never been a single transaction between them. No bookings. No payments. She could swear they'd known each other all their lives, wanted each other just as long. She could swear they were lovers.

When a loud, rapid thumping echoed in, Dosie popped up so fast her neck cracked. Someone was knocking on her door. *Holy shit! It's her! It's got to be her. What do I do? What do I say? What am I going to say? Something stupid. Something romantic. Go before she disappears!*

She clambered out of the tub and tossed a towel around her torso without bothering to dry anything. With each wet step she took, she told herself another knock would come any second, that she'd hear a voice filter through saying, *"Housekeeping!" "Room service!" "Hey, uh, sorry to shout this through your door, but I'm in the room next to yours, and it sounds like someone's getting, like, drowned in the tub or something. Are you okay?"* Someone, anyone, other than the person her wild heart was hoping for, because surely, it wasn't *really—*

"Oh my God, Dosie, hurry up. I need to pee! I can hear you fiddling with the chain!"

Dosie gasped and freed the chain, yanked open the door. "Kaylia! You're here! You're here?"

"Yes, I'm here, and you're naked."

Dosie looked down at her towel dress. "I was in the bath."

"The perfect place to drown in your misery."

"Naturally."

"Okay, but seriously, I have to pee." She shoved her way inside, and Dosie followed her back to the foggy, humid bathroom. She'd grown up sharing a bathroom with anywhere from eleven to eighteen people on any given day and sometimes forgot it wasn't meant to be a communal experience. Thankfully, Kaylia had never cared. The first time Dosie had followed Natalie into a bathroom, the girl had turned her right back around, said, "No," and booted her out the door.

"What are you doing here?" Dosie asked as Kaylia dropped her wide-leg pleated pants and scrap of purple underwear to her ankles and sat on the toilet.

"Um, have you already forgotten that you texted me you were having a 'post-traumatic meltdown?' Am I supposed to just ignore something like that?"

Oh, right.

"Well, yeah, but you're supposed to be in New York. I thought you would just FaceTime me and talk me down. I didn't think you would get on a plane and come back just to check on me. Now I feel bad."

"Okay, slow your roll, Princess." Her laugh was lost to the

whoosh of the toilet's flush. "You sent that text three hours ago. Even with the ungodly prices I pay for first class, I can't make the plane go faster. I was already on my way back."

"Oh." *Duh.* "Right."

"You're special, babe, but you're not *that* special," Kaylia said as she washed her hands, and Dosie felt something unstick itself inside her.

She laughed. "I'm so glad you're here. Thank you for coming."

"Don't I always have your back?" Kaylia checked herself over in the mirror. Dosie thought she looked as amazing as always—sharp, professional, and unapologetically feminine—but she could see Kaylia's grimace. "I feel like I've been awake for three days and am starting to look it."

"*Have* you been awake for three days?"

"Not quite, but.... You know my client that moved to New York?"

"The composer guy you're suing HBO for?" Dosie grinned. "What was his name? Something to do with beef, right?"

Kaylia rolled her eyes. "His name is Angus," she said, and Dosie snorted. "You clearly spend too much time with Natalie."

"Ooh, I should text her. You know she had that hot date tonight with the girl from the morgue."

Kaylia's nose wrinkled. "You realize how fucked up that sounds, right?"

"What? She's a medical examiner at the morgue."

"Yes, okay, so maybe we say Nat had a date—a *date*, mind you, not a *hot* date, because, Dosie, if you have to say 'hot date', it's definitely not going to be one—Nat had a date with a doctor, not 'the girl from the morgue'. That makes her sound like a necrophile."

"Ew. Kaylia."

"You said it." She shrugged. "Can we move this to the bed?" She didn't wait for an answer. "I need to be horizontal."

"Why?" Dosie quickly switched her towel for a robe and followed Kaylia to the bed. "Because you've been awake with Mr. Beefy Music Man for three days? I'm supposed to believe you guys weren't horizontal at some point?"

"Theodosia Grace Fisher!" Kaylia cackled as she kicked off her shoes and crawled under the covers. "Paying for lesbian sex has corrupted you. I love it."

"Oh, *God*." Dosie buried her face in her pillow and groaned until she felt so out of breath she might faint.

"Uh oh. Guess I know who your post-traumatic meltdown is about." She nudged Dosie as if excited to hear about her irrevocable humiliation. "I'm so glad I drank a Red Bull. Tell me everything."

Dosie braced herself and did just that, and when she was finished with the whole ridiculous, emotional spiel, when they'd rationalized and criticized and hoped it all to death, the sky was dawn-bright outside the window, and she was exhausted. Kaylia dozed beside her but sleep still evaded Dosie. Her mind didn't seem to want to sleep or rest at all.

When yet another knock suddenly broke the quiet, her

stomach plummeted. She sprang up in bed, felt Kaylia stir beside her.

"Was that a knock?"

"Yes."

"Did you order room service?"

"Kaylia, you've been with me for the last six hours. Did you see me order room service?"

"Damn. I want breakfast." She sat up, tired eyes widening. "Shit. Do you think it's...."

"Jennifer," Dosie said, mouth dry as the Mojave. Heart buried in the sand.

The Prophet was the first to teach me that there is power in what we wear. Our clothes can be a symbol. They can be a tool. They can even be a weapon.

I remember the day I learned that lesson.

My father hadn't sat for breakfast at the women's table in nearly a year. His sudden arrival was like the trip of an alarm at the back of my brain. At his side, held up partly by his hand and partly by his jutted hip, was a large coil of steel wire. I had no idea what its purpose was, but I knew my father. I knew his body language. That morning, it screamed danger.

As he walked along the table toward his always open seat, he tapped each of us on the head like he was starting a game of Duck, Duck, Goose. He liked that, games, especially when he had a point to make.

Duck. Duck. Duck. Duck.

Goose: Janice.

Like me, my oldest sister Janice had our father's hair, a color our mother called "apple-cinnamon cider," and dark brown eyes. But Janice had edges where I had none. Her face was strong and angled like his, while mine was soft and round like Mother's. Janice was beautiful—everyone said so—handsome and lovely at once. And she was, undeniably and until the end, Father's favorite child.

"Janny," he said and kissed the top of her head, "how about you bless us with the Word this morning, hm? Isaiah 65:2."

His choice made the alarm in my head wail louder. Something was wrong. Someone had done something. Something bad.

"I have spread out My hands all day long to a rebellious people," Janice recited. "Who walk in the way which is not good, following their own thoughts."

Father nodded and carried on down the long table. "Romans 2:4."

Duck. He passed his chair to venture down the table's other side, the side I occupied. Duck.

"Or do you think lightly of the riches of His kindness and tolerance and patience, not knowing that the kindness of God leads you to repentance?"

The verse was barely out of Janice's mouth before she was ordered another. "Revelation 2:21."

Duck. Duck.

Janice was silent a moment, eyes casting back as if visually searching through her brain for the right verse. Like Father, she had a photographic memory, though I wouldn't learn that term for years. On the compound, she was simply "touched," meaning God had blessed her with a divine gift.

"I gave her time to repent," Janice said, "and she does not want to repent—"

"Hosea two, verses six and seven." Father's voice was calm as he cut Janice off, an unnatural kind of calm that made the air hard to breathe, even outside. "Quickly now, Jan. We're all hungry, I'm sure."

Duck. Duck.

The tension built until it felt stiff enough to snap. Then I noticed the looks. At least three of my sisters and two of the commune mothers, mine included, kept glancing to my left.

"Therefore, behold, I will hedge up her way with thorns, and I will build a wall against her so she cannot find her paths," Janice said, and a shiver ran through me.

Duck: Mother Madeline. Duck: Lucy. Duck: Penny.

"She will pursue her lovers, but she will not overtake them."

Duck: Faith.

I froze as Father's hand landed atop my head, but then it popped off again and passed. My relief didn't last. I didn't want any of my family in trouble, but I knew that was what this was, this game he was playing. Someone had to be the goose.

Duck: Trinity.

"And she will seek them, but will not find them," Janice continued. "Then she will say, 'I will go back to my first husband, for it was better for me then than now.'"

Goose: Lara.

The steel coil hit the ground with a thud, and both Father's hands landed on my second-oldest sister's shoulders. Lara tensed under his touch but said nothing. Neither did he. But for the morning birdsong and the dull echoes of the men's breakfast chatter on the other side of the lawn, nothing stirred the silence.

Lara had always been rebellious, never to any unnatural degree; at least, not that I'd ever been aware of. But now she sat so rigidly under Father's touch that I knew she must have done something, and she didn't need to be told what it was. She knew, and he knew, and God knew. And that was enough.

It seemed like hours passed before Father simply let her go, picked the coil up again, and headed back to his seat. When he finally sat, he motioned for a glass of juice, drank it down, and said, "Well, go on then." The coil rested on his lap, visible to everyone. "Eat."

The next morning, Lara didn't leave her bed, and the Prophet emerged from the house with a new addition to his usual attire of khaki pants and button-ups: a thinned strip of steel wire with a crude leather handle fastened to one end. He'd fixed it through his belt loops and tied it in the center, and when he stepped into the sun, the silver caught its brilliance and blinded.

When I saw the long, thin slices between my sister's shoulder blades, she told me, "Father said it was penance. He found out about me and Joel."

I remember being confused by this. Lara was fifteen years old at the time, but I was only nine, and I hadn't yet learned that bodies could wake up like an alarm clock, that they could burn in ways both wanted and sought. I didn't know there were thrills to be had in the touch of another.

I never did find out what transpired between Lara and Joel, but I imagine they shared a kiss or a quiet love confession. Perhaps they'd looked too long or touched one another, slotted their bodies together in that eager way I've since learned so many young, reckless people do.

For that, our father had fashioned a steel whip for Lara and commanded her to tear herself open until she cried for his forgiveness. She finally did, and he finally forgave her, but the wounds had been set and the scars patterned. Her punishment would be permanent, and so would the whip's presence in our lives from that point on.

The Prophet never went another day without it circling his waist, sparkling in the sun. It became a symbol, a tool, a weapon. I still dream about the first time he placed it in my hand, how he'd watched until skinny red strings of flesh spilled down my back like unspooled threads. When I'd finally wailed myself hoarse, he stood, took the whip from my hand, and patted the top of my head.

Goose: Me.

"Shh. Hush now, Dosie-girl. You're forgiven."

Years later, in a deteriorating bungalow on a dead-end street outside Dunsmuir, California, my first-and-only foster guardian, a vintage-obsessed, 65-year-old woman who never left the house without a string of pearls around her neck, would teach me yet another function for clothes: armor.

I often wish I'd learned that lesson sooner.

It wasn't quite dawn when Jennifer stopped reading, but the sky outside her window was lighter. She glanced toward the glass, eyes burning from overuse and too much crying, the entire night she'd spent trading sleep for suffering. Dosie's suffering, years ago. Her own suffering, now.

The familiar scent of Dosie lingered in her clothes, so she hadn't bothered undressing. Even her jacket remained on. But now they felt ruffled and restrictive, staticky, and itchy, and clinging in odd places. She wanted them off.

The ornate molding and high, dark walls of her bathroom relaxed her as she switched on the shower and undressed. As she doffed each layer, she thought of Dosie and of what she'd read. She'd long ago learned the power of purposeful dressing, herself, an incredibly effective tool in her line of work. Seduction. Intimidation. Authority. Jennifer had used her wardrobe to embody, impress, and express each. But if she considered further back, back to her youth, she realized she'd used her clothes then, too. To be invisible. To be forgettable.

She thought of Dosie's dated wardrobe and finally understood. Every time she'd seen her dressed that way was a time when Dosie had been particularly vulnerable and needing confidence, needing to feel *invulnerable*. The first time they met. The first time she let Jennifer pleasure her. Both times they'd been together since the unfortunate triggering incident.

The times Jennifer had seen her in what she imagined to be Dosie's natural style had mostly been by chance. The dressing room. Jennifer showing up hours ahead of their scheduled appointment. Only twice had Dosie *chosen* to present herself that way, and the first time, she'd still had on her pearl necklace. It was such a small and simple thing, but Jennifer always noticed it. How could she not when Dosie's nervous fingers constantly fiddled with it? Now, though, she realized its importance. The second time Dosie presented herself without armor, she'd been completely uninhibited. Dressed down. Neck bare. *Beautiful.* And so very willing to try, explore, *feel.*

Of course, that was the night everything shattered.

Was it any wonder that when Jennifer saw Dosie again after, she'd redonned her armor? Re-fortified her defenses? She'd been vulnerable, and it hurt her. It was only natural she felt the need to protect herself. From her memories. Her trauma.

From Jennifer?

From the way she felt *about* Jennifer?

"I'm pretty sure I'm falling in love with you."

A shaky, wet breath worked its way free. Steam billowed and hazed, the bathroom so foggy it could double as a sauna, but Jennifer still hadn't gotten in the shower. She sat naked on the rug by the toilet, knees pulled to her chest, face buried between. Tears followed her breath, and Jennifer urged herself to get up. Move. Get in the shower. Wash the night away, the worry. Scrub Dosie Fisher off her skin.

"I'm pretty sure I'm falling in love with you."

A cry leapt from her throat. *Fuck.* This was not supposed to happen. Dosie wasn't supposed to fall for her. Others, sure. Anyone else, and Jennifer wouldn't have cared. She'd have done what she'd always done when a client got too attached—a clear conversation about boundaries and reality. If the issue persisted, she would blacklist the client from her bookings and move on with her life. But Dosie, no. Jennifer couldn't, even if she wanted to. And that was the thing: she really didn't want to.

For the first time in her life, a life she'd resolved to never share, Jennifer wanted something more than sex, and the realization made her feel grossly at odds with herself. It was a sensation she hadn't experienced in some time, not since she'd left her old self behind and carved herself a new place in the world, one with power and influence and protection—the feeling of needing someone.

Her chest burned, her eyes, too, as she squeezed her arms around herself and began a soothing rocking motion. Every time her back hit cold porcelain, she was knocked a little farther from her discomfort, until one such thud sent her stacked, discarded clothes tumbling to the floor. They puddled around her like a visual representation of her soul, and Jennifer sank back into her wallowing. Maybe she wouldn't shower at all. Maybe she would pull her messy, Dosie-scented clothes over her naked body like a blanket, lay down on the floor, and cry herself to death. She was a grown fucking woman, but she felt like a child, sick to her stomach over something as paltry as *feelings*. Something as absurd as love.

As she pulled her jacket over her, something rigid in the pocket knocked her leg. She frowned and grabbed it, dug it free. Her brain faltered at the discovery. Her stomach flipped. She turned the hotel keycard over in her hands and found a small sticky note attached to its backside. What had to be Dosie's simple, blocky handwriting was scrawled across its face.

In case what I'm about to do isn't the stupidest thing I've ever done.

Something Jennifer couldn't properly name or identify surged inside her, rapidly overwhelming until she found herself in tears again. She clutched the keycard as every inch of her body went hot then cold then hot again.

"Fuck."

When the door swung open, a shiver shot down Dosie's spine and spread.

"Hi."

Jennifer stood in the hallway in tennis shoes, leggings, and an oversized sweatshirt. Her hair was down and damp, frizzed in places. There wasn't a spot of makeup on her face, and her eyes were a bit spooked, as if she half-expected someone to jump out and scare her. It was the most exposed Dosie had seen her, including the times she'd seen her naked, and if she wasn't certain before, she was certain now. Jennifer Dupont was just as fucked up, weak, and wonderful as *she* was, as anyone was, and Dosie was wholly in love with her.

"Hi," she said, dizzied with excitement. "You knocked."

Jennifer nodded.

"But I gave you a key."

"I found it."

Dosie's stomach sank. Her excitement fizzled as quickly as it had sparked. Was Jennifer there to end things? *Really* end them this time? Wouldn't she have used the key otherwise?

"Dosie." Kaylia's voice surprised them both, then she was at Dosie's side, curling an arm around her back. When her hand settled on Dosie's waist, Jennifer looked as if someone had sucker-punched her. A good sign?

"You aren't alone."

"Right, yeah," Dosie said, "but it's not anything, you know, like that, if that's what you're thinking." She laughed at herself while Kaylia merely narrowed her eyes at Jennifer like she was a contract that needed scrutinizing. "It's Kaylia.

Sorry. I mean, Jennifer, this is my friend, Kaylia. Kaylia, this is my, um.... This is Jennifer."

Jennifer's body relaxed some, and Dosie's pulse accelerated. Another good sign?

"Right. Kaylia." Jennifer's voice smoothed into its usual whipped-butter richness as she held out a hand. "Davis, yes? The friend whose family owns a vineyard."

Kaylia's eyebrows shot up. Dosie felt her own do the same. She'd really remembered that? Maybe she just had a knack for recall like Dosie did. *Or, maybe, she's memorized every moment she's spent with you, just the way you've done with her.* Dosie fought a groan. *Stop it.*

"That's right." Kaylia shook Jennifer's hand. "I didn't realize Dosie had told you about me." She turned back to Dosie. "You good?" she asked, then mimicked Dosie's answering nod. "Okay, I'm going to head home and give you two some space then." She squeezed Dosie to her, face turned inward to whisper in her ear. "Plead your case. All you have to say is the right thing."

Sure. Dosie's pulse hammered. *The right thing. No pressure.*

Kaylia stepped back, and with her back to Jennifer, waggled her eyebrows at Dosie just long enough to turn her red, then schooled her face and turned back around. "Well, I'll be going now."

"It was nice to meet you," Jennifer said as she let her by.

"Sure," Kaylia said, "but break her heart, and you'll wish you hadn't."

Dosie's eyes practically leapt from their sockets. "Kaylia!"

Unbothered, her friend sauntered down the hall, a little wave over her shoulder.

"Don't listen to her," Dosie said and grabbed Jennifer's hand, pulled her into the hotel room. "She's never maimed anyone. Well, that I know of."

"Comforting."

When the door shut them in, the air shifted. Awkwardness infiltrated. Tension. Silence.

Dosie wasn't sure what to say. She wanted to ask if Jennifer loved her too, if that's what she'd come back to say, but at the same time, she didn't. Because Jennifer might answer. And what if her answer broke Dosie's heart?

"I've never seen you so dressed down before," she went with instead. Something safe.

"I know. I'm a mess."

"You're beautiful."

"I'm clean," Jennifer said, "but that's about it. I haven't slept."

"I haven't either."

She shifted closer, turned her hand in Dosie's and squeezed. Her voice dropped to a whisper. "When I left last night, I had a terrible feeling." She closed her eyes. "Like the one I had that night."

Dosie's heart panged. "When you left your sister's house? Why?" She lay her free hand over Jennifer's chest, felt her heart hop beneath it. "I'm fine, Jennifer. Hey, look at me, please." When she did, Dosie rubbed her chest and smiled. "See. I'm fine. Nothing bad is going to happen to me."

Unless you're going to break my heart.

"Bad things *have* happened to you, Dosie," Jennifer huffed and yanked back her hands. Frustration edged into her voice as she moved further into the room and began a slow pacing, like a wild thing freshly caged. "Terrible things. The worst things. So, tell me how, *how*, are you always so optimistic? After everything you've been through, you're still so hopeful. You're so positive. You're so...so... *you*. How? Tell me how. How do I do that? Because I'm what? Ten, twelve years older than you? And I still don't know. I don't know how to do this. I don't know how to just let myself hope and believe the way you do. How? Tell me how. Please."

Dosie didn't try to move closer. She recognized the tension in Jennifer's body, as if the slightest shift in the air might cause her to detonate like a bomb. She knew what it was to be riddled with fear, taut with anger, to have too much going on inside to process and too weak a foundation to contain it. She'd once been the same way.

"I wasn't always like this," she said, voice gentle. "It took years of therapy and work for me to be as balanced as I am, but Jennifer, everything I've been through is *why* I can be so hopeful." Jennifer scoffed, and Dosie smiled. "I mean it. When I was growing up, the hopes I had were limited to such little things, like, I don't know, hoping there would still be hot water left after all my sisters finished their showers. But I never had hope that I would leave the compound, or that I would ever get to make my own choices about my life. I never hoped I would have friends like the ones I have now, or that I would get the chance to kiss a woman or have sex with her or fall in love."

Jennifer stopped her pacing, and Dosie took the chance to inch closer again.

"I could barely even *imagine* those things, they were so outside my reality, so how could I hope for them?" Closer still. "You can't hope for something that no part of you believes is possible." Closer until she could slide her hands down Jennifer's arms again and dance their fingertips together. "But look where I am right now. Look who I'm with. Look at what I'm doing." She freed Jennifer's hands to frame her face instead, pressed her thumb over the corner of her mouth, then smoothed it down to her jaw. "I am living a life I once believed too good to even to be possible."

Jennifer's watering eyes snapped shut as she took a long, deep breath, and when she opened them again, they appeared so deeply troubled that Dosie's racing heart stalled.

"Oh, please don't look at me like that."

"Like what?"

"Like I *shouldn't* be hopeful," Dosie said. "Like you're about to break my heart."

Jennifer brought their foreheads together, pulled Dosie's hands from her face and held them at her chest. "The Director has always been a heartbreaker."

Oh, God. No. "I'm not in love with the Director. I'm in love with Jennifer. With you."

"You don't even know me," Jennifer said, the softest, saddest protest Dosie had ever heard. "How could you possibly be in love with me?"

A shrill siren wailed through the room, and they jumped apart. Dosie cursed and sprinted for her phone on the bedside table. "I completely forgot."

"Forgot?"

Dosie tapped her phone to stop the sound. "That was my alarm for therapy. I have an appointment in twenty minutes."

"So, you need to go then."

"Well, no. It's a video appointment, so I don't have to go anywhere, but I should probably put some actual clothes on. My therapist already knows I'm a mess right now; well, less messy than I was a few days ago, but still not great. Whatever. The point is, I don't have to *look* like a mess just because I *am* one."

Jennifer tensed as if bracing for bad news, as if she wasn't the one on the verge of issuing a rejection. She cast her eyes to the floor, palmed the back of her neck in an odd show of shyness that had Dosie closing the distance between them again. Catching her by the shoulders.

"Hey, this isn't me telling you to go." She stroked Jennifer's arms. "I mean, yes, I'll need you to go during my appointment, but I want you to come back. I want to keep talking about this."

"I hate talking about this."

"I know you do," Dosie said with a laugh. "But we need to. Can you just give me an hour?"

"You need sleep. We both need sleep."

"Okay, well, two hours then? Three? I could take a quick nap after therapy. Or you could come back, and we could nap together. Would that work?"

"Dosie."

"What is it?"

"I've never done this before."

"What?"

"This." A frustrated sigh left her. Energy and overwhelm quaked through her body. "Relationships. Feelings."

Oh, God. "*Is* that what we're doing?" The blend of excitement and anxiety made Dosie borderline queasy. This was going to be *way* too much to cover in her single-hour therapy session. "Are we having a relationship, Jennifer? Are *we* having feelings? Because so far, I'm the only one who's said I—"

Dosie's second alarm cut her off. Fifteen minutes until her appointment.

"Okay, I'm going," Jennifer announced and shot for the door.

"Wait!" Dosie scrambled after her. "Will you come back?"

Jennifer spun at the door, mouth moving wordlessly.

"Please?" Dosie tried and watched the woman crumple. "Why are you so afraid of this?"

With a groan, Jennifer turned back to the door, knocked her forehead against it and stayed put. "I feel like I'm standing on the edge of a cliff, and your hand is on my back, nudging me, and I *want* to jump. I want to fall. I *do*. But I don't have a parachute. I don't have a rope. I don't have wings. I don't even have experience." She set loose a mirthless laugh and looked at her again. "I don't have anything, and it terrifies me."

Oh. Dosie did not know love could feel like this. Her cells were humming.

"Plead your case." Kaylia's voice spilled into her head. This was her chance. *"All you have to say is the right thing."*

She moved in, letting her instincts and the kernel of courage that had gotten her this far guide her. "My hand is on your back, nudging you, because you're wrong, Jennifer." She set her hand exactly there. "I put that room key in your pocket for a reason, and I think you came here for that same reason. You didn't use the key, but I think you wanted to, because we both know you don't have nothing. You have me, and even if you can't say it or accept it yet, some part of you knows that and *trusts* that and w—"

A harsh gasp choked her as Jennifer swallowed her words in a near-feral kiss. The sound barreled into a moan Dosie felt to her toes when her back hit the wall and Jennifer crowded her in. In seconds, she was everywhere, touching and tugging. She was a tide of need, sweeping Dosie up with warm, eager hands and tear-touched kisses. Her still-damp hair smelled fresh and floral, as it swept over Dosie's face, and Dosie buried her hands in it. *What is even happening right now? Am I dreaming?*

"We don't have much time," she said, going with it. What

else could she do? Her body was already aflame. God, would she ever stop wanting this woman this way? At some point, surely, they'd simmer down. Burn out. *But not yet. Not now.* As if on cue, her phone shrieked alive with another alarm. Dosie laughed, dizzy-drunk on their sudden shift. "Ten minutes."

"That's more than enough," Jennifer said as she tugged up Dosie's robe to bare her thighs. "Let me use my mouth."

All the blood in her body shot to the little button between her legs and ballooned. Her pussy wept. *So much for looking presentable at therapy.* "Did you bring one of those dental dam things?"

Jennifer hummed as if pleased. "Good girl," she said, and Dosie's clit throbbed harder. "When was the last time you were tested?"

Dosie blinked, trying to focus. "For STIs? Not since the one I did before my first appointment with you."

"Have you been with anyone else since then?"

"What? No. I've only been with you. But you have, right?"

"No." Jennifer shook her head, sucked at Dosie's bottom lip. "Only you since the last time I was tested."

"Which was when?"

"Two weeks ago. Everyone at my company gets screened bi-monthly. It was clear."

"You haven't had other bookings since then?"

"A few." Jennifer's hands began their roaming again, mindless, and hot. Dosie wasn't sure Jennifer was even aware she was doing it, and something about that made it infinitely hotter. "But bookings vary. Sometimes, I'm just someone's arm candy for an event, but even when it's sexual, that doesn't necessarily mean I'm *having sex*, as in intercourse. It's common for the demographic I work with to get their pleasure through other means. Like objects. Commands. Pain."

"Oh." Dosie recalled Jennifer telling her about the riding crop, how, sometimes, people just wanted something they had control over. That didn't necessarily have to include an exchange of fluids. "Right."

Jennifer's fingers found her jaw. Their gazes locked. "I can show you my most recent test results on my phone, if that will set you at ease, but the rest I'm afraid you'll just have to trust me on." She leaned in, breath puffing over Dosie's lips. "I would never knowingly put you at risk."

"I know."

Jennifer kissed the point of her chin, then licked and sucked her way down to the divot between her collarbones. "Then tell me you want my tongue inside you," she commanded, and Dosie's throat turned desert.

Her alarm sprang to life again before she could say a word. She growled at it. The constant reminder that their time was dwindling set her teeth on edge, but she always set at least four alarms; otherwise, she would never get anywhere at the right time. The fact that Jennifer hadn't commented on the excessive number or volume made Dosie think she had a similar habit. "Five minutes."

Jennifer sank to her knees like she was about to pray. Her

fingers danced around the hem of Dosie's robe as she tilted her head back. Their eyes met. Hers were dilated darkness haloed in blue, looking up at her like someone seeking absolution. Dosie had none to give and didn't care to seek any for herself. If this was a sin, then let her be a sinner. Let her be damned.

"I only need three," Jennifer promised, "and for you to say yes."

Nothing had ever felt this good.

"Yes."

The first true taste of Dosie Fisher was like a freezing sip of water in the middle of the night—a shock to the senses, satisfaction so intense that it bordered on discomfort. She was dewy and swollen from the first lick, and when Jennifer shoved the tip of her tongue inside her, Dosie gasped and bore down.

"Oh God. Oh, my G—*Jennifer*."

Chills spilled down her back at the guttural sound of her name on Dosie's tongue. She wanted to hear it again and again. Endlessly. She flattened her tongue and dragged it roughly up, triggering a deep, achy whine.

"How do you always know exactly how to make me—" She choked on her words as Jennifer sucked her entire clit roughly into her mouth. Dosie gripped her hair and rutted hard against her face, and the heat in Jennifer's body seared.

Heightened until nothing existed but fire and euphoria. The delirium of Dosie's flavor and Dosie's courage and Dosie's love and how much it all meant to Jennifer, how much it excited and inspired and *scared* her. *Fuck*, it scared her.

But this, *this*, she was good at. This, she had mastered. This didn't scare her at all.

"Jennifer, please."

"Almost," she whispered against Dosie's sopping flesh and slid two fingers inside her, sucked her hard, little nub sharply between her teeth again, and reveled in Dosie's answering scream.

She came hard on Jennifer's tongue, tangy and viscous, and Jennifer knew there could be nothing as addicting as the taste. Except, perhaps, Dosie herself. Hadn't she had Jennifer mad for her from the start?

"Look at me."

Jennifer blinked, caught off guard by Dosie's breathless command but, as if powered by it, she shifted back, Dosie's pleasure smearing her chin, and looked.

"Tell me nothing changes when you're with me," Dosie panted, then she dropped to her knees so they were face to face again, nose to nose. Her cheeks were red from exertion, and her chest heaved, but her eyes were steady and determined. She laid her hand over Jennifer's chest. "Tell me you don't feel electric when I touch you." Her fingers skated up to curl around the back of Jennifer's neck. "Tell me you don't burn so hot you could faint every time you hear me say your name." Dosie's bottom lip stuck to Jennifer's, teased her.

"Tell me the entire world doesn't disappear every time we kiss."

And then she was pushing in, taking what she wanted, and it *did*. Jennifer's world *did* disappear. Everything and everyone became a speck of light in a distant universe as she floated into a blissful blankness.

"Tell me you don't love me, because you *don't*," she said, thumbing Jennifer's cheek. "I'll respect your wishes, no matter what, but I just don't see how any other reason could be worth walking away from this."

Jennifer felt like a god and an idiot and a scared little kid, such discord she could hardly think. "Are you really not afraid at all?"

Dosie stared at her for a long, quiet moment, only her ragged breaths in Jennifer's ears. "I'm afraid that when you walk out the door, you won't ever come back," she said. "Not because you *can't* come back, but because you don't want to. Or because you do want to, but you've spent your whole life alone, and you've forgotten how to let someone love you." She smiled a sad smile. "Of course, I'm scared, but I'm also excited. Why can't I make my decisions based on that? Why does fear have to be the feeling we choose to listen to?"

The words struck Jennifer like a battering ram. Knocked her breath loose. Pain followed. Hadn't she made a lifetime of decisions based on fear? Where her personal life was concerned anyway. She'd barely begun to process when a new, different ringtone blasted the quiet, and Dosie whined.

"That's my therapist." She held up her phone to show an incoming call. "I'm late."

"Right," Jennifer said and forced herself up onto wobbly legs. She felt cracked and scattered, like parts of her soul had lurched out of her body to hide about the room. "Okay." *Get yourself together.* "I'll go." She made for the door again, suddenly itching to be alone, to be out of her clothes and out of her body. If she could just sleep for a few hours, just rest her mind. If she could just disappear.

"But you'll come back," Dosie called from behind, more question than statement, more hope than curiosity. "Jennifer?"

The ringing died only to start again, and Jennifer's itch to leave intensified. The ringing. *The ringing.* Her stomach clenched and rolled, clenched again, as fresh tears doused her eyes.

"Jennifer, please."

She opened the door and stopped, looked back at the woman who had turned her world on its head. Dosie was only slightly mussed, not a stitch of armor on her and the glisten of her own pleasure just visible on her lips, transferred in their kiss from Jennifer's mouth to hers. Beautiful. *Devastating.*

And Jennifer wanted to say yes. She wanted to say she would come back, that she would *always* come back. To Dosie. *For* Dosie. That nothing could keep her away, not even herself, not even her fear.

What came out instead was, "I hope therapy goes well."

And then she fled.

14

By the time she reached the lobby, her heart sat like a bitter, dry pill in her throat. Her empty stomach heaved, bile souring her esophagus.

I need to go back. I need to say yes.

Sweat dappled her neck.

Why the fuck didn't I just say yes? I need to go back.

She was going back.

The elevator doors had just closed when Jennifer turned around and jabbed the button. The car jostled a moment, then the doors re-opened, and she stepped back inside. She cast a brief thought toward how ridiculous she must appear on the hotel's security cameras, but it couldn't be helped. Let whoever saw think she forgot something in her room. She *had* forgotten something. Her calm. Her courtesy.

"My mind," she grumbled to the elevator's mirrored

walls, her own face scowling back at her four times over. A few floors ticked by, and she remembered Dosie's therapy appointment. *Shit.* Her heart burned. Her face, too. She couldn't go back up there and interrupt Dosie's session after she'd already caused her to be late. *Shit.* "Shit!"

She didn't know what to do. The idea of knocking on Dosie's door just to say the thing she should have said to begin with, the thing her heart had been screaming even as her mouth floundered, made Jennifer want to find the nearest hole to crawl into and die. But the thought of leaving without clarifying, or rather, *correcting* her earlier nonsense didn't sit right with her either.

The elevator opened with a minor screech, and Jennifer smashed the button to close it again. She hit it a dozen times before it bothered to respond, then with a groan, the tin box lurched back into motion. She couldn't do it. It would be too embarrassing, and she already felt as if her whole body might simply melt itself down to a hideous ooze at any minute. No. *No.* She couldn't go back.

She took out her phone, blinked furiously through budding tears that made her want to claw off her skin. "Oh my God. Fuck *off*." It was barely a breath, an angry, airy whistle at herself as she pinched the bridge of her nose and tilted her head back. She blew cold relief up over her cheeks and put the phone to her ear. "Please pick up."

As soon as the call connected, Dosie was treated to the sight of her own face—a splotched canvas of red and orange—and squeaked like a cornered mouse. "Sorry! Sorry. Oh, God. I'm a mess, I know." She slapped her clammy palms over her cheeks and felt the heat in them, dragged them down until her eyes sagged like a hound dog's. "I was having sex."

For a moment, her therapist said nothing, merely blinking back at her from the laptop screen. But then her booming laugh shot through the speaker. "Good morning to you, too."

"Hi! Hello. I'm going to be problematic today." Dosie grinned and fanned her face. "Fair warning."

"Noted. Thank you. So, morning sex?"

"Yes, and also, maybe, a major emotional breakthrough?" She considered. Sure, Jennifer's visit hadn't ended exactly the way she'd wanted, but the near-nauseating effervescence in her gut didn't feel like disappointment. With that one visit, Jennifer had taken so many steps in rapid succession that it had made Dosie's head spin, and she'd been blissfully dizzy ever since. "I said 'I love you', which is not all that surprising to either of us; you and me, I mean, not me and Jennifer. It *definitely* surprised Jennifer. She ran out of the hotel like a raccoon caught in the trash." The words nagged her ears. "Probably not the best metaphor, because that would make *me* the trash, I think. But anyway." She waved her hand as if to swat a fly. "She left, but then she came back this morning."

"Hence the sex you were having," her therapist supplied.

"Exactly, *but* that's not even the exciting part. Well, no, it *was* exciting. It was really, *really* exciting. But when she showed up here, she wasn't done up *at all*. Like no makeup. Her hair was wet. I mean, if you've been listening to anything I've told you about her, you know how she usually is. For her to come here, all naked and vulnerable like that—well, not *naked*-naked, obviously—" She snorted at herself, then sighed. "I just think it was a big deal for her. It felt like a big deal."

Her skin prickled, a sharp electricity zapping her nerves, but what she noticed most was the feeling in her chest. She was swollen and warm with affection and pride and what she recognized, undeniably, as hope.

"It was intense, all of it," she said as she played the moments back in her mind like a recording. "But it was also... off somehow? Like there was still some kind of barrier between us the whole time. And I could feel it, you know, straining, crumbling, but I could also feel her clinging to it the whole time." The more Dosie said, the faster she said it. "But it still felt like a breakthrough. I don't know. I just feel excited. I mean, I'm scared shitless, as Natalie would say, that I'm reading everything wrong and that what I *think* is happening or what I *hope* is happening isn't actually the case at all, and I'm going to end up getting my big, dumb heart broken. But I really think I'm right about it. About her and us. I really do." She took an obnoxiously large breath. "Anyway, I just hope you're in the mood to analyze the crap out of some stuff, because my kind-of girlfriend-slash-escort is allergic to emotions; well, she's not allergic to having them, exactly, but definitely to acknowledging them, which is somehow both really cute and really sad."

"Trauma responses are not cute, Dosie."

"Okay, well, you haven't seen *her* trauma responses."

"It would be unethical to say I hate you right now."

Dosie cackled. "I told you I was going to be problematic!"

Her therapist rolled her eyes. "Fair enough."

"Anyway, as you know better than anyone, *I* am a pot full of feelings soup, and if I don't talk about what's happening, I'm going to boil over and make a mess. Also, and this is unrelated, I really need to pee."

When her therapist's response was to throw her head back and laugh again, Dosie grinned and stuck her tongue out at her. How grateful she was to have a therapist with a sense of humor; for years, it had been the woman's key to helping her feel "normal," which, of course, was quite the feat for someone who was anything but.

"But! I can hold it," Dosie said. "At least long enough for you to tell me I'm not losing my mind or reading way too far into things. I do that sometimes, you know."

"I know."

The second the car pulled to the curb, Jennifer yanked the front door open and threw herself inside. Carolina stared as if she didn't know her at all, one brow raised, mouth hung half-open. Jennifer buckled herself in. "Say nothing."

"I know nothing, so how can I say anything?"

"I'm sorry to call you on your day off."

"Be sorry about the hour, not the call."

"Right. I'm sorry about that too."

"It's weird that you're up front." Carolina eased the car into the flow of traffic. "Does it feel weird to you? It's weird. It feels weird."

"Should I have sat in the back? No, why would I sit in the back? I'm not your boss today. I'm your friend. In need. I... need you."

"Oh, wow. Are you dying?" Carolina's dark eyes bugged comically. "Wait. Did you *kill* someone? That seems more in character for you."

With an odd sense of relief, Jennifer smiled. "I take it back. I need nothing. Drop me at the next corner."

Carolina glanced at her, unbothered. "You know corpse disposal services are not in my contract, right? I read the fine print."

The laugh spawned surprised Jennifer. It soothed her. "I will fucking throw myself out of this car," she teased, and Carolina shrugged.

"And? You think I would stop you?"

"True. You would probably wave goodbye."

"See. You get me."

Jennifer's laugh muffled as she buried her face in her hands and hinged forward, folding herself in half. Her forehead bumped her knees with each discrepancy in the road, but she didn't care. She liked the rhythmic thump of it, the minor pain. Her eyes stung when Carolina's hand, warm and solid, landed on her back and rubbed two small circles between her shoulder blades.

"So," Carolina said. "You went back. When? Last night? After I dropped you off?"

"This morning." She forced herself up again. "After I found the room key she put in my jacket."

"Mhm. I see. And you didn't call me to take you over there, because you knew I would talk you out of it." She clicked her tongue when Jennifer nodded. "And you made a messy little mess of things because you went back over there before you even had a chance to sort your head out after what she said to you last night."

When Jennifer's breath broke, so did her resolve. The tears she'd been holding back spilled into her lashes until one broke free. *Damn it.* She swiped it away. "I didn't realize I called you for a lecture."

"You called me, because you wanted a friend," Carolina said, "and friends are honest with each other. Sometimes, that means you get a lecture."

"For fuck's sake. Can we at least get coffee before you start in?"

"You paying?"

"As long as you're also going to tell me everything I'm doing *right*, too."

"Oh, for sure." She took a few turns, navigating the streets easily. They'd driven them together countless times. "Hey.

You know that whatever it is, it'll be okay, right?" She reached over, squeezed Jennifer's knee. "It will."

Doubt pooled in Jennifer's belly, dense as mud. She did her best not to indulge it. "Okay."

Shades of green lapped the bay as the sun spilled yellow across its surface. Jennifer stared at it through the white vapors of her coffee's steam. "It's exasperating," she said as she turned to Carolina and leaned her back against the pier railing. "No, it's mortifying. She's in her twenties, her *twenties*, and she's the most emotionally competent person I know." She inhaled the bitter, chocolatey scent of her coffee and sipped. "I've never met anyone more aware of themselves and their issues and strengths and needs. I mean, she's *leagues* ahead of people twice her age, and a month ago, she'd never even touched herself. How does that happen?"

Carolina rested against the railing opposite her. "She's been lucky." She rolled her eyes when Jennifer frowned, said, "Yes, I know she was abused most of her life. I'm not discounting anything she's been through. We know she's suffered, a lot, but that doesn't mean she hasn't also been lucky. In some ways, I think she's been *really* lucky, and I think she would tell you that herself." She pointed to a nearby bench, and they sat. "She's alive, for starters, and uninjured, which is incredible. Even if you haven't finished her book, you know how the story ends. There were less than twenty survivors on that entire compound."

Flashes of headlines and crime-scene photographs blinked in Jennifer's mind like a broken marquee. Her stomach protested each. She wished she'd never seen them.

"From what you've told me, she's been well cared for since everything happened," Carolina said. "And not only that, but she's been in therapy for years. Do you know how many kids in the world are abused and traumatized and never get any kind of help? There are kids who *never* escape their situations, kids who become adults who don't even know that help exists or that they need it. They just go along destroying themselves and everyone around them and wondering why the pain never stops and no one ever stays."

Jennifer felt a twinge in her chest. "You say that like you know from personal experience."

"Maybe I do."

"Maybe I do, too."

They sat together quietly after that, sipping their coffees and watching the foot traffic increase as the sun drifted higher. They sat until Jennifer's muscles released, one by one, and her body finally felt no different than it did any other day. The tension left even her thoughts as she lost herself to the ambience and the secure, calming presence of the woman beside her. When she let out a long sigh, Carolina looked over.

"Feeling better?"

"Yes."

"Good." She held out her hand. "Can I borrow your phone? You had me rushing around after you called, and I left mine on the table."

Jennifer handed the device over. "Sorry."

"It's fine." Carolina traded her empty coffee cup for the phone. "Will you throw this away for me?"

Jennifer took the cup and crossed to the nearest trashcan, tossed her own in with it. When she returned, Carolina handed back her phone and said, "You're welcome."

Wait. What? "What did you do?"

"You and I both know you should have gotten her number from the database weeks ago, like, I don't know, right around the time you had sex with her *off the clock* in a dressing room. All of this could've been avoided if you would've just had your feelings properly instead of all this run-around, but—"

"Yes, I know! I'm emotionally inept. What did you do?"

"Relax. I just sent a text."

"Carolina!" Jennifer opened her texts to see a new exchange with an unnamed string of numbers, the contact not yet saved in her phone.

The first and only message read: *Hey. This is Jennifer. I'm an idiot. I'm sorry. Meet me somewhere tonight, so I can make it up to you? No appointment. Just us.*

When Jennifer looked up at her, Carolina smiled. "Sometimes, the simplest solution is the best one. You need to learn how to humble yourself and stop overcomplicating everything. It's not the end of the world, Jennifer. It's just love. It happens every day."

"Yeah, well, so does murder."

The words of the text warped together as Jennifer read through them for the twentieth time in as many seconds, and then a bubble containing three little dots popped into view. "Shit," she said, showing Carolina, but then the message came through to reveal a GIF of a woman smiling euphorically as she melted out of the chair she was sitting in.

Carolina sputtered out a laugh, and when another text came through asking simply *Where?!*, Jennifer, too, burst with joy. She laughed until she felt so giddy that she could faint. Maybe Carolina was right. It was just love. It happened every day.

She could do this.

"Did you have to call me an idiot though?"

"Say I lied."

"...."

Jennifer fidgeted, spinning her half-drunk whisky highball this way and that, the sweating glass leaving wet streaks and broken rings on the bar top. The polished toes of her black combat boots tapped restlessly against the lowest rung of her stool, their shine in the bar's moody lighting matching the gleam of her button-up. Its black silk rolled down her chest in a thin 'V' that revealed a creamy strip of flesh and a set of three skinny silver necklaces. In her obsidian wide-leg wool pants and oversized blazer, hair tossed at a dramatic part and eyes enhanced to shimmering sapphire by the makeup she'd chosen for just that reason, she was a work of art in all black. She looked good. Damn good. Far, *far*, too damn good to be sitting alone fidgeting.

And yet.

Twenty-five minutes. Dosie was meant to meet her twenty-five minutes ago. At first, she hadn't been bothered. She'd made their dinner reservation for a half-hour later than the time she'd suggested they meet. That way, they could ease into their date—spend some time at the bar, settling their nerves with a drink. But then the minutes had ticked on with Dosie never showing, and Jennifer's phone sat silently. No calls. No notifications. The last message she'd gotten from Dosie was the absurd number of thumbs-up emojis she'd sent after Jennifer gave her the restaurant's address. Surely, there was no way she could've misinterpreted *that*.

She's coming, she told herself. *She'll be here soon.*

She sent a message asking if Dosie was on her way, but it remained unread. Five minutes flew by, and still, she had no answer. Dread crept in on her like a shadow, turning her thoughts dark. What if Dosie had changed her mind? What if she'd realized Jennifer wasn't worth the effort or frustration, the headaches she'd undoubtedly caused every time she tucked tail and ran, every time she'd pulled Dosie close just to push her away, keep her at arm's length?

She's not coming.

"Dupont, right?" The hostess appeared at Jennifer's shoulder. "For two?"

"Oh. Yes."

"Great. Your table is ready if you want to follow me."

"Thank you." Jennifer grabbed her drink and stood, told herself to relax with every step she took. She could give Dosie a little longer. Maybe she was stuck in traffic. Maybe she'd forgotten something and gone back for it. There were so many possibilities. There was no need to assume the worst.

Dosie was coming.

She's coming.

She would be there soon.

She'll be here soon.

When her third knock rendered nothing, Jennifer had to force herself not to sprint for the nearest exit, or trashcan; nausea felt like a second skin at this point. Her heart crashed around her chest like a trapped, terrified bird as she pulled Dosie's keycard from her pocket and slid it into the reader.

"Dosie?" she called as she opened the door a crack. The room's loud, rattling fan was the only reply, so she stepped in and let the door close behind her. It was dark inside with the curtains and drapes drawn, which worried her, but a familiar scent lingered in the air that kept her feet moving. What a torturous experience, to at once be so full of hope and fear.

"Dosie," she said again, breath bursting out of her. She hadn't even realized she was holding it. A razor-thin glow peeked through the drapes and slanted over the large bed, a yellowy white streak cast through auburn hair. The rest of Dosie was a small mass of still shadow under crisp white covers, soundless. Hope bound through Jennifer like an unchained dog, crashing into her darkest corners, her bleakest strands, touching every part of her. Dosie hadn't changed her mind. She hadn't given up on her or stood her up. She'd only overslept.

Or. Doubt pricked Jennifer's mind like a needle. *Or* Dosie *had* changed her mind and had chosen not to meet her and then deliberately went back to sleep.

Stop. Such thoughts had nearly talked her out of going to the hotel, convincing her she'd been stood up, but her gut hadn't let her accept it. Dosie was the most communicative person she knew. There was no way she would've changed her mind without saying so. Jennifer knew this, *believed* it. Dosie wouldn't hurt her, not if she could help it. Jennifer's heart didn't care what she knew. It remained a jackhammer, sending ripples of nervous energy out through her veins, every part of her atremble.

As she moved to the bedside, a muffled jingling hit her ears. It was quiet, distant almost, but she recognized it as an alarm tone. From an unseen location, it sang and sang, until she finally found it stuck down between the mattress and the headboard. How long had it been going off?

She silenced the alarm and sat at Dosie's side. "Hey, Dosie," she said and stroked down her hair, jostled her shoulder. "Wake up, love."

When Dosie woke, it was all at once and in a panic, as if her brain sensed a mistake had been made before it sensed, well, anything else. Awareness remained a half-second behind as she shot up with a gasp, only half-absorbing her surroundings. "What? What's—"

"Whoa." Warm hands took her arms, stilled her. "Relax, darling. Relax. It's just me."

"What?" she asked even as the sound of Jennifer's voice settled her panicked pulse.

"Take a moment," Jennifer said and pushed Dosie's hair back from her face. "You're okay. Just take a moment to wake up."

Dosie grabbed Jennifer's forearms and breathed. Her fatigue ebbed enough for her to focus. She found Jennifer's eyes and everything in her dulled to a hum. "Jennifer."

"Hi. Better?"

"Yes. Thank you. Sorry. What are you doing here?" Then it hit her. "Wait." She a felt a sleepy grin begin to grow. "You used the key."

"I was worried when you didn't show at the restaurant."

"Oh, God!" Dosie slapped a hand to her forehead as reality harshly oriented itself, and she remembered where she was supposed to be. "Our date." Her eyes welled with tears she knew she'd be unable to quell. *No. No, no, no.* "Oh, God. Oh, my God. I'm so sorry, Jennifer. I'm so, so sorry."

Jennifer's shoulders sagged. "It's okay."

"No. No, it's not." Her stomach lurched. A feverish heat spread through her like sickness. "It's not okay. I'm so sorry. I swear I set an alarm. I set, like, ten alarms. I don't know what happened."

With an affectionate smile Dosie felt she didn't deserve, Jennifer took her hand and said, "What happened is you didn't sleep last night. You're overtired." Her thumb drew soft shapes into the back of her hand. "And your phone fell behind the bed, so it wasn't loud enough to wake you. The alarm was going off when I came in."

"I'm so sorry."

"No. I'm glad," Jennifer said. "That you overslept, I mean. Part of me was afraid you'd changed your mind." Her voice squeaked with strain. "I feel like I've done everything so wrong."

Of all the things a person could feel, Dosie's least favorite was guilt. She hated the way it wormed about the body like a parasite. She felt it now, wriggling through her veins, sticking to her insides like glue. *How could I have let this happen?* The image of Jennifer sitting alone in a restaurant waiting for her, heart in her throat as she watched the minutes tick by, thinking Dosie had changed her mind, didn't want her, that she wasn't enough.... *It was an accident.* As if in reprimand, her therapist's voice snapped through her mind. *You apologized. Forgive yourself.*

That would take time, she knew, but even if she couldn't quite soothe herself, she could soothe the hurts she'd caused. The air was cold as she crawled out of the covers in her tank top and sleep shorts and welcomed herself to Jennifer's lap. She wrapped around her—arms, legs, and all—and lay little kisses along her forehead and temples, smiled when Jennifer sighed like she'd just fallen into bed after a long day. "You've done everything exactly the way you needed to," she said and shifted back to look in Jennifer's conflicted eyes. "We both have. That's all we can do until we learn how to do better, right?"

"Every time I'm with you, I feel half out of my mind. I feel so much, so many things I've never felt before, so many things I've never *let* myself feel before, and I can barely think. I can barely process. I don't know how, and it makes me feel fucking incompetent." Her earnest voice broke again, but she didn't look away. Instead, she brought her hand to Dosie's face and held it. "Because *you* are so in tune with your emotions. You are so articulate and open with your heart. I'm terrified you'll lose patience with me."

It amazed Dosie, the relief that that undoubtedly difficult admission gave her. Her ache eased. Her lungs relaxed into their work again as she combed Jennifer's hair back from her warm, slender neck to lay cool fingers there. "That fear you feel? How out of your depth you think you are every time things get serious between us? That's how I feel every time we have sex. Every time you touch me, I feel like an absolute idiot." She laughed at herself and at the horrified face Jennifer made. "No, it's not bad. It's just.... Okay, so, when we have sex, I love it, every minute of it, but I also feel completely lost, like everything is guesswork, and I'm terrified the whole time that I'm going to do something stupid or unsexy or that I won't be able to give you pleasure or take care of you the way you need or want me to."

A shallow frown tugged Jennifer's brow as she traced her thumb over Dosie's top lip. "How do you deal with it?"

"I don't." Dosie laughed and shrugged. "I just let myself be with you anyway because when I am, I feel more alive than I ever imagined was even possible. It's like my entire body is wide awake and aware, and it excites me so much. It makes me, I don't know, just giddy and dizzy in the *best* way." The more she talked, the more Jennifer relaxed under her until Dosie could see a smile beginning to form. "It's like my head is full of hot air and a million-jillion thoughts, and my heart is in my throat and in my chest and in all ten of my fingertips all at once, not to mention *other places.*" When Jennifer laughed, a few tears dropped from her eyes, and Dosie kissed them each away. "And it's so good, Jennifer. It's so, *so* good that I can't help but to trust it and believe it will work out, no matter how much of a fool I might make of myself. It's so good that all that other crap? All that fear and anxiety and crap?" She framed Jennifer's face between her hands, nuzzled the tip of her nose against her cheek. "Oh, baby, it just *doesn't matter.*"

"God." Jennifer lay her forehead against Dosie's, wrapped her hand around the back of her neck and held on like she was afraid Dosie might float away if she didn't. "Where the fuck did you come from?" She peppered kisses over Dosie's cheek and down along her jaw. "How are you real?"

Dosie squeezed her thighs around Jennifer's waist and grinned. "Maybe I'm not," she teased. "You should probably kiss me to make sure."

The brightening of Jennifer's eyes, the playful roll of shadow-dark blue, sent a stampede of shivers down Dosie's spine. "Oh, is that right? Do you think that would work?"

"You never know until you try."

Jennifer kissed her, full and still, and when they parted, wore a dreamy smile as she poked the tip of her index finger into Dosie's dimple. "Real," she said and drew her into a tight embrace, chins resting on shoulders. She turned her face into Dosie's neck and sniffed her, one deep, long inhale that she converted to a comfortable sigh. "All my adult life has been about desire. How did I not know it was possible to want something this much?"

"I don't know. I'm just glad it is."

"Me too."

They sat that way until Dosie grew sleepy again. "Jennifer?"

"Hm?"

"Is it too late to go on our date?"

"I just felt you yawn."

"I don't want to sleep. I want to go on a date with you." She sat back again and rubbed the eye that felt most loath to open. "Please?" She twisted in Jennifer's lap to see the bedside clock. *8:58 PM*. "It's not too late. Can we go? Are you too tired?"

"I'm okay."

"What was that? Did you say, 'Go get dressed, Dosie, because I'm taking you on a date right now'?"

"That does sound like something I'd say."

"Bossy and everything." She popped off Jennifer's lap fast enough to make herself woozy and clicked on the lights. As soon as her eyes adjusted, she groaned. "Oh my God, no. Look at your suit. You look amazing. Were we going somewhere fancy?"

"I always dress like this," Jennifer said. "I dress like this when I go to the dentist."

Dosie gave her a smug grin. "You didn't dress like that when you came to see me this morning."

"That was different."

"I know," she said as she disappeared into the bathroom for her toothbrush.

"You do?"

She applied some paste to the brush and headed back. "You were trying to show me you trusted me enough to be vulnerable in a way you usually aren't," she said in the bathroom's door frame, then popped the brush into her mouth and began to scrub.

Jennifer snorted and wiped the last of her tears away. "You'll have to start charging me for all this therapy soon."

"Unfortunately, I'm not qualified to give you therapy,"

Dosie replied, voice obscured by a mouthful of minty foam. "But I'm happy to recommend someone."

She squawked, toothpaste spraying, and ran for cover when Jennifer sent a pillow flying her way.

As it turned out, their date was comprised mainly of walking. A *lot* of walking. And Dosie loved every second of it. They meandered through the streets, enjoying the night lights and air, popping into whatever shops were still open. Art galleries. Clothing boutiques. Bookstores. They never bought anything, but they talked about *everything*.

Jennifer needed little prompting to voice her opinions, but she often waited for Dosie to share hers first and listened like she would be quizzed at the end of the night. Dosie found it endearing. She found she had to listen just the same, every detail of Jennifer's life like a rare, precious gem she couldn't help but awe at, even the ones that seemed mundane.

She liked Impressionist art because it was "real without being realistic" and made her think of her own work; desire, she'd said, often functioned the same way.

She preferred not to buy her clothes at department stores, even higher-end ones, because a "personal touch" was always better. She most liked to shop where she could have all her desires met to the best of a designer or stylist's ability. Her wardrobe was a huge part of her job, and she tended to it meticulously.

She liked classic rock and crossword puzzles and potatoes all ways, including raw.

"Raw?!"

"With tomato paste."

"Jennifer."

"What?"

"That snack is so sad that it almost makes me want to pray again. For you. And your soul."

"Says the girl who gets turned on by peaches."

Dosie giggled herself lightheaded.

They talked about the odds and ends they encountered, about the architecture of the buildings they passed and about what San Francisco must have been like before it was San Francisco. They talked until the hour grew late and their voices turned scratchy, until Jennifer suddenly stopped and said, "I'm starving." Then they talked about the superiority of veggie pizza as they shared two large slices and whether it was weird to have only ever had New York-style pizza outside of New York. Dosie said they could fix that together someday, and when Jennifer agreed, felt weightless and joy-drunk and wondered if everyone felt this way in love. Maybe it was just her. Maybe it was just them. Maybe they were special. Maybe they were mea—

"How old are you?"

Huh? Dosie blinked. "Twenty-six. Where did that come from?"

"I was just thinking," Jennifer explained, a sudden stiffness in her spine that troubled Dosie. "You said 'someday', and I.... Dosie, you know I'm quite a bit older than you. Right?"

"I figured it was somewhere around ten years, yeah."

"It's fourteen years. I'm forty."

"Oh, okay. Or is that *not* okay? Does it make you uncomfortable or something?"

"Does it make *you* uncomfortable?" Jennifer asked. "Have you even thought about it? Because it's not a gaping chasm, but it's not nothing either."

"But does that even matter if we want to be together? It's not like I'm a child." She pulled Jennifer to a stop and faced her, stroked the backs of her arms. "And hey, you know, *I've* even been married before. Where's your experience, woman?"

Dosie could practically see the anxiety seep out of Jennifer, warping the air like fumes. One eyebrow ticked up in that defiant fashion she favored, as if she found the prospect of a challenge amusing. "You've already experienced my experience," she said, and Dosie flushed with heat.

"This blushing." Jennifer grinned and took her by the waist, shuffled her closer until their lips were just a fraction apart. "I've never seen someone blush so much."

"Ugh, I know," Dosie said and rolled her eyes, fanned her face with both hands as Jennifer held her in place. "It's a stress response, apparently. Like any kind of stress, even good stress. I didn't learn that until after I left the compound though. When I was growing up, my mother said I blushed like this because God made me honest."

Jennifer pinched her lips together, and Dosie rolled her eyes again. They broke into a laugh at the same time, voices melding together, harmonizing in their joy. As the melody dwindled, Jennifer looked her over, eyes scanning as if trying to memorize every shade and angle and line. "Well," she said on a soft breath, "you are honestly beautiful."

"Stop," Dosie whined as the heat in her body flared. "Before my eyebrows catch fire."

"That would be impressive," Jennifer teased, "even for me." She twined their fingers and steered them back into a stroll, their clasped hands swaying between them. "But about before, our ages, I guess what I meant was that it's not an issue for us right now, but what happens when it becomes one?"

"What do you mean? Why would it become an issue?"

"Because, by no measure would I call myself old, but at some point, I will be, and it will be before you. What happens then? When I'm old and wrinkled, and you aren't, do you really think you'll still want me?"

Dosie's head swam. When she'd gotten the apology text, she'd been so hopeful that Jennifer might want to give them a shot, some kind of trial-run relationship to see if the strange, wonderful magic they had could last or even grow. But Jennifer wasn't talking like she wanted to try a relationship with her. Dosie supposed they already had one in all the ways that most counted. No, she was talking about growing old with Dosie. She was talking about a whole life.

The wild excitement flurrying about her gut made her

want to squeal like a child. She didn't, but Jennifer still seemed to pick up on her energy. "Please be serious," she said despite the smile Dosie could see forming. "These things matter."

"I know! I'm serious. I promise. I just don't think this is as big a deal as you think it is," Dosie told her. "It's fourteen years, Jennifer, not forty. So, yes, when you're old, I'll be younger than you, but I'll still be old. When you're ninety, I'll be seventy-six. That's old."

"Not as old as ninety," Jennifer grumbled. "You'll resent having to take care of me."

"I have crappy genes," Dosie said, playfully swinging their hands between them. "You could easily outlive me."

Jennifer gasped. "I wouldn't dare."

With a laugh, Dosie looked at her feet. She needed to make sure they were still on the ground. Wasn't she lighter than air? Wasn't she floating? "Honestly, the way I see it, who even cares?" she said. "As long as no one is being abused, taking care of the people you love is just what you do, warts and all, and age is only one of a million little factors that play a part in that."

"And my work?" Jennifer asked.

"Your work?"

"Will it be a problem for you?"

"What? Why would it be a problem for me?"

"Because I have sex with people for money, Dosie."

Dosie couldn't help it. She laughed. "I'm sorry. You just sound so serious."

"I *am* serious."

"Well, I obviously already know that about you, Jennifer. I *am* one of those people." When Jennifer's only answer was an annoyed huff, Dosie pouted at her. "Oh no, honey." She brought Jennifer's hand to her lips and kissed her knuckles. "Please tell me you didn't bring a whole list of reasons why we shouldn't be together to our first-ever date?"

"An actual list? No." She cut her eyes toward Dosie, bumped their shoulders together. "You're right. I'm sorry. I told you I've never done this before."

"You're doing great." Dosie kept her voice light despite the weight she could sense in the air. It was timid and bold at once, Jennifer's anxiety, and she knew it would take them both a while to learn how best to navigate it. In the meantime, Dosie could be gentle, and she could be patient, and she could remember how much harder it was to even just exist before she learned how to handle her issues and feelings in healthy, beneficial ways. "You don't have to apologize for being scared or confused or worried. Feelings are normal. It's always okay to have them, and it's always okay to tell me about it. Okay?"

"Okay." Jennifer cleared her throat and kept her head down, breath heavy. Her steps remained steady, however, and her hand was gentle in Dosie's. "I don't mean to be negative."

"I know," Dosie assured her with a pulse of her hand. "And I know we have a lot to talk about. I'm excited to have those conversations with you, but we don't have to have them all at once or even right now. My therapist calls that worry-bombing—when you pile all your worries onto something because you're afraid to have it or lose it or even just to accept that it's real. It's the easiest way to talk yourself out of trying something you want to try, and I really don't want to do that to us."

"Right." Jennifer blew a loud sigh and relaxed, reeled Dosie in by their joined hands to wrap an arm around her shoulders instead. "That makes perfect sense."

Dosie leaned into her side, arm looping her waist. "I'm really glad you're talking to me about it, though, and trying to say what you're afraid of rather than—"

"Running?"

"Or shutting me out." Dosie kissed her shoulder. "Another thing I learned in therapy is that when we don't have the right tools or don't know how to use them, even simple tasks become difficult and can overwhelm us. It's the same with our emotions and experiences. If we don't have the right tools for dealing with them in healthy ways, like how best to cope with our anger or fear or whatever else, then—"

"Then even the most basic thing, like having emotions, becomes difficult."

"Right, and then we get overwhelmed, and when we're overwhelmed, our brains and bodies go into survival mode. And when we're in survival mode, we revert to survival instincts."

"Like fight or flight?"

"Or freeze," Dosie said. "People always forget that one,

but it's really common. It's what happens to me. You've seen it firsthand."

"Yes," Jennifer said with a grimace. "I don't think I'll ever forget."

"I know. I'm sorry. I'd love to tell you it won't happen again, but it's not something I have any control over. I just recede into my body sometimes, like a kid hiding under a blanket, praying whatever monster lurks on the other side will leave if I just wait long enough. But then I get stuck there because the monster isn't outside. It's *in me*, in my head. In the past. Does that make sense?"

Jennifer hummed and held her tighter.

"Anyway, my point is: I don't know all your whys. I don't know what all your monsters look like or why your instincts are what they are, but I do know what it's like to be afraid of good things and good people because of the terrible things done to you by bad people. I know how hard it is to train yourself out of living in survival mode when it's the only way you've ever lived. So, I don't want you to ever worry that I'm going to give up on you when you struggle with this. I'm never going to do that. Okay?"

Jennifer said nothing, eyes fixed on the pavement, watching their feet carry them about the city. So, Dosie let her be, knowing she'd been heard. It was up to Jennifer to believe her.

They continued in silence as the foot traffic slowed, and the city grew sleepy, and Jennifer guided them into the Presidio. "This is my favorite place in the city," she said as she drew Dosie deeper into the park, "other than the couch by my fireplace."

Dosie smiled. She wanted to know all Jennifer's favorites. "Tell me why."

The path they chose led them between the deep green of sparingly moonlit eucalyptus. The air smelled like ocean brine and camphor, and it was like an instant balm to Dosie's soul. It never failed to amaze her how even small doses of nature could be so healing.

"I love the city," Jennifer told her. "I love the feel of it, its energy, all the noise and chaos of people everywhere, living their lives. But I grew up surrounded by trees, and I miss it sometimes. I miss the way they make the air smell and how clean it feels in your lungs. And the sounds. The insects and the birds. The wind in the branches. I don't know. It's a different kind of noise. Better, sometimes."

"I know exactly what you mean. It's one of the reasons I wanted the land I grew up on. Most people think it's cursed now. I've even heard people say they think it's perverse that I would go there at all, let alone live there. Maybe it is, in a way, but I don't know. It still feels like home to me. I know the land, the weather. The trees. They're my favorite part, and all my favorite ones are still there, still standing and growing. As hard as it is to be there sometimes, like now, I still also feel the most myself when I'm there. The air smells familiar to me there, and for some reason, I find that comforts me more than most things." She rubbed her fingers around a leathery leaf, then another. "That could change one day, but for now it's where I want to be while I figure out the direction I want my life to take from here. You know?"

When no reply came, Dosie turned to find Jennifer watching her. "What?"

"Nothing."

"Something."

"I was just thinking I want to kiss you."

"So then why don't you?"

"Because the way I want to kiss you, Dosie..." She held Dosie's gaze, let that one rebellious eyebrow slide north. "... wouldn't be appropriate for public."

It was edging toward midnight, but Dosie's body burned like a bright, summer day. Her mouth went sandy dry as she slid her hands around the back of Jennifer's neck and said, "Do it anyway."

Jennifer's kiss was like a tidal wave, sweeping her up and carrying her away, and Dosie gave herself over to it. Potential passersby be damned. Let them be scandalized or disgusted or unbothered. She didn't care, would pay them no mind, because in that moment, she felt not even an ounce of shame, and if she won at nothing else in life, she had that. And that was everything.

When they parted, lips still just touching, Dosie shivered under Jennifer's hands. She felt her heart climb right up onto her tongue, did nothing to stop its escape. "Jennifer, I lov—"

"Shh." Jennifer pressed two fingers against her lips, and fear exploded through Dosie's brain like a firework. Bright red and warning. "Don't, Dosie."

Oh, no. Please, no. "Why not? Do you not feel the sa—"

Jennifer's voice crackled with a nervous laugh as she muted Dosie's lips again and said, "Just wait." Her fingertips were cold against Dosie's cheeks as she mapped her in little twitches of movement that Dosie felt like sparks popping beneath her skin. Something was happening, she knew—something significant. "It's my turn."

Oh. Dosie held her breath, every inch of her body prickling with anticipation.

Jennifer slid her hands down to Dosie's and threaded their fingers. When she spoke again, it wasn't loud or firm or even confident. It was hushed and slow and honest, and it shook Dosie down to her cells. "*Everything* changes when I'm with you," she said and drew one of Dosie's hands up to her chest. "Everything." Higher, she spread Dosie's hand over her throat, then urged the other back to bury in her hair. Her eyes fluttered when Dosie's nails scratched along her scalp, and suddenly, Jennifer was everywhere. Gripping Dosie's waist. Pulling her closer. "I feel electric when you touch me." Her fingers wriggled beneath Dosie's top and splayed over her lower back, forcing her spine to bend so their pelvises were crushed together. "And *every single time* I touch you."

Dosie shuddered, felt a twitch between her legs. "Jennifer."

"*Fuck*, Dosie. Every time you say my name, I burn so hot I could faint."

Wait. Adrenaline flooded Dosie's system as she recognized the words. They were *hers*. A desperate, hungry sort of want took over, a wild, reckless kind of love as Jennifer kissed her silly. Kissed her silent and stupid and brand new.

"Nothing exists right now but you, Dosie," she murmured between presses. "Nothing but us, because—"

"When we kiss, the entire world disappears," Dosie said, voice wobbling as tears flooded her eyes. "Oh, Jennifer. I said the right thing."

"No, darling, you *are* the right thing. The right one." She wiped Dosie's tears away the moment they fell. "The only one."

The smile that spread Dosie's lips couldn't have been tamed. She didn't think bodies were meant to feel so much at once, because everything was hot and dangerous, thrilling and unsteady and bright and *wonderful*, and Dosie had never felt higher. She was a flaming fucking star, and her brilliance couldn't be captured or manipulated or snuffed. She was invincible, untouchable. She was in love.

She grabbed Jennifer by the front of her shirt and said, "I feel like I could fly."

"Funny," Jennifer said and drew their foreheads together. "I feel like I'll never stop falling."

"*No*." Dosie clutched her chest. "Stop. You can't be hot *and* dreamy." Jennifer's loud, sudden laugh made her stomach flip. She bit her lip. "Come back to my hotel room with me."

"Actually," Jennifer said, "I was hoping you would consider coming home with me tonight."

When Dosie's back struck plaster, she moaned and urged Jennifer against her. The gritty laugh that vibrated from her lover's throat as she braced a hand on each side of Dosie's head sent ripples through her thoughts like gaps in airwaves. Her brain was static and purpose in equal measure.

"I thought we came back to the hotel so you could get a change of clothes."

"We did."

"Mhm." Jennifer smirked. "That certainly seems like what we're doing."

Dosie whined. "I can't help it." Her hands roamed, a messy cycle of innocent exploration and blatant groping. "Have you seen yourself?"

"I have."

"Then you know. It's impossible not to want you."

"I *do* masturbate often."

Dosie nearly melted down the wall. "*Jennifer.*"

Another mischievous little laugh burned a direct path to Dosie's already aching sex as Jennifer evaded her seeking mouth with impish glee and kissed instead at the corner of her lips, the soft edge of her jaw. Dosie cried her frustration when Jennifer's tongue licked into her ear and coated it with wet heat. "Stop whining and tell me what you want."

Dosie's knuckles whitened around material undoubtedly too expensive to be handled in such a way, but Jennifer didn't seem to mind. In fact, Dosie could swear she liked it. "I told you: *you*. I want you. I want to...."

"What?" Jennifer's eyes were pure, dark hunger when she met Dosie face-to-face again. "You want to what?"

Her voice had a ring of authority that made all the fine hairs along Dosie's lower back stand on end. Everything prickled and ached and *needed*. "I want to touch you."

"Where?"

"Everywhere."

Jennifer guided Dosie's hands to the clasp of her pants. It hardly made a sound as it opened, and then the pants were on the floor, pooled around Jennifer's boots. "Be specific," she ordered, and with one hand, brought Dosie's fingers to her mouth. "There are so many places and so very many ways to touch someone, Dosie." She sucked two tips between her teeth then used them to paint a wet path over her bottom lip. "Is this where you want to touch me?" She next drew them to her chest, under the edge of her shirt to the swell of her breast. "Or here maybe?"

With her other hand, she guided Dosie between her legs and over her thin panties. "Or is it here?" Dosie could feel the heat emanating from beneath, and a whimper flourished and died in her dry throat. Her body roared like fire as Jennifer dragged their stacked fingertips roughly over herself, over and over until the material was soaked through. "Is this where you want to touch me?"

Her voice deepened as she spoke, roughening around the edges, and Dosie recognized that Jennifer was excited by this

—the talking. The more she spoke, the tighter her grip became and the more her breath shallowed, and every time Dosie reacted—a shudder or sound—Jennifer's pupils dilated a little more. Clearly, she enjoyed the way her voice wound Dosie up like a toy, and that made Dosie *want*. More touching. More trying. More sex. More pleasure. More Jennifer. More of the strange, beautiful expansion she felt pulling in her chest every time they found their way back to one another. Just *more*. Dosie had never felt so gleefully greedy in her life. It was as if she was drowning yet had no desire for air.

"Yes," she panted against Jennifer's lips and shifted her fingers to the edge of her underwear. "Tell me to go under."

"Tell me why you want to," Jennifer volleyed, more controlled than Dosie but just as eager. Her hips seemed to rock of their own accord, body seeking the same release Dosie's sought. "Be specific."

Dosie didn't know what to say or how to say it. She'd never done dirty talk, and if she was honest with herself, she wasn't entirely sure if this even qualified as dirty talk or if Jennifer just wanted her to be more assertive. *Or*. A delicious thought entered her mind. *She's just as affected by my voice as I am by hers.*

She was working up the courage to say something when gentle fingers tilted her chin up. "Don't overthink it," Jennifer told her, and she laughed and leaned into her.

"I swear you can read my mind sometimes."

"I'm reading your body," Jennifer said, "but I want you to use your words. Just try for me, please?"

All I have to say is the right thing. The last time she'd been confronted with such a challenge, she'd simply said the words that had been flitting about her heart like anxious birds. She'd told the truth. *Right. I can do that.* Though, this time, she would pull from a source farther south.

She closed her eyes and focused on the thrum of Jennifer's pulse between her legs and the mess of her underwear. "Feeling you like this isn't enough." Jennifer's small intake of breath made no sound, but Dosie felt it. It encouraged her. "I know you're wet, and I know how amazing it feels to touch you when you are. Like this, through your underwear..." She toyed with the damp edge, let the tip of one finger slip under then out again. "...it isn't enough. I want you coating my fingers." Jennifer trembled, and Dosie's ego swelled. Her blood rushed in her ears. "I want to feel you dripping down my wrist."

A guttural sound was the only warning Dosie got before Jennifer had her by the throat, long fingers cuffing Dosie's esophagus then gripping her chin, forcing her face up. Jennifer's tongue was in Dosie's mouth a beat later, and there was no more resistance. Their voices melted into a harmonic grind as Dosie took initiative, pushing her last barrier to the side and finally sliding between Jennifer's dewy lips.

"I want you inside me." Jennifer caught Dosie's hair between her fingers and pulled. "Now." Dosie's clit throbbed as her head snapped back to expose her neck. Jennifer's teeth scraped down the length of it with just enough pressure to sting. "*Now.*"

So, Dosie had her right there, standing, pants around her ankles and boots still on her feet, fucking her to a breathless series of clipped directions, Jennifer's voice sharpening with each one. Unfortunately for Jennifer, the sharper it got and the more adamantly she made demands, the more excited Dosie became, until she found herself slipping up on a few orders just to hear the rebuke that followed. Jennifer was so sexy when she was in control, even sexier when that control was tested.

An airy laugh wisped across Jennifer's lips as she curled her hand around Dosie's neck again. She put the tip of her thumb to the underside of Dosie's chin and pushed, tilting her gaze up. "Are you deliberately edging me, Ms. Fisher?"

It took a moment for Dosie to process the words, dazed by Jennifer's overwide pupils and flushed cheeks, the smirk tilting one corner of her mouth. She was surprised to realize she didn't feel embarrassed at all as she admitted, "I don't know what that is."

"You keep bringing me to the edge of orgasm only to back off or change your rhythm before I can come. That's called edging—deliberately preventing orgasm at the brink of it."

"Oh. No, I definitely want the orgasm to happen."

"Well, it *does* eventually happen," Jennifer said. "The point is to stave it off first in the hope of building to a more intense and satisfying one."

"Right." She tried to focus on what was being said, but it was a bit hard when she was still three fingers deep inside

Jennifer and could feel every thump of her pulse from the inside. "Okay."

"Dosie?"

"Sorry. Yes, sorry. I was just trying to make it last longer. The way you were talking to me, demanding. Your voice. I just really, *really* liked it."

"Don't be sorry. Edging is good, *very* good. Just ask beforehand next time. That way, I'll know it's deliberate."

"Yes, ma'am," Dosie said with a goofy, pleasure-drunk grin and a ridiculous salute. "Director, ma'am."

"Good girl," Jennifer said and hiked her leg up to sling it around Dosie's ass. "Now, make me come."

"*Yes.*" Dosie shuddered as Jennifer's muscles squeezed viciously around her fingers, sucking her in deeper. She was so wet that every stroke sounded lewd, and when she ordered Dosie to add a fourth finger, the air seemed to catch fire. They gasped like they were suffocating, oxygen thinned under the thick of their desire, and Dosie watched all but her thumb disappear inside Jennifer's dripping cunt.

"Oh wow," she whispered. "You feel *so* good."

"I'm close," Jennifer panted. "Fuck, Dosie, I'm going to come so fucking hard."

Dosie was near dreadful with arousal, and those shaky words didn't help. Her breath grew painfully tight as the throb between her thighs became adamant.

"Tell me you want me to come," Jennifer demanded, and Dosie's tight breath burst out of her. Her stomach clenched itself into a ball.

"Please, please," she begged because she wanted it whether she survived it or not. In that moment, she wanted Jennifer's pleasure more than anything in the world. "I want you to come."

Jennifer's scream cracked at its peak, and then her orgasm went silent. Breathless. Frozen. Hard. *Hard.* So hard that Dosie's joints strained. One knuckle popped. The nails in her skin dragged, making lines in her neck and over her scalp, and then finally, the tension released. Jennifer relaxed, head to toe, melting against the wall. When she smiled at Dosie under dazed, lazy eyes, Dosie wondered how she'd ever lived without this. Without her. Without them.

"Mm." Jennifer fought to catch her breath. "That was really good. *Really.* Thank you."

"You're so welcome. I can't feel my hand."

Jennifer dropped her foot to the floor again, grunted as Dosie pulled free and flexed her fingers. A second later, all four were in Jennifer's mouth.

"*Oh.*" Dosie moaned as pleasure rattled her body like an earthquake.

Jennifer caught her as she rocked forward. Her blue eyes shot wide, kiss-moistened lips parted in awe. "Was that...? Did you just fucking climax?"

Dosie didn't answer. Truthfully, she didn't know. Whatever it was, it wasn't enough. God, nothing would ever be enough again, would it?

"Kiss me." She pulled Jennifer's mouth to hers. The scent of sex invaded, and Dosie could have cried. She could have screamed. "Kiss me," she urged again, mindless, starving. "I have to know what you taste like."

"*Baby.*" Jennifer kissed her slow and deep, her flavor sharp and tart and hooking like sour candy, and then she laughed at Dosie's delirious sigh. "Well? How do I rate?"

Dosie licked her lips and teased, "Preliminary scores are good."

"Oh?" Jennifer grinned. "Perhaps you require a more direct sample to accurately assess, hm?" She poked Dosie's dimple with her thumb. "I'm afraid 'good' isn't going to work for me. I'm an 'exceeds expectations' kind of girl."

Dosie's nerves felt like firecrackers, little bang snaps rupturing at the thought of having her mouth on Jennifer. "You're teasing me, but I've actually been thinking about that a lot lately. Using my mouth, I mean. Like, *a lot*, Jen."

That devilish eyebrow arched again, and as if an invisible string had been tied between the two, Dosie's clitoris jumped in response. "You know it does wicked things to me when you call me Jen," she said, then kissed the place her thumb had just been, the dip of Dosie's dimple. "Soon, love."

"But there's a bed right there," Dosie whined and pointed across the room. "And look at this." She turned her finger toward her own face. "I have my mouth with me and everything. I'm ready."

Her squeal rent the air as Jennifer suddenly squatted and scooped her off the floor. "We. are. here. to. pack. a. bag." She punctuated each word with a grunt as, with her pants still around her ankles, she shuffled awkwardly to the luggage rack and deposited Dosie beside it. "Here. Pack. Quickly. I'm going to use the bathroom."

Dosie's pout got her nowhere, so she began shoving clothes carelessly into her suitcase.

"Oh, and Dosie?"

"Yeah?"

"I've been thinking about it, too."

Dosie's mouth went powder dry. She whipped around to find Jennifer leaning against the bathroom doorframe, a downright bawdy smirk on her suckle-swollen lips and her pants still puddling the floor around her feet, long, skinny legs on display. She looked ridiculous, and stunning.

"A lot," she said, and Dosie's knees went weak. Her ankles, too. Her soul.

"You realize this is not helping me hurry, right?"

Jennifer's only response was a witchy little laugh as she vanished into the bathroom again.

Dosie vibrated with joy as she returned to her chaotic packing. "Grab my toothbrush when you come out," she called without much thought, and then, as if the floor had opened beneath her to an empty sky, Dosie's stomach plummeted and took the rest of her with it. The sensation of freefall overwhelmed even as she stood perfectly still in her hotel room, the ground as solid beneath her as it ever was, because she realized what she was doing—the enormity of what, ultimately, was a very simple thing.

She was packing an overnight bag because she was going to Jennifer's house. She was going to Jennifer's house to spend the night. There would be no exchange of payment, no time limit. They would close their eyes together and open them the same way. They could do things they'd never done before, like have a shower together or breakfast. They could say things they'd never said before—dear things, delicate things.

This was their true beginning. Wasn't it? This would make it, *them*, something real and recognized, something tangible, haveable. Something official.

"Toothbrush."

Dosie startled as Jennifer seemed to pop out of thin air at her elbow, toothbrush in hand with the lime-green travel cap already on. She smiled and took it, shoved it into her bag. "Let's go."

15

Nothing in Jennifer's life had ever been easy. She'd built herself up from the ruins of all she lost and made something of herself, something she was proud of, but no part of the process was easy. Every step she'd taken felt heavy and wayward, not at all sure, not at all safe. She'd found her way little by little, error by error, ache by ache. Dosie's journey, she knew, had been much the same.

But this. *This.*

Dosie stepped over the threshold and into her home as if she'd made the walk a thousand times before, kicking off her shoes in the exact place Jennifer always left her own, and something inside Jennifer, some unconscious tension she'd carried in the heart of her for decades, released. She closed the door behind herself. It pressed coolly through her top as she leaned against it and toed off her boots, as she watched Dosie flow through her pathways like a petal caught in a current. Spinning this way and that, she gaped at the high ceilings and ornate molding, the large, cushioned bay window seat, and the dazzling view beyond. The open shades painted cloudy, milky moonlight through her hair as she turned to smile at Jennifer, and nothing had ever been easier than smiling back at her. Following her quiet exploration. Taking her trailing fingers and allowing her to lead.

"Are you going to show me around?"

"I thought you were showing yourself around."

"Well, I am, but show me anyway." She slotted herself into Jennifer's arms. "Give me the official tour."

"What do you want to see?" As if on cue, Dosie's stomach grumbled. "Right. To the kitchen then?"

Dosie's laugh was raucous and perfect. "Yes, show me the kitchen and the many snacks you hopefully keep there. Show me everything." She bounced on the balls of her feet like a kid after too much sugar. "I want to see it all. Where you like to sit when you read. Where you stub your toe the most. The mirror you make faces at yourself in."

"Who says I make faces at myself?"

"I do," Dosie said and tugged her long hair. "Everyone does that." When Jennifer only stared at her, her jaw dropped. "Stop. Everyone doesn't do that? You don't make this face at yourself?" With ridiculous ease, she tucked her top lip above her teeth and flared her nostrils, waggled her eyebrows up and down, and Jennifer fucking *lost it*. "Stop laughing! You don't do that?" She jabbed a finger into Jennifer's chest. "Am I even more of a weirdo than I knew?"

"I'm messing with you," Jennifer said as she calmed. "I make faces at myself. Maybe not *like that*, but yeah, I think everyone probably does that, at least every once in a while."

"Let me see one of yours."

"Oh, not a chance."

Dosie rolled her eyes. "Chicken." She glanced around. "Show me something you never show anyone. Show me...." When her eyes found Jennifer's again, they were lazy, dark magic slithering about Jennifer's soul. She cupped Jennifer's cheek, thumb rubbing along her bottom lip. "Show me where you go when you cry."

And nothing cracked. Nothing broke. Miraculously, Jennifer's stomach neither bottomed nor bubbled. Her lungs didn't seize. Her heart didn't heavy itself with dread. Her joy didn't shatter like thin, fragile glass. It wasn't thin. It wasn't fragile.

And *this*. This wasn't hard at all.

"Okay."

Every step was slow and seamless, every breath free and full, as she led Dosie through to the bedroom. Her heart didn't race but danced, a gentle sway of a beat as she crawled onto her bed and into her spot, cheek finding its home on her pillow. She patted the ever-empty space beside her.

Dosie wriggled into place and stroked down Jennifer's arm. "What are you thinking?"

For a moment, Jennifer could only look at her. "I want to sleep with you."

Dosie's smile was impish, infectious. "And you acted like I was the insatiable one."

Jennifer snorted. "No. Well, not *no*, obviously. But I meant sleep. I want to sleep with you. I want you here, in my bed, whether we have sex or don't." She took Dosie's hand and laid it over her heart so she could feel the way it quickened just for her. "I've never wanted that with anyone. I've never even brought someone home with me before, not like this."

"Really?"

"Only you."

Dosie's poor attempt to hide her satisfaction with the confession was adorable. Her pursed lips quivered with the smile she tamed, and she was so perfectly kissable that Jennifer had to kiss her. So, she did.

When they parted, Dosie sighed against her lips and said, "This is your safe place." Another kiss—quick, sweet. "You brought me to your safe place."

She was crying before she'd even processed the prickle in her eyes. *Fuck.* Her cheeks were damp in seconds. A sob lumped in her throat.

"Oh, sweetheart." Dosie wiped her cheeks. "You've been so lonely, and you didn't even know it," she said, and Jennifer felt a tremor in her soul.

"I love you." A quiet eruption but just as awesome, just as devastating. Jennifer was grounded and soaring at once, drowning and surfing, burning and gelid and *just right*. "I love you." It was so very easy now. It flowed. It flew. She breathed it into Dosie's gasping mouth as she rolled atop her, tears dropping from her lashes, disappearing into Dosie's hair. "I love you." She painted it along her jaw in languid, wet kisses and down the column of her neck. "Fuck, I love you."

"Show me," Dosie pleaded, so Jennifer peeled off their clothes, each move slow, deliberate. Neither sluggish nor passive, it was wide awake and heedful, slow because it had to be. Every inch of skin had to be touched, sucked, experienced. Every cell had to tremble. This was a journey, just beginning. They wouldn't rush it, couldn't. Jennifer had denied herself, denied them both, long enough.

Neither said a word as they explored, discovering and rediscovering, gradually making magic to the tune of labored breath and wet flesh ground together. Time forgotten. Hunger traded for a deeper, more vexing need, a more exquisite satisfaction. It was true what they said: *Love hurt*. Not in the way most expected but in that overly full way. The ache of being at capacity and still growing, of having everything you wanted and still wanting it with all your heart—wanting it closer, hotter, for longer. At the same time, and always, there was the fear of losing it, harming it, abusing it, finding yourself ultimately unworthy of having it. A fear one could only feel if they also felt the opposite: unyielding, insurmountable joy. It was perfect anguish.

Dosie pulsed around her fingers, climaxed with little more than a gasp and a whimper, then quivered her way down Jennifer's body to taste her for the first time. She broke their strange, reverent silence with an intoxicated moan the moment her tongue penetrated. The pads of her fingers dug into Jennifer's hips, anchoring them both, as she lapped at her in messy, eager strokes that lacked any knowledge or precision. That would come with time. Until then, Jennifer was content to have her wild and overwhelmed.

They were saying something to one another, something writers and artists and lovers alike had been trying to translate for millennia. This was sacred communication; it didn't matter that it wasn't seamless or masterful. It was honest. It was organic. It was rich. It couldn't have been better, not then. Maybe never. The way Jennifer felt—how could anything else compare?

Her orgasm wasn't explosive but smooth. She crested and stilled, one hand in Dosie's tangled, sweaty hair, the other gripping her headboard. She waited for Dosie to come up for air, to kiss her thighs, smile up at her from between them, make some painfully dorky comment about how much she enjoyed the taste of her. When instead she felt Dosie's hot tongue prodding her again, Jennifer laughed and tossed an arm over her damp face.

Who needed sleep when there was ecstasy?

Dosie's stomach bellowed her awake with little care for her exhaustion. She opened her eyes to mellow morning light and nothing else familiar. Well, nothing except Jennifer. *Mm, Jennifer.* In an instant, Dosie was wide awake, her body a lightning rod of awareness. She was naked, fully, swollen and sticky between her legs, and all along her back: *heat.* Presence. She wasn't alone. She was with Jennifer, in Jennifer's home, in Jennifer's bed.

When she'd finally dozed off, they'd been face-to-face, hands clasped between their chests. Now, they lay back-to-back, both clearly more accustomed to sleeping alone. Dosie rolled over and was greeted with Jennifer's long, obsidian hair, her rich scent, tinged with stale sweat and sex. *Mm.* She slinked an arm around her waist and shuddered at the feel of naked flesh under her fingertips. She drew a tender line between Jennifer's shoulders, and up the back of her neck. Dosie breathed deeply again, taking more of her in, and when she exhaled, caught another scent.

Her body reacted unbidden. The arm cradling Jennifer clenched as Dosie bunched her knees and squeezed her thighs together, a sudden ache brewing between. She'd spent the night doing the one thing she knew she excelled at: worship. What she lacked in know-how, she made up for in devotion until Jennifer's pleasure had infiltrated all her senses. It filled her nose and coated her tongue and mouth and throat. She felt it, dry and tacky, still clinging to her fingertips.

Desire flared low in her belly, and Dosie nearly laughed at herself. It was absolutely ridiculous. She'd gone her entire post-puberty life, including a short marriage, experiencing little-to-no arousal, but now she couldn't escape it. For weeks, she'd not been able to make it more than a few hours without a thought of Jennifer, and inevitably, her clitoris would begin to throb like a devoted fan chanting, *"Jen-ni-fer! Jen-ni-fer!"*

When Jennifer stiffened under her arm, Dosie froze, afraid to spook her in case she, too, woke having briefly forgotten their circumstances. But then her lover relaxed against her, spine folding into the curve of Dosie's body. Her hand covered Dosie's, fingers caressing her knuckles. When she spoke, her voice was gravel. "Why are we awake?"

Dosie kissed her back, gnawed at it. "Hungry."

"Still? After all the eating you did?"

"I don't think that counts as a meal."

"And yet you sounded so satisfied."

Dosie closed her eyes, bit her lip through a smile as she pinched Jennifer's fingers between her own.

"What?" Jennifer prodded. "No cute little quip to come back with?"

"No," Dosie told her, "because I can still taste you, and it's making me want to do it again."

Jennifer's tired voice was lost between a groan and a guffaw as she buried her face in her pillow. "You cannot be serious." She rolled over and tangled their legs together. "You already devoured me. I'm half-convinced my clitoris isn't even there anymore."

"That would be so sad."

"You would have only yourself to blame."

"So, are you saying you *don't* want me to do it again?"

Jennifer squinted in the soft light. "I don't recall saying that."

"Oh, good. So, first, regular breakfast, and *then*, second breakfast." Dosie giggled with nearly every word, spent and starving and deliriously in love. "Which, in case it wasn't clear, is you."

"Are you always this animated in the mornings?" Jennifer's warm fingertips walked Dosie's cheekbone then smoothed over her hair. "Or are you high on sex fumes?"

"Sometimes," Dosie said, "and *definitely*." She shimmied closer, smushing their breasts together, the fleshy friction like a drug she had no desire to kick. "But mostly, it's you. Us." She kissed Jennifer's chin, her mouth, the shallow dip of her philtrum. "Can I tell you something?"

Jennifer yawned and nuzzled her, wrapped her up to pull her closer. "You can tell me anything," she said. "Tell me everything."

"Do you remember, I told you I was married right out of high school? Well, obviously, now that you know who I am, you know I never actually went to high school. It's just what I always say when people don't know my story, because it's the easiest way for people to assume I was young and dumb and not-at-all thinking things through. So much easier than explaining what my marriage really was. Not that it wasn't those things, too, because it was, but it was mostly—"

"A trauma bond?" Jennifer guessed as she rubbed her eyes to wake herself up a bit more.

Dosie nodded. "Not all trauma bonds are bad, but ours

was. I mean, we weren't even interested in each other, but we'd been through something together that no one else could even come close to understanding. And it was comforting at first, but then, you know, instead of encouraging each other to heal, we just became each other's enablers. We ended up perpetuating our abuse, because we didn't know anything else and were too afraid to try something new. Afraid we would damn ourselves to Hell if we did, and at that point, we already spent half our time thinking we were damned anyway just for surviving."

"I'm sorry, Dosie."

"No, it's fine. I've made my peace with it." She shook her head at herself, huffed a laugh. "Wow. I just chose *the most* depressing way to try to tell you that this is all new to me, too. All of it. I *was* married, but I've never been in love. No one's ever been in love with me. I'd never even been on a date before last night, which was wonderful. Thank you." She smiled, pulled Jennifer closer to kiss the tip of her nose. "This is a lot to wake you up with. I'm sorry. I'm not so concise when I'm tired."

"And hungry."

"And hungry, yes." Her stomach growled as if triggered. "Ugh, so hungry." She planted a furious flurry of kisses all over Jennifer's face. "Okay, I'm done talking. I was just trying to say that this is new for both of us, so it's normal that we're anxious about it and afraid to mess things up. But I've also never felt healthier or more excited about something in my life, and I'm hoping, if it's okay with you, that we can just lean into that feeling instead. Instead of being scared. Is that okay?"

"Yes," Jennifer said with an ease that surprised her.

"Really?"

"Really. You may have to pull me back from the edge sometimes, but yes, really. Excitement, please. *Please*."

When they kissed this time, it was fuller, deeper, and Dosie didn't even care that they both had morning breath, that her mouth still tasted like Jennifer's pussy. Maybe Jennifer *liked* that. Tingles floated down her back, vibrated through her thighs.

"Mm, I felt that."

Dosie didn't feel the slightest bit embarrassed. "Good."

"I love how responsive your body is."

"I love how much you make it respond."

Jennifer chuckled. "Can I tell you something now?"

"Is it, 'You're in luck, Dosie, because I make a real mean omelet,'?" she asked. "Because I might cry."

"Last night was my first real date, too."

Dosie's chest turned to goo, her voice to a whisper. "Really?"

"Really," Jennifer said again and kissed Dosie's eyes as they teared up anyway.

"Did you have a good time?"

"I'm *still* having a good time." She thumbed Dosie's chin, smiled. "Aren't you?"

Before Dosie could say a thing, her stomach saw fit to remind them, once more, that *it* was not having a good time, not at all. It was being neglected. It was near passing away. This was its death rattle.

"Come on, then," Jennifer said and sat up. "Let's get you fed." The covers fell around her naked waist and pooled, so that she briefly looked like a marble statue.

"Dear God." Was she just going to wake up to that regularly now? Just a casual weekend in San Francisco with *that* wrapped around her? That was just going to be her life now? Her mouth watered. "Do we have to get dressed for that? Because I *really* might cry then."

Jennifer's expression could only be described as offended. "If you even look at an article of clothing, I will riot."

Dosie followed her to the kitchen like a starving dog, staring at Jennifer's beautifully bare ass all the way. "Hey, I was thinking, after breakfast—"

"Breakfasts."

"Yes! *Breakfasts.*" She cackled and grabbed Jennifer, ringing her waist as they wobbled and nearly fell. "I knew you wanted me to do it again."

"Oh no, maybe we shouldn't." Jennifer laughed. "All the sex we've been having has done diabolical things to your ego, my love."

An unexpected rush of emotion hit her. Glee stampeded, spreading joy to every inch. "I'm your love," she whispered and held Jennifer tighter. "You love me."

She expected another tease, another joke. Instead, Jennifer turned in her arms and looked her right in the eyes and said, "Yes."

When Dosie released her next breath, it felt like weight leaving her body. It felt like shadows creeping off and away, leaving her to shine. "You're mine, too."

Like two puzzle pieces, they connected in a perfect embrace. Jennifer was warm under her hands and exact against her measure, and Dosie could see the image they made so clearly in her mind. So radiant it threatened to reignite her belief in God. Any god. Instead, she chose to believe in the divinity that was simple nature, the nature of attraction and communion, desire and care. She believed in Jennifer and in herself and in what they could be together, the kind of joy and purpose they could carve into each other's paths. *That* was sacred. That was holy. That was more than enough meaning for a life, two lives. Any life.

"One omelet, coming up," Jennifer said and kissed the corner of Dosie's mouth. "You can get the plates and glasses down." She pointed to the right cabinet. "And there's juice in the refrigerator. Apple. Maybe some orange, too. I might've finished that, though."

"Apple is perfect."

"What were you going to say before?" Jennifer asked as she washed her hands at the kitchen sink, dried them with a sage-colored towel that lay folded over its lip. "You were thinking after breakfasts...?"

Dosie chuckled at Jennifer's use of the plural again. *Second breakfast* was definitely happening. "I was thinking," she said and pulled two plates from the indicated cabinet, "if you're not too busy today—"

"I'm not busy today."

"Great!" She added two glasses to the countertop and clapped her hands together. "So, then, how would you feel about a road trip?"

The steady crunch of loose macadam under tire finally skittered to silence as Dosie brought the car to a stop and cut the engine. Their road trip, as it happened, was just a few short hours and brought them somewhere Jennifer had already been. She looked out the windshield at Dosie's looming abode, well-worn from the years it had housed too many and from the years that followed when it housed only ghosts.

"Well," Dosie said, looking out at the same view as if she expected to see those ghosts peering back at her from the windows. Maybe she did.

Jennifer wondered what bubbled to life in the black of Dosie's thoughts each time she saw the face of her childhood home. What comforted her? What hurt? How would *she* feel if confronted with her own childhood home? Wasn't it also riddled with echoes of both happiness and horror? A sharp knot formed in her throat as she imagined the door that had haunted her for years. She wondered how often Dosie woke to the four walls she'd been terrorized within and felt that same jagged lump bobbing at the back of her tongue.

She lay her hand over the console, palm up. When Dosie

covered it with her own, Jennifer thumbed her knuckles and said, "Ready?"

On her nod, they left the cozy bubble of the car.

The air smelled oxygen-rich and woody, and a mild breeze crept through the surrounding foliage. It was nice. Jennifer grabbed Dosie's two modest bags from the backseat, the second collected from Dosie's hotel room before they'd left the city. She slung one over her shoulder and held the other out of reach when Dosie tried to take it from her. "I have them."

"I can help."

"I don't need help."

"Let me help."

"Let *me* be chivalrous."

"Oh. Is that what's happening? Okay, sorry. You're very chivalrous. Thank you."

"You're ruining it."

Dosie chuckled and led the way up the porch to the front door. She slotted a brass key in the lock, but when the door creaked open, she made no move to go inside. Her smile drifted as she stared in, seemingly trapped where she stood.

Jennifer knew the breadth of her knowledge concerning Dosie's traumas and triggers was negligible. She'd learned precious little over the course of their involvement when compared to a lifetime. Dosie herself clearly hadn't uncovered them all. But there was one thing she *had* learned, one thing that instantly came to mind as she watched Dosie struggle.

She knew exactly where to look, having watched her pack the rest of her things at the hotel, and in less than a minute, she had them. Careful not to startle her, Jennifer eased into the space behind Dosie and lay the string of pearls over her collarbones. After a few tries, she managed to clasp its ends under Dosie's hair and let it fall into place.

"There," she said and kissed the back of her head. "Armor on."

Dosie ran her fingers over the necklace then spun in Jennifer's arms. The afternoon sun caught a few tears in reflector flashes, but Dosie wore a dazzling smile. A second later, she pressed it into Jennifer's mouth. Her bags hit the porch with two dull thuds, and then time accelerated.

They shuffled over the threshold, fear and hesitation trampled under the ardent weight of want. Dosie's back cracked against the door, Jennifer crowding her in a fashion that stirred memory. *"My name is Jennifer."* And further back. *"I want you."* And even further back, to Dosie's first tremble at her command. *"I would have the lay of you, Ms. Fisher."*

Dosie's fingers tangled in her hair as they rolled along the walls in stumbling steps until they tumbled into Dosie's living room and onto her couch. It was dark and red-washed in the curtain-filtered afternoon light, and no sounds but their own panting and the rustle of discarded clothes stirred the air. Dosie parted her thighs and pulled Jennifer between them, on top of her, gripped her arms like she was afraid the ground might open beneath them and swallow her whole.

In that moment, she was Dosie's anchor. Her steadiness. Her safe place. And she realized, with surprisingly easy acceptance, that was really all she wanted to be for as long as she possibly could. Dosie's anchor. Dosie's distraction, her reassurance, her comfort. Hers. So, she closed her eyes and gave herself over to it, to her lover's frantic rutting and relentless grip, to her desperate, consuming need.

A whine erupted as Dosie quickly approached climax. Her cunt was still swollen and dewy from the two rounds they'd enjoyed before they left San Francisco, and it felt *amazing*, sliding over Jennifer's pelvis and the top of her slit, slicking her pubic hair. She pushed one of Dosie's legs up until her knee was bunched over her breast and her vulva spread like a sun-soaked rose. Jennifer coated it with her own and moaned. *That* was even better.

The direct contact of their wet, throbbing flesh had Dosie sobbing. "Oh, God," she cried. "Oh, God, Jen."

"I have you. Let go."

And then she was gone, disappearing into a storm of tremors and strain, every muscle rigid, every vein popping. When she crashed back into the couch cushion, she pulled Jennifer with her and held her tight to her chest, both arms around her, squeezing her nearly breathless. "Thank you," she murmured into Jennifer's naked shoulder. "Thank you."

"A good way to say, 'Welcome home'?"

When Dosie let free a lovely, small laugh, Jennifer knew she would be okay.

"Consider it my housewarming gift."

"I've lived here for months now."

"That's why I made it extra good."

"Oh, right. No wonder I can't feel my legs." She shifted so they lay side by side, facing one another. "Thank you for coming out here with me. I know it's a long drive, and you can't st—"

"Shh, Dosie. I'm here now. Let's just enjoy it."

It seemed all Jennifer's worries had been cast like ash into the wind the moment she'd given herself over to loving Dosie Fisher, the moment she'd agreed to lean into her excitement instead of her fear. Of course, she knew they would eventually find their way back around to her, her worries, her dark spots, but for now, she was content to let them be. She wanted Dosie to feel that contentment as well and embrace it. They'd had enough turmoil to last both their lifetimes.

"You're right," Dosie said. "Thank you for not letting me spiral."

"Is there anything you want or need to do?" Jennifer asked. "Or should we just continue to occupy your couch naked?"

Dosie pondered for a moment, one eye squinted shut, bottom lip pinched between her teeth. "A shower would be nice."

"Agreed."

"And food."

"You are the hungriest person I know."

"But for now, naked on the couch is perfect."

Perfect. Yes, she agreed.

When Dosie rolled in her arms, Jennifer filled in her spaces from behind, buried her nose in her hair. How incredible, to hold someone she loved. To have not just passion with someone but simplicity, quiet, ease. She'd not felt the comfort of connection in decades, not since her family, her sister.

The afternoon passed into evening, and Jennifer lay still and blissful and awake despite Dosie having fallen asleep in her arms hours earlier. She'd come close to drifting off a few times herself but always found her head too full to allow it. Her thoughts didn't race but pulsed pleasantly as she absorbed the minutiae of the room around her in a way that she'd never had time nor care to before. Every color and texture. Every piece of furniture. Unhung art and half-gone candles, pencils and packing tape and a few random tools.

A small box sat in one corner, the stacks of books inside piled too high for the flaps to close. Jennifer could see the books were all the same, recognized them immediately from the print on their spines. Dosie's memoir. She thought of where she'd last stopped reading, the dog-eared page of her own copy waiting back home. She could get up now, slip off the couch while Dosie slept, and grab a book, pick up where she left off. She could finish.

But she knew what was coming. There wasn't much of the book left, which meant only tragedy awaited, worse even than what she'd already read. The end of Dosie's time with her family, the end of so much life and of Dosie's life as she had always known it. Even knowing that she survived, that she went on to have a better life, one full of joy and friendship and kindness, one Jennifer was lucky enough to be part of now, she dreaded reading what came before.

A tiny hum called her back to the moment, a sleepy, satisfied sound emanating from Dosie's throat as she turned in Jennifer's arms without waking and burrowed into her chest. Warmth surged through her, collected right at the spot where Dosie's breath puffed against her skin, just over her heart. She threaded her fingers through Dosie's hair, careful not to tug, and lay featherlight kisses along her temple.

Oh, she was wide open. Exposed. Vulnerable. But she was breathing. She was soaked in light and seeing paths and possibilities she had never even dreamed of before. When she'd met Dosie, she had seen only a challenge, a gardener presented with a bud that hadn't blossomed. She would give it heat and light, wet it just right, and make beauty and color and life where no one ever had before. She'd never expected that Dosie might be a gardener too, that she would make Jennifer's hostile heart into a home, and all the things she'd long believed dead and gone would begin to grow again.

She sighed and held Dosie a little tighter. No, she would leave the book be for now, come back to it another day. They had no need of the past, not when they were reveling in the present, sowing a future they once believed too good to be true.

About the Author

Corrie MacKay is an American writer with an extensive background in genre writing and editing and an inability to sit still for long. New adventures are always calling! MacKay is a proud lesbian and feminist using her fiction to explore the themes that have dominated her life and to share the lessons she has learned along her journey. Her stories are maps of wonder, hardship, and healing. And heat. Don't forget that! More than anything, Corrie seeks to leave her readers with a rich and enduring sense of hope and a desire to live and love.

instagram.com/writefreemackay

*The following pages contain a brief excerpt from MacKay's forthcoming novel The Depth of You. *

The Depth of You
Excerpt

The wall cracked, puckering where the lamp's base made contact. A single second, a ripple of energy that lasted only as long as it took Dosie to wince, and then the porcelain shattered. Thick shards shot from the point of impact before clattering to the floor and skidding out of sight.

"Dosie."

A wisp of a word, a crackle of breath and hurt. When Dosie looked up, the shock of what she'd walked into sapped away. Pain took its place, the kind of heartache she'd not felt in ages. The familiarity of it stole her breath.

Jennifer stood across the room in a pair of running shorts and a sports bra, her long hair pulled back in a frizzy ponytail and her skin sheened with sweat. Every muscle was taut, and her chest heaved, breaths shallow and wet. Her eyes were rimmed with red, and tears streaked her cheeks. One of her hands still jutted forward from throwing the lamp. "You aren't supposed to be here."

Dosie's eyes stung. Her throat felt tight and unyielding. She had never seen Jennifer like this, this emotional, this out of control. It scared her. It broke her heart. "I was worried about you," she said. "You didn't sound like yourself on the phone."

"That's because I'm not," Jennifer snapped, a sudden burst of irritation splintering the brief surprise of Dosie's arrival. "That's why you shouldn't be here."

"Or maybe it's why I should be," Dosie argued and chanced a step toward her girlfriend. "You don't have to be alone."

The tension in Jennifer's body wobbled then gave. Her body shook as if she hid earthquakes under her skin. "I didn't want you to see me like this."

www.ingramcontent.com/pod-product-compliance
Lightning Source LLC
LaVergne TN
LVHW100504110826
845146LV00002B/506

* 9 7 9 8 9 8 8 7 4 4 5 1 1 *